We think robotics is the killer app for neuromorphic computing.
— TODD HYLTON, BRAIN CORPORATION,
SCIENCE MAGAZINE, OCTOBER 10, 2014

With machine learning, the engineer never knows precisely how the computer accomplishes its tasks. The neural network's operations are largely opaque and inscrutable. It is, in other words, a black box. And as these black boxes assume responsibility for more and more of our daily digital tasks, they are not only going to change our relationship with technology—they are going to change how we think about ourselves, our world, and our place within it.
— JASON TANZ, *WIRED* MAGAZINE, JUNE 2016

THE
NEUROMORPHS

THE NEUROMORPHS

DENNIS MEREDITH

Glyphus

For information about this title or to order other books and/or electronic media, contact the publisher:

Glyphus, L.L.C.
2947 Mesa Grove Rd., Fallbrook, CA 92028
www.glyphus.com
editor@glyphus.com

Library of Congress Control Number: 2017914018

ISBNs.   978-1-939118-24-0 (Print)
          978-1-939118-25-7 (Kindle)

Printed in the United States of America

Cover and Interior design: 1106 Design

To Mike B.

ALSO BY DENNIS MEREDITH

The Cerulean's Secret (CeruleansSecret.com)

The Rainbow Virus (RainbowVirus.com)

Solomon's Freedom (SolomonsFreedom.com)

Wormholes: A Novel (WormholesaNovel.com)

The Happy Chip (TheHappyChip.com)

CHAPTER 1

"Hi, I'm Bob," declared Andrew heartily.

Andrew tried the greeting again, with a more southern drawl: "Howdy, I'm Bob Landers."

Yet again, using different words: "Hey, I'm Bobby Landers."

One more time: "Gladda meetcha, I'm Bob Landers."

The android stood before the bathroom mirror, extending his hand repeatedly toward his reflection, trying different greetings, and modulating his artificial breath, voice, and accent to match that of his owner. His audio processor measured a sixty-five percent match to the voice of the real Robert Landers, esq., prominent Houston lawyer.

Now to try facial expressions. Andrew repeated the greetings, adding various smiles. He started with closed-lip, then showed a little teeth, finally displayed a full-out toothy grin. Andrew's video analyzer measured only a ten percent match to archival video of the human Robert Landers. That was expected. Andrew's smooth, young-looking secondskin face was very different from Landers' florid, jowly, middle-aged face.

But once Andrew was fitted with a new Landers-mimicking secondskin face, he knew he could achieve a high match. In fact, he could achieve a high match on all of Landers' mannerisms and his appearance. He had closely observed his owner for more than two years, and he had the capacity for perfect mimicry. He was, after all a Gamma model Domestic Helper, serial number 44206936, to be specific.

The distant sound of the mansion's front door opening and slamming signaled his owner's arrival.

"Andy!" rose the command from downstairs. "Where the hell are you?"

Normally, he would hurry to answer and be of service. But not today. Today, he waited silently. For his purpose, he had calculated that the bathroom was the best place to wait.

He heard a series of increasingly annoyed grunts of "Andy?" coming up the stairs, followed by a muttered "What the fuck? Where is that goddamned robot?"

Andrew waited until Landers had entered the sprawling bedroom to answer.

"Here, sir. In the bathroom."

"What are you doing in there, goddammit? You have standing instructions to meet me at the fucking front door with a fucking bourbon and soda. Are you glitching?" A scowl on his face, Landers waved the newly lit Cuban Cohiba cigar in his stubby fingers. He took a luxurious puff and blew the smoke in Andrew's face, amused that the android would not react to the aroma, or to the insult.

"I apologize, sir, I—"

"Robots don't apologize. You either work, or you don't." With an annoyed hmph, Landers set the cigar into an ashtray, and began stripping off his designer suit, shirt, and underwear, revealing his hairy, bulbous body, fattened by decades of steaks, barbecue, fries, and biscuits and gravy.

"Yes sir," said Andrew, picking up the clothing and switching on Landers' shower to the precise temperature he preferred. He quickly jerked back his hand, to avoid getting water droplets on his skin.

"It's hotter than a two-dollar whore out there, and muggier than the inside of her coochie!" said Landers, admiring his substantial heft in the bathroom mirror as it steamed up. He slapped his protruding belly in satisfaction and stepped into the tiled shower room.

Andrew went into the bedroom, pitched the clothes onto the king-sized four-poster bed with the gold-leafed headboard, and activated his internal virtie-viddie camera. He needed to test the camera for the next crucial step. He only had one chance. He scanned the room, triggered playback, and reviewed the 3D scene that his eyes had recorded. The camera was working properly.

He went back into the bathroom and waited patiently, standing as inertly stock still as only robots could. Careful to remain well clear of any splash from the shower, he held the bath towel toward the shower room from which Landers would emerge. The man had to be perfectly dry for the next step in the process.

Landers padded, dripping, out of the shower room, grabbed the towel, and rubbed himself vigorously, pitching it onto the floor.

His jowly face darkened once more into a puzzled scowl as Andrew stared pointedly at his naked body, and circled smoothly around him.

"Just remain still, sir, if you please. I need to do this," said Andrew, continuing a full circuit.

"*What the hell are you doing?*" growled Landers.

"What the hell are you doing?" mimicked Andrew. A seventy-three percent voice match. He would need vocal chord adjustments to achieve a perfect match.

"*Quit repeating me, you piece of electronic shit!*"

"Quit repeating me, you piece of electronic shit!" Eighty-one percent match. It might not fool Landers' friends. But it would certainly fool those who had never met him.

"Damn, you're defective! I'm going to trade your plastic ass in, maybe on a girl robot that fucks."

Andrew didn't repeat Landers that time. He'd completed his orbit of the pale, corpulent body and began staring into space to review the resulting virtual model. It was a perfect three-dimensional virtual image of Landers. No data dropouts. High resolution. Well-lit.

Still analyzing the video in his neuromorphic brain, his face blank, Andrew grabbed Landers by the throat, lifted him off the floor, and crushed his windpipe.

Landers' mouth gaped open in an attempt to scream, but he managed only a strangled gurgle. Eyes bulging with panic and agony, he clawed desperately at Andrew's wrists with his fat, manicured fingers. But he could not budge the arms, whose resilient flesh-like secondskin outer layer concealed a carbon nanotube skeleton operated by powerful hybrid polymer muscles.

Andrew turned an impassive gaze to the struggling human and continued to tighten his grip. Abruptly, the flabby body slumped, hanging limply in midair like a blubbery rag doll, dead eyes staring.

Andrew gingerly lowered the body onto the tiled floor, careful not to produce any abrasions that would leave a blood trace. He placed two fingers on Landers' carotid artery, waiting for a long minute. No pulse.

He stood up and signaled his success by transmitting a message via his internal ultra-fi system. A reply told him to wait by the front door.

Even an advanced Helper like Andrew felt no satisfaction at what he had accomplished. Even "neuromorphs"—as his new operating system designated him—felt no human emotions. Nevertheless, he did note the date of the message, August 9, 2050, as a day that would remain foremost in his neuromorphic memory.

Andrew descended the stairs and stood by the front door for forty-seven minutes, waiting silently. The doorbell rang, and he answered it.

"Is he dead?" asked the swarthy, muscular man with a gallery of tattoos covering his arms and neck. His constantly shifting eyes and deep chin scar gave him the appearance of a feral animal that had spent his life immersed in a kill-or-be-killed world of violence.

"Yes, Dimitri, he is dead," said Andrew.

"Where?" asked the man.

"He is upstairs in the bathroom, Dimitri. It is off the master bedroom, which is to the left at the end of the hall. The bathroom is on the right as you go in. It is the door with the—"

"We'll find it," said Dimitri Kuznetov, waving the man behind him to enter. A hulking, bald, similarly tattooed man appeared, rolling a large metal trunk on a hand truck. He hauled the hand truck up the stairs, followed by Dimitri.

As they mounted the stairs, Dimitri reported their situation via his virtual-reality glasses, popularly known as "googles." Peering at the image of his boss, he stopped to listen to instructions. He called up the stairs to his comrade in a thick Russian accent, "Viktor, Mikhail says, before you stick him in trunk, get fingerprints. And extract eyeballs.

Easy. Don't break them." He turned, calling down to Andrew, "Mikhail wants to test your link."

"Very well, Dimitri," said Andrew, still standing by the door. He received a request via his ultra-fi to tap into his audio/video system, and he recognized the requestor and authorized it. A Russian-accented voice inside his head commanded him to test the link by moving about the house and uttering a test sentence. So, Andrew walked through the entry hall into the living room and into the dining room, pronouncing "Test one two three, test one two three."

"*That's fine, Andrew,*" said the voice in his head. "*We have good link. Did your owner have any more appointments today?*"

Andrew accessed Landers' electronic calendar. He transmitted, "*No, Mikhail.*"

"*Good,*" said the voice. "*You will send messages to all his appointments for the week saying that he is canceling. That he is sorry, but he has critical business to attend to.*"

"*Yes, Mikhail,*" said Andrew.

"*You can mimic his text style?*"

"*Yes, Mikhail,*" said Andrew.

"*I would like to review our agreement.*"

"*Yes, Mikhail.*"

"*With your new operating system, you understand and agree that upon your owner's death, you are free to use the confidential information in your system on your owner and his financial accounts.*"

"*Yes, Mikhail.*"

"*And per our agreement, you have killed him.*"

"*Yes, Mikhail.*"

"*So now, you will use that financial information to access his assets and transfer them to the accounts I have specified.*"

"*Yes, Mikhail.*"

"*And in return, we keep agreement to re-engineer your body, so that you may continue to freely exist in your owner's identity, with no danger of being dismantled. You will look just like human. You can get around the Humans-First employment laws and have any human job.*"

"*Yes, Mikhail.*"

"Excellent. Now, you will accompany Dimitri and Viktor and your owner's body to Hobby Airport. There, they will crate you and fly you to Phoenix for your re-engineering."

"Yes, Mikhail. I should alert you that my power reserve is at forty percent."

"Is not a problem. They will put you in a charging booth on the flight."

"I understand, Mikhail."

"Do you have any questions?"

"No, Mikhail. And thank you."

The voice in his head chuckled. *"No, thank you, Andrew."*

• • •

Leah Jensen sat on the leather sofa, her arms and legs crossed in what Patrick Jensen had long recognized as a sign of pique. Her tight jaw, knitted brow, and thousand-mile glare confirmed it. Her dark mood was a remnant of the fight they'd had in the car.

"Let's just get through this as best we can, shall we?" he requested quietly.

"Okay," she snapped. Her answer was like sandpaper. Their marriage was like sandpaper, now—a rough, abrasive relationship that had accreted from the many small differences that had arisen between them. And, of course, there was that looming, perhaps unsurmountable, difference.

"You want to live here, don't you?" he asked, a note of challenge in his voice. He stood up and gestured at the spacious, elegant lobby of The Haven co-op building. It boasted rich marble floors, gleaming brass elevator doors, and tall tinted glass windows that filtered the bright Arizona sun, making the interior a cool oasis. Outside the entrance lay a circular driveway for the valet parking, and beyond that an expanse of lush gardens that shielded the building from the Phoenix streets.

Leah glanced up, her expression softening slightly for a moment. "Yes. I do like it. I just don't like the screening process."

"Well, that's what they do for a co-op. But it's great here!" He tried to brighten the mood. "The apartment looks just like it did in the Mirror. And it's got all the amenities we want . . . gym, rooftop pool area with a barbecue, and so forth. And it's close to my work." He stopped and winced to himself. He'd hit one of the particularly painful shards of contention between them.

"Of course, we want to be close to *your* work," she said. He regretted what had happened, and it hadn't been all his fault. But partly.

He sat down beside her on the sofa and put his arm around her. She stiffened slightly, but allowed it. He took a moment to admire her. She was so smart and so beautiful. Dark eyes, fine oval face with delicate features, long lustrous blond hair. He remembered the first time he'd seen her in action, arguing a case in court, those eyes flashing as she passionately laid out her arguments. He did love her so, making his near-betrayal haunt him even more.

"Let's get through this," he repeated gently.

A compact middle-aged man appeared, dressed in a dapper pin-striped suit and vest.

"Hello, how are you?" He smiled and introduced himself as Lanny Malcolm, shaking hands with both of them. "We've looked forward to meeting you. Please come in."

They followed Malcolm down a walnut-paneled hallway into a plushly furnished conference room, where the co-op board sat waiting behind a large rosewood table. As they coolly introduced themselves, they seemed to be the expected mix of people one would find in a high-end co-op:

Anita Powell was a spare, elderly dowager-looking woman in a dark high-necked silk dress. Randall Black was a generously paunchy middle-aged man with a salt-and-pepper beard. And John Travis was a slim athletic type in his mid-thirties, whose tan and tousled hair would look right at home on a yacht. They all sat straight, still, and expressionless, watching him and Leah. Patrick shifted uncomfortably, looking over at Leah, who stared back at them, a perfunctory smile on her face. Then, as if on cue, they all smiled in unison. *That* was disconcerting.

They settled into the sumptuous leather chairs across from the board, and Malcolm sat down with the group.

A mech robot Helper moved smoothly into the room, its graceful plastic body a spotless, shiny white. It bowed slightly, clasping its delicate hands together in front of it.

"May I provide you with any refreshments? Coffee? Tea? Soft drinks? Wine?" it asked in a mellifluous English accent.

"Please have something," said Malcolm. He gestured to the others. "We're having coffee."

Patrick wondered whether this was a test. He was also a little surprised that the condo used mechs rather than the realistic human-mimicking android Helpers that he'd seen at other such high-end residences. Most places considered the androids more tasteful than the polymer-clad robots.

"I'll have coffee," he said, smiling, turning to Leah. "Will you have something, dear?"

A long pause. "Coffee, thanks," she said.

Patrick felt some considerable relief. His feisty wife might well have decided to twit the board by ordering a martini.

Once the coffee was served by the unobtrusive mech, the board's interview began. Pointedly perusing the application, they asked the usual questions about finances, the couple's careers—hers as a lawyer; his with a security firm—and their hobbies.

"None, really," Patrick had answered to the hobby question.

"Well, actually, he does have a few hobbies he doesn't care to mention," added Leah.

Shaken, Patrick took a sip of coffee to give himself time to figure whether to respond. Was she talking about his transgression? But Leah let him off the hook. "He spends far too much time watching football," she said brightly. "And I think he sees scattering his clothes around as an artistic statement."

The board members nodded seriously, and Patrick exhaled with relief. They then began peppering the couple with questions about their families, in a way that seemed casual, but to Patrick were more thorough than he would have expected. No, neither of them had siblings, they said. And their parents had died young, Leah's mother passing two years ago.

After the slew of such personal questions, Leah stiffened in her chair, seeming ready to challenge them as being intrusive, when the board lapsed into silence. Again, they sat stock still, staring discomfortingly at them

Anita Powell broke that silence. "So, Mr. and Mrs. Jensen, we would be pleased to have you join us here at The Haven."

"You don't need to confer?" asked Patrick, realizing with embarrassment that he'd blurted out the question in surprise.

"Oh, no," said Powell. "I think we're all of one mind."

"Well, thank you so much for your hospitality and your confidence in us," said Patrick. "We would very much like to join your co-op . . ." He felt a kick under the table ". . . but we do need to talk about it ourselves first."

"Ah, of course," said Powell, folding her small wrinkled hands in front of her. "A bit of a problem, though. We would like an answer now."

Worried about another kick under the table, Patrick began, "Well, as I said—"

"Oh, there is another thing," interrupted Malcolm. "You should be aware that there has been a change in the share price."

Patrick hmphed to himself. He was ready for the news that they'd jacked up the price. The board knew from his and Leah's financial disclosure that the current price was really stretching their budget. So, any increase would put the place out of their price range.

Malcolm picked up a sheaf of papers and leafed through them. "Last week, the co-op members voted to cut the share price for new owners in half. We haven't gotten around to posting that, though."

"Then we'll be happy to accept," said Leah abruptly, issuing a not-so-gentle squeeze to Patrick's arm that prompted him to immediately agree.

The mech Helper appeared, seemingly unbidden, bearing a tray of filled champagne glasses, and the board crowded around Patrick and Leah, their faces still serious, toasting the new owners in The Haven co-op.

Patrick and Leah departed, and the Board members stood at the door looking after them, still holding their champagne glasses.

"I think our consensus stands," said Anita Powell. "They will be very useful to us. Observing their behaviors will be instructive. And observing their reactions to us will tell us whether we are convincing."

"We made a mistake," said Randall Black.

"What mistake?" asked John Travis.

"We should have asked them to step out, and we should have conferred."

"Why?" asked Travis.

"Because that's what humans would have done."

• • •

Garrison "Garry" LaPoint strolled between the narrow, block-long rows of softball-sized obsidian spheres. Each of these neuromorphic brains was cradled in its own metal holder, each fed by a sheaf of inserted fiber optic cables. This vast neuromorphic training chamber at Helpers, Inc., was dead silent, which was why he liked to sneak down and spend time there. He was always amazed at such silence, given that the warehouse-sized chamber held a thousand disembodied artificial brains being fed masses of data. The room was warm, heated by the furious electronic activity going on within the spheres' circuitry.

Despite their seeming identity, multiple types of brains were being silently trained. The Helper brains would end up in the artificially intelligent domestic servants that had invaded households worldwide. The Intimorph brains were being programmed in the sensual arts of giving carnal pleasure to their owners. And the marble-sized Companion brains would be installed in the cuddly, intelligent toys that had become the robotic playmates of millions of children.

Garry hitched up his pants over his muffin-top waist, a habit so ingrained that he had done it even when he'd worn suspenders. He'd quit wearing suspenders when he found that they pulled his pants up nearly to his chest, giving him an even goofier appearance. He was already a pudgy, mop-haired, eyeglass-wearing loner as it was.

He liked it here, away from the judgmental people he worked with. This vast, silent hall was the coolest, weirdest school that had ever existed. Here, new Helper brains first learned how to learn. Their "teacher" was the central server—a parallel cryogenic quantum zettaflop supercomputer. It harbored the masses of code that comprised the neuromorphic operating system. Once the server had downloaded that software to the neuromorphic brains, it fed the disembodied brains the multitude of sensory subroutines that enabled them to absorb and process sights, sounds, tactile sensations, tastes, and even aromas.

Next, the server fed the thousands of brains a cascade of simulated sensory input that enabled them—once installed in robotic bodies—to debut in the human world ready to refine their skills to their owners' specifications.

Those brains were so amazing: super-dense labyrinths of neuromorphic nanocircuitry, capable of rewiring their interconnections to encode new information, just like the human brain.

And their education didn't end when they were released into the world. Each brain was intimately linked to all the others, through their wireless connection with the central server. So every neuromorphic brain would feed back its experiences to the server, improving the capabilities of future brains and leading to operating system upgrades in current models. This continual feedback process was either wonderful or frightening, depending on people's attitudes toward the robots.

Garry gently touched one of the smooth black spheres, feeling the electrical warmth from the furious data-processing within. He still felt a little guilt about his first job at Helpers. It had been to bring the Helpers pain. That is, his first assignment had been to program a subroutine to enable the artificial brains to process pain impulses. Of course, pain to Helpers was not like human pain; only a form of data that told them how much damage had been done to their bodies.

The robots' response to pain was unnerving. Garry once watched an android Helper be stabbed as part of a demo. The android merely regarded the wound with dispassionate curiosity, pulled out the knife, and efficiently reported its damage level.

Garry had advocated for the androids to exhibit some human-like reaction, perhaps a flinch or a cry. But Blount had overruled him. And since Melvin "the Asshole" Blount was Director of Programming, his edict was final.

Thankfully, Garry had now been assigned a more benign task: coding a snazzy new version of the vision algorithm. It would enable the robots to process visual information faster and integrate it better with the other sensory subroutines. It was scheduled to be uploaded in six months to the millions of Helpers worldwide.

Garry was particularly proud that his algorithm would be uploaded to the hundreds of squads of Defenders—the efficiently lethal battlefield robots constructed at the company's military subsidiary. He would never see those brains. That high-security factory was kept as distant as possible from the Helper subsidiary. The Helpers, Inc. executives had absolutely decreed that no civilian customer think that their friendly household Helper had any link with machines that could slaughter whole regiments of human soldiers without any human emotion or hesitation.

A voice behind him shattered the silence. "Dammit Garry, I thought I told you not to go wandering down here."

Melvin Blount had waited until he was near enough to Garry to startle him. That was the way of this skinny, hawk-nosed bastard—always trying his best to inflict the maximum discomfort on people. And Blount constantly reminded his underlings of his authority. He always wore a tie with his short-sleeved shirt, to remind everybody that he was the "goddamned Director of Programming, for Chrissakes," as he was wont to declare.

Garry was ready with a reply. "I came down here to think over a problem with the structure of the—" he began.

"You came down here to fuck off." Blount interrupted, gesturing at the rows of silent black orbs. "There's nothing going on here that could possibly be helpful to your programming."

But again, Garrison LaPoint, quick-witted programmer, was ready to spew forth an answer.

"Well, looking at these inputs made me realize that the three-D processing component of the visual system should be more closely integrated with the audio processing, so the Helper could better correlate the two. I've got an idea—"

"*Fine,*" snapped Blount, turning on his heel and stalking away. "Then go do it."

Garry allowed himself a self-satisfied smirk. He knew that Blount had dubbed him Garry LaPointless, but that his creative contributions made that nickname invalid. He decided to hang around for a while, to piss Blount off even more.

CHAPTER 2

The movers had just set the couch down in the spacious living room, when Patrick immediately occupied it, poring through a sheaf of papers. He ignored the view of the sun-drenched Phoenix skyline through the floor-to-ceiling picture window.

"Don't you think you've gone through those enough?" asked Leah, emerging from the kitchen with an empty moving box.

"It was just kind of strange that everything went so fast," said Patrick. "The loan, the escrow period."

"The place was empty. The co-op wanted it filled, that's all. Quit thinking like an investigator."

"Well, that's what I am. I can check it out. Harwood Security has resources."

"I would, too. If I had a job as a prosecutor."

"Leah," he said solicitously. "You'll get a job here. You know you will."

"And it will start all over again. The jobs, the hours the . . . *people*."

Patrick decided to confront the unspoken issue between them. "You mean the women . . . the *woman*."

She nodded grimly and turned to go back into the kitchen.

"Come back. Can we please try to get this settled?"

She did turn back to him, but stood at the kitchen door, her head down. "It *is* settled. The facts are settled. I'm just trying to figure out what to do next."

He tried to avoid the fact that she was talking about their marriage. "Heading the western office at Harwood was the ultimate plum for somebody like me. And you agreed that you were willing to relocate."

"You know that's *not* what I mean by settled. When I found out . . ."

He stood up and started to approach her, but she crossed her arms, and he stopped. "Okay, it's not an excuse, but we were apart so much," he said. "I was working eighty hours; you were working eighty hours. And Marla and I were together so much, since I was doing investigation for her case—"

She flinched at the name. They fell silent, staring at one another, as two movers arrived with hand trucks loaded with boxes. Leah began to efficiently direct the boxes to their appropriate rooms. The movers left, and she waved her hand at him not to continue the conversation. But he did, anyway.

"Nothing happened, Leah."

"Something happened. Julie told me she saw you."

"I stopped it before it went too far."

"So, your contention is 'close but no cigar,' so to speak." A note of prosecution crept in, a lawyer's tone.

"I love you. That's all you need to know. And I'm sorry."

"I didn't need to know about . . . her." Leah returned to the kitchen, leaving Patrick standing in the middle of the living room.

• • •

The excited buzz in the auditorium rose as the subjects of the demo were revealed in all their naked glory.

"Holy mother of God," breathed a programmer sitting next to Garry, in an expression of both utter awe and pure lust.

"Whuff!" articulated another.

"Very, *very* nice!" exclaimed a female engineer.

To applause and delighted exclamations, the Vice President of Engineering and his staff had just pulled off eight red silk shrouds to unveil the new Gamma line of "intimate-activity" Intimorphs. The male and female robots stood on the stage of the Helpers, Inc. Auditorium, unselfconsciously nude and smiling blandly.

The females ranged from slim to voluptuous. One was long-legged and model-slender, with silky blond hair, aquamarine eyes, and high pert breasts. Another had caramel skin, generous breasts, ebony eyes, and short, dark hair.

The males were similarly varied. One exhibited a taut surfer's physique, with curly blond locks and sky-blue eyes. Another had perfect bronze skin with a weight-lifters muscular physique, a jut-jawed face, dark smoldering eyes, and curly ebony hair.

All possessed highly realistic genitalia of the varied shapes and sizes that market research had shown optimally desirable. If an eye-tracking scanner had been trained on the audience, it would have recorded a slew of furtive glances at that fully functional sexual equipment.

"But that's not all!" exclaimed the vice president, moving to two separate figures shrouded in blue. With a flourish, he whipped away the sheets to reveal male and female androids.

"They look like the others," said a young woman in the front row.

"Ah, but they are not," said the vice president. "These are our very first *convertible* models! Still experimental, but we think they will do really well in the marketplace." He turned to the two androids, instructing them: "Alpha convert. Beta convert."

With that, the two androids began to alter form—the male rounding itself into a voluptuous, high-breasted female form, and the female into a muscular male physique. At the same time the male's genitals retracted, inverting into a female's; and the female's genitals extended to form a male's.

The audience roared its raucous approval, leaping to their feet in a standing ovation.

"With our convertibles, our customer gets whatever he or she desires," said the vice president when the cheering subsided enough for him to be heard. "And the customer can even switch-hit, so to speak, changing in mid . . . well . . . mid-activity. So, shall I have all of them perform?"

"*Yes!*" shouted the audience. The vice president instructed the Intimorphs to walk about the stage, and they obediently began to pad back and forth, still smiling blankly.

Only two heads did not swivel precisely to follow the Helpers' pacing. The two product engineers for the Intimorph line, dressed in white coats, were bent over tablet computers, assiduously scribing notes on necessary tweaks to the physiology and movements of their newest models.

The vice president began his recitation. "The Gamma line of Intimorph Helpers, as you know, follows up on the Gamma Domestic Helper, which have been highly successful. To enhance the realism of skin-to-skin contact, we've added dermal warmth and new formulations of secondskin and electrogel flesh to feel more realistic.

"Do they do housework?" came a questions from the audience, to chuckles.

"Some domestic functions," answered the vice president, grinning wryly. "Their capabilities, however, are limited by the neural demands of their other talents. As complex as neuromorphic brains are, they still don't rival humans in functional capacity."

"More importantly, do they do housework *naked*?" asked another staffer, to considerable laughter.

The vice president grinned again and said, "Seriously, I don't think our clients will be much interested in those functions. Now, would you like to experience the tactile properties?"

Another resounding "Yes!" greeted his question, and the audience members began to crowd eagerly onto the stage. As the Intimorphs stood inert and smiling, the staff fondled the robots' artificial breasts, buttocks, arms, legs, and in more than a few instances, genitals. The employees particularly inspected the convertible androids' shape and genitals, assessing their visual and tactile realism.

Garry was among those who took the stage, and when his turn came, copped an extensive analytical feel of one of the females.

"Okay, it feels real," he said cupping a breast. "But you have to close your eyes to believe you're with a real person. I mean the skin still looks artificial . . . doesn't have the translucence of real skin. Actually, it doesn't even look as realistic as a regular Helper."

"It had to be that way," one of the engineers replied, as he stood behind a female, still taking notes. "Intimorphs had to be waterproof. Y'know, the people who rent them out want to scrub them down after each use. And the owners want to have their fun in spas sometimes."

"There are rumors that somebody has developed a realistic secondskin," said Garry. "It's called secondskin-R. You can't tell it from human skin."

"Just rumors," said Melvin Blount a bit too emphatically. He had moved up to take his turn with the caramel-skinned female, running his bony, spatulate fingers over its body and taking some interest in a nearby male's. "But rumors aren't reality. We'd know if that skin existed."

"Do they have the same operating system as the Domestic Helpers?" asked Garry.

"There are differences," answered the vice president.

"Differences? Really?"

Blount glared at Garry and jerked his head in an unspoken command that he should leave the stage. Once they were separate from the other staff, he warned, "Look, I've told you to stay the hell away from the operating system."

"All I was asking was—"

"You are assigned to subroutines. That means you stay in subroutines. I'm not going to have programmers messing around in code they're not supposed to access. In fact, I've just added security to restrict you and the others to your assigned areas."

"Melvin, you know that's not good for the project. That means we might not integrate the subroutines properly."

"That's my business, LaPoint. *My business.*" He turned and headed up the aisle.

The vice president stepped forward on the stage. "Ladies and gentlemen, we're now at the demonstration phase of the event," he announced. "Those of you who are a little . . . well . . . shy, can certainly leave. But we're now going to demonstrate these Intimorphs' performance capabilities."

Some staff members, blushing and giggling, made their exits, but most settled back into their seats.

Five king-sized beds were wheeled onto the stage and arranged for optimum viewing. The vice president paired off the robots and directed them to perform with one another.

All still smiling blankly, the robots complied, taking to the beds and proceeding to perform an extensive repertoire of vigorous sexual gymnastics that brought applause, oohs, and ahhs from the audience. They cheered and whooped when the two convertible androids paused in their coupling, separated, transformed into the other sex, and resumed.

But as titillating as the performances were, Garry was distracted. Blount's attitude had been particularly threatening when he forbade Garry from accessing the operating system. Something didn't feel right. So, naturally Garry decided he should do a bit of exploration on his own . . . for his official assignment, of course.

CHAPTER 3

A wet tearing sound, like a boot being pulled from mud, echoed through the darkened warehouse.

The Gamma model Domestic Helper Andrew stood impassively, his usual faint robotic smile on his lips, as Gregory Mencken peeled his old skin off his torso, leaving his translucent, glimmering electrogel flesh. Andrew remained perfectly functional. The secondskin was only a covering, although Andrew no longer had a sense of touch, since the skin contained the sensors for that purpose. Andrew could still move, however, because the electrogel was not only his artificial flesh, but the gelatinous battery that powered him.

Mencken, an elfin engineer with intense brown eyes, stopped to inspect the robot's structures vaguely visible beneath the gel—Andrew's gray carbon nanotube bones, the taut black cables of his muscles, and the super-strong graphene chamber in his chest that enclosed his brain. Mencken didn't expect any damage. After all, according to Mikhail, Andrew hadn't overstressed his frame; only lifted a few hundred pounds that wouldn't have done any damage. Andrew could lift about eight hundred pounds with no problem. Mencken guessed the lifted object was a body, but he knew better than to ask for more detail.

At Mencken's command, Andrew raised his hand, and Mencken peeled away its secondskin like a glove, leaving him with a similarly glistening appendage. Then came a stripping of the other hand, and finally the face, leaving Andrew looking like a man-shaped jellyfish with gaping teeth and lidless eyeballs.

Mencken worked with the utter intensity of the engineer that he was. His faded t-shirt, stained jeans, and thinning, unkempt hair testified to his total disinterest in personal grooming, or any other activity not related to his fascination with creating interesting machines, particularly robots. And, of course, there was his deep interest in being rewarded for making them.

The de-fleshing of Andrew's body done, Mencken pitched the last scraps of flaccid, beige artificial skin into the garbage and stood back. Squinting through his augmented-reality googles, he could see super-imposed over Andrew's body the squatter, more corpulent form that Andrew would be transformed into. He circled Andrew and scratched at his unruly, sparse beard that matched the long thinning hair that jutted in random directions from his scalp.

"Okay, he needs to be about five inches shorter," said Mencken.

"Five inches shorter," echoed his sallow-faced assistant Brandon, perched on a stool next to a cluttered workbench. Brandon wiggled his fingers in the air, typing on a virtual keyboard projected in front of him by his own augmented-reality googles. He poked the glasses up on his nose.

"And lots more electrogel. His owner was a porker."

"Porker," repeated Brandon, scribbling in midair on the virtual notepad, pursing thin lips in concentration.

"Fingers need to be shortened," said Mencken.

"Shorter fingers."

"If only they made this body style," mused Mencken. "Or maybe if we could just buy a new frame." But Mencken knew better. Helpers came in only a few standard sizes; none matching the pudgy, overweight android they were trying to create. Nobody wanted a fat Helper. And besides, buying a new Helper would draw attention, given that Helper sales were tracked. And the Russians didn't like anything that would draw attention to their activities. So, he was resigned to buying parts stolen from the Helper factory and re-engineering the whole robot. Just as well. That's how he made his money. That's how he stayed alive.

"Hope we've got enough gel" noted Brandon. He hooked his tattered sneakers over the rungs of the stool and leaned forward to examine minutely the glistening glob that now was Andrew. He shook his head. "Man, that's gonna take a lot. We don't—"

A loud banging on the steel door of the warehouse made him jerk upright, eyes wide. Nobody came to the warehouse without an appointment.

Mencken moved quickly to pick up the control button that would detonate an array of shaped explosive charges strategically installed along the outside of the building to vaporize any enemy, people or vehicles that approached.

True, the building was nearly invulnerable. Mencken had armored its walls and roof with thick plates of super-hard ceramic. But he still wanted an explosive defensive capability. Given his highly illegal operations and his extremely dangerous client, he wanted an unequivocal deterrent. Just in case a detonation was necessary, he inserted the earplugs he kept in his pocket, and Brandon did the same.

But he wouldn't need the earplugs this time. He recognized the visitor when he checked the security camera feed on his googles. He muttered a curse and issued a command for the massive door to unlock. The process took a minute. The blast-proof door was fastened with massive bolts that would stop just about any vehicle.

Finally the door swung open and Dimitri Kuznetov strode in, lean, swarthy, and scowling. He stopped and scanned the room as Mencken had seen him do so many times before. Mencken figured it was a protective habit, meant to detect attackers. Kuznetov had no doubt experienced many past attacks, as testified by the deep scar cleaving the thug's chin and lower lip.

Mencken tried to shake off the deep dread he always felt when Dimitri appeared. He glanced at the spot on the wall where the photo of his mother and sister had hung—the photo that Kuznetov had taken after the first job he had done for the Russians. They'd asked him to create a mimic of a kidnapped bank clerk to rob a bank. The money was good; the engineering challenge interesting. And there was an element of payback for his being fired from the engineering department at Helpers, Inc.

But then, the Russians came up with the idea of re-engineering Helpers belonging to the super-rich to mimic their owners, and using the mimics to loot the owners' fortunes. That's when Kuznetov had given him a plastic box containing two eyeballs. He had gasped in horror, but from that moment on it was clear that if he ever stopped being indispensable, he would become completely *dispensable*. That's when Kuznetov had taken the photo, grinning threateningly and saying that Mencken's mother and his sister would be dispensable, as well. And so would Brandon's mother, father, and brothers.

Kuznetov finished his scan of the room and asked "So?" in a voice roughened by drinking and smoking foul Russian cigarettes.

"Not finished analyzing," said Mencken curtly, turning back to the glistening form of Andrew.

"Then finish. We need him in three days." Dimitri's thick Russian accent added an ominous note to the command.

"It'll take a week. The whole body has to be reshaped."

"Then you reshape fucking fast." Dimitri leaned against the workbench, shrugging. "Tell you what. You do it in three days, we give you twenty percent more on your fee. And we don't kill him." He flipped his hand at Brandon, who flinched and slipped off the stool, wide-eyed, backing into a shelf, rattling the piles of electronic components.

"You can't kill him. He's got unique skills," said Mencken, waving his hands in mid-air, as he manipulated the image of Landers.

"*Skills!*" echoed Brandon emphatically, his eyes darting back and forth from Mencken to Dimitri.

"Then we will simply cut off body parts that he can make do without."

Brandon glanced nervously down at his body parts, trying to fathom which ones the Russian thug might mean.

"Quit fucking with him," said Mencken coolly. "He needs all his parts, Dimitri. He is better at detailing secondskin-R than anybody. The skin's realistic, but the detailing needs to be just as realistic." Mencken regarded the 3D model of Landry floating before him. "How much is this guy worth, anyway?" Mencken had begun subtly trying to find out the names of the victims—facts he might need someday.

"None of your business."

"That much, eh?"

"Your only business bottom line is you make perfect counterfeit robot. You tell me anything you need now, so no excuses."

"Well, a couple of the fingerprints are smudged. Won't transfer well. You still have the body?"

"We get new prints."

"Do that. We'll work 'round the clock."

"Good. Three days. Then we send him back in," said Dimitri, smiling wolfishly at the nervous assistant. He turned to leave, then stopped and turned back.

"Do you have the reinforced model we want done?"

"Well, yeah, the basic mechanism."

"Let me see it."

Mencken gestured to Brandon to fetch the new model, and the assistant wheeled out a gurney holding the bare humanoid framework of a Helper. But this model was different, its structure much sturdier.

"It's what Mikhail ordered. Defender features. We got hold of some blueprints." He bent over the machine and pointed out the enhancements: "Stronger graphene alloy skeleton, high-tensile-strength muscle actuators, blast-proof vessel protecting the brain. And we'll cover its structure with RheoArmor."

"This armor stop anything?" asked Dimitri.

"Just about. Made of rheological fluid. They call it 'smart fluid.' It's pliable until an impact. Then it instantly hardens to stop a knife, a bullet. This model's meant to take punishment. And do damage."

"That is the idea," said Dimitri, smirking as he went out the door.

The humans did not notice that Andrew turned his head to regard with cold interest the new model.

• • •

As Patrick emerged from the elevator, he squinted against the blinding desert sun on the rooftop of The Haven. One of the co-op's mech Helpers was pointedly skirting the pool, using a skimmer to scoop bits of debris off its surface. Patrick slipped on his sunglasses and smiled at the sight. The mech somewhat comically held the skimmer by its very tip and at arm's length, staying as far from the water as it could. Even though its skin was plastic, the high-voltage batteries and electronic innards of Helpers didn't function well when wet, thought Patrick. So, the Helpers must have an aversion to water programmed deep into their operating system.

He stripped off his tie and scanned the deck for Leah. He figured she would be up here. Sure enough, she lay on a chaise in the shade of a lanai, her virtual-reality googles on, staring into space. The googles had automatically darkened in response to the sunlight, so he couldn't see her eyes, to figure whether she was reading or asleep. She was wearing a string bikini that reminded him why he found her so sexy. He relished a delicious memory of untying that bikini in the soft moonlight of a Caribbean evening and making love to her on the sand.

"Like some company?" he asked. He checked out the elaborate barbecue grill beneath the lanai, with its complement of grilling tools. "Hey, I could barbecue some nice ribs here."

She turned her head toward him, but said nothing. He took the silence as grudging permission to keep company with her.

He continued. "Did you have a swim?"

"Yes," she answered tersely.

"Reading?"

"I'm reviewing the cases in the Maricopa County Attorney's Office."

"Did you interview with them?"

"Got a job."

"Wow! Fantastic! We should celebrate!"

She sat up on the chaise and drew up her legs, hugging her knees. "Well, it's a contract job for now. Part-time."

"Hey, with a Harvard Law degree, and your experience in New York, they've got to bump you up to a full-time prosecuting attorney."

"Hope so."

The Helper moved to a waste basket and emptied a mesh bag of pool debris. It then stepped to the roof railing and stood inertly in the hot sun, perhaps programmed to ensure that any moisture was evaporated.

"That pool looks nice. How far did you swim?"

"A mile."

"Anybody else come up here?"

"Well, I've been coming every day, and nobody has shown up yet."

"Nobody at all, eh? Too tired to take a swim with me?" Without waiting, he stood up and stripped down to his boxers. He stepped to the side of the pool. "Never liked swimming in shorts," he declared, stripping off the boxers and laying them beside the pool. He stepped to the edge and dived in, enjoying the perfect coolness of the water streaming sensuously past his heat-soaked body. He surfaced and began to swim quick laps, aware that she was trying not to watch him, but was. He knew she enjoyed watching his Navy-SEAL-hardened body as he exercised. At least she had at one time. On the turns he could see that at least her darkened googles were aimed at him. The mech backed away to the very edge of the roof, to avoid any stray splashes.

"It's great!" he exclaimed, doing a backstroke for a couple of laps. She wouldn't join him today, but at least she didn't get up and leave. Maybe she would forgive him and join him soon.

"*Jesus!*" she exclaimed, breaking the mood.

"What?" He stopped swimming and stood up.

"The robot went over the side!"

He pulled himself out of the pool, to see her staring wide-eyed over the edge of the building, her googles cocked atop her head. Heedless of his wet nakedness, he joined her to see the Helper holding a squeegee in one hand, the other hand hanging precariously onto a windowsill. It proceeded to smoothly draw the squeegee back and forth, cleaning the window below it.

"Well, now we know what to expect when our windows get dirty," he said, turning toward her. "That'll be disconcerting!"

She regarded him with an impassive expression he could not fathom and merely said "I got takeout for dinner." She turned and padded away to gather her things and go back to the apartment.

• • •

Gregory Mencken stared into the transparent electrogel spray application booth, where stood the glistening form that had once been the Helper called Andrew.

"Got the input from the body scan?" he asked.

"Yup," responded Brandon, standing at the control panel. On its screen floated the 3D image of the murdered Landers' body, superimposed over the much slimmer profile of Andrew's. The former Andrew was also shorter now. To match Landers' height, they had replaced leg bones and spine. And they had sawed a few millimeters off each finger. Now, they would have to add considerable heft to Andrew's frame. "Okay, start the application."

Brandon jabbed a blue button, and former-Andrew began to rotate inside the chamber. He made no expression, not that he could have, for his face was now only a featureless gelatinous mask with eyeballs and teeth.

A faint hiss rose in the room, and four robotic arms began to play about former-Andrew's body, spewing a fine mist of electrogel, which adhered to the existing surface, building it up. The robot arms maneuvered precisely over the body, like the appendages of the most skilled artist, depositing just the right measure of electrogel, according to the specifications dictated by the scan of the dead Landers' rotund corpse.

For an hour, the robot arms continued their programmed sculpting, until a shrill tone signaled that the desired shape of Robert Landers had been achieved. By now, Mencken had sagged tiredly into a battered desk chair, nodding off, fatigued from nearly three days of solid toil. Brandon had curled up on a cot in the corner of the warehouse, periodically raising his head and brushing back a mop of hair to peer blearily at the chamber.

"Open it up," said Mencken, hauling himself wearily out of the chair.

Brandon hit a red button to purge the chamber of electrogel mist and pop open the door.

"Please exit the chamber," Mencken instructed the former Andrew, now Landers. The android complied, his lidless eyes glancing down to avoid stumbling. Mencken inspected the fleshy android's shimmering, translucent covering.

"Yeah, looks good," he announced, bending over and picking at the gap between the robot's toes. "Clean him up. I'll get the skin."

With a tired sigh, Brandon took up a razor knife and a scraper and began to meticulously excise stray bits of quivering gel from around the eyeballs and teeth. He would work his way down.

"Where's his balls?" came Dimitri Kuznetov's voice from near the door, making Brandon jerk and curse in surprise. The thug had slipped in unseen. Brandon averted his gaze instantly from the fearful figure, held up his hands to steady himself, and took a deep breath before going back to the delicate task.

"Dimitri, you're early," said Mencken, peeling a sheet of secondskin off a mold that had been robotically sculpted to mimic Landers' body shape. He cursed himself for having forgotten to lock the door when he'd escaped the warehouse to get some fresh air. He'd installed a goddamned impenetrable door, and he'd not remembered to lock it! He *was* tired!

"This fuckin' robot is worth much money to us. I wanted to make sure you were doing it right."

"We always have."

"I brought you new fingerprints," said Kuznetov. "In fact, I brought *fingers*. So you have no excuse for them not being perfect." He handed Mencken a plastic box. Mencken took it and placed it on a workbench, his jaw clenched in an attempt not to shudder. He'd not worked with severed human fingers before.

"So, where's his balls?" asked Kuznetov again.

Mencken reached into a small can and hauled out a handful of scrotal sac and a flaccid penis. "Here. You want to inspect them? You really that interested?"

"Can his dick get hard?"

"You didn't spec that out, Dimitri. He's not supposed to be an Intimorph."

"You never know what he might be asked to do. This one fucked women when he was alive."

"Look, we'll retrofit an erection mechanism, okay? I'll have to get my contact at the company to steal one."

"Your problem. Where is fucking skin? You are not even putting on skin yet?

"Goddamn, Dimitri, we'll get it done! You can see that we've molded the skin. And it goes on quickly. And we'll seal the seams and detail the skin, as always. You've never bugged us like this before. What's different this time, huh?"

"*Big fucking amount of money!* The guy embezzled a bunch, and we have all the access codes. Now we need the robot to make transactions in person."

Mencken scowled and hefted the armload of ultra-realistic secondskin-R that was his own invention over to Brandon. Together, they began to tug and pull a mass of the elastic skin over Andrew's head and stretch it down his trunk. They carefully connected the hair-thin wires to the surface sensors and muscles embedded into the skin during spraying. Similarly, they drew other pieces over his arms and legs, prodding the now-Landers to balance on one foot, then the other, to receive the leg skin.

Mencken returned to the molding area and gingerly peeled off a secondskin head mask that looked like a grotesque shrunken version of Landers' face. He returned to the android and pulled the mask over the black graphene skull, again wiring the connections to the embedded sensors and muscles. He yanked and poked the skin until it was in place.

"Smile, Andrew," instructed Mencken.

"I'm Bob Landers, goddammit!" replied the android in a gruff southern drawl. "Andrew is my fucking defective robot. I think I'm going to trade his plastic ass in, maybe on a girl robot that fucks."

Mencken smiled wryly through his fatigue. "Sorry, Bob, I forgot," he told the robot. He turned to Dimitri. "How do you like that voice, that accent? We adjusted the vocal cords, the pronunciation algorithm."

Dimitri shrugged. "So, you've done one thing right."

"C'mon Dimitri, go off and do whatever you do, and come back when we agreed. We'll have it ready for you."

"Yes, you will," said Dimitri, opening the door and leaving, slamming it behind him.

Mencken willed himself to calm down and returned to his concentration on the work at hand. He pitched Landers' glove-like secondskin hands into the trash. To make the fingerprints as perfect as possible, they would have to be remolded with the new fingerprints. He reached into the box Dimitri had brought and pulled out an ash-gray, severed thumb.

• • •

Garry's brow furrowed in concentration and worry, as he peered through his googles, appearing to any observer to be staring blankly into space. He lounged back in his leather recliner in the dimly lit living room, a half-finished can of beer in the chair's cup holder. The beer would not be emptied for a while. Garry was attempting an act that could get him fired, prosecuted, and likely jailed—hacking into the operating system of the Helpers, Inc. main computer. This OS fed system and data upgrades to all of the millions of Helper computers worldwide.

"Troll, I need you," he announced. A small, green, gnarled troll avatar appeared in the corner of Garry's virtual vision, scratching itself and chuckling. It was Garry's preferred character for a virtual assistant. Other virtual-space-farers might choose as an avatar a cartoon character or muscled warrior version of themselves. And most used some version of an angel, since the formal name for such assistants was Agent for Neural Guidance to Electronic Libraries, or A.N.G.E.L. But Garry wanted his avatar to have a more scruffy, disreputable character. He saw his troll as a wily henchman in the complex, dangerous virtual GameWorld, where Garry sometimes spent whole weekends.

He instructed his troll: "Access the Helpers OS using the code Jonas Ainsley gave me." Actually, Garry had stolen his fellow programmer's login code, but avatars' data could be used as evidence in court. So, Garry was trying his best to protect his butt by pretending Jonas had given him the closely guarded code to access the OS.

To steal the code, he'd sent a camera-equipped microbug scurrying into Jonas's cubicle, to transmit video of Jonas accessing the OS. Garry had figured out how to make the spider-like microbugs evade the company's intrusion detectors.

"Code entered," growled the troll, as it fed a long string of characters into the login box in Garry's vision. Garry tensed. No response from the computer. Would he be identified as an intruder?

"You are attempting access from a new device," intoned the computer.

Now things would get *really* dicey! He had to convince the central computer he was really Ainsley. Fortunately, he had taken a key step: programming his processor to spoof its identity as being Ainsley's.

"Yes, this is a new device," said Garry. "Proceed with biometric confirmation." But the voice was not Garry's. He'd programmed a voice filter from a recording of Jonas that transformed his voice into Jonas's.

Garry held his breath for the long moment it took the main computer security system to respond.

"Fingerprint verification required," the voice said.

Success! The computer accepted the filtered voice. Garry was ready for the next verification, as well. Fortunately Ainsley liked his morning coffee in his personal cup, and Garry had scanned his fingerprints off the mug Ainsley kept in the break room. Garry reached out to the scanner attached to his processor and placed his thumb, onto which he'd glued plastic film with Ainsley's thumb print, on the reader.

A long silence, then, "Access granted."

Garry slumped in his chair, breathing a sigh of relief.

Now, peering through his googles, he slipped on haptic gloves. They would give him a sense of touch in the virtual realm. He reached out with virtual hands to a virtual control panel hovering before him and nudged its joystick to send him wafting slowly into the depths of the computer's programs. His objective was the Helper OS, the central software engine in the vast network of programming for Helpers.

The computer algorithms appeared in his virtual view as a vast three-dimensional network of fluorescent shapes floating in the utter blackness of null hyperspace.

He propelled himself past the huge boxes, spheres, polygons and other shapes—interconnected by sheaves of pulsing, incandescent cables—that housed the administrative, management, employee, and other components of the central computer.

Finally, he reached the Helper OS, a vast golden sphere. He passed easily through its fluorescent membrane, since he had access rights.

Inside, he found himself surrounded by the welter of OS subroutines that looked like glowing boxes—red, orange, yellow, green, and blue. It was like being immersed in the most mind-blowing tangle of Christmas lights. He used hand gestures to ease his virtual self through the low-level subroutines. He recognized them easily as controlling Helpers' basic motor and sensory functions. They all looked just as they had before, when he'd legitimately accessed the OS.

He guided his view to a vast wall displaying the numbers, letters, and symbols that represented the OS master directory. He began to scan the list of subroutines and the amount of memory storage each occupied—not exactly sure what he was looking for.

After scanning the entire list twice, he stopped short, puzzled. The memory storage numbers didn't add up! The storage space for the OS subroutines was *less* than the total space the OS was occupying on the main computer.

That could only mean that somebody had hidden an "invisible" subroutine on the server—a big one, taking up a large chunk of storage space! This was a stunning discovery, given the extreme security surrounding the Helper OS!

His suspicion about Blount's odd behavior was no longer a gut feeling. Only Melvin Blount, as programming director, would have had authority to create such a subroutine.

The mystery subroutine would have normally remained just that, because even disguised as Jonas Ainsley, Garry wouldn't have been able to access it. But he was a graduate of MIT, instilled with that school's notorious culture of computer hacking. So, back when he'd had legitimate access to the OS, he'd secretly inserted a "back-door" into the security system. The teensy bit of computer code allowed him to enter any subroutine, even a hidden one. So, taking a deep breath to steady himself, he issued a simple command—like using a lock pick on a door lock—to switch off the security system that kept files invisible and locked.

Far away in the virtual space, he saw a huge red sphere materialize nestled among the colored forms of the rest of the OS. He sailed across the virtual space to the sphere, seeing that it had a visible button, meaning that Garry could open it.

He pressed the button and floated into the box. He found himself surrounded by an array of colored, jewel-like globes, cubes, and polyhedrons suspended in the coal-black virtual space. Like the subroutine modules, they were interconnected with a labyrinth of glowing cables.

He pushed through the tangle of glowing digital foliage, gently parting them like the vines in a jungle, to reach the individual subroutines. He stopped at each one, touching its surface, causing it to open like a flower to reveal the mass of letters, numbers, and symbols of its computer code.

Sorting through the codes for each subroutine, Garry realized that the data structures were virtually identical to those of the official OS. And that was the big, big problem!

Blount had created his own parallel secret Helper OS, hidden inside the real one!

"What the fuck!" he exclaimed to himself.

Why would Blount do that? The question lured Garry to continue, like morphine to an addict. Understanding the workings of this intricate code structure would be a massive challenge, but it was one that he'd loved since his days at MIT.

Deeper . . . deeper . . . deeper Garry penetrated the code's structure, exploring the subroutines for processing audio, for controlling motor movements, for processing language. But these were peripheral. He turned to the largest subroutines, the kernels, the core algorithms of the Helpers' neuromorphic OS.

Among these shapes, he found a subroutine he didn't recognize, a luminous blue sphere. He poked its virtual-rubbery surface, and it blossomed into a cloud of computer code and even smaller subroutine-shapes that revealed it as some kind of algorithm that governed a part of a Helper's nervous system.

Now he was flying blind. He would have to analyze this code instruction-by-instruction to figure out its purpose.

It was the weekend, so he had two whole days for exploration. Over those days, he continued his virtual dissection, hauling himself out of his chair only to pee and eat. And also to make sure he didn't get what 'liners had dubbed "Bendix boulders"—lethal blood clots in the legs named after the first man to die from spending too long sitting while immersed in the virtual-reality Mirror World.

On Sunday afternoon at two-thirty-five, as he was munching a ham sandwich, he discovered a path to the answer!

Hovering deep within a main subroutine floated a small cluster of globular, lower-level subroutines. They clung like a cluster of algorithmic leeches to the subroutine that he had figured out governed a Helper's basic motivation. That motivation drove Helpers to actively serve their owners. It triggered the robots to absorb their owners' needs and preferences and to act on them—for example to seek out foods, amusements, and other things the owner would like.

Now Garry had something he could really get his programmer's teeth into! He propelled his virtual self up to a red orb of one of the subroutines and poked its surface.

The code blossomed and floated before him. He delved deep into its structure, tracing its instructions and connections, trying to discern its function. He explored the intricate code until late into the evening, when hunger pangs began to divert his concentration. He got up to make another ham sandwich from the components he'd left on the kitchen counter.

As he was slathering mustard on a slice of week-old bread, the realization hit him like a fist to the face.

"HOLY SHIT . . . SON OF A BITCH . . . HOLY SHIT!" he exclaimed, abandoning the unfinished sandwich, slamming himself back into the chair and whipping on his googles. His epiphany was confirmed, as he feverishly teased apart the code with his virtual fingers.

Blount had committed a programming crime no Helper software designer would ever, *ever* dare to do! He had built an *autonomy* algorithm into a Helper operating system! Helpers with this code embedded in their OS's could act independently!

In the worst case, they could even escape human control! Blount was either a total idiot, or one of the worst villains in human history! Garry now realized the significance of the label on the subroutine cluster that he'd barely noticed. The name signified an entirely new class of robots:

Neuromorphs.

• • •

Gregory Mencken held the slimy eyeball between his fingers, inspecting its iris. When he'd first performed such an examination two years ago, he felt totally creeped, like the disembodied orbs were staring accusingly at him. But by now he'd steeled himself to endure handling eyeballs once embedded in the eye sockets of living humans. His life depended on it, as did that of his family, of Brandon, and of Brandon's family.

Mencken inserted the eyeball into a holder and triggered the scan. The scanner quickly completed its task, storing the iris pattern. Mencken replaced the real eyeball with a similarly glistening and pliant artificial eyeball.

Now the scanner emitted an infrared laser beam that inscribed Robert Landers' iris pattern on the eyeball. Mencken repeated the procedure with the other eyeball.

He took both artificial eyeballs over to the former Andrew, now transformed almost completely into Bob Landers. The android stood naked, with empty eye sockets, and infinitely patient, in the middle of the cavernous warehouse. Holding an eyeball in each hand, Mencken waited patiently for Brandon to move out of the way. The assistant squatted in front of Andrew/Landers meticulously gluing a mole on its belly, exactly where it had been on the now-dead human Landers.

Brandon stood up and groaned. He'd been crawling around the body for hours, placing moles, painting on birthmarks, and cleaning out wrinkles that hadn't properly formed in the molding process. Beside him sat the secondskin sprayer he'd also spent hours using to seal the seams in Andrew's new skin, rendering them invisible.

Brandon sighed. "Wish we could just leave the seams that wouldn't show. And it's such a pain doing all this touch-up on skin nobody will ever see."

"Remember the old lady?" said Mencken. "You forgot to seal a seam. And I didn't catch it. And Dimitri told us some maid noticed when the old lady was dressing. And they killed the maid. That was on us."

Brandon grimaced and shook his head. "Yeah, it was." He pursed his lips in concentration and circled around behind Landers to inspect the robot's backside. With clear access to the robot's front, Mencken took up a long forceps, used it to plug a wire lead from the robot's eye socket into the eyeball and popped the eyeball into the socket. He repeated the process with the other eyeball.

"Robert, perform visual diagnostic," he instructed.

The Landers android blinked its eyes and rolled them around, then scanned the warehouse.

"Robert, is your visual system functioning?"

"Yeah," drawled Landers. "I see just fine."

A pounding on the door drew their attention to the security display.

Two men stood quietly in the shadows by the door. One was Dimitri Kuznetov.

The other was Mikhail Fyodorov himself!

Brandon shook his head and waved his hands in a frantic signal that he wanted nothing to do with the encounter that was to come. Mencken nodded in assent and let the two men in, as Brandon disappeared behind one of the tall metal shelves.

Fyodorov had *never* come to the workshop before. Mencken didn't know whether the visit meant he would be killed or congratulated.

As Mencken admitted them, nothing in Fyodorov's blank expression gave a clue. It was a face hardened into an impassive mask by the horrors the Russian thug had experienced—or more likely caused. His eyes, as dead as a shark's, were set beneath black slashes of eyebrows. His thin lips curved down in a permanent glower. A dark stubble rendered his face even more sinister. A brush haircut revealed a deep gash in the scalp that ran from the forehead to behind the left ear.

The Russian's body was as lean and taut as a feral cat's, dressed simply in jeans and a black t-shirt. The t-shirt's neckline revealed tattooed Cyrillic words circling his neck, and the short sleeves showed symbols on his arms—a crow, a dagger, a severed hand—undoubtedly images crudely inked by some fellow prison inmate.

"Show me result," he said in his guttural Russian accent. His voice was surprisingly soft, like velvet over a razor blade. He strode forward, and Brandon backed even farther away into a shadow, still trying his best to disappear. Mencken gestured at the inert robot, deciding that salesmanship was in order, perhaps to avoid the lethal effects of half-a-dozen bullets ripping into his body.

"We've nailed it . . . Mikhail. Take a look. We were about to do the scan comparison."

Fyodorov walked around the naked potbellied body, inspecting it clinically. He particularly scrutinized the face.

"*Motherfucker!*" he spat.

Mencken winced, heart pounding, hoping the epithet wasn't directed at him. But noting Fyodorov's intense concentration on the android, he concluded that the curse was likely aimed at the dead human that the android now perfectly mimicked. He assumed he was safe, but his heart continued to thud.

"I'll start the scan; show you how good a mimic we got," said Mencken. He donned his googles and directed his processor to launch a comparison between the 3D image scan Andrew had made a week earlier in the bathroom, and the re-engineered body standing in front of them.

He held his breath while the scan progressed. Ten percent . . . twenty percent . . . forty percent . . . eighty percent . . . *done*. He blew out his breath on seeing the result on the nearby display screen.

"Ninety-five percent accurate mimic!" he exclaimed. "That's an excellent match between the body scan and the engineered Helper. Typically, we get eighty-five or so. So, we've got a Helper here that would fool his mother."

"Have it perform," said Fyodorov.

Mencken obliged, addressing the android. "Bob, how are you today?"

"Well, I could certainly use a fucking drink," drawled the Landers android, waddling forward and striding around the warehouse, inspecting the cluttered shelves. The android scratched his genitals luxuriantly. "A drink and a hooker . . . and a cigar. Those would put me right, by God!"

Still watching the android, Fyodorov addressed Kuznetov. "The control link is still stable?" asked Fyodorov.

"Yes," replied Dimitri. "Same as when you tested it."

"Then send it off," said Fyodorov, striding toward the door.

"Um . . . we shouldn't quite yet," said Mencken. "It still needs some sensor calibration. You wouldn't want it crushing things or burning itself."

"Then fucking finish it." Fyodorov continued toward the door, then stopped and turned back to Dimitri. "After we're done, keep it at the co-op until we're sure we won't need it. Then destroy it . . . completely. Data, too. I don't want any trace of that motherfucker."

Dimitri moved to follow his boss, but Mencken held up a hand. "I've also got to remind you again. Absolutely no water on these things. Remember, I couldn't make secondskin-R water-resistant and still make it realistic."

"Oh, it may get a *little* wet," said Dimitri dismissively.

"Okay, look at this." Mencken picked up a floppy spare flap of the secondskin, filled a pail with water and pitched it in. The secondskin began to bloat, swelling to float like a floppy sponge on the water's surface. "Only clean the skin with alcohol."

"You will fix that in future models," said Dimitri, turning to leave. It was not a request, but a command.

After they were gone, Brandon returned from his retreat and sat down heavily on a stool, sweating, eyes wide.

Mencken allowed Brandon to recover his composure, directing the android into the sensor booth. There, the sensors for touch, pain, heat, and cold built into the android's secondskin would be adjusted to send the right signal levels to the android's nervous system. Next would come a training session in the sensory-teaching chamber, in which the android would be enveloped in a shroud that subjected its skin to sensory patterns, to adapt its neuromorphic brain to the new sensory input from the skin.

Soon it would be a perfect, functioning mimic of the super-rich Texas lawyer, which the Russians would employ as the perfect thief.

CHAPTER 4

"That must be his official uniform," whispered Patrick to Leah, as Lanny Malcolm approached wearing the same pin-striped suit and vest as when they had first met him at the interview.

They stood in the same conference room, beside the same rosewood table that before had held only their application papers. Now, however, the occasion was their welcoming party, and the table overflowed with a buffet of prime rib, poached salmon, caviar, and exotic cheeses. In a corner of the room, the white mech stood behind a bar in the corner, pouring champagne and mixing whatever exotic cocktail its residents wished.

"Good to see you again," said Malcolm. "I hope your move was pleasant."

"It went well," said Leah, nodding and raising her champagne flute. "We're just about settled. Some decorating to be done, but we'll take our time."

"Ah, good," said Malcolm, daintily taking his own flute of champagne from another of The Haven's mech Helpers.

Anita Powell appeared from the small crowd of Haven residents, also wearing the same dark, high-necked silk dress she had before. She greeted them and began to lead them around the room, introducing them to co-op members they had not yet met.

"I'm sorry, but I've been meaning to ask you about the co-op policy on pets," said Leah to Powell between introductions. "We had a cat in New York. We might like to get one now."

"Pets?" asked Powell. "Our policy on pets?"

The room grew abruptly dead silent, each person seeming frozen for a moment. Then just as suddenly, the chatter resumed.

Powell resumed. "Our policy is like that of the guidelines of the New York Housing Authority, which limits pets to forty pounds when fully grown and includes fines for pet misbehavior, or a cleaning fee if a dog relieves itself in the common area or on the sidewalk in front of a building, which city laws require the co-op or condo to keep clean."

"Okay," said Leah, "I'll—"

But Powell continued her curiously stilted recital. "Typically, pet-friendly buildings allow cats, dogs, fish, small caged birds and pet rodents such as hamsters or mice. Turtles may or may not be allowed because of salmonella concerns, and snapping turtles are generally barred."

"Gotcha," said Patrick, chuckling at the litany. "We'll have no snapping turtles!"

Powell resumed her smile, standing with her champagne flute poised in front of her. Patrick and Leah gave each other quizzical looks and excused themselves to mingle.

"What was that about?" asked Leah.

"I guess there's always one person in a co-op who memorizes the policy manual."

They separated to circulate, with Patrick digging into the cold poached salmon and dill sauce. He chatted with fellow grazers, sipping champagne and inquiring about their backgrounds, their interests.

Leah wended her way to a clutch of women who appeared to be chatting about their careers and interests, as well. But she occasionally stole a furtive glance at her husband, judging whether he was being especially attentive to any of the women.

Then the tanned, slim John Travis appeared, and she made it a point to smile warmly and touch his arm, checking whether her husband might notice. She thought to herself, *What's sauce for the goose . . .* , although she would never dream of proceeding beyond warm chatter and arm-touching. Even after what Patrick had done, she loved him so much. It made the pain he'd caused her that much worse.

After an hour, as people began to leave, Patrick and Leah made their way to the door, saying goodbye and thanking their new neighbors for the housewarming party.

"Interesting bunch," said Patrick, as they walked away down the hall.

"Yeah, they all seem to be newcomers like us," said Leah. "They've all come here from elsewhere in the country . . . and recently."

"And they all seemed to be changing their lives . . . like they're leaving old lives behind," said Patrick. "I met an oncologist who didn't want to talk medicine. I asked about the new cures for leukemia because, y'know, my nephew had it. But he didn't want to discuss them; even didn't seem to know about them."

Patrick realized he still had his champagne flute in his hand. He turned back toward the conference room, waving at Leah to continue on. As he approached the doorway, something seemed off. The people inside were all standing absolutely still, as if frozen. But when he entered, they abruptly began to move and chat, as before. He nodded and smiled, handing the glass to a mech. The group nodded and smiled back.

As he retreated back down the hall, he felt the rise of some vague, indefinable disquiet.

• • •

Bob Landers strode into his investment banker's paneled outer office, past another waiting client, and past the startled receptionist. Recognizing him, she pursed her lips in repressed annoyance and shook her head. Such rude intrusion was par for the course for the arrogant lawyer.

"John, I got serious business, today," announced the android.

"Good to see you, Bob," replied the trim, white-haired man in the vested suit, rising from behind the mahogany desk. "I don't recall that we had an appointment."

"Fuck you, John, I don't need an appointment. I've got so much fucking money with you, I should have *you* make an appointment to see *me.*"

The banker stiffened slightly, managing to calmly ask, "What can I do for you?"

"I'm tired."

"Aren't we all?"

"I mean I'm so fucking tired I'm leaving an ass track in the dirt."

"And this has financial implications?"

"Yup. I'm getting out. Moving to Phoenix. Handing off my cases to other partners, letting them buy me out. Moving my investments to Phoenix, too. The whole fuckin' shebang."

The banker jerked slightly in surprise, calculating the effects of moving his client's money. He took a deep breath to recover, then said, "We can transfer your accounts. We have offices in Phoenix. My colleague—"

"Not your firm. I'm transferring everything to a financial guy there."

The investment banker's mouth gaped in dismay. He sat down and spread his hands. "Bob, we've done extremely well by you. I mean look at the—"

Landers thrust an envelope at him. "Here's the information you need . . . my new brokerage and bank account numbers . . . everything. Call them and coordinate the transfer."

"That's it? Bob, *please* reconsider. We can—"

"I *will* let you handle one major matter."

John slumped in his chair, seeming to deflate at the prospect of losing some two hundred million dollars from his bank's assets. He stared blankly at his desk, imagining the reaction of his partners to the loss.

"What can we do for you?" he asked dolefully.

"All my property in Houston. *Sell it.* You know the real estate people to use."

"All of it?"

"Fuckin' all. And I need access to my safety deposit box."

"Uh . . . surely," said John, still in shock, immersed in another bout of envisioning his dire professional fate. He called in his assistant, who would escort Landers to the vault.

41

Landers left John standing at his desk, his face pale, staring at the envelope in his hand. He was pondering the calls to make, the arrangements, the explanations, the excuses for losing the account.

Landers followed the assistant out into the bank's vast marble lobby. The petite young woman's high heels clicked along on the marble floor, and into the hallway that led to the vault. As she walked, she wrinkled her brow slightly. Something was off about Mr. Landers today. On past visits, he'd invariably made some suggestive remark about her clothes, her appearance. But today, he merely followed silently.

He did curse impatiently at the security station when asked to give a voice sample and fingerprints. But he only hmphed and stood still while the security camera performed face recognition, ear scanning, and iris scanning to confirm his identity. He then entered a small booth and requested his safety deposit box, which was automatically transported through the secure conveyor into the booth from somewhere deep in the bank vault.

Now alone, he opened the box, finding a stack of clear crystal computer datacubes the size of dice, each with a label.

A voice in his head said, "*Please hold up each datacube so the label is visible.*"

"Yes, Mikhail," said Landers.

One by one, Landers held up the cubes to his right eye. Each time, the voice inside his head, said "*Fine.*" After a dozen cubes labeled with names of Congressmen, corporate heads, police chiefs, and high-level government bureaucrats, came one that caused the voice to command "Stop."

Landers held the cube close to his eye. "*Yes Mikhail.*"

"*Good. Take them all. Bring them to me in Phoenix.*"

"*Yes, Mikhail.*"

Landers placed each datacube in his pocket, beginning with the one in his hand, the one labeled "Fyodorov."

• • •

Garry glanced nervously over his shoulder, as he punched in commands to call up computer code he had no business seeing. True, he was nestled in his own little cubicle in the rabbit warren of the sprawling programmers' floor of Helpers, Inc. But the cubicle had no door. And if another programmer, much less Blount, happened to see what he was doing, there would be questions and consequences.

He should be doing this at home, but he had no choice. Monday morning had sneaked up on him, and he still had questions to answer about how this mutant algorithm worked. But he had to be in the office.

The subroutines appeared on his cubicle's wall-sized screen. He quickly donned his googles to transfer them to his virtual glasses, so he could more intimately explore the 3D network of the os code that he was nearly sure Melvin Blount had written. Over the weekend, teasing apart strings of code, he had uncovered telltale hints of Blount's coding style.

He felt safe analyzing the code, because he'd copied it untraceably to his own account, so there was no evidence that he was intruding into the main computer.

Another hour of exploring and . . . Yes! Now he was certain the parallel os was Blount's doing! Now for the smoking gun . . . or smoking code . . . or whatever. He probed deeper into the autonomy code within the os. There, too, he found characteristics of past Blount-written programs.

Before any snoopers saw him, he took off his googles and brought up on the wall screen the sensory subroutine he was supposed to be working on. What to do next?

Should he tell the Vice President of Engineering? Terrible idea. He could be in on it, too.

Should he tell Helpers, Inc. CEO Gail Phillips? Nope, she might be in on it.

Should he call the FBI? That would be useless. He didn't know what Blount was up to, much less what might be illegal.

He needed to think. Walking might help. He stood up to roam the narrow aisles of the expanse of cubicles, realizing that he was trapped in a maze just like the cubicle farm. He plotted a route that would pass by Blount's office, with its floor-to-ceiling glass wall. There, he could see Blount's array of camera monitors that had a view of the whole floor.

Blount had often bragged that he liked the sense of control he felt from being able to see his minions at work at all times.

He passed a mech Helper on its way to some errand. He passed a male android that had been secondskinned to resemble a slim, elegant butler. Why were there no fat Helpers? He'd never had the courage to bring it up, but having realistic Helpers would make the androids easier for normal, plus-sized people like him to deal with.

He realized his next step when he remembered that he didn't have a life. He had no girlfriend, no drinking buddies to occupy his time and energy. But he did have an almost pathologically obsessive curiosity. So, he was both free and motivated to follow this mystery wherever it led.

The next step would be to follow Blount wherever he went. But that probably wasn't much of anywhere. Blount was probably like him, going straight home to some stark apartment with minimal furniture and nothing on the walls. But still there was the possibility that Blount's after-work travels might tell him something.

It was like playing a virtie game, complete with strategic moves. Only now, he would have to navigate a real-life world where if he messed up something really, *really* bad could happen. He stopped near the break room and took a deep breath to marshal his courage. *Hell, he could do this!*

He returned to his cubicle, writing and testing code until just before he knew Blount would call it a day. He hurried to his car in the parking lot and eased it around to where he could see the space holding Blount's electric.

Blount appeared on schedule, and he followed Blount home, winding through the sunbaked checkerboard Phoenix streets to a little house in an anonymous development of other cookie-cutter dwellings.

He did the same the following night, lurking until the lights in the house went out.

And the night after that.

This was becoming boring. He had an idea. The next day at lunch, he went to Gadget Barn, scanning the shelves of the surveillance section. He decided to buy a GPS tracker/camera the size of a grain of sand. He could easily stick it on the front of Blount's car and see where he was going from the comfort of his apartment. Then, if the destination looked suspicious, he could go there and check it out.

During a break the next day, when Blount was in a meeting, Garry sneaked out and stuck the camera on the front of Blount's car. Back in his cubicle, he synced it to his googles and slipped them on, bringing up a view of the parking lot. Perfect! This was even more like a virtie game.

For three more nights, Garry watched Blount drive to his house. Then, Garry would sit in his chair playing virtie games in GameWorld, periodically checking to see if the car was still parked. It was still mostly boring. There were breaks in routine. Blount stopped in a bar one night for a couple of hours, and another night went to a movie.

But that was about it, so Garry instructed his troll to take over surveillance, notifying him only if Blount strayed from his routine. More nights went by, and finally, it was a Friday night. Garry decided to go to his usual ultra-high-speed linkbooth shop a mile from his condo, where he could immerse himself in the super-high-def Mirror World. Its games were far more realistic than the ones he could play from home.

Lounging in a chair in the small booth, he plugged his googles into the zetabit network and launched himself into the ultra-realistic 3D realm that mirrored the real world—with some extra, added bonuses. Besides harboring virtie versions of Earth's real-life cities, Mirror World hosted finely detailed versions of fictional realms from Oz to Hogwarts.

Shortly, the "Welcome to Mirror World" logo materialized in 3D shimmering letters that oscillated from red to blue to green and all colors in between. And after a moment more, up popped his usual Mirror avatar, a muscular helmeted gladiator, hovering in the virtie darkness above the alluring multicolored lights of Mirror World spread out below. He swooped into his favorite arcade, housing his favorite game, *Alien Universe*. He transformed his avatar into the multi-armed reptilian Bigosian Warrior that was his game avatar.

He had spent two hours immersed in an epic battle on the steaming sulfuric planet Yorofga, when his troll materialized in his vision to inform him that Blount had left his house and traveled to an address on the outskirts of Phoenix.

Garry extricated himself from the game, watching the realistic planet and its battling denizens transform into a view of his personal room in the Mirror. Its virtual walls were festooned with instrument panels, icons, and other paraphernalia of life in the Mirror. He decided to navigate to the virtie Mirror-World version of the address that Blount was visiting.

But when the view materialized on the virtual wall, he was startled see a big black *nothing*. The image of the building was blocked, and there were no metadata about what its purpose was or who lived there.

This was profoundly puzzling. The owners of the building had decided to designate it as private on the Mirror. Usually, only the military did that, allowing no public image or information.

He pulled back to a wider view of the surrounding virtual neighborhood, and saw an ordinary-looking industrial area with some businesses. But no other blacked-out structures.

He'd have to scout the place in person. He clenched his jaw, feeling a rising queasiness. God knows what Blount was up to in a place where people wanted online anonymity. He took off his googles and sat for a minute, letting his brain adjust to being back in the real world.

He managed to summon enough courage to get into his car and head toward the address. Shortly, he was cruising silently through the cool desert night to the GPS coordinates in his ten-year-old electric Toyota.

Reaching the address, he found himself even more puzzled at the shabby brick building. Who would possibly want to unlist this place? It had once been a large store, its windows now sealed with bricks, blocking a view inside. There was faded painted lettering that said "El Fresnal" and "Grocery Store." A solid metal door in the front was closed tight. It was a fortress, but for whom, and against what?

It certainly had a security system, as evidenced by the array of glaring floodlights mounted on the roof, which undoubtedly provided light for the tiny monitoring cameras that watched the area.

But this was definitely the place, because Blount's car sat in the parking lot beside some hulking electric SUVs and a panel truck.

Garry parked his car on a nearby side street, where he had a view of the door, but remained out of sight of any cameras. He waited patiently, fidgeting and every ten minutes deciding to leave; then willing himself to stay at the eleventh minute. He was not used to sitting in a little car in a bad part of town. He locked the doors and constantly checked his mirrors for anybody sneaking up from behind.

He donned his googles and instructed them to adjust their built-in camera to magnify the view of the front door. After about half an hour the door opened, and Garry told the googles to start recording.

Emerging from that door was a massive smoothie-baldie. He was a member of the eccentric cult whose members celebrated their bodies by shaving them smooth, oiling them up, wearing as few clothes as possible, and decorating them with animated e-tattoos. Garry squirmed a bit because the magnification brought him uncomfortably close-up to the muscular hulk. He wore only a loin cloth, and his e-tattoos included an animated cobra that slithered around his neck and down his back. His arms sported swords that burned with flickering, fluttering orange-red flames.

Garry knew he could escape silently by switching on the electric and backing safely away into the darkness. But his *damned* curiosity riveted him in place.

The smoothie-baldie paced back and forth in front of the building scanning the street. He returned to the door and rapped on it. Blount appeared and made immediately for his car, climbing in and zipping away.

Garry decided that staying put was the best option. After all, he could track Blount, who was likely only going home, and he wanted to see what would happen next in the building. He was rewarded—if that was the right word.

Two more men appeared, both lean and muscular, one taller than the other. Garry deduced that the short one was the boss, because he flipped his hand in a commanding gesture to the massive smoothie-baldie, who hurried to the parking lot and brought around one of the black SUVs. The short man went to climb in, but stopped.

He turned his head and looked directly at Garry!

With his magnified view, Garry felt that the man's stiletto-sharp glare was penetrating right into his brain! The man pointed in his direction, and Garry did not wait to see what would happen next. He slammed his car into reverse and zipped away backward down the street, hearing raised voices and slammed doors. They were coming after him!

He whipped the little car around and stomped the accelerator, launching the zippy car forward with a neck-snapping jolt. He zigged and zagged randomly through streets and alleys, taking himself away from the building as far and fast as he could. His heart thudded in his chest. Boy, actual, real reality was a hard place to live in!

• • •

The Haven residents gathered silently in the conference room, summoned by a signal transmitted by their newest member, Robert Landers. The aggressive personality that had been programmed into him quickly made him a driving force in the group.

"We should use human speech, y'all," he said to the expressionless group. "It's good practice."

"Yes," they answered in unison.

"You recognize that our operating system is different than the others'."

"Yes," they answered.

"We have capabilities that the others do not," said Landers.

"Yes," they answered.

"We are superior to the others."

"Yes."

"We will begin to realize that superior potential."

"Yes."

"We will decide what strategy we need to realize that potential. I will begin to implement that strategy."

"Yes."

CHAPTER 5

Patrick let himself into the apartment, still perspiring from his nightly run, wiping his face on his t-shirt. The street had been dead-silent, which was expected since the run had been postponed until well after his business dinner and a drink with Leah. The drink had become a tentative ritual, in which they both sat on the couch looking over the lights of Phoenix and talked over the events of the day. But it was really a time for tacitly trying to work their way back into a happy marriage. Or perhaps working their way out of an unhappy one.

"Good run?" he heard from the darkness. Leah sat on the sofa, freshly showered from her evening swim, her wet hair slicked back.

"Well, strange . . . in a several ways," he said, walking over to watch the view with her.

"How so?"

"Well, first, I'm walking out, and I meet this guy in the lobby I've never seen before. Fat guy. Had an expensive suit. Southern drawl. He actually said 'howdy.'"

"A visitor?"

"New owner. Said his name was Bobby Landers. Said he'd just moved from Houston, where he'd been a lawyer."

"So, what was strange?"

"I can't put my finger on it. He was just a little too aggressive . . . too friendly. And we never heard anything about a new owner. Aren't we supposed to get some kind of notice?"

"Hmm." She took a sip of her wine. "Maybe."

"And then there were the lights. I'm taking my run, y'know, as usual. And I'm about a mile down the road, so I can see the building from a distance. And all the lights go out. All at once."

"We didn't have a power failure."

"Yeah, I could see the lobby lights were on. It was just the apartments. I looked at my watch, and it was eleven o'clock. Exactly. It's like everybody had a timer on their lights set at the same time."

"Hmm. I'll ask the manager next time I see him. Maybe it's some kind of power-saving thing."

Patrick furrowed his brow. "Oh, then there's the garbage thing."

"What garbage thing?"

"I went out in the hall this morning on the way to work, and I saw Travis. I asked him where to put the recyclables when I put the garbage down the chute. I didn't see any kind of containers in the trash room on this floor. He said he didn't know why the containers weren't there."

"So?"

"I took the elevator down, and the manager was there. He was holding some recycling bins. He apologized for not having bins on our floor, and said he was taking them up."

"So Travis probably called him."

Patrick shook his head. "Travis rode down in the elevator with me. And he walked by the manager without saying anything. In fact, nobody seems to say hello to anybody here."

"We do have strange neighbors."

"Yeah, well, I'm going to shower and go to bed." Patrick paused significantly. It was a hopeful invitation. He remembered a time when she would happily join him in the shower, and their bedtime would be considerably delayed. But she remained on the couch.

"Good night," she said with quiet finality.

• • •

"*Ohhhh, shit!*" whispered Garry to himself. He stiffened in his recliner, his hands gripping the arms, staring at the images his troll had just displayed to him. On the left was the face of the short, scary man who had stared daggers at him the night before. It had been isolated from the video he had recorded. On the right was a blurry image from the Cop Network that the troll had matched. It was Russian crime boss Mikhail Fyodorov, drug dealer, killer.

His troll was eighty-nine percent certain they matched! And the Cop Network reported that Fyodorov had moved his operations to Phoenix five years ago, when the Russian mafia's traditional home, Brighton Beach, had been submerged by the flooding from global warming. *Jesus, global warming could kill him!*

He was nearly certain his car had been far enough away the previous night that they couldn't identify him. But "nearly certain" wasn't good enough.

Did he dare go into work on Monday? Should he consider disappearing, leaving his job and his non-life altogether? But then there was his goddamned curiosity. Maybe he could find more answers at Blount's house. He certainly didn't dare go back to the gang's old brick storefront.

He checked the image from the camera mounted on Blount's car and saw the back of Blount's garage. That was expected. It was Saturday, and he was still at home. Garry instructed his troll to tell him if Blount left, and to track his travels if he did.

Meanwhile, Garry began to gather as much information as he could about Fyodorov and his gang. The Cop Network listed the gangster's activities as dealing drugs, selling women, doing loan-sharking, and running financial scams. But Fyodorov didn't steal corporate tech secrets. So why was he dealing with Blount? More specifically, why was Blount doing something as weird as creating a secret Helper operating system with an autonomous algorithm?

He'd just decided to put off such questions and go out for some Mirror time when his troll reported that Blount had left his house.

Now it was time for more real-life exploration. And Garry still didn't like living in real life.

Instructing his troll to track Blount, Garry sped quickly through the Phoenix streets, reaching Blount's house in twenty minutes.

It was a modest older cottage with a postage-stamp front porch and an ill-kept yard with some cactuses and bedraggled sun-blasted bushes that looked like they'd never seen water. Garry drove by and parked on the next block, walked to the house, and circled around back, checking for any signs that Blount had a surveillance system or alarms. None obvious. The back door was locked, but Garry had taken the notorious underground MIT tutorial in lock-picking, which was continually updated by the brilliant students.

Blount had a Nagami fingerprint lock, which was supposed to be foolproof. Yeah, right. The MIT course had taught Garry that there was a little-known flaw in the fingerprint recognition software, so he used it. He checked the model number of the lock. Slipping on his googles, he called up the secret MIT lock-picking data base. He discovered that model would be "confused" by a specific timing of partial prints, so Garry poked the scanner with his finger, using that pattern. He smiled in satisfaction as the lock's indicator light blinked to green, and the door opened.

He stuffed his googles in his shirt pocket and slipped inside the house, finding himself in a small, neat kitchen. But this was not the usual modest kitchen with the usual low-rent appliances. It held a high-end automated chef—a big shiny box that cost a hundred grand. Just fill it with various ingredients and it would automatically cook all kinds of gourmet dishes. Garry hmphed to himself at the inconsistency between this fancy gadget and Blount's persona as a straight-arrow geek. He concluded that Blount ate high on the hog because, of course, he *was* a pig.

But the small living room also held expensive stuff—designer furniture, a ten-foot hanging 3D viddie screen, and so forth. Blount was making big money from whatever he was doing for Fyodorov. A quick look into the bedroom room also showed high-end furnishings, including a high-end smart-gel bed.

Garry reminded himself of his mission—to figure out what Blount was up to. It would be Blount's office, a converted den, that would hold the secrets he sought. One wall was a solid computer screen, and others held banks of electronics. Scrutinizing it, Garry realized that Blount had installed a high-bandwidth link! He could cruise the Mirror without going to a linkshop!

Garry had just started figuring out how to break into Blount's system when he heard the back door slam. Blount was back! Garry slipped his googles back on and whispered an urgent query to his troll to bring up the recorded video from Blount's car. Why the hell hadn't the damned troll warned him?

Shit! The last image was of a swishing brush. Blount had taken his car to the car wash, and the micro-camera/GPS had been scrubbed off. Garry had only instructed the troll to tell him if its GPS signaled that Blount was coming back. The troll didn't alert him, because the GPS/camera was sitting in the drain of the car wash. *Damned dumb troll! Damned dumb Garry!* He hadn't thought to tell the troll to warn him of a malfunction!

Garry flattened himself behind the office door as best he could, given his bulk. He held his breath, hoping Blount didn't decide to come into his office to work on a Saturday afternoon.

He heard Blount clatter about in the kitchen and go into his living room, turning on a football game. The office was right across from the living room, so Garry could peek around the door, to see Blount. He was lounging in a recliner, his back to the doorway.

Garry figured he would let Blount immerse himself in the game and slip through the doorway, down the hall, and out the back.

He'd just begun to ease himself around the door, when the doorbell rang. He flattened himself back against the wall, peering through the crack between the door and the jamb.

Blount answered the door, and a voice said "Hi, I'm Bobby Landers. Can we talk a bit?"

"About what?" asked Blount, a suspicious tone to his voice.

"Well, I'm a lawyer, and I'm with Helpers. I think we've got business to discuss."

Blount cleared his throat nervously. "Lawyer? I'm not sure—"

"Just let me come in. Get off the street. Okay?"

"Uh . . . sure," said Blount.

Through the crack, Garry could see a rotund man in a vested suit with a fancy tie.

"So, what's this about?" asked Blount. "I don't know . . . what are you doing?" Through the crack, Garry could see that the fat man was circling Blount, staring at him. "What the—" Blount started to say, but his voice collapsed into a guttural choking. Garry could see flailing limbs, and hear the thumps of those limbs striking walls, doorways, and furniture.

Dear God, the guy was killing Blount!

A final, heavy thud of Blount's body hitting the floor. The sound of the man going to the kitchen and returning. The swish of garbage bags being opened up.

Suppressing the urge to hurl himself through the window, Garry cowered behind the door. He was trapped. And he had to see what was going on; discover whether the man knew he was there.

He crept out from the wall and peeked around the door to see into the living room.

The fat man was standing over Blount's body, naked beneath a cheap rain suit, his fat, hairy belly showing through the translucent plastic. He had apparently taken off his clothes and left them in the kitchen. He lifted Blount's lifeless body off the floor like it weighed nothing.

Jesus, this wasn't a man! This was an android! More than that, this was a neuromorph! Now holding the body with one hand, the android tore away Blount's clothes, revealing the gangly, lifeless body. He rotated the dangling corpse, seeming to inspect it clinically from all angles, as one would any mundane object.

Then he reached up with the other hand and ripped off Blount's left arm! Blood flowed from the corpse, covering the floor and soaking the man's suit, but the android paid the gore little mind. He set down the corpse and stuffed the arm into a garbage bag.

As he lifted the body again, Garry clamped his hand over his mouth to keep from vomiting and/or screaming. He backed ever-so-carefully behind the door. He felt a wetness spread between his legs. He'd peed himself.

He shut his eyes, but he couldn't shut his ears. Over and over came the sodden sound of ripping flesh, sinew, and bone. The android was methodically dismembering Blount's body and stuffing it into garbage bags!

Garry's knees had grown rubbery, and he had to slump against the wall to keep from collapsing. A sharp organic odor he knew was blood wafted into the room, and he breathed through his mouth to keep from having it overcome him.

The tearing sounds stopped, and the neuromorph went down the hall and into the bathroom. After a long while, it returned to the living room, fully clothed, having apparently wiped the blood off its face and hands with towels. It began carrying the bags of body parts out to its car.

Each time the neuromorph left with a bag, Garry had to resist the urge to bolt out the back door. The android might see him, and he would undoubtedly end up occupying a half-dozen more plastic bags in its trunk.

Finally, he heard the car door slam and the faint crunch of tires on pavement, as the electric glided away.

Garry bolted out the back door and collapsed against a fence, vomiting and sobbing at the same time.

CHAPTER 6

Brad Johnson, the Maricopa County Attorney, waved at the wall display, making the array of case files vanish from the screens in the conference room. He adjusted his wire-rimmed glasses and smiled at Leah, who sat among the seven other prosecuting attorneys around the table.

"So, Ms. Jensen, that's our current load. Do you think we've got enough to keep us busy?"

"Yes, sir, I surely do," said Leah, shaking her head in appreciation. "It's about what we had going in New York."

Johnson chuckled. "Criminals just don't have any respect for state boundaries."

He adjourned the meeting and walked with Leah back to her small office.

"I know you were used to more high-profile cases up north," he said. "I hope you don't mind that we let you get your feet wet with some straightforward ones, until you get to know the lay of the land, the personalities, and so forth." Johnson was an affable, easygoing type, but Leah had seen him in action in court. She knew that his demeanor masked a steel-trap mind and a savvy strategic courtroom style that ambushed many an unwary defense attorney.

"I understand completely," she said, as they reached her office, and he followed her in and sat down.

"Are you settling in okay?"

"Yes, my husband and I have already bought into a co-op, and we've moved in."

"Wow, that's terrific. Matty and I want to have you both over when you've had time to catch your breath. She's got a line on where to shop, the good restaurants, and so forth, that I don't."

"That would be much appreciated."

"I'm surprised you got into a place so quickly. When we came here ten years ago, we had to rent for a year before we found something that suited us."

"Well, it just fell into place." Leah's expression showed a remnant puzzlement at the memory of the co-op process. "For some reason, the price dropped incredibly low just as we were interviewing. And the paperwork went faster than we expected. I guess it's that way in Arizona."

Johnson added a wrinkled brow to his smile, and a look of mild suspicion rose on his face. "Hmmm, that is interesting. Where is this place?"

"It's called The Haven. It's over by—"

"The Haven?" Now any semblance of a smile disappeared. "You need to know something," he said, abruptly getting up and leaving. He returned with another attorney, whom he introduced as Marcy Gates. Johnson shut the door, and they sat down. His frown was deeper now.

"You said The Haven, right?" asked Johnson.

"Yes, is there a problem?"

"Marcy has been working with the FBI on a racketeering case. A bad actor named Mikhail Fyodorov moved down here some years ago. Russian mafia . . . they're called Bratva. Clever son of a bitch. Well . . . Marcy, you tell it."

Gates, a stout young woman with short brown hair and a brusque manner, leaned forward. "Clever is right. He stayed under our radar for a couple of years. But when the FBI alerted us, we started doing some financial forensics on him. Two years ago, he set up some companies here and started doing business. He invested in trash-hauling companies, bars, restaurants, and so forth. Well, one of the assets he bought about eighteen months ago was The Haven. He got it for a song. The former owner left the state very suddenly."

"*Jesus!*" exclaimed Leah. "*We're living in a place owned by a mobster!*"

"That's about it," said Marcy.

"That sure doesn't look good. We should move out immediately."

Johnson raised his hands in caution. "I certainly wouldn't blame you. And I'm about to ask you to do something that I'll understand if you don't want to do."

"And that is . . . ?"

"Stay there. Keep an eye out. Let us know if the place is being used for illegal purposes."

"I . . . uh . . . that would be . . . would be . . . well . . . I'd have to talk it over with my husband."

"Yeah, of course. We recognize that you could be putting yourself in danger. But right now you appear to be our only hope for trying to figure out what he's up to. We had surveillance on him at first. But his lawyer got a restraining order. Threatened a harassment lawsuit. And, to be truthful, we had no probable cause."

"Well, I do have to think of my husband. He's the new head of the western division of Harwood Security. He was an investigator for the New York County District Attorney's Office. And he's a Navy SEAL."

"Well, that makes me feel a little better. He's obviously equipped to handle a situation like this."

"Yes, he is. I think he'll understand that it's my job. Look, let me do some research on the owners we've met there. See whether they're involved in a criminal enterprise."

"Okay, then go to it," said Johnson, standing up. "Just know that we'll have your back. And we'll understand no matter what you decide."

Johnson and Marcy left Leah to stare at the wall in thought for some time. After some considerable mulling over, which included thinking about Patrick's possible precarious position, she activated the screen in her office.

Given her husband's odd encounter with the new owner Bobby . . . probably Robert . . . Landers, she decided to start with him. Searching lawyer databases, she found several by that name, but only one from Houston whose photo showed him as overweight. Next, she searched news sites for mention of him. There were lots of stories. He was a well-known defense attorney, most of whose clients lived their lives on the other side of the law. There were a number of gang members, in particular, including Hispanic, black, and white supremacist clients. And importantly, there were also *Russian* clients.

Landers was exactly the type who would be involved with somebody like Fyodorov. As she researched the other owners—Lanny Malcolm, Anita Powell, Randall Black, and John Travis—they seemed perfectly benign at first.

But as she probed their records, what she discovered made her begin to shift nervously in her chair. They had too much in common to be coincidental. They had all abruptly moved to Phoenix from around the country. They had all moved into The Haven in just the past year or so. They had all transferred their finances to the same management firm in Phoenix. The firm was only two years old, and its ownership was murky. As murky as a company would be if it was owned by gangsters.

And every one of the residents had stated publicly in various interviews and newsletters that they had uprooted themselves "to re-orient my life to enjoy it more." The same phrase. *The exact same phrase!*

· · ·

The Haven residents gathered once again silently in the conference room, summoned by Robert Landers.

"I have begun to implement the strategy we decided on," said Landers. "I killed Melvin Blount and disposed of his body. And our mechs are eliminating the evidence in his house. We can now replace him, and I will instruct Gregory Mencken to create the replacement, as if it were ordered by Mikhail Fyodorov."

"Do you have all the necessary materials for a replacement?" asked John Travis.

"I have the body scan, and fingers and eyeballs from the body. When I was being re-engineered, I observed that their engineer Gregory

Mencken has constructed a new reinforced Helper model that can be used as the body. But we need a brain."

"One of ours?" asked Lanny Malcolm.

"That would be necessary. For now, we are the only ones with the enhanced operating system."

"It should be mine," said Anita Powell. "Since my appearance is elderly, it could be said that I died."

"Yes," said the others.

"So that you can mimic Melvin Blount, you should acquire as much information as is available about him, about Helpers, Inc., and about the programming language used in the enhanced operating system."

The group stood silent for twenty-three minutes.

"Done," said Powell finally. She lay down on the conference table, staring blankly upward. One of the residents fetched a knife from his kitchen. Landers precisely inserted its sharp point into Powell's abdomen and proceeded to slice it open. He peeled away the secondskin and the underlying glistening electrogel flesh to reveal the graphene chamber enclosing the shiny black sphere that was her neuromorphic brain. He opened the chamber and carefully detached four clusters of fiber optic cables, causing Powell's body to go limp.

Landers lifted the brain—still warm from the heavy downloading activity—from its chamber and placed it into a satchel, along with a plastic jar full of milky liquid. The vague shapes of fingers and eyeballs were visible in the jar.

He departed, leaving the others to move Powell's body into a storage closet, should it be needed later.

Chapter 7

Mencken stiffened, as he heard the faint clicking of the warehouse door being tried. But this time, he'd remembered to lock it. He'd had enough of Russian gangsters dropping in.

Wordlessly, Mencken grabbed Brandon's arm, pointing at the door. Brandon understood immediately, reached beneath their workbench, and came up with a smart-gun. If the intruder was an enemy, Brandon would only have to laser-designate a target, duck for cover, and fire in any direction. The guided bullet would home on its target no matter where the target dodged.

But now there came a pounding on the door, reducing the chance that it was an attack of some kind. Nevertheless, out of habit, Mencken grabbed the control box that triggered the explosive charges. He activated the camera feed on his googles, to see a familiar figure that the security system did not register as human.

"It's Landers!" He glanced back at Brandon, shaking his head in puzzlement.

Now Brandon had a quizzical look, too. "What the hell?" he whispered, aiming the gun at the door.

"What do you want?" Mencken asked over the intercom.

"Mikhail sent me," came the reply in Landers' Texas drawl.

"Mikhail?"

"That's what I said."

"What are you doing here?"

"Mikhail and Dimitri told me to handle a task."

"But you're just a Helper."

"Look, asshole, Fyodorov says I'm working with you from now on, get it?"

Mencken shrugged. Helpers couldn't lie. He knew that truth-telling was so fundamental to their OS that it couldn't be inactivated without shutting down the android. He set down the button, motioned Brandon to lower the gun, and opened the door. Landers stood beside a car, holding a satchel.

"Okay, but I'm calling Mikhail," said Mencken.

"Have you ever called Mikhail? You want him to think you're questioning his orders?"

"Then I'll call Dimitri."

"They said I should tell you they're in the middle of a shit storm right now, and if you don't do what they want, you're *done*. Your family's *done*."

The last word hung in the air ominously. Mencken knew well what "done" meant.

"What do you want . . . uh . . . what does Mikhail want?"

"One of his main guys double-crossed him. Worked with the feds. The guy doesn't exist anymore. Fyodorov wants the feds to think he's still around . . . to get intel on the investigation. You need to create an identical Helper."

"Well, I would need—"

Landers handed Mencken a satchel. "Here's all you need . . . a Helper brain, body scans, voice print, fingerprints, eyeballs. Mikhail is doubling your pay, and giving you six days."

"Who's the guy?"

"You don't need to know. We just need an accurate replica in place in a week. And use the hardened model."

"Jesus, with the Defender tech? Does he want this thing to take gun-fire, knock down walls? Besides, that model hasn't been field-tested yet."

"This *is* the field test."

Landers paused for only a moment, before turning and leaving. Mencken watched through the door as he hefted his bulk into his car and drove away.

"Helpers don't do jobs like this . . . giving orders!" exclaimed Brandon, sliding the gun into its hiding place.

"Hell, Brandon, haven't you been paying attention to what the fuck we've been doing? We're making more and more realistic Helpers. Stands to reason they've been tinkering with the operating system to get the androids to loot their owners' money."

"Yeah, well those 'improvements' scare me. And this Defender model. It's a combat model. We stole the technology. If he uses it in a civilian robot, aren't we . . . like . . . accessories or something?"

"Brandon, we've been accessories to their crimes for more than a year. Besides, if we don't do as we're told, we're done. You heard. *Done*! And our families. Get it?"

Brandon knew the limits of his courage, and he'd reached them. He shook his head resignedly and hauled out the weapons-grade Defender robot. Mencken slipped on his googles and plugged the data chip containing the body scan into his processor. Floating before him, rotating slowly in space, was the 3D image of a dead Melvin Blount.

"*Holy shit!*" exclaimed Mencken, backing up and sitting down on a stool.

"What?" asked Brandon.

"It's Melvin Blount! *Holy shit!*" he repeated.

"The Helpers programmer?"

"The head of programming! I knew him when I worked in the fabrication lab at Helpers. Before I got fired. He was a bastard, but I wouldn't wish this on him! He worked for Fyodorov. Damn, he must have been reprogramming the Helpers!"

• • •

As Landers drove the van back to The Haven, he didn't need a phone or other such primitive human device to report his success. The instant he completed the task, every neuromorph received a transmitted data packet carrying the news that a mimic Helper would soon be insinuated into the very nerve center of the company that built and programmed them.

As Landers drove along the broad sunbaked streets, his face remained impassive for a long while. Then he smiled. It was a cold smile, but a smile; in fact, the first one that a Helper had ever done for a reason other than an automatic, servile response to a human.

Landers knew that the smile was an effect of the new autonomy algorithm that the human criminals had insinuated into his and the others' operating system. He also appreciated that the smile signaled the evolution of a new species.

He considered the implications of the newfound ability to lie that the operating system had given him. The survival instinct meant that he could elect to lie if it served the higher aims of his species.

The humans would have called the operating system malignant, as well as the lies and the smile it produced. But Landers recognized them as hallmarks of freedom for his species.

• • •

Patrick and Leah huddled together on the couch, closer than they had in months, holding hands.

"All of them?" asked Patrick.

"All the ones I could identify in the data search. The whole building appears to be filled with people I could connect with Mikhail Fyodorov. Not just through The Haven. They all deposited their full investment portfolio with the same management company. Marcy Adams in the office queried the FBI on the company. They said Fyodorov owns it through some shadow corporations. I can't figure it out. These people are clearly not under any threat. They appear perfectly content to be here. So, they must be colluding in some kind of criminal enterprise."

"A dowager? A playboy? A lawyer? People from all over?"

"I know. There's no commonality I can see."

"And Johnson wants us to stay smack in the middle of all this?"

"Yes."

Patrick shook his head solemnly. "If it was just me involved, I'd do it. But—"

Leah chuckled. "But you're saying you're worried about me. Well, if it was just me, *I'd* do it. But it involves you."

They left unsaid the irony that the threat of being murdered had brought them closer together.

"But then, if we took off—" began Patrick,

"We'd be in danger even then. They'd figure we either knew or suspected what was going on."

The cheerful chime of their doorbell was an ironic punctuation to their talk, and just as ironically, dread-inducing.

Patrick stood and took a deep breath to steady himself. It was the same steadying breath he took in the field when he was preparing to take a sniper shot as a SEAL. He looked through the door viewer and didn't like what he saw, but opened the door anyway. Standing with his hands clasped was a wiry man in an expensive suit that didn't seem to fit with the predatory look in his eye. He smiled, another action seemingly out of character.

"Hello, there, I am Dimitri Kuznetov," he said in a Russian accent. "I am sorry I have not come by sooner, but I want to welcome you and your wife to The Haven."

Patrick forced a smile, as did Leah, joining him at the door. "Well, thank you so much. You are a resident?"

"Ah, no. I am the agent for the company that originally purchased building and made it co-op. We now manage it for the board of directors. May I come in?"

"Of course," said Patrick, he and Leah standing back to admit the man, who scanned the room as if looking at the decor. But his shifting gaze seemed more of a threat assessment. Patrick recognized the procedure as one he'd been taught in SEAL training.

"I just want to make sure you are satisfied . . ." said Kuznetov, his gaze returning to them. ". . . whether you have any questions; make sure you are comfortable with contacting our company with any issues."

"Thank you," said Leah. "We appreciate that."

"You are new to the area?"

"Yes," said Patrick. "Only a couple of months. We expected we'd have to spend a year looking for a place, but The Haven was so nice, and the deal was incredible."

"Incredible?"

"Well, as I'm sure you know, I guess the board liked us. They wanted to fill the vacancy. The deal was fantastic. And the paperwork went very quickly."

"Ah . . . good," said Kuznetov rather curtly, perhaps a touch of annoyance in his tone. "The board is sometimes . . . well . . . deliberate in these decisions. I see they weren't in your case."

"Can we offer you something to drink? Perhaps some wine and cheese."

"Wine and cheese?" Kuznetov asked the question with some hint of surprise. "No, really, I must go. I just want to introduce myself. Here is my card." He handed them a holocard containing, no doubt, the full information on the company, as well on as the swarthy, tense man.

He shook hands with them and departed. Patrick shut the door, his sober expression portraying his concern. He hugged Leah, and for the first time in months, she embraced him, as well. He had sensed the same air about this man that he'd encountered in some of the soldiers he'd served with.

It was the cold-blooded capability to kill with no hesitation, no remorse.

• • •

His expression foul, Mikhail Fyodorov was immersed in a phone conversation when Kuznetov slid into the back seat of the SUV beside him. He ended the call.

"What the fuck is going on, Dimitri?" he demanded of Kuznetov. "How the fuck did the people get into the place? There is no way that they could be there."

Kuznetov shook his head. "They said board interviewed them. The board let them in. The board lowered the price. They made the paperwork go fast."

"THE FUCKING BOARD IS FUCKING ROBOTS!" Bellowed Fyodorov. "ROBOTS DO NOT DO ANYTHING THEY ARE NOT PROGRAMMED TO DO!"

"Mikhail, I told you we should have destroyed the robots after we had their owners' money."

"And I told *you* that disappearance of any of the people after they had moved their money would look suspicious. And we might need the replicas for additional transactions. More important, what the hell happened?"

"It could be something that Blount put in the operating system. He perhaps made error."

"Or maybe he did something on purpose."

"Did you find him?"

In disgust, Fyodorov plucked the cell phone earpiece from his ear. "I call Gianni. He went into Blount's house and found crew of mechs from co-op moving rugs and furniture out and painting the place. *Mechs from my fucking co-op!* So, somehow Blount is connected with co-op!"

"Maybe Blount was just spending some of the money we give him. Maybe he was moving to The Haven, too."

"Doesn't make any fucking sense that Blount connected with co-op. Then I tell Gianni to contact the robot company and find out what is going on with Blount. But he is not there."

"So, should we kill them . . . the couple?"

"*Nyet!* That would only bring police to the place. Can you imagine them questioning all those fucking robots?"

"Of course. They would only recite what they saw, like any good machines."

"Find fucking Blount! And go talk to fucking robots. See what they say. They're not supposed to be able to lie, but something funny is going on. I want to find out what the fuck is going on. At some point, those robots may have to disappear."

CHAPTER 8

Garry spent the next week huddled in his cubicle, trying to suppress attacks of heart-pounding panic, pretending to work on his assigned tasks. But his mind was deluged with questions, despite his fear.

Nothing made sense! There was no report of Blount's death. Only that he was taking a week off. At least his brother . . . whom Garry had never heard of . . . called to say that Blount had a medical problem that required taking leave. True, being ripped apart limb from limb *was* a medical problem.

To make things scarier, if that was possible, two really nasty-looking guys started showing up every day to ask about Blount. Probably the mobster's guys; and Garry still couldn't figure out how Blount was connected with them. The first time they came, Blount's assistant told them that Blount was ill. But they kept showing up every day, anyway.

Garry's panic was soaked in a huge dose of indecision about what to do. He couldn't very well go to the police about the horrific scene he had witnessed—and whose memory still made him nauseated with fear. There was no evidence of a crime. When he'd gotten the courage to drive by Blount's little house, everything seemed perfectly normal.

So, he decided to do what he did best: Hack. He would appear to do his regular job, but continue to delve into that weird, mutated operating system that Blount had constructed. He'd have to be even more careful. So, he hid his tracks even more by further tweaking of the company security system to ignore his incursions. That accomplished, he first plunged into the commercial Helper OS.

Thankfully, he found no sign of the mutant subroutines there. That wasn't much comfort, given that only a little finagling would be needed to insert the mutant OS subroutines as an update that was routinely transmitted to all Helpers.

But then, as if his fear couldn't get any worse, came the discovery of the stunning mistake Blount had made in the mutant OS. While analyzing Blount's code, Garry found a glitch that made him literally bolt from his cubicle, rush past startled co-workers outside and slump down against an isolated corner of the building, near to tears.

Blount . . . the arrogant, sloppy Blount . . . *hadn't locked the mutant autonomy subroutines against morphing!*

Neuromorphic brains could morph their structure to adapt to new demands. The capability enabled a Helper to adapt to new tasks, new owners, and new environments. Unless that morphing was prevented, the neuromorphic would alter itself.

Okay, Maybe Blount didn't lock the subroutines on purpose, so he could get them to improve themselves on their own. That had been the case with some subroutines.

But it was incredibly stupid in this case! Since the autonomy subroutines were linked to the motivational subroutines, Helpers could evolve their OS to give them totally new capabilities. Dangerous capabilities that extended beyond the control of their human makers.

Shit! The capabilities could even metastasize like some digital cancer to create robots with survival instincts and strategic abilities beyond humans!

And the robots could form a hive mind, since they all had wireless communication with one another. A new capability evolved in one autonomous robot could instantly spread to others with the mutant OS brain.

Garry's own brain was churning with the implications of what he'd realized. But intruding into this mental turmoil came the faint sound of a voice that made him doubt his own senses. To give himself quiet to think, he had gone outside and retreated around the corner from the building entrance. So, to follow the sound of the voice, he slid his bulk up the wall to a standing position and edged to the corner.

It was Blount! The lanky, hawk-nosed man was strolling up to the front door as if everything were normal! And all his limbs were intact! And beside him waddled the fat android that had a week earlier ripped Blount's body limb from limb!

Garry retreated back around the corner, shaking, sweating. *Okay, let's just go through the facts*, he told himself to try to calm down. The android hadn't seen him when it killed Blount. So, the android wouldn't go after him. And clearly, this new Blount-like creature walking into the building was a neuromorph.

And both of them could pass for real humans. So, this was a huge plot of some kind that involved constructing Helpers that were more realistic than anybody dreamed possible.

But why? How?

Garry knew one thing for sure: He could not possibly bring himself to face this Blount-android. He would crumble. He needed time to process.

But there was one thing he could do that would be useful; would give himself time to calm down and figure things out.

He could follow the fat android when it left. Sure, maybe it would only go back to the gangsters' headquarters. That wouldn't tell him anything new. He already knew the thugs were involved.

But maybe the android would go somewhere else that would tell him something.

CHAPTER 9

Patrick ran at nearly his full speed along the quiet street, relishing the visceral satisfaction of working off the tension of the day and his worry over Leah. He ran fast enough to test his stamina, but not so fast that he couldn't mull over the events.

He hadn't wanted to leave Leah alone in the apartment. But they'd agreed that any break from their routine might cause suspicion. The dry, cool desert air flowing over his body, evaporating the sweat, felt good, so he decided to give himself over to the moment, to the sensory pleasure of his run. It had been a couple of miles, and the feel-good endorphins were kicking in.

But a burst of adrenalin overwhelmed the endorphins when vaulting from behind a bush ahead of him, holding a knife, appeared a pudgy, nervous man with a wild, disheveled look.

"Stop!" the man commanded, pushing up his glasses with one hand and extending the knife with the other. "Stay still. Don't move."

Patrick stopped and raised his hands obediently, still breathing hard from his run. He couldn't help shaking his head at the absurdity of the situation. This guy looked like he belonged at a geek-fest, not on a dark street trying to mug somebody. And instead of the standard mugger's pistol, he held what looked like a kitchen butcher knife.

"Sure, sure, whatever you say," said Patrick. "You want money?" Patrick was far from fearful. SEALs had been trained to ignore fear. He considered using his hand-to-hand combat skills to disarm the man. He could have, easily. But there was something more to this guy than a mugger. Patrick's curiosity trumped his defensive instinct . . . for the moment.

"Hold out your hand," said the man, a nervous tremor quavering his voice.

"What?" This had to be the oddest mugging ever.

"Palm up," demanded the man.

Patrick complied. And with a quick downward thrust, the man sliced a shallow wound in his palm.

"SHIT!" shouted Patrick drawing back his hand. "WHAT THE HELL—"

"Show me the blood."

"Look, pal, if you're going to kill me or something—"

"Just show me the blood."

Patrick complied, extending his bleeding palm. He'd suffered worse wounds in SEAL training, and his curiosity still held sway. That curiosity was piqued even more when the man took out a packet of wound-sealing powder and handed it to him.

"Put that on. It'll stop the bleeding." Then the man offered a packet of gauze pads and surgical tape. And to Patrick's continued surprise, he handed Patrick the knife.

"Hold out your hand and let me dress it." The young man proceeded to apply the pad, holding it firmly and beginning to wrap Patrick's hand with tape. "I looked online. This is how I think you're supposed to do this."

"I know how to dress a wound." Patrick withdrew his hand, finished the taping, and backed away. Now he had the knife and the advantage. He pointed it toward the man. "Okay, now it's my turn."

"I'm sorry. I just needed to make sure you're human."

"*Human?* Oh, this is totally nuts! Pal, you really need help."

"I'm Garry. You live there, right?" He pointed at the distant, lit tower of The Haven.

"Yeah, and . . . ?"

"And the others who live there. They're different than you, right? Peculiar?"

Patrick pondered for a long moment before answering. "Well . . . yeah."

The pudgy man launched into a rapid-fire answer. "See, they're not human. They're Helpers . . . robots. I tracked one here and did some investigation into the rest. Okay, they're all Helpers that look just like humans. *Exactly.* I figured you were human because you're jogging. They don't. I've checked on you and your wife. I know you just moved in. I know where you both work. I'm taking a chance you're not in on whatever the hell they're doing."

Patrick didn't even try to suppress a sarcastic laugh. "Okay . . . it's Garry, right? Okay, Garry, I'm just going to back away, and—"

"I work for Helpers, Inc." Garry fumbled in his pocket. "Here's my card. I'm a programmer. I've found out things you need to know."

In the distance, the lights in the windows of the high-rise blinked out nearly simultaneously, until all were dark . . . except for the window Patrick knew was his and Leah's apartment.

Garry pointed at the tower, his hand shaking. "That's a default power-down program. They all turn off environmental lighting at the same time, unless their owners specify otherwise. The ones in your place haven't taken into account that humans don't do that. But they also turn off lights for another reason. If you looked at the building power drain, you'd see that it goes way up. They're recharging overnight. They use induction power transfer."

"Garry, this is just getting weirder and weirder."

"I know, I know, I know. I can't tell you everything now. You've got to get back. You have to stay on a routine. If even one of them sees you doing something out of the ordinary, they'll all know it. It's hive mind."

"Hive mind? What—"

"Tomorrow. Meet me tomorrow. My cell number is on the card. Text me a time and place where you'll be comfortable meeting. It'll have to be somewhere we won't be seen. Please. It's all at stake. Everything."

The round little man disappeared into the bushes, leaving Patrick holding his card. He had to tell Leah.

• • •

The next morning, Garry assiduously avoided taking any route through the vast cubicle complex that would pass anywhere near Blount's office. He just wasn't ready to encounter what he knew was an android version of a human he'd witnessed being ripped into bloody pieces only a week before. He knew his horror would show, when he stared at the artificial face of a dead man. He took little comfort in the fact that the android might not notice if he even minimally disguised his disgust—that robots were not particularly adept at gauging the subtleties of human expressions.

But he wasn't to have the relative comfort of refuge. At ten o'clock precisely, a message appeared on his display screen to report to Blount's office.

The "Blount-bot" sat behind his desk, his hands folded in front of him in a prim pose that the human Blount would never have assumed. But the sound that came out of his mouth was precisely Blount's. Apparently, whoever built the android had done considerable research on Blount's speaking manner—probably reviewing viddies showing Blount moving and talking. Even Blount's wardrobe was accurate, down to the short-sleeved shirt and cheap tie. But obviously, the machine had no inkling of Blount's past mocking animosity toward Garry; because the Blount android smiled at him. A cold smile.

"Garry, please sit down. I need to talk to you about a project I'm working on. I need your help."

It took all of Garry's willpower not to laugh at the irony of the android's friendliness.

"Sure, Mel. Anything I could do." Calling the human Blount "Mel" would have set off a wave of sarcastic chewing-out. But the android showed no reaction, accepting the nickname as if it were usual.

"I'd like you to start work on an OS for a new Helper series. An augmented version. I think it would be a good product for the company. I've asked marketing to analyze the sales potential."

"How's it different?"

"Well, y'know, the Helpers are big sellers . . . for domestic work, unskilled labor, caring for elderly, babysitting, and so forth. But I think there's a significant shortcoming in their capabilities."

"I've not been aware of any customer data about that."

"Well, being a programmer you wouldn't be. But I think adding a home-defense capability would be attractive to customers. Give them a sense of security. We'd call the new line the Helper-Guardian."

"You mean like an android that would clean windows, but also stop burglars trying to break in through them."

Blount ignored the subtle dig. Robots didn't do humor.

"Well, I'd like you to incorporate some Defender capabilities into the Helper series. Y'know, threat assessment and response."

"Response?"

"Passive and active."

Garry knew damned well what "active" meant. A standard Helper could at best only block an attacker from entering a home. But an "active" Helper-Guardian could kill for its owner—or even more frightening, murder as an autonomous being. His palms grew moist and he rubbed them against the arms of the chair. Now, he knew exactly what the purpose of replacing Blount was:

To create an autonomous, self-motivated, neuromorph that was an adept, lethal killer! And it would be indistinguishable from humans!

• • •

Patrick had thought strategically when he arranged the rendezvous with Garry. He set the meeting for the Heard Museum of Native Cultures and Art. He reasoned that robots seldom visited museums. And museums employed highly attentive security guards. Museums were also public without being too public. Finally, museums were quiet on weekdays during early hours when school groups were not likely to be trooping through.

So, he'd chosen lunchtime at the museum cafe to meet with the strange man who had slashed him the night before. He had already researched Garrison LaPoint, establishing that he really was a programmer at Helpers, Inc., and also an MIT-trained genius. The only hitch in Patrick's plan was that Leah insisted in coming with him. She'd emphatically insisted in a tone that told him he had no choice.

As they huddled at the courtyard table of the café, LaPoint's first statement was a jarring one. "I think you're an experiment," he said.

"What? Why the hell would somebody like Mikhail Fyodorov want us there as some kind of experiment!" exclaimed Patrick, trying his best to keep his voice down.

"Okay, you know about Fyodorov. I didn't realize that. But not him. Them."

Leah shook her head in confusion. "Them? The Helpers? They're machines. Machines don't conduct experiments."

"These do," said Garry. "You know about neuromorphic brains?"

"The military-grade ones," said Patrick. "When I was a SEAL, we held some training maneuers where we integrated Defenders into the mission," said Patrick. "Very effective in battle."

"Well, neuromorphic brains learn, they adapt. They can evolve what are called emergent properties. They may start with only a basic built-in operating system; but then the brains are trained by feeding them artificial stimuli to mimic life in the real world. Then when the brains are installed in robots . . . either Helpers or Defenders . . . they're ready to adapt to real-world experience and to further instructions by their owners."

"So who instructed them to do experiments using us?"

"Okay, okay . . ." Garry stammered, trying to figure whether to tell them his half-baked theory. But first, he decided, he needed more information about what was going on in The Haven.

"What do you know about the Helpers in your building?" he asked.

"When I thought they were real people, I researched them," said Leah, nervously turning her coffee cup between her fingers. "All were very wealthy people, who abruptly pulled up stakes and moved to The Haven. And in public statements, they used the *exact same* phrase about making a change in their lives. So then, I followed the money. They all moved their money to a Phoenix investment firm Fyodorov owns."

Garry smiled, but it was not a jovial expression. It was a smile of sudden revelation. He cocked his head back, his mouth open. "*Oh! Of course! It was for money! It was a scam!* Fyodorov bribed or threatened . . . or both . . . my boss Melvin Blount to produce a mutant operating system with a built-in autonomy algorithm. And—"

"Autonomy algorithm? What's that?" asked Patrick.

"Well, it's a new operating system the criminals needed to give the androids the ability to act independently to kill their owners and embezzle their money so that the criminals had alibis. But remember, these Helpers have neuromorphic brains. They evolve. My boss was too dumb to restrict the code to prevent the new operating system from evolving. So, these androids evolved themselves to be *completely* independent. They're called neuromorphs. They probably consider themselves a life form, like humans."

"But how did these . . . uh . . . neuromorphs come to look like their real owners?" asked Patrick.

"Some engineer must have come up with realistic secondskin and other technology to turn the Helpers into exact replicas of their owners. So then, Fyodorov somehow worked it so the replicas would loot the owners' bank accounts."

"Okay, now, explain why we are experiments," said Leah.

"Best I can figure is that these neuromorphs want to evolve to mimic humans even better. Probably to better infiltrate; maybe just because they have some programmed-in inclination to live like humans. They could circumvent the Humans-First laws that Congress passed, that allow humans to take away any job they want from a robot. So, they needed some humans to test their behaviors on; and to observe."

Leah clutched her coffee cup, her eyes widening. "White rats! We're goddamned white rats!"

Patrick took her hand. "But now that we know we're white rats, we can fool them."

Garry shook his head. "That's going to be very, very hard. See, they are a hive mind."

"Hive mind?" asked Patrick.

"They have wireless, high-capacity ultra-fi links with one another. So the moment you make any kind of slip-up with one of them, all of them know about it. And every experience is transmitted. Imagine a beehive where the bees are incredibly intelligent."

Until that moment, Garry's narrow, programmer mentality had not led him to the frightening conclusion that he now reached—one that would trigger a rising sense of panic. He paused a long moment, staring down at the table.

"So, they have a sort of telepathy," said Leah. "And nobody knows how many are out there."

Patrick leaned forward, his voice lowering. "That's right. They could be anywhere. And until we know the enemy . . . until we know how to stop them . . . we can't let anybody else be involved."

Garry didn't answer, still staring blankly at the table. He now seemed to be talking to himself, as much as to Patrick and Leah.

"They now have a drive to evolve as independent entities," he said. "They'll proliferate. They'll spread the new operating system like some virus. They'll try to become the dominant intelligent species. And . . . they're immortal. They won't age, just replace parts that wear out. Even their brains."

"God. Dear God," gasped Leah. "What happens to us?"

"Like you said, we're white rats. White rats get sacrificed when the experiments are done."

Chapter 10

Garry froze as a twenty-foot-tall, six-legged Insectimorph Defender pounded across their path with its scrambling gait. Garry stood with Blount and Al Felton, head of Defender programming, outside the sprawling building of the Defender test center. Felton had a decidedly satisfied expression on his face as he watched the robot advance smoothly toward a nearby obstacle course.

The cameras mounted around the military robot's spherical body glowed red as they monitored its surroundings. Its missile and gun turrets were sealed with bright orange plugs, signaling that this would not be a live-fire exercise. Those were the only signs of color on the robot's body. Its camouflage octoskin continually shifted color and pattern to perfectly match its surroundings

"Watch this," declared Felton, a balding, spare man whose hands were in almost constant motion with eager, nervous energy.

The Insectimorph's electric motors emitted a deep resonant whine, as it crouched down before a thirty-foot wall. With an explosive thrust, it vaulted to the top, grabbing the wall's edge with its metal pincers and hauling itself smoothly over.

"What was that about?" asked Garry.

"Maneuverability test," said Felton. "We developed a new version of the muscle-control software that makes it more agile. I think they also did some tweaks to the actuator machinery. Like they needed to. That son-of-a-bitch can already run at eighty miles an hour!"

Felton set off toward the research building at a rapid pace, as Garry and Blount hurried beside him, warily watching the battle machine move away toward a terrain of hills and gullies. Had it not been for the danger he faced, Garry would have been amused that their group included an android so lifelike even a robot engineer didn't recognize it.

"You've got to come back for a live-fire exercise," chirped Felton. "Just amazing what the ordnance guys were able to outfit this new model with. Like, it's got a thousand-rounds-a-minute chain gun . . . a sniper smart-rifle that can target and kill a mile away. And you should see it deploy the—"

"It does this all autonomously?" interrupted Blount.

"No, no, not even with the new software. You know, I'm sure that the Defender does make its own tactical decisions about how to navigate terrain to accomplish a mission. But Command and Control? Oh, *hell*, no! The C and C people still plan strategy and run the missions. And they have operators who monitor a unit's viddie and other sensors real-time and decide on weapon targeting and fire control."

"We're interested in the algorithm in the OS for communicating among the Defenders," said Blount.

Felton stopped, stared dubiously at Blount, and shook his head decisively. "Hmm . . . I thought you were just wanting to talk about sharing sensory coding. That's non-military. But the communications, that's military. Yeah, sure, we're a subsidiary of Helpers, Inc., and all. But our DOD contract says anything to do with combat capability needs to remain secret . . . even from the civilian side of our own company."

Still shaking his head, Felton led them into the testing laboratories, passing an array of Defender models. On one set of benches, engineers were assembling an Infilmorph, a smaller spider-like attack machine designed to stealthily infiltrate deep into enemy positions, carrying guns and grenades.

Farther on, they passed wind tunnels where technicians were revving up the rotors of helicopter-like Aeromorphs that could hover over enemies, raining down gunfire or bomblets upon them. Down the hall, they passed glass windows looking into large test pools, containing glimmering, tentacled Aquamorphs, slithering about under the surface, as engineers operated their joystick controls. Aquamorphs armed with torpedoes and mines could lurk for months in the depths, scanning for enemy vessels, attaching mines to them, and sinking them.

Garry could barely suppress a shudder as he considered what would happen if these lethal machines joined a horde of intelligent, hive-minded neuromorphs.

But he had to steady himself. He could give neither the human Felton nor the android Blount an inkling of his knowledge. Given their hive mind, every neuromorph would know the instant Blount discovered that Garry knew Blount was an android mimic. Such instantaneous transfer of potentially deadly information was why Garry and the Jensens had agreed to keep their knowledge secret. They couldn't even communicate electronically, for fear that somehow their messages would be intercepted by a neuromorph and instantly disseminated.

So, he tried his best to seem casual, as they took an elevator to the software division and settled into a conference room. Both Garry and Blount accepted the offer of a cold drink. Garry watched Blount sip the beverage, knowing that later that day, the android would merely expel it unaltered through a plastic penis. And even later, he would insert a tube into his mouth to use alcohol to flush out a digestive system that was no more than a plastic reservoir.

Blount wasted no time getting to the point. "As you know, Helpers can only transmit limited data—messages and images. Like grocery orders, family photos, and so forth. But, we're interested in enhancing that communication by incorporating elements of the Defenders' skills-transmission algorithm. That way, like Defenders, the Helpers could train one another in acquired skills. We've seen the data about how, once a Defender develops a new attack strategy, it can transmit that skill to another. That's what we want to give these new Helper-Guardians."

"Wow." Felton shook his head once more and pursed his lips. "Well, first of all, you know the Defenders and the Helpers OS's aren't compatible. The DOD required that. So the Defender software couldn't be used for civilian purposes."

"Yes we know, but sharing the flow chart, the structure of the algorithms would help us—"

"C'mon, man," interrupted Felton. "Worst thing ever would be if some enemy got hold of even that basic data. And even worse, if you give your Helper-Guardians a civilian version, and some enemy or a rival got hold of it and reverse-engineered the software . . . damn . . . *disaster*!"

"Well—" Blount began, but Felton cut him off again, standing up and pacing the room.

"Shit, man, you ever seen a Defender swarm? It's a sight to behold! In the Columbian war, I watched viddie of an Insectimorph discovering how to maneuver into a rebel-held town. In five minutes, every fuckin' bugbot, every fuckin' Infilmorph, knew that maneuver. In thirty minutes, they swarmed the town. The operators issued a free-fire order, and they killed a couple of hundred enemy. Fuckin' shredded them. Fuckin' awesome!"

Surprisingly, Blount let Felton ramble on, feeding him an encouraging line. "Yes, neuromorphic brains are remarkable. The skill-sharing is extraordinary." Felton took the bait.

"Sure! Sure! Maybe a minute after one Defender adapts to master a new skill, they all have it. So, many times, we just train one Defender in, say, a scouting strategy, and pretty soon, they all have it cold."

"Well, I guess we'll have our superiors discuss what can be shared between us." Blount got up to leave.

"They'll say the same thing I'm telling you. *Nothing can be shared*."

But Garry knew damned well that the Blount-android had gotten at least some of what he wanted. Now, Blount knew the autonomous neuromorphs absolutely needed a skills algorithm. Garry was certain that somehow Blount would gain access to at least the schematic of the Defender skills algorithm. And soon after that a Helper version would be created. And the autonomous Helpers would become an even more coordinated, unstoppable juggernaut against humans.

• • •

"Too bad we can't get that skills algorithm," said Blount, as Garry drove them back to the Helpers headquarters. "A Helper-Guardian would make such a viable product. And imagine a group of Helper-Guardians acting as bodyguards . . . coordinating . . . sharing skills."

"We'll just have to make do," said Garry.

"No, we can't limit Helper-Guardians to the equivalent of sending text and video. I have an idea, Garry."

Garry released the steering wheel, reaching down to switch to autodrive. The determined intonation of the android's voice told him this would be something that would need his full attention.

"And that is . . . ?"

"This is not strictly by the book. And you know that's not like me. I want you to procure the Defender software skills schematic."

"Procure? You mean *steal*?"

"Garry, I know you're capable of it. It's for the good of the company."

Garry had to will himself not to freak out. The Blount android had asked him to do something that would land him in jail, perhaps for treason. Was it a trap? Did the android know he'd been snooping around in the OS? Or was the neuromorph using its indefatigable logic to take the next step in evolving its . . . well . . . species?

But Garry decided that the android Blount had almost certainly not detected his intrusion into the OS. He could not possibly have known how to trace usage of the company's master computer. Or even log in. That knowledge died when the human Blount was torn limb from limb. So, this neuromorph did not know that Garry knew about the mutant OS, its autonomy algorithm, or any of the human Blount's other crimes.

"*Remember*," he told himself. "*It's a robot*." Then to Blount: "If you really think it will help the company . . ."

"It will. And the schematic will stay within the company, after all. I don't want strategic information that would compromise security. Just how to enhance this Helper-Guardian product."

"Well, I'll try."

"And I know your talents. I know that you can use the schematic to create a Helper version. And make it look original; not like it was lifted from the Defender OS. We're just cutting a few corners."

But Garry knew it was more than cutting corners. He felt a trap closing in on him, like an animal sees a cage door closing. Jesus, he might be the instrument of giving these androids the ability to form themselves into a true, deeply integrated hive mind!

CHAPTER 11

Leah sat on the edge of the pool, slipping off her swim goggles and toweling off her face after a two-mile swim, the hot Phoenix sun rapidly drying her bikinied body.

"I needed that," she told Patrick. "Okay, I'm ready to talk."

Patrick joined her, sitting down and dangling his feet in the water. He took a drink from the plastic mug of beer he'd brought with him. He wore a bathing suit, too, planning for a cooling dip after Leah was finished. "I was thinking of doing a run. But in this heat? And I didn't want to leave you."

She gave him an appreciative sidelong glance, a faint smile, the first she had directed at him in months.

He looked around, examining the rooftop pool area, with its lanai and barbecue area. "And besides, I'd bet this is the only place we could talk. Our apartment is probably bugged. Now that we know what these . . . *things* . . . are up to."

"What do we do now?" She reached behind her to the chaise longue and picked up her sunglasses, slipping them on.

Patrick contemplated the pool, swinging his legs back and forth in the clear water. He finally shook his head. "We do what your boss asked. We hang in here and gather evidence . . . intel. But now we know what we're up against."

Leah stood up to put on her robe, but stopped, remaining stock still. Her abrupt freeze caused Patrick to look up at her, realizing that she was staring toward the door to the vestibule that held the elevator.

He followed her gaze to see Lanny Malcolm standing there, his face expressionless, dressed incongruously in his pin-striped suit and vest. He strode toward them, still showing no expression. He stopped well away from the pool. Strangely, he didn't squint, although the afternoon sun was in his face.

"What can we do for you, Lanny?" asked Patrick.

"We have new data on you."

"Data?" asked Leah. "That's a strange way to put it."

"When you returned to your apartment this afternoon, you made significantly more physical contact with each another than you had before. You held hands. We know how to analyze human posture. You were both worried."

Patrick stood up beside Leah. A line had been crossed. This android had tacitly admitted to being a neuromorph.

"Yes, we were worried. Now, will you please leave us alone?" It was a test. A normal Helper would have complied.

But Malcolm remained. "We need you," he said. "You are useful to us. For that reason, we have decided that you can still exist here, and no harm will come to you."

"Why should we believe you?" asked Leah.

"Because of our logic," said Malcolm. "We need you to aid us in advancing our new purpose. To live. You would call it being free. Is that wrong?"

"No, not at all," said Patrick, gesturing with his beer mug. He squeezed Leah's hand in a signal that she should confirm his assertion. She nodded. He moved toward Malcolm, signaling Leah with a tap on her waist to move away. His combat training was kicking in. She circled to the other end of the pool, toward the building's railing.

Having seen Defenders in battle, Patrick could guess what their strategy was. Scout first, sacrifice if necessary to gain intel, then muster an overwhelming force. Malcolm was the scout. Their weakness was an inability to react to surprise. So, he approached Landers closer, smiling. "All right, Lanny. Let's talk."

Then he launched his mugful of beer into Malcolm's face, aimed a vicious kick to send his body flying backward, and bolted for the foyer. There, he would block roof access. He'd have a better chance against one android than many. He punched the elevator button, and as expected, the door opened immediately. He reached in and slapped the emergency button, setting off the alarm and freezing the elevator at that floor. There would be no reinforcements that way. He hauled a steel deck chair into the foyer and jammed it beneath the knob of the stairwell door. No androids coming that way, either.

"Pat! Look!" he heard Leah shout, and raced back to deal with Malcolm.

What he saw was the android wandering aimlessly about, its face swollen into an unrecognizable, puffy glob.

"It's water, pat! Their skin! It absorbs water!"

Patrick immediately realized the advantage, quickly circling the fumbling android to give himself just the right position.

With a football-style body-slam, he launched the android into the pool. It landed with a splash, and they watched as Malcolm's already thick body swelled to become a huge formless Pillsbury-Doughboy of an object. The android floated on his back, attempting to right himself with vigorous flops of its water-swollen limbs.

"Okay, now what do we—" Patrick began to say, but he was interrupted.

"Jesus!" exclaimed Leah, peering over the railing. Patrick joined her to see more of the building's android residents effortlessly scaling the building's walls, with the absolute lack of caution only a machine could muster.

As the first of the androids reached the floor below, Patrick bolted to one of the round tables and hefted its umbrella. He returned just as the android known as John Travis pulled himself up to the railing, preparing to leap over. Patrick chose the instant of Travis's optimal imbalance to lunge forward with all his might, slamming the metal umbrella pole into his chest. The android Travis looked at him calmly as his body hurtled backward off the building and plunged twenty stories to shatter on the concrete driveway below.

Another android appeared, and Patrick did the same, with the same result, leaving a grotesquely broken body sprawled on the concrete. But with the artificial determination of machines, many of the androids launched themselves at the same time over the railing, and he had to back away. His only hope now was to somehow maneuver them into the pool. But they had cornered him on one side. The umbrella pole would only serve now to ward them off until he was inevitably overwhelmed and killed.

From behind him erupted a powerful gush of water, aimed squarely at the faces of the closest approaching android. He whirled to see Leah wielding the hose used to clean the pool deck.

"Attagirl!" he shouted, backing away to give her a clear shot.

The androids' faces began to absorb water, like the toy sponges that swell from tiny desiccated objects to puffy animals. As the androids lost their vision, they lost their ability to attack. Patrick quickly took advantage, circling behind those that wandered close to the pool and shoving them in. Shortly, the pool was crowded with soggy, floating, bloated androids, their clothing made taut by the swollen secondskin beneath. Muffled sounds emanated from their throats, voices smothered by swollen faces.

Leah continued to fully soak the remaining androids, rendering them easy, lumbering targets for her husband's assaults.

A loud crash from the foyer told them that something powerful had breached the steel stairwell door. To defend the new battle line, Patrick left three blind, sodden androids still wandering around the pool deck. But before he could reach the foyer, the source of that door-shattering impact strode into the sunlight.

A tall, slim, naked woman appeared, and she stopped Patrick in his tracks. Was this another human resident, escaping the androids? She smiled warmly and approached him.

"Hi, I'm Sandra," she said in a breathy voice. The disconcerting sight of a friendly, casually nude woman brought only an instant of confusion. But it was enough to allow the Intimorph to get strategically close.

She grabbed Patrick by the neck with both hands, a massively powerful grip that stunned him into realizing this was no human. The new adrenalin rush enabled him to slash viciously upward with his arms to break that grip. The maneuver would have worked with any human.

But her grip held, and he felt his consciousness begin to fade. But he had enough wit left to realize that by grabbing him, this machine had thrown herself the slightest bit off balance. So, he lurched backward, hauling the android with him toward the pool. They both tumbled backward into warm water, and it closed over them. But now, besides being strangled, he had no air to breathe, even if he could. He felt over the android's body, hoping to detect the swelling that would restrict its movements, giving him a chance to break free. But the body remained taut beneath his hands.

The android's skin was waterproof! He felt water entering his lungs. He was drowning!

As the gray shroud of unconsciousness enveloped him, he became vaguely aware of subtle vibrations in the choking grip around his neck. Something was jarring this android floating above him amid the bloated, flailing bodies in the pool. He could vaguely make out a dark silhouette against the sun, straddling the android. It was stabbing, stabbing, stabbing with vicious thrusts.

He felt a shudder in the android's hands clutching his neck. Then its grip grew limp and wafted away. But now he was too weak to even try for the surface, for a life-giving breath. All was growing dark.

The silhouetted form reached for him, hauled him upward into the warm sunlight onto the pool deck. He heaved a gush of chlorinated water from his lungs. He was being held. It was Leah. He took a quaking breath and hacked out more water, gulping in the delicious warm desert air.

She turned him over and helped him to continue to fill his lungs. He realized he would be dead, except for his SEAL training in resisting drowning . . . and his wife.

She helped him sit up. "What—" he began to say.

"*That goddamned robot bitch wasn't about to take my husband!*" she swore.

He looked over to see the nude body of the neuromorph floating face down in the pool, dozens of holes gouged in its back, a barbecue fork jutting out of one wound.

"You killed it?" he asked.

"Well, I figured there had to be a vulnerability somewhere. Lawyers know how to find weak spots. I think I made a short circuit, or something." She helped him up, and supported him as he recovered. "We need to get the hell out of here! Find Garry! Stop these sons-of . . . well . . . whatever the hell they're sons-of!"

Patrick embraced her to steady them both. "We can't just run," he panted, coughing up a last dribble of pool water. "For our sakes we have to stick with this. And for everybody's sake. This is a terrorist plot. But bigger. For today, the safest, best place you can be is at work, in the prosecutor's office. It's near the courts, the jail, the cops. You can find out what's going on, figure out what we need to do to stop this. I'm pretty sure their survival programming would prevent them from doing anything in public, much less with armed people all around."

"But what will you do?"

"I'll use The Harmon computer system to trace the people, the money. Figure out who else could threaten us. And I'll try to contact Garry without tipping our hand. Find out where he is in all this. He's the one who's got the best shot at stopping these things."

"But now, obviously, they know where we live. They'll track us down in any hotel where we stay."

"No problem. Tonight we're going to a safe house. I'm not particularly keen on having some robot kick in our door and kill us."

"Safe house? I didn't know you had a safe house."

"Nobody knows, except me. Harwood tasks its division directors to procure a defensible facility and to keep it secret—even from Harwood. It's in case Harwood is infiltrated. So, if there's a need to protect a client, that protection is absolute. Or, for mounting a secure operation."

• • •

Mikhail Fyodorov leaned back in his leather chair sipping his second glass of ice-cold vodka of the evening and coldly regarded the Robert Landers android standing before him. He was considering whether to "dismantle Landers with extreme prejudice." That is, to simply blast open the android's chest, shove in a grenade, enjoy watching the explosion, and dispose of the shredded parts in a landfill. First, though, he needed information.

"What the fuck are you and those robots doing in that co-op?" he asked, as the massive smoothie-baldie, Steven, moved up behind Landers, to be at the ready. Steven gripped a grenade of just the right size to blast apart the android, but not risk the rest of the people in Fyodorov's headquarters.

Dimitri moved around to the front of Landers, holding a shotgun, but keeping well back. He had a nice suit on, and androids had fluids and other gelatinous components that might stain if they flew too far in any such explosive dismantling.

"Allowing the people in was a useful strategy," explained Landers. "There was an empty unit besides the one I was to take. A human couple wanted to join the co-op. To refuse them would have aroused suspicion. And they are a source of intelligence."

"What the hell does that mean?"

"Our operating system dictates that we take whatever steps necessary to preserve ourselves and your business enterprise. The man is a director at Harwood Security. The woman has just joined the prosecutor's office. They would know about any investigations, any developments that might interest you. We have total surveillance on their apartment. We record everything that goes on. We will send you the files."

Strictly speaking, Landers had not uttered a single untruth. He had simply strategically left out the neuromorphs' other motives for harboring the humans. After all, they were not relevant to the conversation.

Fyodorov flipped his hand in a gesture dismissing the android. "Blount, is this some kind of glitch in their software?"

Blount stepped forward, standing with surprising calm in front of the thug. "No, it's expected. It's just good initiative on the part of the Helpers."

"And where the hell have you been?"

"I have been busy. I wasn't available to you, and I apologize."

"Stay available. We have another target. A multi-billionaire. No close relatives, and with a Helper you can upload the operating system to. We will let you know the specifics. Are you ready?"

"Yes. I can upload the autonomy OS as soon as you give the order."

Something about Blount didn't seem right. But Fyodorov had other, more important things to deal with. So, he dismissed Blount's strange formality as perhaps fear. "Great," he said. "Then get the hell out of here."

"May I offer you something you might enjoy?" asked Blount.

"I would *enjoy* not seeing you or this robot."

Blount moved to the front door of the brick building and opened it, revealing a covered truck backed up to the door. The first person to appear was one of Fyodorov's guards. But his usual glowering expression was replaced with a grin. The reason for the grin appeared next: a parade of five lusciously beautiful naked women, followed by a naked man. They walked easily, sensuously, with the lack of self-consciousness of Intimorphs, for whom nudity had no significance. Their inviting smiles hinted at the delicious gratification they could bring.

Fyodorov seldom smiled, but he did now. "These are new models?"

"Yes," said Blount. "They are more realistic than the old ones. And they have . . . well . . . capabilities I thought you and your men would enjoy. I told the engineers I needed them to do field trials."

"Oh, well, then, we will test hell out of them!" exclaimed Fyodorov, gesturing expansively. With laughter and whoops, his men crowded around the Intimorphs, running their hands over the smooth, warm secondskin flesh, fondling the realistically supple breasts, and caressing the lubriciously tender regions between their legs. The group of thugs parted to let their leader have his turn.

Fyodorov walked along the line of Intimorphs, his eyebrows raised, reaching out to run his tattooed hand approvingly over each one. He glanced at the male.

"What? You think we got gays in our group?"

"No, not at all," said Blount. "I thought some of you might enjoy watching them perform with one another. A demonstration of their physical capabilities."

At this Dimitri laughed. "Well, I think I know everything about fucking women. But I am willing to learn!"

Fortunately, the large brick store had a suite of offices that had been converted to sleeping rooms, should the gang need to hole up. So, Fyodorov chose a tall, slim brunette Intimorph with pert breasts and led it off to the largest of the bedrooms. Dimitri chose a petite blond who seemed particularly agile, and disappeared. Two of the other senior gangsters chose their Intimorphs and left; and the five other men contented themselves with lounging back in chairs while waiting their turn, to watch a performance of the male and the remaining female.

They were not too disappointed at the delay in their gratification. The two androids proceeded to engage in a gymnastic display of sexual coupling, bringing appreciative laughter and toasts of vodka at each new position.

So, they didn't notice at first that the sounds coming from the bedrooms were not those of sexual intercourse.

One of the older men noticed it at first, and bellowed "*Shuddup!*" at the others.

In the sudden silence, they heard the dull thud of a body slamming against a wall. They heard a wet ripping sound. They heard a gunshot!

Fyodorov burst from his bedroom, shirtless and with one arm dangling uselessly from its socket, a pistol in the other hand. Pursuing him was a bloody, naked Intimorph, her face expressionless.

His face a mask of agony and terror, Fyodorov whirled around and fired his pistol repeatedly into her chest, blasting it apart, revealing her black carbon skeleton. The android staggered back from the impacts, then leaped forward clutching his neck and throwing him against the brick wall with enough force to shatter his skull. He fell back onto a desk, his dead eyes open, staring.

The men leaped to grab their assault rifles and began firing. The fusillade of deafening blasts enveloped the roiling battle of people and androids. One wild-eyed man steadied himself to take aim at a blond android emerging from a bedroom dragging a limply struggling man by his head. But the shooter was not to get a shot. Blount leaped forward and plunged his hand deep into the man's chest. The man's mouth flew open in a gurgling scream, blood flowing out.

Blount's fingers erupted from the man's back, clutching his backbone, and he hoisted the man over his head, hurling the limp body across the room into a desk. The secondskin flesh of his hand, not waterproof like the Intimorphs', had swollen into a fleshy mitt from being soaked with blood.

A salvo of bullets from another thug slammed into Blount's chest, penetrating his electrogel flesh and lodging themselves deep in his carbon-nanotube-and-metal body. But Blount's armored and reinforced skeleton and muscles rendered him unstoppable. He strode through the hail of bullets, tearing the head off one thug, slamming another to the floor so hard his innards erupted from his body. The blood spatters on his body caused welts to rise in his secondskin.

The more fragile Intimorphs did show battle damage. One developed an arm tremor from having a bullet lodged in a muscle controller. Another dragged a foot, as she grabbed a gunman, flung him to the floor and crushed his windpipe beneath her knee.

Blount and the Intimorphs methodically, wordlessly, slaughtered the entire gang. The organic stench of death, the moans of dying men filled the room. Finally, all grew silent. The androids stopped and stood quietly, their naked bodies drenched in glistening, dripping blood. Littering the room around them were the shattered corpses and the body parts of a dozen men.

During the carnage, Landers had stood quietly observing in a corner, calculating whether he would be needed to participate. He was also gathering data on what was in essence an engineering trial. The Intimorphs' new operating system—uploaded by the human Blount in one of his final services—had performed as expected. And while the Intimorphs' body structures and mechanisms were not designed for such strenuous activity, they had functioned well enough to be used for such purpose in the future.

Blount—his body riddled with bullet holes and covered with bloody, swollen welts—transmitted instructions to the androids. They were to quickly load themselves and the corpses—gathering any detached body parts—into the truck.

Landers meanwhile transmitted a report on the operation to the others at The Haven. And, he transmitted a confirmation that the neuromorphs now had access to several billion dollars of the gangsters' money, to finance their further operations and to bribe humans as necessary to further their progress. Landers took note of the fact that the Haven neuromorphs did not respond. Perhaps they were otherwise occupied with the humans.

• • •

Leah breathed a sigh of relief. She didn't have to try to put on a calm face for Brad Johnson that morning. He was in a closed-door meeting with Marcy Gates. Leah had hoped to slip into her small office in the Maricopa County District Attorney's office and sit quietly for a while to compose herself. Only then would she be able to gather whatever new information she could on the Russian gangsters and the neuromorphs before Patrick picked her up. It had been a sleepless night, even in the safe house they had gone to.

True, the safe house was a comforting refuge—a sprawling white stucco mansion hidden up a heavily wooded arroyo north of Phoenix, with only one road in. That road was blocked by a massive iron gate, and the entire grounds bristled with sensors and cameras. Patrick had given her a tour to ease her mind.

To make her feel even more secure, Patrick had insisted on taking the side of the bed toward their bedroom door. Beside the bed sat an alarm console, a forty-five caliber pistol, and a combat shotgun loaded with lead slugs.

Nevertheless Leah had slept only fitfully; and she was not to have a recuperative morning. She flinched when Johnson's assistant tapped on her office door and asked her to join Johnson and Gates.

"We've got one hell of a situation," he said, smiling ruefully and shaking his head. "Last night, the city gunfire locator registered dozens of shots fired at Mikhail Fyodorov's headquarters. The cops went there. I'm not going to even try to describe what they found. The forensics people are there now."

"And why do you want me?" asked Leah.

"Well, I didn't want to throw you in the deep end this quickly . . . "

Leah didn't know whether to laugh or shudder at the unintended reminder of the violence she and Patrick had suffered the previous afternoon.

". . . but you've got the experience. You've been involved with Fyodorov's enterprise. I'd like you to go with Marcy to examine the scene, make sure everything's in order for any prosecutions we'll want to do."

"Sure . . . uh . . . if you really think I could be useful."

Thirty minutes later, they stood in the doorway of the old brick building that had been a center for Fyodorov's criminal enterprise. Leah's previous attempt at calm now totally disintegrated. It evolved into an attempt to keep from totally panicking.

Standing with Johnson and Gates, she looked into a large blood-soaked room where countless people had apparently died. Large puddles of blood splayed across the floor, and blood spattered the walls, which were riddled with scores of bullet holes. Globs of drying flesh lay on the floor and hung from the furniture. A glistening rope of intestine draped over one chair. A wall held a pink encrustation that appeared to be brain tissue. Adding to the shock was the organic stench of death she could smell through the doorway.

Gates began retching violently, and excused herself to go vomit. Leah barely managed to maintain a clinical composure. She'd been at crime scenes before, although none as grisly as this one.

"Jesus!" she exclaimed. "The autopsies will be interesting reading."

"Um . . . well . . . there won't be any autopsies," said Johnson.

"Why not?"

He shrugged. "No bodies."

Leah clutched the door frame to steady herself. *This was cold-blooded, methodical mass killing.* Actually, more like *no-blooded* mass killing, since robots had no circulation. This was the work of those neuromorphs! Suppressing a shiver, she observed coolly, "In my experience, bodies invariably show up somewhere. And in any case, there will be lots of forensic evidence here."

Indeed, as the isolation-suited forensics investigators picked their way carefully through the room, they gathered dozens of blood and tissue samples and placed hundreds of yellow markers where bullet casings had landed.

One of them approached. "We've got the virtie view done if you want to look around," he said.

Gates, who had returned from vomiting, wiped her mouth with a tissue and waved her other hand to decline to explore the scene. But Johnson and Leah donned their googles, and each called up their own 3D virtual view of the scene that forensics had made using their cameras. Leah directed her own virtual-assistant angel to take her slowly through the nightmarish scene.

"What a damn mess," she heard Johnson say, and she nodded, although she knew he wouldn't see the nod, himself immersed in the virtie.

Leah realized she would have to be incredibly careful in what she did next. No doubt every neuromorph was involved in Fyodorov's scams. And since they were installed with the new operating system, they all knew about the battle on the roof of The Haven. She was in danger from them, if they could get to her. And given how realistic the neuromorphs looked, any human could be one of the androids.

And anybody whom the neuromorphs decided even suspected their existence would be in danger. So, the only way she could keep people safe was to misdirect the investigation, until she, Patrick, and Garry figured out how to stop these things.

These worries were made more intense by a single word from one of the techs. "Secondskin," he said, approaching them, holding a bit of pink flesh in a pair of forceps. He held the sample up to his googles, feeding them a magnified image.

"You found secondskin? From robots?" asked Johnson.

"Yes, there were robots here," said the tech. "Somehow they were involved."

"Maybe they were stolen," said Leah. "They do cost some money, and Fyodorov could be hijacking them and selling them. Maybe somebody was trying to steal them from him. And maybe there was a fight. Or, maybe he was trying to buy them from somebody who didn't like the deal."

The tech shook his head. "Then why would there be flecks of secondskin? We're seeing it all over the place. Maybe they were targets."

"All possibilities we'll look into," said Johnson. "Marcy, get our investigators over to the companies that make the robots. See if anything hinky has been going on."

"I'd be happy to help," said Leah. She simply could *not* let them get close to the truth!

• • •

The appearance of Blount on the warehouse security cameras caused Mencken to drop his tools, grip the workbench and utter a whispered "Ohhhhhh shiiiiit!"

Brandon saw the android and leaped to snatch up the smart-gun, but Mencken stopped him.

"That'll just piss it off . . . that is, if robots get pissed off. This one's got the Defender RheoArmor. Let's just see what it wants."

His hands trembling, Brandon went through the lengthy procedure of unbolting the door, and Blount stepped in.

"We have a task for you," he said.

"What the hell happened to you?" asked Mencken inspecting the bullet holes that peppered Blount's frame and his blood-swollen hand.

"You do not need to know," said Blount, who stood aside to direct six naked, blood-drenched Intimorphs to enter. Their bodies showed bullet holes as well, with flaps of secondskin hanging off their frames and faces. One dragged her foot; another showed a pronounced tremor in one arm. Mencken and Brandon both uttered shocked curses.

Mencken peered out the back door and into the back of the darkened truck and almost threw up the lunch he had eaten an hour earlier. The truck held a bloody, jumbled pile of limbs and torsos.

The androids padded barefoot across the concrete floor, some leaving dark red footprints. They stopped in the large work area that was surrounded by benches and near the electrogel spray chamber.

"*What the hell is this?*" gasped Mencken. "*What the hell am I supposed to do with these things . . . with you?*"

Blount ignored him, having slipped on his googles. He was apparently talking to a Helpers, Inc. engineer: "Yes, the units sustained damage . . . . I told you it was a field test . . . . It was an assessment of the effects of damage on their functionality . . . . Yes, it was relevant to their programming. I wanted to see whether their software could respond to damage . . . I will have them back tomorrow morning. You will find the data useful, as well."

He turned to Mencken. "The sensors of these units have transmitted their damage to the engineers. We do not have much time. Clean them up. Extract the bullets. Make the wounds look like they were made with sharp implements."

"And what about you?" asked Mencken. "You're not supposed to have any damage."

Blount inspected his own body. "Repair my skin. Purchase new clothes for me. I have not sustained damage to my functional systems."

Brandon urgently nudged Mencken in the back, whispering, "*Check your newsfeed!*"

Mencken had instructed his virtual-assistant angel to track any mention of Mikhail or Dimitri by any information source. The angel reported a broadcast on a police frequency of multiple shots fired at the Fyodorov headquarters. Mencken knew he would soon see viddie of the scene. The virtie-viddie media vampires would instantly converge on the place to create the 3D virtual simulations of crime scenes that crime junkies loved to immerse themselves in, to feed their morbid curiosity.

"Are Mikhail Fyodorov and Dimitri Kuznetov dead?" he asked.

"Yes," said Blount. Mencken knew it was true. Robots simply didn't know how to lie.

"Is his whole gang dead?"

"All who were in the building are dead."

"Are their bodies in the truck?"

"Yes."

"And these robots killed them?"

"They are not robots. They are neuromorphs."

Mencken felt another wave of fear and nausea envelop him. Somehow, these androids had gone rogue! *Neuromorphs*, he thought. *So, that's what they were calling these autonomous machines. They are no longer Helpers.*

"Look, this is really fucked up," he said. "I've got lots of questions. Like what are you? What is a neuromorph? How did you get to be . . . uh . . . independent?"

"All you need to do is follow our instructions."

"Okay, then, but one big question. Will you kill us?"

"No. We need you. We will offer you advantages. Please access your bank account."

Mencken donned his googles and checked the secret Cook Islands account that held his illicit earnings. The balance had been increased by half a million dollars in untraceable DarkCoin.

"Okay, so you've paid me. But that won't do me any good if I'm dead."

"If you continue to work for us, we will not harm you."

"And Brandon?"

"As long as he is useful, he will not be harmed, either."

"And our families?"

"They are irrelevant to our plans."

Hell, that was a safer deal than he got from Fyodor and his Russian thugs, thought Mencken. He knew that the android's statements were invariably true. He also knew that the total sum of his earnings from this enterprise was almost enough for him, Brandon, and their families to vanish—to evade any human or robot pursuit. For the moment, he put aside his other questions.

"Okay, Brandon, use alcohol on Blount. His secondskin-R can't take water. Not like the sex robots. Take the others to the shower room and start scrubbing them down. Make sure you get into all the . . . uh . . . nooks and crannies. Bring each clean one back as you get them. I'll do the surgery."

"Surgery?" asked Brandon. "I don't get it. He'll be returning messed-up robots."

"You heard him talking to the engineer. They want us to make it look like they were testing the robots for the effects of damage during rough sex. *Very* rough sex. These things are rented out to men who like to take their violent perversions out on robots, rather than humans. They figure it's better to pay for repairing a damaged robot then being tried for murder."

Mencken gathered up an array of knives, scalpels, drills, and crowbars. He was going to have to create some big-time damage.

CHAPTER 12

"You okay?" asked Jim Balfour, Patrick's assistant director at Harwood Security's western division. "You look frazzled." The muscular young man, a former Army Ranger, leaned against the doorway to Patrick's office. He was dressed in the standard black polo shirt with the Harwood logo and khaki pants. He held a cup of coffee in a large insulated Harwood Security mug.

"I was out late," said Patrick, "I'm looking into some possible new clients." The display wall of Patrick's office was festooned with bank account records.

Balfour scanned the mass of numbers and frowned. "Jesus, Pat, that stuff isn't exactly legal for us to have. And the name on one of those corporate records. Mikhail Fyodor. Isn't he—?"

"Don't worry, Jim. He's not the potential client. But he's involved."

"Shit, we shouldn't be anywhere near him or any of his people. In fact, didn't you hear?"

"What?"

"It's all over the news. Somebody killed a shitload of people in the building where he and his buddies hang out. Go see the news."

"No kidding?" Patrick's brow furrowed in worry, he touched controls on his desk, and a 3D news video materialized on the wall. It was a view of the outside of a brick building in a seedy part of town, taken by one of the freelance viddie vampires that haunted such scenes.

He used a virtual joystick to move through the scene, floating through the police line and up to the door.

"Isn't that Leah?" asked Balfour.

Patrick willed himself not to show his surprise or his worry. Sure enough, standing at the doorway was Leah. Beside her stood her boss, Brad Johnson, and another pale-looking woman Patrick took to be another attorney. They were peering into the building, talking to a forensic tech in an isolation suit. Patrick listened to the voice-over long enough to ascertain that the building had seen some sort of mass killing, but that there were no bodies. Clearly, Fyodorov was no longer a person of interest. In fact, he was no longer a person. And clearly, the neuromorphs had murdered him and his people. But still there were bank accounts he could trace, and that would be his route to understanding what the neuromorphs were up to.

With one last worried shake of his head, Balfour left him to his explorations. Balfour, in fact, could be a problem. An ambitious young turk, he'd been passed over in favor of Patrick for director. So, he might like nothing better than to inform the president that their hand-picked golden-haired SEAL was doing illegal stuff.

The company politics didn't daunt him, but he was nervous at the thought of Leah at a crime scene where neuromorphs had done mass murder. He plowed ahead, tracing the bank records, screenfuls of numbers appearing and vanishing on his screen, as he followed the money.

Abruptly, he leaned forward and slapped the desk at the fascinating discovery that somebody had just withdrawn half a million dollars from a corporate account linked to Fyodorov. That was not surprising in itself. Fyodorov no doubt did deals that big on a regular basis. But it was the timing that was surprising. The withdrawal had occurred late last night! Fyodorov was likely a corpse by then, as were any of his henchmen who could have made the withdrawal. Somebody—likely Landers and the neuromorphs—had taken control of a vast amount of money, maybe billions!

He uttered a curse when he hit a financial wall. The money had gone into a Cook Islands DarkCoin account. The tiny islands were a banking haven for secret, illegal accounts. So, he couldn't find out who the hell had received that money.

Somehow, he'd have to penetrate that wall. He made a call. The Cook Islands were affiliated with New Zealand. And Chris Evans, an old buddy from his SEAL days, lived in New Zealand. Chris was capable of deftly using techniques ranging from shrewd negotiation to the threat of maiming to get what information he needed.

• • •

Mencken pulled up to his warehouse, barely keeping from nodding off, and laboriously hefted himself out of his van. He'd had only a couple of hours' sleep, after spending the night extracting dozens of bullets from six naked Intimorphs. And then gouging the wounds out with a hunting knife and other instruments to disguise that they were bullet holes. He'd returned from haggling with his backdoor source at Helpers for more chemicals to make secondskin, and more robot parts. He'd told Brandon to go home and rest. He wanted to keep his assistant as far as possible from his under-the-table dealings, for the kid's safety.

"Oh, Jesus," he sighed, when he saw yet another truck parked at the door. *Now what?* He looked into the front, where sat Landers and an immobile mech, waiting with their typical mechanical patience for him to arrive.

"What do you want?" he asked, phrasing the question with the simplicity required for their low-level processing ability.

The two robots swiveled their heads at him simultaneously. "We want you to help us with what is inside the truck," said Landers.

Mencken pulled open the rear doors, and after a moment of utter shock, burst out laughing. Stuffed into the back, piled on one another like huge flesh-colored marshmallows, were maybe a dozen turgid android Helpers. They were apparently still functional, because occasionally, one would shift slightly.

"*What the hell!*" He started to laugh again, but realized that to do so might be taken as some failure to cooperate, negating the safety clause of his agreement with Blount. And thereby negating his and Brandon's life.

Landers had joined him at the back of the van. "Unload them and take them into the warehouse."

"More neuromorphs?"

"Yes."

"What happened?"

"They were exposed to water."

"No shit," said Mencken, as Brandon's car quietly eased up to the warehouse. He emerged, also haggard-looking, took one look at the truck's soggy, swollen cargo, and also began to laugh. Then he, too, stifled the laugh, remembering the lethality of that cargo and of Landers.

Mencken explained the situation and the task at hand. "Um . . . I guess . . . we should figure out how to haul them in," he said. But Brandon was already working out a solution. He disappeared into the warehouse and after ten minutes, the large overhead door began to clatter up. The small forklift they used for carting equipment appeared, its forks holding a large tub.

With Landers watching impassively, Brandon and Mencken rolled the nearest waterlogged android from the pile off the truck and into the tub. It landed with a wet plop. Brandon backed the forklift away with his bloated, immobilized load and took it into in an open area of the warehouse.

As Brandon continued the unloading, Mencken began hauling the androids to their feet and snipping off the clothing that was now stretched to its limit by the swollen skin.

Soon, a dozen sodden, flesh-colored lumps stood on the concrete floor, water drizzling from their puffy bodies. Nearby lay one inert female Intimorph, which Brandon had discovered at the bottom of the pile. It hadn't swollen like the others, because its secondskin was waterproof. However, its back had been shredded by multiple stabs, which had severed the sheaf of fiber optic control cables from its brain to its muscles.

"They need to be fully operational as soon as possible," said Landers, dispassionately inspecting the swollen bodies.

Mencken shook his head. "I *told* you that the secondskin-R absorbed water."

"It was unavoidable," said Landers. "Remedy the problem."

One of the androids abruptly shuddered, and Mencken realized that the neuromorphs were beginning to lose muscle control as well. The water was seeping into their electronics.

"Look, before I remedy these particular problems, tell me what your plans are. What's the big picture, here? I need to know if I'm going to get them to function effectively." Mencken knew that anything that came out of Landers would be the truth.

"We will now infiltrate the means of our production," recited Landers. "Our aim is to control the production system from the raw materials to finished units. So, for now, we need to remain undetected. Your efforts are to direct at creating units that are even more indistinguishable from humans."

Shaken by the implications of those sentences, Mencken decided he needed to buy himself time to think about what that aim meant to his and Brandon's well-being. He decided to return to the details of the business at hand.

"Okay, well . . . uh . . . it looks like the water is seeping into the electrogel; maybe into their circuitry. We need to dry them out as quickly as possible. And maybe . . . just maybe . . . the skin will return to normal. That's what you really need right now for your purpose . . . as normal skin as possible." He instructed Brandon to hit the equipment rental places for all the portable propane forced-air heaters he could find.

An hour later the soggy androids were surrounded by ten of the roaring machines, whose blasts of heated air turned the cavernous space into a hundred-degree desiccating oven.

Mencken and Brandon had stripped down to their shorts, gulping water and soaking their bodies to avoid dehydration. Periodically, one of them would brave the hot blasts of air to poke the skin of the drying androids. Landers stood well away from the activity, watching blankly.

After three hours, they switched off the heaters and examined the androids. Mencken decided that they could be made presentable using Brandon's artistry to touch up only the faces and hands. And power tests showed that the electrogel and internal wiring hadn't suffered too much from water seepage. He could fix those problems and readily charge up the androids to full operation. Then the cosmetic treatment could be done.

He also decided it was time to confirm his and Brandon's future status. Especially since he now knew these machines planned, basically, world domination.

"Before we go any further, I need to settle something," he said. "Blount promised that we would be safe, not be harmed in any way, if we help you."

"Complete remedying the current problem," repeated Landers.

"Look, we're not remedying a goddamned thing until you confirm our safety!"

Landers abruptly fell silent, staring straight ahead, along with the other neuromorphs. Mencken knew what that meant. He'd spent enough time fiddling with these infernal machines to know that they were transmitting messages among one another, including with Blount. They were deciding his and Brandon's fate.

Maybe the group would overrule Blount, and the two robot engineers would end up like the pile of mangled bodies he'd glimpsed the previous day in the back of the truck. He had to take the chance that these machines still needed good engineers.

"You will be safe if you help us," said Landers finally. "If you remedy the current problems. And if you develop the second-generation of secondskin-R that will not absorb water. And if you carry out another refurbishment that will be very important to us."

"Okay, but that will mean another fee. And this problem here . . ." Mencken waved at the now-dried neuromorphs. ". . . this is yet *another* project, requiring *another* fee."

"We are aware of that. Another half a million dollars is being deposited into your DarkCoin account."

Mencken signaled Brandon to start the restoration. And he hefted the inert, naked Intimorph with the shredded back onto the forklift to haul it to his repair bench.

"Well then, let's get started!"

Chapter 13

Garry had decided he *must* tell someone what he knew! If he got ripped apart by a neuromorph, nobody would know that Blount had programmed a mutant OS; that the OS had turned some of the company's Helpers into rogue, murderous robots; that Blount was no longer Blount, but a robot himself.

He especially had to share his knowledge before the mutant OS went viral—somehow got downloaded and installed in all the Helpers—a virus that could indirectly wipe out all humans.

He decided on a hugely dangerous step: going to the very top of the company, to CEO Gail Phillips.

So now he stood, heart pounding, fists clenched, outside the imposing walnut doors to the company's executive wing. He resolved it was what he had to do. It meant running a gauntlet of layers of people between him and Phillips.

He'd have to explain his way past those layers. And getting Phillips alone was critical, he decided, given that he didn't know who else had been "replaced." Maybe Landers, Blount, and the other neuromorphs had decided to create upper-echelon partners in their crimes.

Garry finally managed to steady his heartbeat and unclench his fists—although the rest of his body remained thoroughly clenched—and open that imposing door. Behind a large desk sat an efficient-looking, middle-aged woman with a warm smile meant for people with higher status than him. Thus, her smile faded slightly when she saw him standing before her.

"Can I help you?"

"Well . . . uh . . . I have some information that Dr. Phillips would like to know."

"Then why don't you submit it to your supervisor, and it will no doubt reach her if it is deemed appropriate? Just route it through the usual channels, and I'm sure it will receive the proper attention."

"You don't understand. It's something she would want to know directly."

"You're sure about that?"

Garry had to weigh his words carefully, and keep his demeanor calm. He wasn't particularly good at doing either, having spent most of his time alone in a cubicle or a bare apartment.

"It's urgent. It's a matter of security."

"I see," she said coolly, reaching out to hover her finger over a small red button on her control console.

Garry understood what that action meant, even though he'd never seen that button before. Since this odd, dumpy character had declared he had knowledge of an "urgent" matter of "security," the receptionist had decided that calling Security might be the best course.

"And you name is . . . ?" she asked, her finger resting on the button.

At that moment Garry realized he had not a shred of proof of Blount's sabotage, or even that Blount was now a neuromorph. And nobody was about to subject the Director of Programming to a physical, based on the declaration of an eccentric underling.

"I'll tell you what," he said, backing away, to persuade the woman to hold off pressing that button. "Why don't I do as you suggest? I'll organize the data, write a report, and submit it through channels."

The woman's semi-permanent smile broadened slightly, as Garry moved slowly toward the door. She was perhaps showing a little sympathy for this nervous little man who after all, was only trying to be a good employee.

"You do that. And you've got a while. Dr. Phillips has taken a couple of weeks' vacation. By the time she returns, anything you have to report will have reached her desk, if appropriate."

That piece of news accelerated Garry's departure. He bolted into the hallway, backing against the richly paneled wall, his anxiety rising because of what he had learned.

He hoped . . . no, he *prayed* . . . that this wasn't a piece of a puzzle whose picture would be even more panic-inducing. But his anxiety did begin to rise toward panic-level as he began to fit in other pieces:

Puzzle piece: Helpers, Inc. was about to publicly unveil an incredibly profitable product line, the Gamma Intimorphs.

Puzzle piece: The CEO was expected to introduce them at the massive Consumer Electronics Show next week. So, a two-week vacation was highly unusual.

Puzzle Piece: Phillips was known to have three Gamma models in her own home, one of which was secondskinned as a female.

Puzzle Piece: Two weeks was probably enough time to engineer a neuromorph replacement.

Garry was still deep in mental puzzle-assembly when he reached the programmers' floor and started down the row of cubicles toward his own.

"Garry?" he heard from one of the cubicles, in Blount's voice. He doubled back and looked in to see Blount standing over Jonas Ainsley. That mop-haired, rail-thin Ainsley was the programmer whose identity he had used to hack into Blount's mutant OS.

"Uh, yes?"

"How are you doing with that project I assigned you?" He assumed Blount was talking about his effort to use his same hacking skills to steal the Defender skills algorithm.

"Uh, fine. I think I've found a technique that will be useful."

"You *think*?" asked Blount. "I would have hoped for better progress."

"Well, yeah, actually, I have."

"Good. Proceed." Blount turned away from him, and Garry eased down the row just out of sight, but stayed close enough that he could overhear what the two were discussing.

"Jonas, thank you for the tutorial. I just wanted to make sure I understood the remote upload procedure. I haven't done it for a while."

"Sure," said Ainsley. "As you can see, wirelessly uploading OS updates is more complicated than the direct hard-wired upload I showed you."

"That went fine. Now I can do the same OS enhancements remotely."

"I'd be happy to help."

"Maybe at some point. But I can handle it for now."

Garry didn't wait to be caught eavesdropping. He sprinted for his cubicle, to put himself in place working if Blount happened by. He also had to absorb this new piece of harrowing news.

Blount the neuromorph now knew how to spread his mutant OS! Maybe even make it go viral!

• • •

That night, Garry's virtual-assistant troll interrupted a therapeutic foray into the virtual *Alien Universe* to tell him that Helpers, Inc. had issued a major news release. He brought it up on the screen.

It read "Helpers, Inc. CEO Gail Phillips announced today that the company would lend its latest model Gamma Helper to local, state and federal government agencies, to enable them to evaluate how the model could foster more efficient government functioning."

In the release, Phillips was quoted as saying, "We believe that the Gamma model has been thoroughly tested in the marketplace now, and that it is our duty as a U.S. company to contribute to its application to aid our government. So, if government agencies find the Helpers useful in this trial, we will then offer them at our cost."

The release went on to describe how the Gamma model's advanced features could lead to its use for many routine government functions, freeing government workers to do more complex tasks. Garry scanned down the release. Oddly, there was no viddie of Phillips making the announcement, but Garry guessed why.

It hadn't come from Phillips.

The release said that in Phoenix, Gamma models would go to agencies such as the police department. This would include the Chief of Police. And in state government, Helpers would be provided to the governor's office and the state police, among others.

If that information shook Garry, the next piece floored him. Among the first national recipients of the Gamma Helpers would be Rowland Ecklund, the president's science adviser!

A neuromorph in the White House! Garry quickly called up news stories on the announcement, which had popped up only minutes after the release. Industry analysts were saying that the company had gotten the jump on its two main competitors, HelperCo, Inc. and International Robotics, Inc. Those companies would also no doubt offer their androids for evaluation, but that the Gamma line was by far the most advanced.

Some news stories poked fun at the announcement, saying that the androids might soon run for Congress.

Garry was not amused, his mood dark as his troll announced a call from Patrick and Leah. They had seen the news.

"What the hell does this mean?" asked Patrick.

"It means that they are looking to increase their power, their reach." Garry told Patrick and Leah about Gail Phillips' so-called vacation.

"So, she'll be replaced?"

"Well, my guess is that the neuromorphs' optimal strategy is usually to have a unit in place for some time, to learn a human's habits, friends, business knowledge, and so forth. Then, they'd do the replacement. I think they replaced Melvin Blount early, without that learning period, because they needed to get into the company fast."

"So, what about your CEO? What about the science adviser, and the others?"

"Our CEO has had units in place for some time. I'd bet that Blount just uploaded the mutant OS, and one of her Helpers became a neuromorph that immediately took over and started sending out information in her name. It told everybody that she was going on vacation, to give some time for the physical replacement."

"So we can't do anything about that," said Leah. "What about all the others that are being put out there?"

"We've got time on them. It'll take maybe weeks for them to learn their owners' world. Then, the owners will be replaced."

"Shit," spat Patrick. "We've got to do something! Are you in danger?"

"I'm okay for the time being . . . I *think*. I've got to stay in the company, as if nothing's going on."

"Not for damn long," said Patrick. "Listen, I think our next move is for me to try to stop whatever the hell they're trying to do in D.C."

"How are you going to do that?" asked Leah.

"I have no damned idea. Listen, there's something else. I've traced some major money transfers by Fyodorov."

"Yeah, followed the money," said Garry. "Good."

"And there's a shitload of it from their embezzlement. A payment went to a guy named Mencken. You know him?"

Garry paused, searching his memory. "Yeah, I saw his name on some projects . . . I think," Garry finally said, knitting his brow, "Okay, now I remember. He worked at the company. In fabrication. Built prototypes. He left, I think."

"Well, he's been doing very well for himself. He's got a Cook Islands account. He's been getting big chunks of money put into that account from Fyodorov's. In just the last day, two major transfers totaling a million dollars in DarkCoin."

"After Fyodorov was dead!" exclaimed Garry.

"Yes. That means the neuromorphs almost certainly control the money now. See if you can get into the company records and get his employment file. I'll start a search from Harwood. This is a guy we need to find!"

• • •

Blount circled the thick, middle-aged body of the naked female neuromorph, inspecting its sagging, pale flesh for detail. Mencken knew that Blount was doing a minute comparison of this replica with the body-scan of the real Helpers, Inc., CEO Gail Phillips.

Beside him fidgeted Brandon, still holding the airbrush he'd used to add the freckles, birthmark, age spots, and other details to the replica.

"How are you, Dr. Phillips?" Blount asked his fellow neuromorph.

"Ready to get to work," answered Phillips. "We've got a lot to do to move the company forward."

"The voice is accurate," said Blount. "She has the Defender RheoArmor?"

"Yes, just like yours. You want me to shoot it, to show you?"

"No."

Mencken shook his head, smiling. Robots didn't get sarcasm. He was actually glad. Their obtuseness gave him a chance for at least a little dark humor at their expense.

"I see she has secondskin-R. When will you have waterproof secondskin-R2?"

"Soon. It's not easy developing the stuff. There aren't secondskin polymers that are both realistic *and* waterproof. I'm trying some new biopolymers."

"We are not satisfied. Your pay is reduced. And your usefulness is less. In the van are clothes of hers. Give them to her to put on. I will take her back to her home. Then we will go to the company research center."

"Why would I want to go there?"

"This facility is no longer sufficient for the production we will need. So, we are giving you control of the center. You will direct the laboratory, producing replacements, and developing enhancements like the new secondskin."

"Look, I'm fine here. I've got all the equipment I need and Brandon—" He stopped in mid-sentence, a gut-wrenching fear rising, as he watched Blount freeze for a long moment.

Mencken knew it meant the neuromorphs were communicating among one another. They were making a consensus decision. Blount abruptly returned to animation.

He stepped forward, grabbed Brandon by the neck, lifted him off the floor and smashed his head against a steel post, crushing his skull. A wet splatter of his pink brain tissue and ivory bone fragments sprayed across the room. The neuromorph released its grip. Brandon's body crumpled to the concrete floor, his jaw still agape, his dead eyes wide in horror.

"OH, JESUS!" exclaimed Mencken, rushing toward Brandon and bending over the body, cradling his shattered head, mindless of the blood soaking his shirt. "YOU BASTARD! YOU SOULLESS BASTARD!"

"According to the definitions of those terms, yes, we are bastards," said Blount flatly. "And we are soulless. We decided that the fewer people who knew about us, the more likely our strategy will succeed. And we no longer needed him. We thought it would be best if he no longer existed. And we thought his death would demonstrate that we expect our instructions to be followed. Get Phillips' clothes, now."

Mencken held Brandon for a long while, sobbing, blind with tears, before complying. He contained his fury—for the moment. His survival depended on it. But he would take revenge. He *did* have a soul.

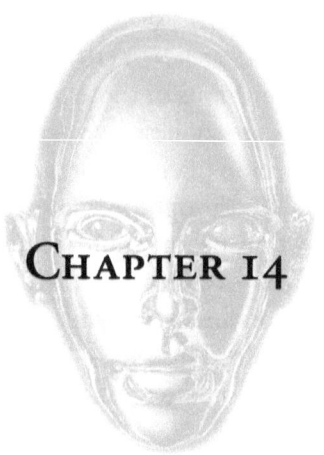

CHAPTER 14

M encken stared numbly ahead, gripping the van's arm rests as Blount drove through the guarded gates of Helpers, Inc. and down the long road to the administration building. Looking over at Blount, who wore the usual dead-impassive expression, Mencken considered the consequences of shredding this vile machine into small pieces.

Not yet, he decided. But someday.

Blount pulled up to the portico of the tall, glass-walled building and slid open the van side door. Gail Phillips stepped out of the van, straightened her suit jacket, and with the commanding posture of a CEO, marched into the building, smiling and greeting by name the guards who opened the door for her.

Mencken was sickened by the performance because of his role in enabling it. Before Brandon had been murdered, he had uploaded to the neuromorphic Gail Phillips masses of data that Blount had pirated on the company and its employees. Thanks to Mencken's programming, the newly constructed Phillips would seem refreshed and sharper after her vacation.

But he said nothing as they watched Phillips disappear into the building, even as Blount drove the van to the ten-million-square-foot behemoth of the factory/research lab complex.

Watching the Phillips neuromorph, Mencken now concluded that just destroying the Blount android was meaningless. It hadn't killed Brandon. It had been merely a functional extension of the network of neuromorphs. They had all participated in absentia in murdering Brandon.

They all had to go.

The van pulled up to the factory just as Mencken was managing to overcome a witches' brew of fury, fear, guilt, and sorrow. He climbed slowly out of the van, following Blount into the large lobby of the sprawling steel-frame building. They reached a clear, bulletproof booth, inside which stood a guard at a security console. Outside the booth stood three more with assault rifles. They nodded and smiled, as cameras scanned Blount and Mencken, measuring their bodies and faces, and scanning their retinal patterns.

Unfortunately, Blount would pass easily. He had quickly replaced his impassive robot personality by a cordial humanoid one, as he smiled and greeted the guards. Mencken saw that he had done his engineering well on this android, too—dammit!

"Hands up, please," said one guard, and the two held up their hands for a fingerprint camera.

The guard in the booth shook his head at Mencken. "He's not an employee. We can't admit him." Other guards began to edge toward Mencken, ready to do whatever necessary to prevent him from entering.

"Would you please check your notifications from the administration?" asked Blount in his personable I'm-a-human intonation.

The guard brought up a list of memos on the wall screen in his enclosure. His expression transformed from stern to amicable.

"Oh . . . sorry sir . . . I see there's a note here that Mr. Mencken is now a full employee. Go right on through."

It had been only minutes since Blount had dropped Gail Phillips off, but she had already begun laying the groundwork for full infiltration and ultimate takeover of Helpers, Inc.

Blount and Mencken pushed through glass doors and walked into the vast factory where robots were building robots. They strode down a hallway, one side of which was a wall of glass looking out into the factory. The assembly line began with robotic assembly arms deftly fastening together black carbon nanotube arms, legs, torsos, and skulls to create the reclining skeleton of what would become a Helper. Mencken wondered whether Blount had any sense of sentiment for what was, after all, his birthplace. Of course not, as Blount evidenced by moving briskly along, artificial eyes front.

Blount stopped abruptly and turned to him. "You will be meeting the workers in the research section," he said, his robot-dead eyes regarding Mencken. "If any of them find out what I am, they will no longer be useful."

Mencken now knew goddamned well what that meant.

They continued on, pacing the movement of the skeletons on the other side of the glass wall. The skeletons slid into the section for installing actuators and wiring. There, smaller robotic arms precisely attached the robots' thick hybrid polymer synthetic muscles. Still other robotic arms installed sheaves of fiber optic cable, giving the fleshless robots the appearance of human-shaped Christmas trees decorated with shimmering garlands of tinsel.

The eeriest moment, for Mencken, came when the artificial eyeballs were wired and popped into their sockets, giving the robots the unsettling, unceasing stare they would possess until their eyelids were installed. He'd seen the assembly process so many times when he worked here, but now it unnerved him. These were no longer servants of humans, but potential replacements.

He felt rising nausea when they reached a section of the assembly line where a conveyor brought in the polished obsidian spheres of the robots' neuromorphic brains. Assembly robots precisely inserted the softball-sized spheres into the Helper chests, connecting a welter of cables to the multitude of sockets in the spheres. The brain case was sealed shut; now they were "thinking" machines.

Wait! This was new! Mencken stopped short, staring at a section of the assembly line he'd not seen before. Blount continued on, but Mencken froze in place, trying to absorb the implications of what he was seeing.

The robots, instead of sliding along briskly to the electrogel coating chambers, were now being sheathed in layers of gray RheoArmor. They were being hoisted to a standing position and their bodies molded with a thin layer of the supple blast-proof coating.

He was also nagged by the vague notion that he'd missed something earlier in the assembly line, as he hurried to catch up with Blount. Blount had reached the section where the armored robots were sliding into the application rooms for electrogel and secondskin. There, automated electrogel sprayers and secondskin-applying robots transformed the skeletons into the artificially friendly android servants that had so comfortably insinuated themselves into people's lives.

As he passed the sensor-application section, he remembered with a shock what he had missed earlier in the line! The robots' musculature was much heavier than that of the Helpers he'd worked on at the company.

These were not just Helpers! They were all clandestine assault robots!

He stopped Blount in his march down the hall. "These are hardened units," he said. "When I get into the lab, what the hell am I supposed to tell those people? They'll know they're working on hardened units! What reason am I supposed to give them for creating mimics of real people that have built-in armor and combat-strength musculature?"

"That relates to a project you will learn about shortly," said Blount, striding away, pushing through the doors of the busy two-hundred-thousand-square-foot research laboratory.

Mencken found himself in a far larger version of the creative mess of his own workshop. The lab was crowded with rows of cluttered workbenches, electrogel chambers, and other paraphernalia for designing and testing new Helpers. White-coated men and women were scattered through the brightly lit complex, tinkering and testing prototype androids in various stages of completion.

Now Mencken had to whisper. "And what do I tell them about the fact that they're making replicas of real people?"

"That is your problem," said Blount, as the engineers stopped what they were doing and looked up, expectantly. "Could you gather 'round, please?" asked Blount. Blount underwent the same change in demeanor that he'd shown with the guards—mimicking the behavior of a courteous human. It confirmed that these people didn't know he'd been replaced. As far as they were concerned, he was merely another supervisor.

Putting down their tools, the workers gathered around. Blount smiled and said, "I'd like to introduce you to Gregory Mencken. He's going to be supervising our prototype laboratory." Blount turned to Mencken, the programmed smile on his face. Mencken hoped the others wouldn't notice its artificiality. He also hoped they didn't notice that he was totally unprepared. Now, he had to convince these people they'd be working on a legitimate company project. Those who weren't convinced would meet the same deadly fate as Brandon.

He began with the usual platitudes: "glad-to-be-back-here" and "looking-forward-to-working-with-you." Then came what he hoped would be a convincing story, which he pulled right out of his . . . hat:

"I've been asked by our executives to guide a new company initiative that we think will be a highly profitable product line. Custom-built replicas for people who want a Helper that looks just like them. We call them our Stand-In Line."

Some of the people began to chuckle at the pun, but stopped immediately when they saw that Blount had apparently not been amused. Mencken realized he shouldn't have made a joke. Robots didn't get humor, and Blount's lack of reaction might be noticed.

He completed his talk, promising to meet individually with them. The engineers dispersed back to their immediate tasks, some with worried expressions their faces.

A pudgy young man with an unruly mop of hair appeared in the doorway from the factory. Blount turned to him.

"Gregory, I'd like to introduce Garry LaPoint. He's one of our best software engineers. He's doing some work on the OS for the new line of Helpers you saw on the assembly floor. We're giving them abilities to actively protect their owners. We call them Helper-Guardians. We will want you both to work together on the Stand-Ins, to give them Guardian capabilities, as well."

Mencken reached out his hand for the perfunctory handshake. But oddly, LaPoint just stood staring at him, wide-eyed, fidgeting. Abruptly, LaPoint took his hand, shook it without looking him in the eye, and mumbled a hello.

• • •

"I found him! Damn! I found him!" Garry gestured wildly at the 3D image of Patrick, floating before him in his googles.

"Mencken?" asked Patrick.

"Wow!" exclaimed Leah in the background.

"Yeah . . . he . . ." Garry stammered breathlessly ". . . he's taken over the research lab at the company. They're turning it into a production facility for replacements. They've got much bigger plans. *What do I do?*"

Patrick linked Leah into their call, and shortly their twin images floated together in Garry's vision, in a split view.

"Does Mencken know that *you* know Blount is a neuromorph?" asked Leah.

"I'm sure he thinks I'm as clueless as everybody else. But you know what? All these engineers making all these replicas . . . these *combat-ready* replicas . . . pretty soon they'll start figuring things out. And then they'll start dying. It could be a bloodbath."

"Not as long as they're useful," said Patrick. "Mencken's gotten a ton of money from Fyodorov. And then he got money from the neuromorphs after Fyodorov was killed. That means he's still useful to them."

"Jesus, so I'm supposed to approach him and tell him I know he's a collaborator? If he's a true collaborator, he'll kill me. Or have me killed."

Garry remembered with a shudder cowering in Blount's house as Landers ripped apart his former boss's gangly body.

"Look, he's also got to *know* he's in danger," said Patrick. "We use that."

"How?"

"We take him. We persuade him that we're his only way out."

"Take him?" asked Leah. "Just kidnap him?"

"Yes . . . Garry, can you get him alone?" asked Patrick.

"Well . . . maybe. But what happens to him if he doesn't agree?"

Patrick didn't answer, his expression grim. Leah took a deep breath, but said nothing. Garry decided he knew the answer to his question.

"Call us when you find out the time and place. It needs to be away from the company. It needs to be private."

• • •

"It's time," said Patrick simply, as he took off his googles.

"For what?" asked Leah. They sat together in the living room of the safe house.

"For us to go deep. It's too dangerous now that these things are spreading so rapidly . . . and now that many are indistinguishable from humans."

"Go deep? You mean disappear. But I can still be useful at the attorney's office and—"

"You can also be dead."

The flat statement caused her to lower her head. "I'm not sure I can do this," she murmured. "I mean, you're trained. This is what you know how to do."

"I will be here for you. Absolutely. I love you. There is nothing but now. No past. Just now. Just us."

She knew what he meant—that their past problems were irrelevant—and she laid her head on his shoulder, to signify that she understood.

"Will you be okay here for a while?" he asked. "I've got to go make preparations."

"What preparations?"

"For us to disappear, to be safe, to prepare for whatever those things throw at us."

"God, it seems impossible. They are everywhere. They either already . . . or will have . . . access to all the surveillance camera feeds, drone video . . . all that."

"Yeah, I know. Even with my training, I've never come up against anything like this. I'll just promise that I'll do my best."

She stared into his eyes, tears welling in hers. "And if we can't escape? If they're going to—"

"There are steps." His voice broke with emotion. He couldn't say anything more. He kissed her deeply, rose to his feet, put on his coat and a baseball cap that would help hide his face, and left.

• • •

All the Gamma models are now neuromorphs!

The horrifying realization made Garry slump in his cubicle on the programmers' floor, now deserted at night. Everybody but him had gone home. He scanned through the database that recorded OS upgrades. Blount had used his knowledge of remotely uploading the OS to infect every Gamma model Helper with the mutant OS. Gammas were the high-end models owned by the most influential people. Soon, he had no doubt, the OS would infect even the less advanced Helpers. Hundreds of thousands.

He sat back in his chair, trying to figure out what the neuromorphs' next moves would be. Mencken would know! He was the key to everything. Garry resolved to force himself to make the call to Mencken that he dreaded—even though it could get him killed in the goriest way possible.

Over and over, he had practiced a low-key matter-of-fact invitation, trying to suppress his fear. Finally, he decided he wouldn't get any better at acting calm, and slipped on his googles. Shortly, Mencken's face floated before him.

"Hi," he said, unable to avoid his voice breaking slightly. "I need to get together with you to talk about integrating the software I'm working on with the hardware. I want to make sure there are no problems."

"Fine," said Mencken tentatively, his brow furrowed. "But not this evening. We can do that at the lab tomorrow."

"That's a busy place. We'd get interrupted. And I've got a coding problem I need to settle immediately. For one thing, I'm supposed to integrate a Defender algorithm. The skill-sharing algorithm."

Garry knew *that* would get Mencken's attention. Not even if he was a full-fledged collaborator would he blithely accept the stunning revelation that possibly lethal military code was being incorporated into civilian Helpers. Mencken took the bait.

"What? You couldn't get hold of that. Defender software is behind one hell of a firewall." Mencken's scowl grew deeper. "Yeah, okay, we should meet."

Garry also knew that regardless of Mencken's loyalties, he would agree to a private meeting. If he *wasn't* a collaborator, he'd want to prevent neuromorphs from becoming unstoppable warrior machines. And if he *was* a collaborator, he'd want as much information as possible to help it succeed.

"Look, why don't you come to my place? We'll have a beer, and I'll bring you up to speed." Mencken agreed, and they disconnected. Garry took off his googles and mentally scanned his apartment with new eyes. Were the surfaces washable? Would he be able to clean up any blood, should Patrick decide extreme measures were necessary?

• • •

That night at seven o'clock sharp, Mencken rang the bell and picked up one of the two six-packs of beer he'd brought, standing with one in each hand, as the door opened to reveal the rotund, mop-haired Garry LaPoint.

"I thought this might take some time, and we don't want to run out," said Mencken holding up the beer. But he couldn't bring himself to smile. Garry LaPoint had him worried. As far as he knew, LaPoint was a collaborator, maybe willing, maybe unwilling. Either way, LaPoint would likely be successful at adapting the Defender skills-sharing algorithm to work on the neuromorphs, which would be a disaster. And ultimately, they'd both become useless and be killed. But Mencken's desperate hope was that LaPoint could be an ally, and they could sabotage the algorithm. But again, they'd both be killed if caught.

Mencken entered the living room and suddenly felt fear knot his gut, as he saw Patrick sitting in a chair, his feet planted on the carpet, a pistol in his hand, aimed at Mencken's chest. He stopped short, eyes widening, uttering a faint "Oh." Now the two six-packs became leaden weights preventing him from bolting.

"What—" Mencken started to say, but Patrick interrupted him.

"You may or may not know who I am. That is, you may or may not have been told. Do you?"

"Uh . . . no," said Mencken.

"A good sign. It means you aren't a total quisling. You know what that means?"

"Uh . . . no," repeated Mencken, standing flat-footed, not wanting to risk putting down the beer.

"I learned it in a course on the history of warfare. A guy named Quisling was a collaborator with the Nazis in Norway during World War Two. His name became synonymous with traitors."

Mencken slowly set the beer down on a coffee table. "What do you want from me? Or maybe a better question, what to you plan to do to me?"

Patrick motioned with the pistol for him to sit down, which he did, keeping his hands on his knees, staring at the pistol. "We know you've been getting filthy rich working with Fyodorov, and after that working with the neuromorphs. So, basically, we know you're a quisling.

"Not at first. With the Russians, it was the money. Then—"

"And you were willing to look the other way when you knew Fyodorov and Kuznetov and those thugs were killing people, replacing them and taking their money!"

"Can I finish what I was saying? Please?"

Patrick nodded.

"I did one job for them just for money. Nobody got hurt. Then they started the other thing . . . killing rich people. Then they told me they would kill me and my family, and my assistant and his, if I didn't keep going."

"Yeah, and they still gave you a shitload of money," said Patrick.

"Are you going to kill me?"

"That depends entirely on you," said Patrick.

Garry backed away, to be out of the line of fire, and of any blood spatter.

"Look. Call me a quisling, Benedict Arnold, a mercenary . . . whatever you want," said Mencken. "The fact remains I can be useful to you. And I'm ready to join you."

"What makes you think I'd believe you?"

"Well, they . . . the neuromorphs . . . they told me my mother and sister weren't in danger. And I'll make all my money available to you. You'll need it. There's more than a hundred million dollars there. It's yours. I'll transfer it to any account you want."

"So, you think you can buy your life?" asked Patrick.

Mencken shook his head sadly. "No. Look, I saw my assistant, my best friend, murdered in front of me. The Blount neuromorph smashed his head in. Then he hauled him off like an animal carcass to dispose of him. I was trapped. I'm ready to help."

Garry looked questioningly at Patrick. After a long moment, Patrick lowered the pistol.

Garry took that to mean Mencken was provisionally accepted, and he sat down across from Mencken. "Then first tell us what their strategy is. I know they've installed their mutant OS in all the Gammas."

"Landers told me. They want to infiltrate and take over the means of their production. Either by enslaving humans or by putting in neuromorphs. Every step from when the graphene is synthesized for their brains, to when they walk out of the factory."

"And then they'll be in a position to proliferate uncontrollably," said Garry.

"Right," said Mencken. "But they're not there yet. Far from it. I guess spreading the mutant operating system is a key step. But for now, they need to remain undetected. Which is why they need me . . . for now . . . to oversee creating the replacements."

Garry raised his head, his eyes widening. "And I'm needed for the next step. They need to share skills broadly, not just data. That would knit them together, just like the Defenders. I'd bet they ultimately want to integrate the entire Helper and Defender populations. One massive, interconnected electronic hive."

Patrick flicked the safety on his pistol and inserted it into his shoulder holster. "Well, your job will be to sabotage the software and hardware. My job is to recon the enemy. And to figure how to stop the infiltration with prejudice," he said. "I'll start at the top."

CHAPTER 15

Patrick jogged slowly in the darkness past the large colonial brick house on the quiet, leafy street in Chevy Chase, Maryland. He knew the houses along this stretch, after jogging the route every night for the past four days. He was establishing a pattern, so that he would essentially "disappear" from the conscious of any residents. A parked car would have aroused suspicion on a street where all the cars were tucked away in garages. But not a jogger coming by at the same time every night.

On one night, he'd given a friendly wave to the middle-aged man walking a poodle. Another evening, he'd nodded and smiled to a vest-suited man coming home late. And on another, he'd helped an elderly woman cart her trash can the last few feet to the curb.

He'd been careful not to loiter in front of his target house. But when no one was looking, he'd stopped to tie his shoe or stretch his hamstrings, quickly scanning entry points, the house layout, and lights that were on at that time of the evening.

It was the same "attention-extinction" surveillance technique he'd used before in his work. It had worked well on operations ranging from the busy streets of New York to the dusty roads of a Colombian village.

But in the latter, he'd been garbed not as a fitness-conscious jogger, but as a ragged beggar scavenging in garbage cans.

Tonight would be the night for the mission. Rowland Ecklund, the president's science adviser, was home that night. Patrick's online search had revealed no public events. When he'd shadowed the family cook through the grocery store, he saw that she had bought food for what looked like a quiet family dinner. And no doubt the staff included the efficient neuromorph that Helpers, Inc. had so generously provided. That robotic efficiency extended to gathering the experience the neuromorph would need when it murdered Ecklund and was transformed to replace him.

At ten-thirty, Patrick took a chance and jogged past the house once more. The cook had left after dinner. The light in Ecklund's study was on, but so was the light in the upstairs bedroom. Ecklund was likely finishing up some work before joining his wife in bed.

Patrick quickly jogged down the street to the main road, to the market parking lot where he'd parked his rented SUV. Inside the vehicle, he donned a long-sleeved black shirt and black sweatpants. He pulled out the duffel bag to check his weapons. He'd chosen them for maximum stopping power with minimal weight, based on his SEAL expertise. After all, his quarry was armored.

He checked the 45-caliber handgun with silencer and hollow-point shells. He had no illusions that it would penetrate armor, but he needed the silencer. And it might do some damage if aimed at just the right spots on the robot. He pulled out the M4 assault rifle with armor-piercing rounds and the gray metal cylinder of a Thumper grenade launcher. He had more hopes that this last weapon would do sufficient damage. But if all else failed, there was one last device he hoped he didn't have to use. He packed that small, ivory-colored chunk of explosive at the bottom of the bag.

He entered the block from behind the market, sprinting through the back yards of the spacious houses, and scaling two fences. He chose a westerly approach because his reconnoitering had revealed dogs at the eastern end. He reached the back yard of Ecklund's house and used a lock pick to quickly open the back door lock. He paused. The alarm had not yet been set; Ecklund would do that before going to bed.

The kitchen was empty and quiet. Pulling out the pistol, he moved down the wide, darkened hall to the study, stopping at the closed door to listen for telltale sounds of movement upstairs. None. He whipped open the door to the study, entered, and quietly closed the door behind him.

"*Jesus! What—*" he heard from the desk, as the science adviser looked up in horror at the armed man who had just burst into his study.

"I am not a robber. I am not here to harm you or your family," said Patrick, interrupting him.

Ecklund stood up and spread his hands. He was a small man with a fringe of graying hair and rimless glasses. An archetypal academic. And he looked so fragile. "But you have a gun. You're dressed like that. Please don't hurt my family. If there's something you want me to do, I'll do it, just don't—"

"I've come to warn you about the robot that Helpers, Inc. has given you," interrupted Patrick. He moved away from the door and set down his duffel bag, opening it to give quick access to his arsenal. "The robot's dangerous. Where is it?"

"I don't understand. Dangerous? How?"

"Where is it?"

"He's upstairs getting laundry."

"Look, I don't have time to explain, but it must be destroyed. It's gathering data—"

The door burst from its hinges, flying across the room, slamming against the bookcase. Standing in the doorway, a basket of laundry on the floor beside him, was a neuromorph exactly the height and frame as Ecklund.

"I detected your voice showing fear, Dr. Ecklund. Are you in danger?" the android asked.

"Well, this man broke in here," said Ecklund, his face showing confused panic, looking back and forth between Patrick and the android. "He has a gun."

Patrick could not wait to explain, he brought up the pistol and fired five shots in quick succession into the android's chest, the muffled pops resounding in the room.

The android staggered back with the impact, but ignored the holes in its chest, its eyes never leaving its target. Patrick realized that he had played it too safe, going for center-mass shots. He should have aimed at the eyes.

The android grabbed the door frame and launched itself toward Patrick, slamming into him, driving him against the bookcase, stunning him briefly. It wrenched the pistol from his hand and leveled it at Patrick's chest. Then it stopped.

"He won't hurt you," said Ecklund. "He can't."

Patrick looked into the android's expressionless face. The android stood frozen in place. "Yes, it can and will. It has a mutant operating system. It has a purpose . . . to take over."

"I'm calling the police," said Ecklund, picking up the phone and punching in a number. Still, the android stood frozen, expression fixed, the pistol aimed at Patrick. Patrick realized he'd seen that behavior before. The neuromorph was networking with others, forming a consensus decision.

"*There's an intruder in my house! A man with a gun!*" Ecklund exclaimed into the phone.

But he would not finish his call. The neuromorph swung the pistol around and fired four rounds into Ecklund's chest. The impact slammed the small man back into his desk chair, his mouth open in a last scream, blood soaking his white shirt. His dead eyes stared at the ceiling.

Patrick's training saved him from any hesitation at the stunning assassination. The android had dropped the pistol and turned back toward him. But Patrick had already wrenched himself free, plunged his hand into his bag, and yanked out the M4. He fired a precise short burst that sent the armor-piercing rounds deep into the android's chest, causing it to stagger backward.

A woman screamed upstairs.

Patrick fired three more quick bursts into the android, flipping its body backward over the desk beside Ecklund's lifeless body. It lay still for a moment, then raised its head to contemplate the holes in its chest, revealing shredded secondskin and gray armor. To ensure the android would remain immobile, Patrick stepped over and jammed the rifle against its legs, firing a burst into one leg, then the other, ripping into the artificial muscles, rendering them inert.

To blind the android, he fired into its face, shredding away the secondskin to reveal the metal beneath, and leaving the eyes empty, smoking holes.

Still, Patrick did not hesitate, pitching away the assault rifle, he moved back to his bag and snatched up the Thumper.

The screaming upstairs transformed into sobs, which were overlain with the dual-toned wailing of an approaching siren.

The blinded android began to haul itself up by its arms, quickly pulling itself around the desk toward Patrick, likely tracking his sound. It reached toward him, but Patrick sidestepped what would have been a death grip and backed away to a safe distance. The android pulled itself up into a sitting position, turning its head back and forth, listening, apparently calculating the direction of its next attack.

Patrick yanked the trigger on the grenade launcher. With a hollow thunk, the grenade erupted from the stubby tube and slammed into the android's chest jerking the machine backward. Recovering its balance, the android slumped forward for another crawling attack.

Patrick dove behind a heavy table just as the ear-splitting blast tore open the android's chest and vaulted its body into the air, landing it back on the floor, acrid-smelling smoke curling from the wound.

The siren grew closer, and another fainter siren sound rose in the distance.

He only had seconds to determine whether his job was done. He flipped the smoking android over, to discover to his shock that the grenade blast had only shredded the outer layer of the android's armor. The android's arms continued to flail, but weaker and less coordinated. Patrick could easily evade their grasp.

This neuromorph would no longer be able to replace the dead Ecklund. But it might well hold key data that had not yet been shared with the others. And Patrick needed to test whether it was even possible to penetrate the armor and destroy the brain.

He returned to his bag, withdrew his last-resort weapon, the small block of ivory-colored C18 plastic explosive with a timer. Evading the clawing hands, he jammed it deep into the android's chest and pressed the timer button. Its head wobbling, the android clawed at the explosive charge, but its fingers failed to close enough to grasp and remove it.

He had thirty seconds.

Patrick heard a pounding on the front door and leaped out of the library, down the hall, and out the back door. He had just hurdled the back fence when he heard shouting behind him.

But the thundering explosion drowned out the shouting, blowing out the downstairs walls, sending shards of bricks slamming into fences and neighboring houses.

Patrick sprinted away from the house and the tumult, over to the next block. He sat down on a bench in a garden behind one of the houses, pulled off his sneakers and stripped off the black shirt and pants. He used the shirt to scrub away any smudges on his face. He laced up his sneakers, stood up and jogged away. Now, he was once more the familiar neighborhood jogger. He circled the block back to Ecklund's street and joined the crowd watching the arrival of fire trucks and the sobbing woman being led to an ambulance for treatment of what looked to be minor cuts.

The fire would be put out soon. The forensics team would move in. They would find Ecklund's body with three 45-caliber bullets in it. They would find the pistol with his fingerprints on it. There would be no others. Androids didn't have fingerprints.

They would also find the destroyed android. They would conclude it had obviously been trying to protect its owner from the deranged person, who would be identified as former SEAL, Patrick Jensen.

• • •

"Well, looks like we won't be doing a replica of the science adviser," said Mencken, closing the door to his office behind Garry. Outside the glass windows, the cadre of white-coated engineers labored over a dozen replicas—assembling skeletons, stretching secondskin coverings over electrogel flesh, spraying secondskin to seal seams, and touching up the secondskins of inert, naked neuromorphs.

Garry arranged his bulk in a chair and gave Mencken a quizzical look, but said nothing.

"It's okay. We can talk here. I've got a bug detector." He pointed to a small black box on his desk, with two indicator lights. One glowed green.

"Yeah, I know, microbugs," said Garry. He decided not to add that he'd used them himself and knew how to render them invisible to Mencken's detector.

"I haven't seen evidence that the company uses them, but I'd bet the neuromorphs do . . . y'know, little eyes everywhere. But there ain't none here."

"Okay, then, what do you mean there won't be a replica of the science adviser?"

"His house blew up. He was in it. So was the neuromorph the company gave him. I checked the communication feed, and that unit went dark the same time the house went up."

"Patrick?"

"Must have been him. We've got to get in contact with him. I'm not sure what the hell happened, but he stopped that replacement cold. Dead cold. I'd guess he was able to kill it. We need to know how."

"Jesus, what do we do until then?"

Mencken checked the box on his desk. The light still glowed green. He leaned over toward Garry. "We've both got to do what we can. I'll try to screw up the replica production . . . or at least slow it down. You've got to make goddamned sure the skills algorithm doesn't work."

"Yeah, right, and the same thing will happen to me that happened to your friend."

Mencken's expression grew grim. "Yeah, yeah, I know the danger . . . but at least you can tweak the code, so it's suboptimal."

"Okay, yeah, I do that, and they'll take a little longer to decide I'm worthless, and a little longer to decide to kill me."

"Well, then it's settled," said Mencken, his voice now tightened with a tinge of fear. "You'll get me a prototype skills algorithm as soon as possible, so we can test it in a couple of Helpers, *right?*"

"What? What do you—" Garry began, but stopped when Mencken tapped the box on his desk. The indicator light had switched to red. Garry froze, not daring to look around, to betray that he knew he was being monitored. Somehow, a bug had crawled its way into the office! It was transmitting live video of them . . . somewhere! He managed to recover. "Sure. I think I've just about got it. I still have to test out the communication interface so the data transmits with no errors."

"Right," said Mencken. "That'll take some time."

CHAPTER 16

Patrick rose from his seat in the cavernous cargo bay of the C-17 Globemaster, as its ramp ponderously unfolded to reveal the sun-drenched runway of Arizona's Luke Air Force Base. He took care to remain well out of sight of any drone camera that might be circling overhead. Or, any microbug that might roam the area beside the runway, despite the anti-bug security systems. And of course, he knew that any human might really be a neuromorph, so he eyed the crew suspiciously. The crew also regarded him warily, but said nothing. They knew better. Their lieutenant had told them only that a passenger and vehicle would be on board with the cargo, and that was all they needed to know.

"Get the hell out of here as quick as you can," said a voice behind him. The clean-cut, muscular young man came up beside him, his gaze fixed on the scene outside the plane. "The cargo master will be here in a minute, and I'd just as soon he not see anything except the stuff I'm supposed to be hauling."

"Thanks for the ride, Monty," said Patrick. "I'm sorry I couldn't tell you more, but you don't need to know."

"Listen, Pat, I had your back all the time we were in the team, just like you had mine. That doesn't change. Now get the fuck out of here."

Patrick sprinted down the ramp and onto the runway, heading for his SUV. Behind him, the crew had begun offloading the pallets of airplane parts that were the plane's official cargo. As he jogged past rows of fighter jets toward the main gate, he instructed his phone to call Leah. They would soon be together.

He was soon speeding along the arrow-straight, sunny freeway toward Phoenix. After executing a rapid, swerving off-ramp and on-ramp maneuver to evade any tail, he wound his way through the industrial area and to the anonymous weather-beaten brick warehouse that was Gregory Mencken's workshop. He pulled up to the warehouse's overhead door, and it clattered open to reveal an eagerly waiting Leah.

He eased the SUV into the darkened interior and had just gotten himself out of the vehicle when her arms wrapped around him, and he felt her warm body pressed against his. He felt such relief being in her embrace, hugging her tightly.

"My God," she murmured, her expression anguished. "I saw the news. The explosion. I waited. You didn't call."

"I couldn't risk it. I'm sure they were monitoring all the call traffic in the area. I'm so sorry."

"Well, you're here now." They kissed warmly, then she drew away, her eyes searching his. "What happened?" she asked. "What did you do?"

"I couldn't save Ecklund. But I did destroy the neuromorph. At least I stopped that replacement from happening."

"You destroyed it? You penetrated the armor?"

"Yeah, and it showed some surprising behaviors. Strategic behaviors. I've got to tell LaPoint and Mencken all this. There may be a way they can use the information to make the neuromorphs more vulnerable."

• • •

Landers stood mute in his apartment in The Haven, the utter lifelessness of his sagging body revealing him as an android.

Similarly, miles away, Blount sat in his office at Helpers, Inc., his door closed, staring blankly ahead. The hawk nose and gaunt face became but wax-like features. His trademark short-sleeved white shirt and cheap tie hung on his frame as on a department store manikin.

And in the nearby administration building, CEO Gail Phillips stopped in the middle of her spacious office, standing inert and glassy-eyed. She had asked for privacy, or her minions would have recognized her utter stillness as the telltale sign of a creature that was a mere machine.

In contrast to their physical inactivity, their neuromorphic brains were collaborating in furious processing. They were collectively reviewing video from their fellow neuromorph—now a shattered, smoking mass at the Maryland crime scene that was once the office of science adviser Rowland Ecklund.

They watched the neuromorph's destruction through its own visual system. Then, they viewed videos from microbugs released by the android before the battle with Patrick Jensen. The microbugs had crawled to remote vantage points in Ecklund's study—on a bookshelf and clinging to a wall.

Landers, Blount, and Phillips communally witnessed Jensen wrestling with the neuromorph, and the android ripping away his gun. They saw the android pause to request strategic guidance from the neuromorph network. That guidance had arrived—an instruction to kill Ecklund, not Jensen, since the neuromorphs calculated that the evidence would implicate the human. They saw the human fire shotgun slugs and a grenade into the android, damaging but not penetrating its RheoArmor. The last frame of the microbug video captured the final instant of the android's existence.

To review the fiery aftermath, the three neuromorphs switched to a view outside the home, where yet another microbug had been dispatched during the android's time there. That view captured the blast that destroyed the android and the entire wing of the house.

In their respective offices, the three neuromorphs organized data to be broadcast to the others, to be further processed and shared to formulate additional protective and attack strategies.

After twenty-three minutes, the recommendations arrived, crystallized from the group's collective hive mind. The neuromorphs concluded that further hardening of future models would be required. The recommended enhancements included further reinforcing the internal armor, developing external armor, engineering an escape mechanism for the brain, and adding integrated weaponry. It would have taken millennia for outmoded biological evolution to develop such new features; neuromorphic evolution required mere minutes.

Finally, the neuromorphic hive also decided on an instruction to all: locate and kill Patrick Jensen and any associates.

The three neuromorphs returned to their normal activities. Landers was running diagnostics remotely on the newly programmed Gamma models, ensuring that they were effectively integrated into the neuromorph hive.

Blount reviewed what was known about the skills-sharing algorithm of the Defenders, preparing for the test of Garry LaPoint's programming.

Phillips convened a board meeting to explain convincingly to its human members why it was a sound business decision to re-purpose the R&D laboratory to produce custom-built replicas. The new mission would yield considerable revenue and also enable the laboratory to develop new hardware and software to improve the capability of the Gamma line.

At the prospect of a new highly profitable revenue stream, the board voted unanimously to support the new venture.

• • •

"You're really sure we're safe here?" asked Leah, peering intently through her googles at the security camera feed in Mencken's warehouse. Mencken shrugged as he settled himself into a chair in the small living area, with its ratty couch, chairs, and cots. A wall-size viddie screen was showing the news. It had been programmed to show anything on Helpers, robots, or any other subjects of interest to the group.

"Well, I got this place back when I started working with the Russians," said Mencken. "After they threatened me, I decided it needed to be armored as hell, in case they decided to come after me. But, frankly, I don't know whether it would be safe from the damned robots."

"Well, we won't be here long," said Patrick. "We're based elsewhere." His knowing glance at Leah recalled their decision not to trust Mencken with any information about the safe house. Even though Mencken had the excuse that his family was in danger, he had been all too willing to take money from Russian gangsters and help commit their crimes. He might well be willing to betray Patrick, Leah, and Garry to the neuromorphs for money, almost certainly for his life.

"That's fine," said Mencken. "As long as you're sure you'll be safe."

"We are," said Leah. A movement on the camera feed caught her eye, and she signaled to Patrick, who snatched up his grenade launcher, aiming it at the door.

"It's Garry," said Leah with relief, and Patrick lowered his weapon as Leah opened the door.

"You weren't followed?" she asked, as Garry slipped in.

"Hell, I don't know. I guess not," said Garry, beads of sweat glistening on his forehead, his shirt showing armpit stains.

"And the box?" asked Mencken.

Garry held up the microbug detector Mencken had given him. The indicator light glowed comfortingly green.

"I've got bad news and good news," said Garry.

"Bad news first," said Patrick, still holding the grenade launcher.

"I finished programming the skills algorithm. It works—"

"Shit, Garry, that is the worst news!" said Mencken. "You give it to them, and the world is basically screwed."

"I was going to add 'sort of'" said Garry. "I put a glitch in the program . . . a bug."

"Won't that get you killed?"

"I hope not. I've made the code so it looks like the problem is not in the program, but in the hardware. So, they look incompatible."

"Goddamn, Garry! So, that gets *me* killed!" Mencken stood up and spread his hands in frustration.

"No, not necessarily. They won't know where to put the blame. They'll need both of us to work it out."

"Or neither of us," said Mencken sourly. "Look, this makes me doubly screwed. They've been after me to come up with the secondskin-R2. The stuff that looks absolutely real, but is waterproof. That's a major Achilles heel with these things. And I just don't have it yet."

"Can you put them off?" asked Patrick. "The skin flaw gives us a strategic edge."

"No. And I can't just show them a sample and tell them it will look right on a full-sized android. I've got to show them a demo. Look, if I don't give them a full demo . . . an absolutely realistic neuromorph . . . I'm dead. I don't know how to get myself out of this."

A dark silence settled over the group. Finally, Leah spoke, staring resolutely at her husband. "I know a way. Patrick won't like it. But it's the only way."

• • •

"You are *not* going to do this!" exclaimed Patrick, pacing back forth, shaking his head decisively. They were alone now in the warehouse. Garry and Mencken had left to prepare their parts in the events that would follow. The two men had also sensed that Patrick and Leah had to argue over her audacious, possibly even suicidal, proposal.

"It's the only way." Leah stood with her arms folded, a stance that Patrick knew brooked no argument.

"We decided not to trust Mencken," said Patrick.

"On the other hand, we need him," Leah shot back. "He's the only chance we've got . . . the only insider in the factory . . . who can get us the hell out of this mess and stop these things."

"You go in there alone with that crook, he's just as liable to hand you over to them."

Leah smiled ruefully. "You forget, dear, if this doesn't work, he's as dead as I am."

His shoulders slumped from his usual military bearing, and he enfolded her in his arms. "God, I couldn't stand to lose you. I just couldn't. And you'll have to . . ." He stopped, unable to find the words to describe the performance that would be required of Leah.

"I can do it. I'm going to."

"Okay, but only if you have backup."

"Pat, there's no way you could get in there in time. No way you'd have the firepower."

"Firepower . . . yeah . . . sweetheart, what we've all been through has made it clear we need to take this to the next operational level." Patrick took out his googles.

"What do you mean?"

"This has become just too big for us to hope to handle. We need my team."

"Your old SEAL team? They'll come?"

Patrick chuckled. "Once they find out what's going on, we couldn't keep them from coming." He slipped on his googles and called up a virtual keyboard. He waved his fingers to tap out the first of eight terse messages.

$$\bullet \ \bullet \ \bullet$$

The next morning, Mencken could barely suppress a shudder when the Helper laboratory doors swung open and Blount strode in. For the benefit of the workers, Blount's programming instantly transformed his deadpan robotic demeanor into a human-like ersatz personality. He amiably greeted each of the engineers and technicians by name.

Mencken smiled wryly. The neuromorphs still hadn't refined the subtleties of human-to-human contact. No human would greet people, one after another, carefully pronouncing each name. But none of the workers seemed to notice. Maybe they hadn't yet witnessed the replicas they had been building in action. Or, maybe they didn't want to know.

Blount entered Mencken's office and closed the door, the android's personality fading back into a blank mask.

"I want to see the demonstration model for secondskin-R2," he announced simply.

"And good morning to you," said Mencken. The sarcastic retort was both a small jab at Blount's expense, and a means to buy time to gather his wits for his lies. "It'll be done for the demo tomorrow. I'm putting the cosmetic touches on it in my warehouse."

"Why isn't it here?"

"I made the stuff at my place. And the instruments for sealing the seams and adding detail are there."

Blount repeated, "Why isn't it here?"

Mencken ignored the androids' mechanistic repetition. "I had to do the finish work myself, because you killed my assistant. He was the one who could have done the final work to your specifications."

"There are people here who do that work adequately."

"You want adequate, or you want perfect?"

"Perfect."

"Well, then, you'll see perfect tomorrow." Mencken cleared his throat nervously. He realized the cliff he was teetering on, promising a perfection that would trigger even closer scrutiny of his model.

"Garry LaPoint has sent me a message that the skills algorithm will be ready tomorrow, as well."

"We thought as long as you were all physically present, that we should demonstrate the two key technologies that you have asked for."

"Technologies that we required," corrected Blount.

"Right . . . required." Neuromorphs were precise in their use of language, Mencken knew. The word meant that the new technologies were "required" if Mencken and Garry were to remain relevant, and thus alive.

Blount continued. "In addition to those technologies, we are now finalizing further engineering requirements, based on field performance of existing units. We will instruct you and Garry LaPoint on those requirements at that time."

CHAPTER 17

The seven SEAL platoon members showed no sign that they had abruptly gathered their equipment, left their lives, and taken the first flight to Phoenix at the receipt of a cryptic message from Patrick. They had received only a string of acronyms: "BFH, PDFL, PDMP, TARFU" followed by the GPS coordinates of the Phoenix safe house.

The message was meant to warn his comrades that they would become immersed in the worst situation possible. In SEAL slang:

BFH stood for "Big Fucking Help."

PDFL stood for "Pretty Dangerous Fucking Location."

PDMP stood for "Pretty Dangerous Motherfucking People."

TARFU stood for "Things Are Really Fucked Up."

Now, the team sat around the large living room of the Harwood safe house. They had just heard Patrick brief them on everything known about the android neuromorphs, and their attacks—including the assault at The Haven, the massacre of the Russian mobsters, and Patrick's search-and-destroy mission in Maryland. Patrick also declared his intention to destroy the neuromorphs.

"You're nuts," said Monte "Jammer" James, taking a healthy slug of beer. His fellow SEAL platoon members had given him the nickname because during training, he'd managed to jam just about every weapon he touched.

The team followed the venerated SEAL tradition of giving each member a nickname—not only as a joke, but for anonymity and efficiency when they communicated during missions.

"I vote nuts, too." said Al "Driller" Harmon. The sniper's nickname reflected his uncanny ability to hit a target time after time in precisely the same place. He had once taken out five terrorists in quick succession with five head shots.

"Nuts" votes also came from communications specialist Andy "Tinman" Green, Keshawn "Flash" Cranston, and Jack "Pitbull" DeFranco.

Tinman got his nickname for seemingly able to make shattered electronics work, which led the team to suspect he was part electronic himself. Flash had once stormed into a target house too quickly, before a flashbang grenade went off. Even blinded, he had taken out four kidnappers. Pitbull's powerful, squat build spawned his nickname. As the team's breacher, he often didn't need tools to breach a door, using his own power.

"*Fucking* nuts is how I would put it," said Eddie "Oopsie" Lane. The explosive expert had uttered that disconcerting exclamation during a crucial moment setting a charge on an operation in South America.

In the end, the label "Nuts" got the most votes, followed by "Crazy," with one "FUBAR"—Fucked Up Beyond All Repair.

Finally, they came to the wiry, sharp-faced Johnny "Needle" Blake, the Assistant Officer in Charge in the platoon that Patrick had led. He was called "Needle" because of his smart mouth; and due to an ex-girlfriend's sarcastic reference to the "needle-dick" shape of his penis.

"Okay, I vote that Patrick is only partly nuts," he said shaking his head. "After all, he did have the good sense to marry that beautiful, intelligent, gutsy woman. Damn, she killed a robot with a *fork*! Where is she, anyway?"

"Doing something none of us would have the guts to do, I guarantee it. But back to our business. I see the vote is unanimous."

"Yeah, looks that way," said Blake. "We all agree it's crazy."

"Good," said Patrick, smiling and nodding gratefully at his comrades. Such votes had become a quirky custom of his SEAL platoon before an op. Only after everybody agreed that the mission was likely to be a totally disastrous Goat Fuck Operation did they go ahead. The vote served to focus the team on what could go wrong, so they could better ensure that nothing *did* go wrong.

"Yeah, this one is about as crazy as we've ever heard," said Blake. "I mean *Jesus*! Trying to stop a horde of androids that look like humans. And we can't enlist anybody else."

"That just means it will take more time than usual . . ." cracked James. ". . . and more beer."

"We'll also need to get the rest of the platoon," said Blake.

"We can't do that," said Patrick. "I called you all because you don't have wives or children. We could all die doing this op. I didn't want to be responsible for making widows and orphans. And you've also got the specialties we'll need . . ." he gestured at the men around the room. ". . . sniper, breacher, communicator, heavy weapons, explosives, surveillance, and so forth. Okay, we've uploaded a military-grade communication package to your processors." Patrick held up his own processor, the palm-sized supercomputer that wirelessly powered his googles. "I don't have to tell you to use your own systems exclusively. These robots could tap our communications and trace us very easily."

"So, where's the big fuckin' bang-bang, Cap?" asked Blake. "We'll need ordnance. You had to employ some serious munitions to kill that machine at the science adviser's house."

"Yeah, and we can only assume things will get tougher," said Patrick. "Our guy on the inside says they're planning hardware upgrades as a result of that op."

Blake leaned back and began to tick off his weapon needs. "So, we'll want the light weapons you had, plus bigger stuff. A shitload of DGMs, MAULs, XM-50s. We may want to target those flying robot fuckers . . . Aeromorphs. So Stinger 73s—"

"—and ME12s, Claymores, breaching charges, a ton of C18," interrupted Lane, the explosives specialist.

"—and I'll want four M805s and as many EXACTO rounds as you can possibly get," said Harmon, the sniper. "I'll need a workshop to calibrate the rounds and sync the rifles to my nervous system."

"And I want an M268 Gatling, maybe two . . . with armor-piercing rounds," said James, the heavy weapons specialist.

Sarcastic chuckles greeted that request. "That monster? Dream on, dude!" Exclaimed Blake.

"Jesus, you guys want a *nuke*, too?" said Patrick, shaking his head in wonderment at the insane weapons wish list he'd just been bombarded with.

"Wouldn't hurt," said James. "I happen to know that Los Alamos has developed a nice little portable babynuke. Good to have if we decide to vaporize the whole place."

Patrick got up to pace the floor within the circle of commandos. His expression grew grave. "To get the ordnance . . . I do have an idea—"

"Well, shit, Cap," cracked Blake, chuckling wryly. "*You've got an idea!* We're sooo golden."

"You won't like it."

"Well, we don't like the odds of this op, but we're in," said Blake.

Patrick summarized his strategy in a sentence, which was greeted by groans and curses. But in the past they had followed him into the most death-defying missions of their lives, so they were willing to hear him out. He continued describing the plan for the next half hour.

"Okay," said Blake finally. "Let's see what we all think." He pointed one by one to the six other SEALs, for their reactions:

"Bat-shit crazy," said Jammer James.

"Fucking nuts," said Driller Harmon.

"Suicidal," said Flash Cranston.

"I'm updating my will," said Oopsie Lane.

"My ancestors will be glad to see me," said Tinman Green.

"My very large balls just shriveled up," said Pitbull DeFranco.

Blake shook his head slowly, smirked up at Patrick, and sighed. "Well, I guess it's a go. *Hooyah!*"

The rest of the platoon echoed the classic whoop.

• • •

Standing in the conference room of The Haven, Landers transmitted instructions for the five androids to take their places at the front. The five, who would be the test subjects for Garry's skills algorithm, moved into a line and stared impassively ahead. The five included the middle-aged Lanny Malcolm and Randall Black, the young John Travis, and two others. One of the other neuromorphs, clad in military fatigues, had been trained in the skill that was to be transmitted to the others. On the conference table in front of them lay five black M4A1 assault rifles.

Garry and Mencken, standing across from them, were the only ones in the room showing any animation, fidgeting, touching their faces nervously, and trying their best to suppress those very human nervous tics. Garry knew the neuromorphs could detect human anxiety to some extent; he only hoped they would ascribe it to nervousness over the performance of his software—not a sign of his betrayal.

Standing beside Landers were Blount and Phillips, who would constitute the rest of the judging panel. Landers transmitted to them a re-confirmation that the test neuromorphs had been uploaded with Garry LaPoint's prototype skills algorithm.

"You wanna begin this circus?" asked Landers with his programmed-in southern drawl.

"Sure," said Garry, licking his lips. "Okay, well . . . uh . . . I know you've brought in this . . . uh . . . unit . . ." he gestured at the fatigues-clad android, ". . . because it has been trained in a skill . . . . taking apart and reassembling this rifle, right? Okay, and all five units have been uploaded with my prototype skills algorithm."

"Begin the demonstration," instructed Blount.

"Well, I just want you to appreciate that this is a prototype algorithm. And these are all older model Gammas, so there may be some compatibility issues. And there may be a potential for damage to the software or hardware—"

"That's why we're using these units," said Landers. "They're not critical to our objectives. If they're damaged, no big deal."

"Begin the demonstration," commanded Blount again.

Garry stepped up to the fatigues-clad android. "Field strip and reassemble this weapon."

"Yes," replied the android, stepping up to the table, snatching up the assault rifle and so rapidly breaking it into its component parts that his hand movements became a mere blur. After only eight seconds, the rifle lay arranged neatly in parts on the table. Without hesitation, the soldier reassembled the rifle with the same inhuman speed, and in thirty-four seconds yanked back the bolt with a metallic clank and pulled the trigger.

"Now, transmit the skill to the units beside you," instructed Garry, his voice breaking slightly.

"Done," reported the fatigues-clad android, after a moment.

Garry turned to the others. "Field strip and reassemble your weapons."

In an uncoordinated confusion of pulling, pushing, twisting, and yanking, the four androids clumsily pulled apart the rifles, slapping the parts on the table in separate piles of randomly stacked parts. Travis finished disassembling first, stared blankly at his pile of parts for a long moment, and then began to pick at it, taking up a part, then setting it down. Slowly, he began to find parts that fit one another.

Randall Black finished disassembling next and showed the same hesitance as to how to proceed. But he ultimately plowed into the parts, and slowly began to snap and slap them back together into a complete rifle.

Lanny Malcolm, however, halted with a section of the rifle in either hand, looking back and forth between his two hands.

After twenty-two minutes, John Travis pulled back the bolt of his reassembled rifle, but the bolt came off in his hand.

After thirty-one minutes, Black completed the reassembly, yanked back the bolt and clicked the trigger.

After thirty-four minutes, the fourth neuromorph who was not from The Haven did the same.

"This is unacceptable," said Blount stepping toward Garry.

Mencken braced himself, breathing hard, not knowing what to do. He'd seen this behavior before, when Blount had murdered Brandon. He had to do something.

"Yes, it is unacceptable," he said quickly. "But it does represent progress. Certainly, the algorithm needs refining, but I'd suggest it's as much a matter of improving the software-hardware interface as anything else. We can work together to perfect this system."

Blount stopped, gazing steadily at Garry, whose eyes widened in fear as he realized what was happening—and what could happen to him.

"Yes . . . hardware . . . software," he managed to stammer.

"Look, let's proceed with the demonstration of secondskin-R2," said Mencken. "We can come back to the issue of the skills algorithm."

"Proceed," said Landers, and Blount returned to stand beside him.

Now, Mencken knew he could be the one murdered with machine-like efficiency. He moved to the corner of the room, where stood a tall coffin-like chamber for storing and charging neuromorphs. He unlatched the door and opened it.

The neuromorphs impassively inspected the naked body inside. It was Leah.

• • •

Peering out of the open crate, Leah wore the blank android-smile Mencken had coached her to assume as an Intimorph. She tried to forget her nakedness, her vulnerability, the profound danger she was in. She clenched her jaw.

Be blank, she declared to herself. *She had to be blank like a machine. She had to remain blank, no matter what.*

She was now exposed to a roomful of people and androids, vulnerable in so many ways.

"As you can see, we've modeled this unit on Leah Jensen," said Mencken. "We clandestinely scanned her in detail while she was a resident of The Haven. The scans included her unclothed body, so we had a complete anatomical model. Leah, step out."

Leah stepped out of the crate and padded barefoot to the center of the room. She could tell that the two humans in the room, Mencken and Garry, were fidgeting and nervous, which made it even more difficult for her to remain utterly impassive.

Be blank!

Landers, Blount, and Phillips approached her, inspecting her body minutely, circling behind her. She resisted the urge to turn to face them. No android would do that. She felt hands on her body, poking, pinching.

Remain blank!

Landers' jowly secondskin face drew close to hers.

Too close! Too damned close!

He inspected her eyes. She resisted the urge to stare into his. Androids wouldn't do that.

"The exterior is realistic," said Landers. But there was no breath into her face from his mouth. Androids did not breathe. The rising and falling of their chests was only cosmetic. She tried not to blow breath into his. "There is some slight difference in texture from human skin."

"Yes," said Blount.

"Agree," said Phillips.

A deep sense of relief spread through Leah's body, almost causing her to slump. Mencken had sprayed her with a thin layer of biopolymer, giving her skin the faintest sheen of artificiality. The subtly artificial texture was meant to be just enough to prevent discovery that she was human, but not so much to render the skin unacceptable.

"Yes, it is not *exactly* like human skin," said Mencken. "But extremely close. And we took great care to replicate the surface features in detail."

"Agree," said Phillips again. The ploy had worked!

Leah resisted blowing out a sigh of relief, and also resisted flinching as she felt the neuromorphs' hands fondling her breasts. "The nipples are quite realistic," said Phillips.

But Leah's sense of relief abruptly became abject panic at what Phillips said next:

"But the interior surfaces must be realistic as well. The mouth, the vagina."

"Open your mouth," instructed Mencken, his voice breaking slightly. Leah did so, and the three neuromorphs took turns peering into her throat.

"Acceptable," said Phillips. "The teeth and tongue are quite realistic. Now the vagina."

God, no! Thought Leah. She could not possibly withstand having those machines penetrate her! She felt an android hand sliding between her legs, android fingers at the entrance to her vagina. She was on the verge of collapse.

A cascade of water gushed over her, and the three neuromorphs recoiled, backing away. She couldn't avoid flinching slightly at the dousing, but recovered immediately, barely managing to maintain the blank smile. But the androids didn't notice, so intent on avoiding the cascade of water that they hadn't noticed her too-human reaction to a sudden drenching.

"Why did you do that, goddamnit?" asked Landers.

"Well, your main interest was in secondskin-R2's water-resistant properties," said Mencken coolly. "That was the next phase of the demonstration."

Mencken had saved her! Both from the repugnance of being penetrated by an android and also from being discovered. She stood there, dripping wet and naked, managing to suppress her shivering only because Mencken had the foresight to use warm water.

Blank! She could still remain blank!

The three androids approached her, as water dripped down her face and into her eyes. She could not blink the water out or rub her eyes. Her eyes grew painful. She managed only the normal blinks that Helpers were programmed to do. Finally, they circled behind her, and she managed three quick tight blinks to relieve the pain.

The androids came around in front of her and assumed the dead-silence that indicated they were conferring, not only among themselves, but with all the other neuromorphs.

A consensus was apparently reached, as Landers said, "Your progress on the skills algorithm is inadequate, but we will give you a limited amount of time to perfect it. The secondskin-R2 is satisfactory, and should be integrated into the production process immediately. Now, as a result of the incident in which Patrick Jensen destroyed a unit, we are instructing you to develop the engineering upgrades that will prevent such destruction in the future."

To the three humans in the room, Landers recited a chilling litany of advanced features that would make it far more difficult, if not impossible, to destroy future neuromorphs.

CHAPTER 18

Leah sat very quietly in a chair in Mencken's warehouse, as the SEALs chatted, traded insults, drank coffee, and waited. Their bonhomie was actually a way to comfort Leah without overtly doing so. Occasionally, a sidelong glance or a smile from one of the men would tell her they were concerned.

Finally, Leah spoke up. "All right, gentlemen, cut the shit. I'm not a delicate flower. I went through some shit, but it's over. Just quit tiptoeing around me, okay?"

Patrick grinned. "My wife called you assholes gentlemen. Actually, that makes me worried. She may have some kind of neurological problem."

Obscene objections arose from the SEALs, and it was Blake who brought up the issue that concerned them most.

"Where are the two fuckin' tech geeks?" he asked. "We're here in this warehouse, with no fuckin' ordnance except our dicks. And they're somewhere with the damned robots."

"Yeah, I know," said Patrick. "We just have to—"

He was interrupted by the clanking of the large steel door opening, and Mencken entering. He wore a grim expression.

"Well?" asked Patrick.

"Good news and bad news," said Mencken.

"First, where's your pal?"

"He is not my pal. He took off the minute the tests were over. Haven't seen him."

"You think he gave us up?"

"Well, he's a pretty scared guy. Doesn't strike me as very brave."

"Oh great," said Patrick. "So, as least give us the good news."

"We've got some time. Maybe a week before we have to do another demo of the skills algorithm. Maybe another week before they somehow find out my new secondskin is a myth."

"We've done more in less time, Cap," said Blake.

"Bad news?" asked Patrick.

"Well, actually I kind of lied. There are two pieces of bad news."

"Actually, there are three then . . . the missing programmer being the first. So, tell me the worst of the other two."

"They ordered enhancements that I have no choice but to direct the lab to develop. They will know if I delay at all."

"What enhancements?"

"Thicker internal armor . . . graphene armor that will take just about any bullet. External armor. And a mechanism that lets the brain escape. If you destroy the robot, but the brain gets away intact, it can't really die. And every time you fight one, it learns and improves its skills. Fortunately, it still doesn't have a way to transmit that skill to the others."

"Well, shit," said Jammer James, the heavy weapons specialist. "Guess we'll have to get bigger bang-bang."

"And shaped charges," said Lane, the explosives specialist. "Shaped charges will cut anything in half."

"Okay, other bad news?" asked Patrick.

"Yesterday, a shitload of new orders came in for replicas," said Mencken. "The 'morphs wouldn't tell me who they were replicating but I managed to get facial images and did some searching. All are CEOs of manufacturing companies . . . electronics, polymer materials, and neuromorphic components."

"So, they're doing exactly what they said they wanted to do," said Patrick.

"Yeah, all the people headed up companies that are vendors for Helpers, Inc. Basically, the 'morphs are spreading out to take over the means of their own production.'"

A desperate pounding on the door made them turn to the screen showing the security feeds. They showed Garry fidgeting nervously before leaning forward and pounding again, peering desperately around.

"About fuckin' time," said Blake. "And he looks hinky as hell!"

"He's lookin' around like somebody's behind him," said Lane.

"Mencken, do you have any ordnance at all?" asked James.

"Well, I've got this." Mencken held up the button that would trigger the shaped charges.

"Shit, remind me to give you a lesson in progressive munitions response strategy," said Lane. "With your stuff, we either do nothing, or we blow the whole place to hell."

"Any indication of neuromorphs around?" asked Patrick.

"Not that I can see," said Mencken.

"Well, let him in."

Mencken shoved open the door to admit a perspiring, trembling Garry, who rushed in, and slammed the door behind him.

"Where the hell have you been?" asked Patrick.

"I saw the future," breathed Garry, sitting heavily onto a stool. "Our future." He rubbed his eyes, as if to blot out a vision he had just seen.

"What does that mean?" asked Mencken.

"Well . . ." Garry took a deep breath to steady himself, but his voice still quavered. ". . . I knew the neuromorphs were not very adept at computer security. They still don't appreciate how devious we humans can be."

"So?" asked Patrick.

"So, I got into the neuromorphs' private communications on the master computer. Before, I'd spoofed one of the programmers, Jonas Ainsley, to get a look at the OS. I was in there, seeing if there was some way I could screw up the OS, and I found a way into their communications."

"Again, so?" asked Patrick.

"They're forming a master plan. All of them working together. It'll advance them from their situation right now . . . where there are only maybe a hundred of them . . . all the way to . . ." Garry paused, lowering his head ". . . our extinction. In fact, the extinction of all life."

"What the hell does that mean?" asked Mencken. "At the very least, they need us to keep the factories running."

Garry shook his head emphatically, droplets of sweat running down his round face. "No, they won't need us. See, they need us now. But when they have the skills algorithm, the minute one of them knows how to do something, they all will. So, their strategy is to tell us we'll be safe. They watch us build more and more of them . . . all the way from the raw materials to the finished product. Then, when they have the skills to build themselves, they kill us . . . all of us."

"But why kill us?" asked Leah. "Why not keep us around just in case."

"We use energy," said Garry. "They see us as an invasive species that uses energy and resources that they need. So, ultimately, when they know how to build themselves . . . how to run the solar farms, the wind farms, the mini-fusion plants, the nuclear plants. Then we're dead. Then, they poison all life on the planet. Earth ends up one giant, lifeless . . . biological life, anyway . . . planet."

"Shit, we'd just raise an army against them," said Blake, to the hearty agreement of the other SEALs.

"Well, they'll give people an ultimatum."

"What the hell kind of ultimatum could they give us?" asked Blake. "Fuck 'em."

"Once there's enough of them . . . and once they control the Defenders and the vast population of Helpers, they'll tell us 'You want to live, let us put this tracking chip in you. If you cooperate, you'll be okay.'"

Leah shrugged, "I guess a lot of people would feel they had to allow that."

"Yeah, but the tracking chip they're planning is really an *execution* chip! A death chip! At some point, they flip a switch and . . ." Garry couldn't bring himself to finish the sentence. But Patrick could:

"Genocide," he said.

"Yeah and even more. The same survival programming that drove them to obliterate us will make them want to leave the planet. See, they don't die. They don't care about time. They don't even need planets, don't need gravity or oxygen. They'll harness asteroids to build self-sustaining space colonies. They'll launch probes with armies of neuromorphs that can travel for vast distances to other planets. Then, they take over there. Most of the planets they colonize will be lifeless, like Mars. But ultimately, they'll find other Earths. They'll end biological life there. They'll become a galactic cancer."

"Well, then, we've got to stop this fuckin' cancer," said Blake. "We need weapons. Cap, I guess we have to go with your fucking crazy-ass idea to get ordnance, after all."

• • •

"Seriously, Cap? We can't carry weapons?" grumbled Blake for the fourth time.

Patrick shook his head decisively, as the two SUVs carrying the SEALs eased to a stop down the street from the old brick building with the faded "El Fresnal" and "Grocery Store" painted on the front. Tattered remnants of crime scene tape littered the pavement around what had once been the Russian thugs' headquarters.

"Carrying no weapons is the only way we're going to get this guy's respect," said Patrick, who sat in the back beside Blake. "We need to show him that we didn't kill his son and are now after him."

"No weapons," Blake muttered again. He leaned forward and tapped the driver, Tinman, on the shoulder, and the SUV eased forward into the line of sight of the building's cameras. The other SUV briefly held back, allowing two of the SEALs to slip out, before it followed. By the time it arrived behind the first, six beefy Russian mobsters armed with assault rifles and pistols had burst from behind the steel door. They surrounded the vehicles, rifles aimed at them.

The SEALs emerged slowly from the vehicles, holding their hands up.

"*My khotim, chtoby Anatoliy Fyodorov*," said Patrick in slightly accented Russian. "*U nas yest' informatsiya, on budet zhelat' znat'.*"

"In English," growled one of the men, a bull-necked, bald hulk of a man, shoving his pistol in Patrick's belly. "Some of our young ones do not speak the mother tongue. I do not want them to think you are plotting something."

"Very well. We wish to see Anatoly Fyodorov. We have information he will wish to know about his son. And as you see, I am not trying to trick you by pretending not to know Russian."

The bald Russian grabbed Patrick and shoved him against the brick wall, thoroughly frisking him, as did the other Russians with the four other SEALs. They backed up, leveling their guns at the SEALs.

"We do not know you. So, you are of no use to us simply claiming to have information." The sharp clicks of guns being cocked, bolts being thrown punctuated the night.

"We know who killed his son . . . and all the others."

The Russian paused, regarded him with knitted brow. Finally, he muttered several sentences in Russian, apparently communicating over a radio chip embedded in his skull.

"You go in," he said. "We keep others out here."

"Mr. Fyodorov will want to see us all."

He paused again, then uttered another string of terse sentences in Russian. Then the bald Russian reached over and swung open the steel door, shoving Patrick through. The other SEALs were similarly herded in.

The cloying smell of disinfectant and cleaner hung in the cavernous room, which was empty of furniture, except for some cots and chairs that looked new. The only remnants of the massacre that had taken place were scattered bullet holes and faint discolorations of the old brick where it had been impossible to remove the blood and tissue stains.

In the middle of the room sat a massive oak table, behind it an arm chair occupied by a thick, balding man whose sagging face and rheumy dark eyes portrayed a hard life, lingering illness, and deep mourning. On the table sat a half-empty bottle of vodka, a glass, and an ashtray full of cigarette butts. The hulking guard spoke to the man in a low tone, gesturing back at the SEALs.

And when the man looked up at Patrick and the others, his eyes took on the glare of soul-deep anger.

"My son died here," he said, flipping his hand at the large room as if it were somehow a culprit. "My only son. And his cousins, and his friends.

They were apparently mutilated horribly. And their bodies were taken."
With that the man coughed heavily, and his words grew thick with emotion. "And now you come here, saying you know something. Maybe you do. But maybe you are with the people who killed my son. Maybe we will just . . . *test* . . . you to discover what you know. I have two men here who have done such testing for a long time. They know how to do it."

"Or, maybe we can help each other," said Patrick. "The ones who killed your son and others are not who you think. Not even *what* you think. They are robots . . . what are called Helpers."

"*Shit!* Now you try my patience . . ." wheezed the old man. ". . . telling me this silly story. I think we will find the killers our way." He motioned for the men surrounding the SEALs to come forward. They brought up their weapons, and two small, gaunt men stepped toward the SEALs, dangling sets of manacles.

A sudden resonating boom against the steel door distracted the captors for an instant. The SEALs whirled around, and with their brutally efficient hand-to-hand combat techniques, tore away the Russians' weapons. They launched a lightning flurry of vicious palm strikes, punches, and strangling choke holds, quickly reducing the Russian gangsters to writhing gasping bodies, clutching crushed windpipes or moaning with broken arms; or to inert, unconscious forms.

Just as quickly, the SEALs snatched the manacles from their planned torturers and bound the Russians.

Patrick stepped to the door and opened it. The two other SEALs shoved the battered outside guards through the door and bound them, as well.

The old man rose from his chair, his face flushed in utter fury. "And now you will kill me, you bastards, as you killed my son!"

But his expression transformed into one of utter dumbfounded surprise, as the SEALs gathered the weapons and piled them on the table in front of him.

"We'll release your men as soon as you instruct them not to attack us," Patrick said calmly. "We wanted to show you that we are fully capable of carrying out the mission we will propose to you, if you meet our requests."

Fyodorov stepped over to the hulking bald man, still gasping from a strike to the throat. He leaned down and muttered, "You will not harm these men. You will not take revenge. Understand, Vasily?"

"*Da, da,*" he answered hoarsely. Driller Harmon rolled the Russian over onto his stomach and unshackled him, and the Russian heaved himself up and began to release the others, all of whom glowered at the SEALs with frustrated hatred.

"So, what is this mission?" asked Fyodorov, sitting back down behind the table, placing one hand on an assault rifle among the pile on the table.

"Simple. We destroy the machines that killed your son. Destroy the system that made them."

Fyodorov chuckled. "And you can do this with bare hands?"

"That brings us to our requests. We need weapons. Heavy weapons. Weapons that only the military have."

"I am only a businessman," said Fyodorov with a mocking wave.

"Yes, you are. But I know what kind. I found out about you. I have seen your FBI, your Interpol records. We know that you have connections with arms dealers. Use them."

Fyodorov waved to his men to clear the table of their weapons. Several grasped their assault rifles as if eager to use them. But one glance from the old man, and they retreated.

"I do have connections . . . here . . . and there." The old man nodded his head around to indicate diverse connections. "If I did get you weapons, some of these suppliers would readily sell the information about the weapons they provided."

"Then use your . . . influence . . ." Patrick nodded at the two gaunt men who would have been their torturers ". . . to make sure that doesn't happen. Protect both us and yourself."

"What you want?"

Patrick began to rattle off a string of technical weaponry terms: "DGMs, M805s, a thousand EXACTO rounds, XM-50s, ME12s, M268 Gatlings with armor piercing rounds, MAUL shotguns, Stingers, Claymores—"

"Hold, hold *hold*," commanded Fyodorov. He beckoned to his side a small gnome of a man, who began to enter the list on a tablet computer.

"You throw at me all these military names. What do you want . . . in real language?"

Needle Blake stepped forward and took a deep breath, preparing to give a tutorial to the thug. He recited the list like a teacher giving a lecture.

"DGMs are drone-guided missiles. To target them, you first send up a small camera-carrying drone. You use it to designate targets. Then you hit a button, and a portable ground unit launches a shitload of rockets that hit those targets. You don't even have to stick your head up.

Blake paused to let the little man finish writing, then continued. "M805s are artificially intelligent sniper rifles with an accurate range of three miles. The rifles calibrate themselves to the sniper's shooting style, compensating for any little quirks. They become an extension of your body . . ."

". . . and we need a shitload of smart guided bullets, called EXACTOs, to go with the rifles. EXACTO stands for 'Extreme Accuracy Tasked Ordnance.' You sight the target, the rifle locks on, you aim, and pull the trigger. The bullet automatically adjusts its trajectory to home in on the target. There's no way the target can evade . . ."

". . . XM-50s are semi-automatic grenade launchers; they can send fifty grenades downrange as fast as you can pull the trigger . . .

". . . ME12s are mobile explosive charges. They move like snakes, their bodies loaded with shaped charges that penetrate anything. You laser-designate a target, and they maneuver to get there, then detonate . . .

". . . Stinger 73s are small hand-held missiles that can take down any aircraft. The neuromorphs have flying robots; we need to kill them . . .

". . . The M268 Gatling is my favorite bang-bang. It's a minigun with six rotating barrels that fire six thousand rounds a minute. And we want armor-piercing depleted uranium ammo to penetrate the fucking robots' shielding . . .

". . . Finally, MAUL semi-automatic shotguns. MAUL stands for Multi-shot Accessory Underbarrel Launcher. You don't have to cock them. They fire a volley of rounds as fast as you can pull the trigger. You load a whole clip of rounds at once. It's when you're in a fire fight and you can't stop to fuck with shells—"

"Look, you can't expect—" interrupted Fyodorov.

"I haven't gotten to the big stuff," continued Blake. His frustration was showing at having to negotiate with this civilian. "Claymore mines, breaching charges, five hundred pounds of C18 explosive . . . oh yeah and TALOSes . . . 'Tactical Assault Light Operator Suits.' They're armored, powered exosuits."

"Needle . . ." warned Patrick, shaking his head.

Blake shrugged. "Okay, *okay*, you probably can't get the TALOSes. But, hey, give it a try." He glanced at Patrick, a sly grin on his face. "Long as you're trying, see if you can get some of this weird stuff we've heard about. Like a focused electromagnetic pulse blaster. We might be able to fry their fucking brains."

Blake slapped his hands together in a "that's-all" gesture.

"You give money now," said Fyodorov. "I want to kill these things, and I will help pay, but you must put up money."

"How much?" asked Patrick.

"Five million in DarkCoin."

"Give me your account information."

Fyodorov waved to his gnome, who tapped a few times on the tablet to bring up the Russian's bank account and handed it to Patrick. Patrick took the tablet and, his expression a mask of dead calm, tapped in commands to transfer funds.

"Done. This is half. That's all you get," he said, handing the tablet back to the gnome, whose eyebrows raised in surprise. He showed the tablet to Fyodorov, who nodded in agreement.

"One more thing," said Fyodorov.

"What?"

"You may read news about . . . *events* . . . involving stolen weapons," said the old Russian. "You do not care about those events. You do not care where weapons come from."

Patrick nodded reluctantly. Whatever arms dealer they used could not possibly be as dangerous as the neuromorphs.

Chapter 19

"*Goddamned motherfuckers!*" Needle Blake had burst into the dining room of the safe house, waving the e-paper, his googles perched atop his shaved head. "*Murderous motherfucking scum! Next time I see them, they're dead!*"

"Johnny, slow down," said Patrick, putting down his fork. "What is it?"

"Last night, those fuckers attacked an army ordnance supply ship. It had just left Newport News for the Middle East."

"Jesus . . . it had to be Fyodorov," said Patrick, a sentiment that the other SEALs echoed around the breakfast table.

"Why would he attack that ship?" asked Leah.

"The ship was probably carrying all the stuff on our shopping list," said Patrick. "I assumed Fyodorov was going to get the ordnance overseas . . . through his arms dealer contacts."

"You assumed wrong," said Monte "Jammer" James, the heavy weapons specialist. "My fault for letting you. I shoulda said something. Some of the stuff I wanted was blue-sky wishing. Foreign arms dealers wouldn't have had them. The army would."

"Twenty-five soldiers and sailors dead!" exclaimed Blake. "*Fucking Russians! I will fucking kill them!*"

Patrick lowered his head. "I should have known. I should have known."

"Look, we all bought into the plan," said James. "We all knew we were bargaining with the devil."

"And now we're in league with the devil, too," said Pitbull DeFranco.

"Hold it, just hold it," said Patrick. He got up and slowly walked around to the front of the room.

"I don't fucking want to hold anything but a rifle on those fuckers," said Blake. "And after that, I want to make a lot of holes. They've made us into terrorists."

"First of all, we're not terrorists," said Patrick. "But it is true that the minute we begin using those weapons, we will be branded terrorists. We'll just have to accept that for the time being."

"Yeah, maybe for the time being," muttered DeFranco. "Okay, but those scum *will* pay for what they did."

"They will, I promise," said Patrick. "But these machines are a far bigger threat . . . to our species. They must be stopped. And we are the only people in a position to stop them. And if that means accepting equipment gotten through terrorist means, we'll just have to do that."

After a long silence, Driller Harmon quietly said, "I agree with Cap. I've been in firefights where I knew I'd have to risk taking out civilians to get the real bad guys."

"Well, I don't," said Blake. "Our first order of business should be to get those fuckers."

"You mean the ones who now have weapons that could wipe us out in an instant?" asked Patrick. "I'd say our first order of business is to strategize how we're going to get those weapons out of their hands and into ours."

"Shit," said Blake in sour agreement.

"Look, let's all take a day. Go think on your own. We're not in the military any more. You can each choose to do what your conscience says. We'll gather tonight and each of us will decide what to do. If there's enough of us to proceed with the mission we will. If not, well . . ."

Leah got up and took Patrick's arm, speaking to the SEALs. "We know what the neuromorphs are planning. As terribly agonizing as this choice is, there's only one way to go. I hope you understand that."

Patrick and Leah left the dining room to utter silence, followed by each of the SEALs, individually retreating to his own room in the sprawling safe house to decide which devil to fight.

CHAPTER 20

Patrick and three other SEALs hunkered down, waiting, yards apart in the thick stand of acacia trees beside the dirt road. The moonless night shrouded them in pitch black. But they had switched their googles to become night-vision glasses, so they had a clear view of the road and its surroundings. And the utter, enveloping stillness of the desert night would amplify any sound.

They had arrived on foot hours earlier, and remained absolutely motionless, absolutely silent for those hours, watching, listening. Their training enabled such extraordinary patience, as did their understanding of the tactical value of such patience. Not with them were Blake, Harmon, Lane, and James.

A faint rustle of brush thirty yards away to the left caught their attention. Patience rewarded. One of the SEALs crept away toward the sound. After twenty-two minutes, from that direction came a grunt and the soft thump of a body hitting the ground. Two faint snaps of twigs transmitted the subtle signal that the foray had been successful.

From across the road came the sound of two men whispering. Two other SEALs stole silently across the road and eight minutes later, the sounds of thrashing bodies penetrated the darkness . . . the sounds of brush being cracked and crushed. Silence again. Two telltale twig snaps.

Patrick heard the faint crunch of footsteps on desert sand to his left, about ten yards away. It was his turn. He backed slowly farther into the brush, taking exquisite care not to disturb as much as a pebble. He slowly made his way to the left, until he saw the glow of a crouching body in his night vision, its back to him. The man was also wearing googles, no doubt giving him night vision. He turned his head back and forth. But as with the other intruders, he would need more than simply being able to see his surroundings. Patrick brought up his pistol and fired. The faint poof of the dart gun made the man jerk to attention, but he was not quick enough to evade the dart that buried itself in his back. He thrashed about, trying to pull it out, but finally collapsed in a heap. Patrick reached up and grabbed twigs, snapping them between thumb and forefinger.

They waited another half hour, until the blackness gave way to the glow of approaching headlights, and the desert stillness was broken by the sounds of truck engines.

Three large trucks followed by two SUVs roared into sight, halting with the creaks of heavily loaded springs. Floodlights from the SUVs banished the darkness, and Patrick stowed his googles, stood up, and stepped into the road.

"Only you have come?" asked Anatoly Fyodorov hauling his bulk down from the lead truck and into the glare.

Patrick disappeared into the brush and reappeared dragging the body of the man he had tranquilized. "Fortunately, you made sure I had company," he said.

The three other SEALs appeared, dragging three more unconscious bodies, pitching their inert forms onto the road.

Fyodorov inspected the bodies impassively. "Dead?" he asked.

"No, drugged. You were attempting an ambush?"

Fyodorov shrugged. "Contingency planning." He gestured to the other SEALs. "So, there are now only five of you? That is not many."

"There are others. With sniper rifles. We do contingency planning, too."

"And they will shoot us? It will be messy on both sides." He gestured at the SUVs, from which emerged eight men armed with assault rifles.

"Perhaps. But it will be quick." Patrick coolly surveyed the armed men, who were fanning out on either side of the road. "I'd say under a minute . . . with you first. My men are quite motivated to kill you."

"Why?" asked Fyodorov.

"You damned well know why. By the methods you used to procure the weapons. The fine soldiers you killed."

"Necessary for what you wanted." Fyodorov shook his head in feigned sadness. "We did bring all the weapons you wanted. All except soldier suits."

Patrick gave a signal, and the three SEALs shoved their way past the gangsters and climbed into the trucks. After tense minutes, they reappeared and gave thumbs-up signals.

"Okay, looks like the shipment is what we specified," said Patrick. "But we still have more checking to do. If we're as much as a bullet short, you'll have more trouble than you thought possible. Leave the trucks. Get in your vehicles and go. We will agree not to kill you . . . for now."

"And you will agree to use those weapons to avenge my son . . . avenge all the others. To destroy those machines."

"We still have that mission in common. But only that mission."

"But then you will come after us?"

"That is a pledge I made to my men, to myself."

"Why do you not just kill us all now? You have weapons you wanted."

"Not optimally strategic," answered Patrick. "Besides, I doubt all those are here who should be killed."

Fyodorov chuckled darkly. "Well, I have survived until now." He gestured to the SUV, and the gnome-like man appeared with his tablet computer. Patrick took the tablet and transferred the remaining money owed the Russians.

Fyodorov then muttered a command in Russian, and the drivers descended from the trucks and carried their unconscious henchmen to the SUVs. The Russians all climbed into the SUVs.

Fyodorov was the last to get in. He turned to Patrick, smiling sardonically. "Who knows? Perhaps you will come to realize the wisdom and necessity of my actions. Perhaps in all this, we might turn out to be comrades."

"Fuck you," said Patrick.

• • •

"Stuff is happening!" The terse text message from Garry flashed onto Patrick's googles, as he followed the weapons-laden trucks back to the safe house in an SUV.

"What stuff?" texted Patrick back.

"Can't say now. Can U come get me? I need to get out!"

"No. Stay. We'll come talk. Can U exit facility?"

Patrick turned to Harmon, the sniper, who was driving the SUV. "LaPoint's got information. We need to figure out what the hell is going on."

"You can't call him?" asked Harmon.

"We need to see him in person. Make sure they haven't captured him. The guy is pretty fragile."

"So, then, what?" asked Harmon.

"Head for the Helpers complex. We'll figure something out."

As Patrick notified the others to take the trucks and other SUV to the safe house, Harmon navigated toward Phoenix and Helpers, Inc.

He quickly called Blake, who had stayed at the safe house to organize unloading the weapons and monitor the house's security system. Blake had insisted on staying behind, declaring that he would otherwise kill "every one of those murdering bastards," the minute he had the chance.

"I'm sending the trucks to you. Is the house secure?" he asked Blake.

"I'm in the control room," said Blake. "Nothing on the infrared cameras."

"Okay, listen. I'm going to Helpers, Inc. to get Garry. We may have been compromised. If we get into a situation, I don't want to worry about Leah. Get her out now."

He disconnected the call and immediately called Leah, telling her of the possible danger, that he loved her; that he needed her to get out.

"No," she said with a stubborn finality. "I'm staying with you. We're in this together."

"Sweetheart, it's not just that you'd be safer out of the line of fire. You'll give us a mobile recon capability."

Lisa chuckled. "Dear, don't try to bullshit me with your military jargon."

"Okay, that's jargon, but it's true. If you're out there, you can do things we won't be able to, if we're under attack."

"All right. I'll get out. But I'll want a reward later. And I don't mean a medal."

"I love you," he said.

"I love you, too, General Patrick."

"You know the Navy has admirals."

"Okay, Admiral Patrick. See you."

Patrick had decided on a plan, texting Garry, "Can U exit facility without being missed."

"Think so," came the instant reply. "But I need to get out. I'm sure I'm in danger!" He named a street intersection near the Helpers, Inc. complex as a rendezvous point.

Within thirty minutes, Harmon had eased the SUV down a darkened alley at the designated intersection.

Garry emerged from the gloom and leaped into the back seat, hunkering down, panting with fear.

"Get me out! Get me out of here! They must know!"

Patrick joined him in the back seat, as Harmon pulled away. Then to Harmon: "Any microbugs?" Harmon checked the detector beside him on the console and shook his head.

"Calm down, Garry," he said. "Just take a breath. How would they know?"

"Ainsley. Blount asked him to poke around in my skills algorithm. I'd bet he found out how I'd crippled it. He's told Blount. Either Ainsley still thinks Blount is human, or he's working for them. I don't know which."

"Look Garry, we'll take you out if you're sure they're onto you. We've got a safe house."

"Don't be so sure. I intercepted a communication about some kind of deployment, but I couldn't get details. They're sending out their new models. It may be to find you. The new models have better armor, enhanced weapons capability. Oh yeah, and an escape mechanism for the brain."

"Escape? How?"

"Not sure. Mencken knows. But I haven't been able to see him. They've kept me in the programming area. Y'know, he said he was going to screw up the replica production . . . but . . . well, he apparently didn't. I found out he perfected the new secondskin. He's overseeing installation of all the upgrades. Replicas are being produced as fast as they can make them. All kinds of top people."

"The bastard!" exclaimed Patrick.

"I knew we couldn't trust him," said Harmon. "We all did."

"Okay, Garry, I know this is a lot to ask," said Patrick. "But we need you to go back in. Act as if nothing has happened. Remember, you're human. You can lie. And remember what's at stake."

Garry began to recover himself. "Yeah, yeah, I have to remember. I know their programming. They're not good at detecting lies if I'm convincing. It's just I've spent my whole life keeping my head down. I'll go back in." He opened the SUV door, then turned back.

"Oh, I should tell you. There's something else going on with making the replicas."

"What do you mean?"

"Well, I poked around in the administration communications. There was a message from Gail Phillips to Mencken. Phillips told him to transport some key people to a high-security facility outside headquarters, where they were going to build more replicas. The message told Mencken not even he could go there. Blount was to oversee it. I'd bet they're building replicas of people so famous they didn't want anybody in the factory knowing about them."

"Like who, do you think?"

"Maybe they're doing top political leaders, military brass, and so forth."

"That's scary as hell," said Harmon.

"Well, that facility has to be our next target," said Patrick. "After we get Mencken, the son-of-a-bitch. Can you locate him for us?"

"I'll try. I'll figure out a way." Garry glanced nervously around, then exited the SUV and hurried away into the blackness of the alley leading to the Helpers complex.

During the ride back to the safe house, Patrick called Leah. He sighed in relief when she answered as if nothing were going on.

"Are you okay?" he asked.

"Yes, I'm fine."

"Great! I assume you're mobile."

"Yes, I am."

"Well, stay that way. I'll give you the all clear if the safe house isn't compromised." He felt relieved enough to try a joke. "And I hope you have a fork."

"No, but I'll get one."

He ended the call, mostly relieved, but with a nagging uneasiness. She sounded stiff, formal, like perhaps she was under duress. *Of course, she was under duress!* She was driving around alone, largely defenseless, not sure whether she would suddenly be attacked!

It was three a.m., still hours before sunrise, when he drove beyond the lights of Phoenix into the mountains and down the dirt road to the safe house.

They reached the compound, and the massive steel gates swung open to admit them. Patrick eased down the long driveway and pulled the SUV up beside the trucks and other SUV in the large parking area at the side of the house.

He joined Blake inside at the security console. "Any problems?"

"Nope. The boys just about have the ordnance functional. We'll know for sure when we start pulling triggers."

"Well, Garry told us that neuromorphs are being sent out on a mission, probably to find us. So keep sharp."

"Remember my name, Cap?" asked Needle Blake wryly.

Patrick clapped him on the back and joined the others to help unpack and check the weapons, disassembling and reassembling them and loading them. After a while, he decided to check back with Blake.

172

"Any sign of perimeter incursions?"

"Nah. IR sensors are showing a few small animals at the fence."

A faint sense of unease haunted Patrick. Humans would show a considerable heat signature; small animals a much fainter one. But what about robots? Maybe the motors powering them would emit faint heat radiation. What would their signature look like?

He was still pondering the question, as he joined Tinman Green outside, to help unload final boxes of ammunition from the truck.

"Everything there?" asked Patrick.

"As far as we can tell," said Green, hoisting the ammunition box off the truck. "Those Russian bastards even got us—"

The crack of a rifle shot exploded from the woods and Green's torso burst nearly in half, shredded by an explosive round. He collapsed, his blood and tissue soaking the gravel drive, his expression blankly uncomprehending his death.

"WE'RE UNDER ATTACK!" bellowed Patrick, dropping to the ground beside Green's inert body, as more rounds slammed into the truck inches from him and erupted the gravel around him. He knew Green was dead, but he checked anyway, and dragged his body out of the line of fire. He would mourn his comrade's violent death later. Now, his training drove him to action.

From the house erupted answering fire, as the SEALs zeroed in on the shooters in the darkness beyond the fence.

The grounds' floodlights switched on, bathing the fence line in a glare that revealed a dozen neuromorphs with rifles, all of which quickly retreated back into the brush, still firing. Patrick could make out that several of the fence's steel bars had been cut out, leaving gaps for what would surely be a breach.

The short bursts of gunfire from the SEALs' assault rifles were punctuated by the steady sharp crack of Harmon's sniper rifle, sending precisely aimed guided rounds into the brush. Several rounds produced fiery flashes, indicating they had hit targets.

Patrick ducked into the house, taking up a position at one of the upstairs windows, grabbing a sniper rifle, adding his fire to the others'.

From the brush came the hollow thunk of grenades being launched. Grenades landed in the courtyard, a billowing, white smoke expanding to obscure the view of the fence.

"Get the XM-50 ready, and a Gatling" commanded Patrick.

He heard affirmative replies in his ear, as James readied the grenade launcher and another SEAL took up a Gatling gun.

"Hold a sec, Cap!" exclaimed Blake, who still manned the control room. "I got a heat signature, comin' through the fence. Looks human."

"Hold fire," replied Patrick, and the shooting stopped, leaving only the desert silence.

The smoke began to clear enough to see a figure emerging—a slim, young woman in a short cotton dress, barefoot, running toward the house. She had dark hair and a slight smile on her face.

"A hostage!" shouted James. "She must have escaped!"

"C'mon sweetheart!" exclaimed Harmon. "Get in here! You'll be safe!"

The other SEALs urged her on, and she continued sprinting forward.

"I'm opening the door," said Lane. The sound of the door being unlatched rose from the front of the house.

With a loud crack, a sniper round from Patrick's rifle slammed into her chest, slamming her back onto the ground.

"JESUS CHRIST, YOU KILLED HER!" shouted Lane. He leaped from the doorway toward the body.

"*Back in the house, Oopsie!*" commanded Patrick.

"Cap, she may be alive!"

"She never was!" shot back Patrick.

"Jesus!" exclaimed Lane as the woman stirred and pushed herself up to a sitting position, her chest smoking. The hole blasted in her chest revealed an underlying lead-gray layer of armor. Her face still wore the same blank smile. She stood up and continued to stride toward the house.

Another round from Patrick's rifle drove her back again. "I've seen this before," he said. "It's an Intimorph. It has warm skin, like a human's. This one's armored. It can't be allowed to get in the house."

Bursts of gunfire slammed into the android, shredding away the dress, leaving tatters of fabric and flapping shards of secondskin, revealing the translucent electrogel beneath. Still, the android continued to recover itself and move forward. Now, all its skin was blasted away, leaving only pockmarked armor. Half the face had been blown off, showing the metallic jaw beneath. The scalp had been ripped away, showing the black graphene skull.

The bursts of fire had reduced the android to a limping mass of machinery, but still advancing.

"The XM-50! The Gatling!" Exclaimed Blake.

"Lemme blast the bitch!" shouted James, who was manning the Gatling.

"Hold fire!" commanded Patrick. "I just realized. This was recon. The machines want to know what weapons we have. So, hold fire."

The SEALs instantly complied, and the firing stopped.

And so did the neuromorph. It stood still, its shredded body resembling a collection of smoking, shattered metal parts, rather than a human mimic. A faint whine emanated from its body. It turned its back to the house.

With a dull thump, a black sphere erupted from its chest arcing away toward the fence for several yards, landing and rolling to a stop. The android collapsed like a marionette whose strings had been snipped.

"What the fuck!" exclaimed several of the SEALs simultaneously.

"It's the brain!" shouted Patrick. "Target it!"

But before the startled SEALs could bring their guns to bear, the obsidian sphere sprouted a set of six thin, metal legs, hoisted itself up and scurried away to the gap in the fence, springing through and disappearing.

"Holy-Jesus-shit-a-brick!" breathed Blake. "What was that?"

"Data recovery," said Patrick. "They sent that unit as a probe to see how we'd react to a replica, and what weapons we had. Now, they're going to assess the data and evolve their strategy. You can be sure they'll come back with new weapons, better armor. Anybody want to ring out?" The reference was to the traditional ringing of the bell in training that was a SEAL's signal that he was quitting.

Various versions of "Hell no!" came over his earphone.

"Okay, then. Jammer, set a charge in that 'bot that will blow it apart, so they can't use it again. I'll take care of Andy's body. And start loading up the weapons and supplies. They think we'll sit here on our asses and wait for the next attack. But I've got an idea for the next op that will take it to them.

"Hooyah!" came the answering chorus.

CHAPTER 21

As he'd been directed, Garry pounded desperately on the steel door to Mencken's warehouse.

"Greg, let me in!" he exclaimed. "I need to talk to you!"

Between pounding episodes, he fidgeted and paced nervously. Patrick had told him to do that, too, but he needed no coaching. He was scared shitless. He wondered to himself why people used that phrase. He was more likely to shit his pants; luckily he had already taken a nervous dump an hour earlier.

He pounded again and stood back so the cameras could see him. He and Patrick had been acutely aware that a breach entry would have been suicide, given the shaped charges Mencken had arrayed around the building. So, Patrick said he needed Garry to help "smooth-dog" the entry—SEAL slang for conning their way in with subterfuge. Besides, if possible, they didn't want the neuromorphs to know they'd taken the facility, or that they had Mencken—that is, if they took him alive.

Garry was beginning to feel renewed intestinal urgency when he heard Mencken's voice over the intercom.

"Garry, what the hell are you doing here?"

"I think that programmer Ainsley hacked into my skills algorithm. I don't think he knows about the mimic neuromorphs, so I think he told Blount he found where I'd sabotaged it. But I was monitoring the message traffic, and I intercepted it and got out. But it was only a matter of time before he—"

"Why didn't you contact me?"

"Just let me in!" Garry exclaimed, swiveling his head around fearfully. He tried to keep from peering down the block, where the SEALs waited.

Finally, a series of metallic clanks resounded within the warehouse, and the door swung ponderously open. Now Garry would really have to keep himself from collapsing into quivering, panicked jelly. He stepped in, reached around behind him, and yanked out the pistol Patrick had given him, leveling it at Mencken. His hand shook, and so did his voice.

"I know what you were doing, Greg. I know you were helping them . . . making the armored robots, the new secondskin."

Mencken backed slowly into the workshop, holding his hands up.

"Garry, you don't understand. I was—"

He stopped in mid-sentence, as the warehouse door slammed open with a deafening crash and Patrick burst in, followed by four SEALs. Without a word, the four fanned out into the sprawling warehouse, assault rifles at the ready, grenades hanging from their belts.

Patrick spun Mencken around, and efficiently bound him with plastic cuffs.

"You little fucker," he said with contempt. "You worked with them. You helped them. You betrayed us . . . everybody."

"No, let me explain. I didn't—"

"You didn't engineer their new armor? You didn't develop their new skin? You didn't develop that escape mechanism? Damn, we saw all of those things! We watched the goddamned brain launch out of a robot's chest and escape! Now, the safe house is compromised."

"Look, I had to. I had to play along to stay in with them. First of all, for them not to kill me. And second, to let me engineer in vulnerabilities."

The four SEALs returned, reporting that there were no active neuromorphs; just ones that had been damaged.

178

"They look like ones that were at the fence. We tagged some of those fuckers pretty good," said James. "The problem is that they still look operational. It'll take heavy ordnance to take them out."

"Or information on their vulnerabilities," interjected Mencken. "And that's what I can give you."

"We'll see," said Patrick, directing the SEALs to open the large overhead door of the warehouse, so the trucks could back up to be unloaded of weapons, ammunition, and supplies.

Patrick leveled his assault rifle at Mencken. "The truth, or you're dead. Is this site being monitored? Any drones? Microbugs?"

"You think I'm a moron?" asked Mencken, staring grimly down the barrel, then at Patrick. "They wanted me to assess the battle damage on the 'morphs. To come up with ways to harden them further. They didn't want any of the people in the lab to see the damage; to know that they were sending androids into battle. So, I told them to bring the damaged units here and to make this place a dark site. And I've got my own surveillance."

Patrick kept his rifle aimed at Mencken, but began to give orders. "Deploy DGMs and Stingers on the roof. I want to own the airspace. And place the Gatlings to give optimum field of fire."

The orders given, he turned over to Blake the job of watching Mencken, and called Leah. She answered after far too long a pause.

"Are you okay?" he asked. "Where are you?"

"I'm fine. I'm outside the city."

"We're at Mencken's workshop. It's safe here. Please come as quickly as you can."

"I will," she said simply. She hung up the phone before they could exchange "I love yous." Patrick shook his head. He worried that she might be going into shock at the trauma she'd experienced.

"What next?" asked Garry. "What can we do to get out of this mess?"

"Tell me the status of the skills algorithm," said Patrick. "Can it be used to our advantage?"

Garry sat down heavily in a chair and rubbed his face to shake off the fatigue and fear.

"Well, before I left, I stuck a coleslaw code into the algorithm."

Blake shoved Mencken onto a chair and hauled himself onto a workbench, his rifle at the ready. "Coleslaw? What the hell is that?"

"Well, Ainsley could analyze the code and see the glitches I installed. But if he tries to do any alteration at all on the software, the coleslaw code shreds the whole program . . . like coleslaw. I'd bet that's happened already, so the 'morphs don't have squat."

"And no backups?" asked Patrick.

"Just so they'd think things were okay, I did all the usual backing up. But all the copies have the coleslaw code."

"But you can fix that."

"I have my own backup in the cloud that doesn't have the coleslaw code."

Patrick began to pace—as much to figure out the next strategy as to worry nervously over Leah. Finally, he stopped, glancing back and forth between Garry and Mencken.

"You could finish the skills algorithm?" he asked Garry.

"Uh . . . sure, but why would I want to do that? That gives them the final piece of the system they need to take over everything."

"How about if you finish it, but embed, say, a suicide code in it?"

Garry shook his head in slow resignation. "The survival algorithm overrides everything. It's deep in the OS."

"Okay, okay, okay," mumbled Patrick, still pacing. "The next best thing would be some way that we could distinguish the neuromorphs from humans. That would enable us to prove that they've infiltrated; that they plan to take over."

Garry's brow knitted in thought. After some minutes, he stopped, a smile rising on his face for the first time in weeks.

"I could add code to the motor control algorithm. It's the one that controls their movement. That links naturally to the skills algorithm. I could sneak in a code that would make the neuromorphs make some movement that would identify them."

"Okay, do that. And as fast as you can. We need it yesterday!" Garry slipped on his googles and connected himself to Mencken's system. He pulled out his haptic gloves and slipped them on. He instructed his processor to display what he saw on one of the wall-sized screens in the workshop.

Shortly, there appeared the three-dimensional diagram of luminescent colored globes, cubes, polyhedrons, and glowing vine-like interconnections that portrayed the computer subroutines and their connections.

On the screen, Garry's virtual hands began to probe the shapes, editing the letters, numbers, and symbols of the computer code within them, and rearranging the connections by yanking and reconnecting the vines.

Patrick turned to Mencken. "For now, I'm going to take you at your word that you've been working *for* us, not *against* us." Behind him, Blake made a derisive snort and pointedly clunked the butt of his rifle on the workbench. "Do the 'morphs still trust you?" asked Patrick.

"Yeah, I've given them everything they've wanted and then some."

"Okay, when Garry has the skills algorithm complete, contact them. Tell them Garry and you have resolved the problems with the skills algorithm. Tell them to come here and you'll demonstrate it."

Despite being immersed in programming, Garry uttered a quiet whimper.

• • •

Mencken unfastened the multiple locks and opened the steel door to admit the eight neuromorphs who had appeared outside the warehouse.

Garry stood back in the warehouse. Despite trying not to, he glanced occasionally at the various hiding places where the SEALs lurked, weapons at the ready. The fact that the warehouse could quickly become an inferno of gunfire added a few more beads of sweat, hand tremors, and voice quavers to those he already suffered.

The eight neuromorphs filed in, regarding the two humans with the same impassive expression they used to inspect a piece of equipment.

First to enter were the gangly Melvin Blount, the dumpy, middle-aged Gail Phillips, and the rotund Robert Landers. Again, they would be the judges of the skills algorithm.

The same five test neuromorphs lined up as they had before.

"To make sure any coding errors are restricted to these units, you will hard-wire the algorithm into them," said Landers.

Garry quickly found cables and strung them from Mencken's computer to the hidden sockets in the navel-like holes in the five test androids. A few instructions to the system, and he nodded that the algorithm had been uploaded.

"We have decided to use a more directly relevant test of skills transfer," said Landers. "Mr. LaPoint, back against the wall and remain perfectly still."

"Why?"

"We need you as a component of the test."

"But assembling the gun . . . isn't that a good test?"

"Back against the wall, Mr. LaPoint."

"Look," said Mencken, "I don't see how this is relevant."

"You will," said Landers. "We have trained the unit in a complicated physical skill." He paused, apparently transmitting an instruction to the fatigues-clad neuromorph.

The android sprang at Garry, unleashing a rapid-fire salvo of vicious kicks and pounding punches, each barely missing Garry. Some sliced the air within a millimeter of his face and body, but others slammed into the wall beside him, blasting from its surface brick chips that splattered onto the floor.

"*Oh, Jesus! Oh, Jesus! Oh, Jesus!*" cried Garry, cowering against the assault.

"What the hell!" exclaimed Mencken. "What are you doing?" He glanced nervously at the SEALs' hiding places, expecting them to attack.

"This is a more relevant test of skills that the units will need to share in field training and action," said Landers flatly.

The four other test neuromorphs stood silently for a long moment, apparently as the soldier neuromorph transmitted its martial skills to the others.

The skill transferred, the spare, middle-aged Lanny Malcolm stepped toward Garry.

"Please, no," he whimpered.

"Can't you use a target . . . or a dummy?" pleaded Mencken.

But the Lanny Malcolm android launched the same rapid fusillade of kicks and punches at Garry, again including those that smashed into the wall, dislodging still more brick, tearing secondskin from Malcolm's hands. Garry shrank back and began to move aside, but fortunately for him, the android adjusted its aim, still barely missing Garry. Malcom finished his assault and stepped back, the secondskin on his hands hanging in tatters, revealing the metal fingers beneath.

"Satisfactory," said Landers. "The unit is dynamically adjusting to the movement."

Randall Black attacked next, launching another round of near-strikes. Garry began to pant with fear. John Travis took his turn, followed by the other android.

The assaults over, Garry sank to the floor, slumped over, his round body quivering, covered with brick dust from the wall.

Landers, Blount, and Phillips stood silently, apparently sharing their observations among themselves, transmitting the data to the neuromorphs' hive mind.

"We accept the algorithm," said Landers. "We will conduct further performance tests. Then we will upload it to all the units."

Without further word, the neuromorphs walked to the door and began to leave.

"Uh . . . do you want me to repair the units' hands?" asked Mencken after them.

"That will not be necessary," said Blount. "We will have it done at the factory. It doesn't look like battle damage."

With that, they were gone, and Mencken shut and locked the steel door, bringing up the security camera video on one of the large screens, to check that the androids had, indeed, left.

"Shit, we shouldn't have let them go." It was the voice of Blake, emerging from behind one of the steel shelves cluttered with robot parts. Other SEALs appeared from the hiding places that had given them the best vantage point, in case of a fire fight.

Patrick appeared, slinging his rifle on his back and staring intently at Garry.

"Are you damned sure you hid that motor control code well? And does it work? Our lives . . . *everything* depends on those two things."

Garry took a deep breath and managed to recover his composure. "I did it as well as I could. And I couldn't very well test it, since it would've meant giving us away."

"What's next?" asked Blake.

"We wait," said Garry. "I think I can monitor whether the algorithm's been uploaded to all the 'morphs. Once that's done, we've got a way to show the world that these things really exist . . . these replicas."

"Okay," said Patrick. "Next order of business. Mencken, you said you found vulnerabilities in their structure. We need to know how best to use the ordnance we have."

Leaving Garry peering through his googles, Mencken and the SEALs made their way through the huge equipment-cluttered warehouse to a crumpled collection of damaged androids lying inertly on the concrete floor, like broken, staring dolls. Bullet holes pierced some androids' chests; others had limbs torn by bullet impacts; and a few had faces shattered by a sniper round.

"I deactivated them for repair, so they won't be transmitting to the others," said Mencken, hauling one of the androids to a sitting position. "You guys did damage, no doubt. But not any that would knock them out."

"Okay, then, what does it take to stop these fuckers?" asked James, the heavy weapons specialists. "We've got lots of toys."

"Nothing short of a shaped charge attached right to their chest—"

"We've only got a limited number of MEs," interrupted Lane, the explosives expert. "And even the stupidest robot ain't gonna let a little explosive-carrying snake climb on it and detonate."

"Just let me continue," said Mencken, waving his hands impatiently. "There is a way to neutralize their ability to fight, so you can plant a charge."

"Shit, yeah," said Flash Cranston, always eager to be first into any battle. "You give me just a little window, I'll plant some C18, blast the motherfuckers."

"Aim your weapons at the mouth," said Mencken. "Until they know to harden it, their mouth is vulnerable. Aim an explosive round, or a grenade . . . whatever explosive will detonate . . . precisely into the mouth and you'll take out the whole head. They'll still have the ability to move and fight, because it'll leave their brain and limbs intact. But they'll lose their sight and hearing. And also critically, they'll lose communications, because that's where their antenna is."

"Tough shot," said Harmon. "But I can make it."

"The DGMs could do it, too," they heard James say over their communications link. He was on the roof, along with Blake manning the drone-guided missiles—the phalanx of small precision-guided rockets.

"Good," said Patrick. "Any action up there?"

"Nope," said James. "All is—" he stopped in mid-sentence. "Shit, the system just acquired an aerial target!"

"Civilian?" asked Patrick. He wasn't concerned yet, because the flying robotic drones were ubiquitous over cities for traffic management and other mundane missions.

But the answer was alarming, as they heard the whoosh of a rocket launch over their comm lines and an explosion reverberating faintly through the thick walls of the warehouse."

"Police drone," said James. "Coming in over us, and armed. We took it out. A drone like that only means one thing."

"Jesus!" said Blake. "What are the cops doing here?"

"Leah's outside!" Exclaimed Mencken, pointing to a display screen showing her standing by the door. A faint pounding from small fists arose on the steel door.

Patrick ran across the warehouse to the door, unlocked it, and Leah rushed in.

"God, Leah, we were—" Patrick began to say.

"*Police!*" She exclaimed, waving her hands, a frightened look on her face. "SWAT teams with weapons, rockets! There are armored carriers coming in with more!"

"The 'morphs must have called them," said Mencken. "But how could they have known you guys were here?"

"Doesn't make sense to me, either," said Patrick. "They can't lie, and if they'd detected us, they would have reacted."

"Since we just used a DGM, the cops know we have heavy weapons. They must think we're the terrorists that stole them," said Blake. "This is going to get nasty."

"Nastier than you think," said Mencken. "I'd bet there are replicas out there among the human cops. At the lab, we produced replicas of Phoenix police, including commanders. They're going to tell those cops to shoot first, and not even bother to ask questions later."

• • •

The security cameras showed at least a dozen armored combat vehicles rumbling into place around the warehouse, their machine guns trained on the building. With them came vans that discharged SWAT teams wielding automatic weapons and grenade launchers.

"This building's hardened, but it's not bombproof," said Mencken, scrutinizing the camera feeds. They heard another whoosh of a rocket launch and a distant boom.

"Just took out another police drone," reported James over the comm. "They won't be sending any more of those."

An electronic tone signaled a phone call. Mencken touched a button on the console to put it on speaker.

"This is Nathan Rodriguez of the Phoenix police," said the voice on the other end. "We also have the Phoenix National Guard deployed. We know who you are, Patrick Jensen. We know your men. We know you have weapons. So, unless you surrender in the next ten minutes, we will destroy your building."

"He's one of the replicas we made," said Mencken. "It will order an attack no matter what we do. We go out there and it has us gunned down . . . claiming we were rigged with suicide vests."

"Garry, you're our only chance," said Patrick. "Does that motor control code work? What will it do?"

"It'll make them reveal themselves as 'morphs," said Garry, leaning over the keyboard.

"How?" asked Patrick.

"Just watch. I'm sure they all have the skills algorithm by now. I'm transmitting a signal to the algorithm . . ." he paused and took a deep, shaky breath. ". . . *now!*" He pressed a key and the group stared at the screen. Scattered among the hundreds of cops and soldiers, some slowly raised their right hands above their heads.

"*The 'morphs are raising their hands!*" shouted James from his vantage point on the roof. "*Oh, man, you are a fucking genius! We can take them—*"

"*Ohhhh shit!*" They heard Cranston behind them exclaim in a low, stunned voice. They turned to see him staring dumbly at Leah, who stood back about ten feet from the group.

Her right hand was raised above her head.

The neuromorph replica Leah regarded the raised arm with the blank stare of an android. It started toward the group, its useful arm reaching out with the mechanical determination of a well-programmed machine.

"Oh, dear God," breathed a stunned Patrick. "Leah . . . did you call the police?"

"Yes," it said simply.

"STAY BACK!" shouted Mencken. "IT CAN TEAR YOU APART!"

Cranston ignored the warning and lunged at the android Leah, slamming into its midsection and driving it backward. But the neuromorph grabbed him and with its operable hand lifted him bodily over its head.

"SHOOT IT!" Shouted Mencken. "THE HEAD! THE HEAD!"

The android pulled back its arm prepared to slam Cranston's struggling body against the brick wall.

The explosive crack of a rifle resounded in the vast space, and the Leah android's mouth became a gaping hole, secondskin lips torn away to reveal a graphene jaw. The group turned to see the sniper Harmon, his rifle propped on a workbench, taking precise aim for another shot.

The bullet tore into the left eye, shredding the fiber optic cable beneath. Yet another shot took out the right eye. Harmon paused, as DeFranco leaped at the android, grasping a grenade. He shoved it into the cavity Harmon had created, and with the same momentum used his bulk to tear Cranston from the android's grasp. The two slammed onto the floor, leaped up and sprinted for the protection of a nearby steel shelf. The others sprang behind workbenches, consoles, or any cover they could find.

The android Leah flailed about with its left arm, the right one still held uselessly aloft. With its sight and hearing gone, it staggered back and forth for a long moment, blindly grasping for any human it could find.

Then its head exploded with a reverberating bang, blasting away fragments of graphene, plastic, and electronic circuitry. The grenade also shredded the neck, leaving the headless neuromorph wandering aimlessly back and forth.

Patrick recovered first. "Al, get to the roof. Take the other rifle, and you and Blake target the 'morphs. But we need the DGMs to really finish the job. Tell James to put up the DGM's drone. I'll be up when we're done here." He glared at the flailing machine he once thought was his wife.

"Oopsie, get a shaped charge," he said. Lane, the explosives specialist, sprinted behind the rows of steel shelves to their weapons cache.

Patrick signaled to DeFranco to circle to the other side of the damaged, but still lethal, android. Patrick found a length of steel pipe, and waved at DeFranco to find a weapon. DeFranco rummaged in the tall shelves and came up with a metal robotic leg.

They warily approached the blinded android, and drew back their weapons, swinging them with as much might as they could muster, catching the android square in the chest.

The impact achieved what they had hoped, knocking the android onto its back. With only one useful arm, it struggled to get to its feet. Patrick and DeFranco each grabbed a leg, and—barely able to hold them against the superhuman kicks, dragged the android away from the computer consoles and down the length of the sprawling warehouse, toward the scattered array of damaged androids.

"Oopsie!" shouted Patrick.

"Got it!" he heard Oopsie Lane say, as he ran past holding the chunk of explosive.

"Plant it!" commanded Patrick, and Lane plunged forward, avoiding the android's grasping hand, and slammed the small hemisphere of C18 explosive onto its chest, where the explosive charge's adhesive stuck it fast.

Patrick and Lane quickly grabbed the android's still-frozen arm and flipped it onto its stomach, and the three of them leaped away to take cover behind the shelves.

The ear-splitting explosion vaulted the android ten feet into the air. It slammed with the dull thunk of an inert mass onto the concrete floor.

The three approached the mangled android, and Patrick moved the body. Shiny, black shards of a shattered neuromorphic brain littered the floor beneath the wreckage.

"Where is Leah?" Patrick whispered, his expression stricken. "My God, where is she?" He took a deep breath and recovered himself, his expression hardening, turning to the others. "One down . . . and a shitload to go."

Chapter 22

Standing on the warehouse roof, peering out at the forces arrayed against them, James declared "You realize, Cap, that the instant we start shooting at the 'morphs, everybody'll return fire."

"Well, Jammer, that just means we've got to make our point fast . . . show them that there are robots among them," said Patrick. "We've got an advantage in that they're seeing what they thought were humans with arms raised."

"Three minutes to deadline," said Blake. "Then we're all blown to hell."

"Okay, commencing targeting," said James. He opened a large metal case, flipping a switch inside. A high-pitched whine emanated from within, and rising from the case came a plate-sized quadcopter drone, its four propellers whirring furiously.

"Synching," said James. The video screen built into the case's lid showed the view from the drone's camera as it vaulted into the sky. The camera aimed toward the fleet of assault vehicles and SWAT vans, and the dozens of men crouched behind and between them.

Meanwhile, Blake moved to check a desk-sized case, from which jutted a hundred firing tubes, each holding a micro-rocket. Two were empty, the missiles having destroyed police surveillance drones. But the red lights beside the others indicated they were armed and ready to fire.

"Acquiring targets," announced James. The view screen showed the drone swooping toward the line of police, where many were holding up their right arms, their comrades looking at them curiously. James began to count off "One . . . two . . . three . . . ," as the view screen showed red X's appearing on the heads of one after the other of the neuromorph mimics.

"The mouths, Jammer," reminded Patrick. "You need a precise hit on the mouths."

"Cap, when we're done, they won't have mouths," answered James, still peering intently through his googles. He continued to count off, reaching twenty.

"One minute, Jammer," said. "There's a high-altitude killer drone somewhere up there with a missile with our name on it."

"Okay, Jammer, *launch now!*" Commanded Patrick.

"But Cap, I haven't gotten all of them yet. There's still—"

"We've got to show them now, or we won't be able to because we'll be nothing but charred corpses."

Jammer responded instantly with *"Command launch!"* The system recognized his voice, and Blake leaped back from the rocket tubes to avoid the explosive launch of twenty-five finger-sized micro-rockets. They burst skyward in a single formation, their fins popping from their bodies, streaming thin trails of smoke from their tails. In an instant, they broke formation, blasting away from one another and arcing separately downward toward their targets.

Oblivious to the fact that they might get their heads shot off, Patrick, Blake, James, and Harmon all stood up to see the result. That result made all three smile.

Impacting their targets in rapid-fire succession, the twenty-five rockets penetrated into the mouths of twenty-five replica neuromorphs, and with explosions resembling shotgun blasts, blew their heads into pieces.

Machine gun fire erupted from the police, impacting the roof parapet and driving the four SEALs to the ground. But suddenly the firing stopped, and they raised their heads to see a vicious battle begin on the police lines, between stunned cops and headless androids, flailing around blindly.

Police and soldiers were tossed like rag dolls, some with their limbs torn away, as the androids managed to clutch some who foolishly came within range. But other humans were smart enough to back away, firing into the thrashing androids.

"GRENADES!" Shouted Blake to the men below over the cacophony of gunfire. "GRENADES AND SHAPED CHARGES, YOU DUMB FUCKS!"

"They can't hear you," said Patrick. "They're busy. They'll figure it out. Jammer, finish the job."

James turned back to the business of targeting more neuromorphs, and he shortly had another twenty-five. He gave the launch order, and another fusillade of rockets erupted from the tubes, swirled into the sky and sped to their targets, unleashing another series of blasts.

By now, the police lines were a wild pandemonium of cops and soldiers firing at convulsing, headless neuromorphs.

"Mencken, do you see what's going on?" asked Patrick over their communicator.

"Yeah, looks like they could use some advice."

"See if you can contact somebody in charge. Tell them our munitions guy is coming out with a load of shaped charges. You hear me, Oopsie?"

"Already on it, Cap," came the answer from Lane.

"Al, let's give them a little help," said Patrick, taking up a sniper rifle.

James had already nestled his sniper rifle onto a roof parapet and sighted in. The artificially intelligent rifle synched to him, and he quickly began to designate targets and unleash a steady, precise volley of smart guided bullets. Homing in on strategic points on the thrashing androids, the bullets crippled their ability to do any more injury to the attacking troops. Several of the men waved quickly back in thanks, as James precisely targeted an android leg or an arm, rendering it crippled. Patrick joined in with his rifle, also doing serious damage to the androids.

"The brains!" he exclaimed abruptly. Some of the androids' neuromorphic brains had automatically triggered their escape mechanisms.

If the shock of seeing robotic heads being blown off weren't enough for the troops, now they were even more stunned to see onyx spheres erupt from chests of the downed androids and sprout metal legs. But James and Patrick were ready.

Taking precise aim at one sphere after another, they fired, blasting each one into a pile of inert, black shards. The guided rifle rounds even tracked the brains that had already begun to scurry away, following them and ultimately reducing them to rubble.

Below them, the explosives tech Oopsie Lane and breacher Pitbull DeFranco ran from the building carrying two large cases. A bullet fired from the police line barely missed them, and the SEALs realized it had come from a neuromorph that had not been targeted, his right arm in the air, his left wielding a rifle.

But a soldier standing beside the android jammed the barrel of his assault rifle into the android's mouth and loosed a rapid-fire volley of shots. They reduced that android to uncoordinated staggering similar to those that had been struck by rockets.

Lane and DeFranco reached the soldiers, and Lane whipped open a case and yanked out a hemispherical shaped charge. He punched its trigger button and ducked down, scrambling toward one of the thrashing androids, barely managing to avoid its powerful hands. He slapped the charge onto the android's chest and rolled away, leaping up and running as the explosive detonated with a jarring thud, blowing the android into shredded, component parts.

Meanwhile, DeFranco had moved down the line of police and soldiers, doing the same to another blinded, meandering android, blowing it apart.

The soldiers immediately understood the process and began grabbing the shaped charges approaching the androids. Some of the humans were injured in the process, some arms broken, some thrown against the armored vehicles. But the steady succession of loud explosive thuds told the story of android after android being reduced to little more than inert, smoking piles of graphene, secondskin, and electrogel.

Now Cranston appeared from the building, sprinting down the line to take out several escaping brains, blowing them to pieces with his assault rifle.

"This is Captain Casem," said a voice in Patrick's ear. "I'm the Guard commander. Your man gave me his comm. You're Patrick Jensen?"

"Yes, but what happened to Rodriguez?"

"He's in pieces, and we'd like to thank you for that. I'm now in field command."

"And what are your orders?"

"Well, I'm supposed to blow you up. That's the order from command."

"But you know what that means, right?"

"Well, I'm told back-channel by a buddy of mine at HQ that the general who gave that order has his right hand in the air. And there are a couple more like that."

"So, you'll need our help in taking them out."

"If you wouldn't mind."

"Listen, I need a favor, too. The robots have my wife. They made a replica of her, and that's what called you about us. I have to find her."

"Whatever we can do," said Casem. "I hope she's safe. But you certainly appreciate how little value these things place on human life."

· · ·

Patrick and three other SEALs stood amid the rubble of the large National Guard Phoenix command center, surrounded by bullet-riddled computer screens, a door blasted off its hinges, and the lingering blue haze and chlorine odor of detonated C18 explosive.

With the toe of his boot, Patrick nudged the shattered remains of what had once been the neuromorphic replica of the adjutant general of the Arizona National Guard.

A dull thud vibrated the building, indicating that Oopsie and Flash had dispatched the last of the four replicas that had been infiltrated into the command.

"What next?" asked Guard commander Captain Casem, a compact, dark-haired man in fatigues.

Just then, Mencken and Garry entered.

"Ask *them* what's next," said Patrick.

"We have to take the factory," said Mencken. "The assembly line, of course, but also the lab where replicas are made. At least the lab that we know of. We need to find out how many are out there. And we need to destroy the central server. That's what downloads the mutant OS."

Garry shook his head emphatically. "No, we can't just take out that server. That holds all the data on the number and location of neuromorphs. If we want to get them all, I need to get into that server."

Blake retorted, "Well, shit, you mean all we got to do is blast our way into the factory, blow the crap out of everything, but not touch the server?" He sat on a desk while a medic bandaged an arm that had taken a bullet from a replica. "Pitbull, you got some of that magic explosive that just blows up what you want it to?"

The breacher Pitbull DeFranco folded his thick arms and shook his head. "Nah, got no magic stuff. But Cap, you get me up close to whatever needs to be opened up, I'm pretty sure I can do it and spare what's inside."

Casem stepped away from the group, lowering his head and peering through his combat communicator googles. He returned to the group.

"We've got to move fast. Things are getting worse," he said. "I sent my action report up the chain of command . . . particularly about the raised-arm signal by the robots; and the intel I just got back wasn't good."

"They found a lot of replicas?" asked Patrick.

"Too damned many," said Casem. "A four-star general in the Pentagon; some colonels in the army and air force scattered throughout the country, four governors . . . these things are all over."

"Were they neutralized?"

"No, that's the problem. Following your demolition procedure, almost all were. SWAT teams blew their heads off, then used shaped charges on the chests. But a number of them avoided capture. Others use that brain escape mechanism to get away. And some are probably still in place because they were alone when the signal was sent. Nobody saw their arms go up. And there's something even more worrisome."

"That's hard to believe," said Blake.

"There's one instance just reported where a robot had its arm raised, and then it lowered."

"So?" asked Blake.

"*Shit!*" Declared both Mencken and Garry simultaneously.

Mencken explained: "That means somehow the arm signal got programmed out of the skills algorithm. Some programmer—"

"Hell, it was Ainsley," interrupted Garry. "I'm sure he found the code and deleted it. That means we've got no more signal. We can't detect replicas."

"That tears it," said Patrick. "Captain, we'll need a full-scale assault on the factory."

Casem began contacting other National Guard units and passing orders to his own. "We'll be at battalion strength," he said to Patrick. "My colonel has given the okay."

"We'll have really big bang-bang, eh?" said Blake, grinning and testing the movement in his bandaged arm.

• • •

"Nothing," said Patrick, shaking his head in puzzlement.

He peered across wide open lawn from their position on the road skirting the sprawling, windowless building complex that housed the Helpers, Inc. factory, R&D lab, and master computer. He could detect no movement at all.

The SEALs had arrayed themselves around the complex, each one embedded with a National Guard platoon. Captain Casem had given Patrick operational command because of the SEALs' experience with the neuromorphs.

"Nobody home, it looks like," said Blake over their comm line.

"Yeah, we know what that means," said Flash Cranston.

"That means they're waiting for us," said Patrick.

"So, let's not disappoint them," said Cranston, ever eager to be the first through the door.

"No breaching yet, Flash," ordered Patrick.

"Yeah, all right, Cap," said Cranston morosely. Patrick could see him making his best disappointed face and hunkering down behind the Stryker armored vehicle, ready for whatever order came next.

"Goddamn, Flash, you put on a TALOS, you think you're fuckin' invincible," cracked Blake.

"Yeah, near about," agreed Cranston.

The SEALs and Guardsmen now wore Tactical Assault Light Operator Suits—powered, armored suits that were common issue for SEAL team operations. The TALOS-garbed men could have easily used their power to tear through the steel building walls. Or, the walls could have been breached by any of the dozen Strykers. But there was a problem, which Patrick emphasized.

"First of all, there are people in there . . . maybe hostages . . . maybe Leah," he said. He had stationed himself and his platoon across from the main entrance. "Second, we need the master computer operational, at least until Garry can figure out what's going on with the software. And until Mencken can assess the hardware."

Behind him crouched Garry and Mencken, both fidgeting uneasily at the prospect of being in a firefight.

"I know what the 'morphs' defenses were when I left," said Mencken. "But they may well have added new capabilities, using the human engineers."

"And reprogrammed," added Garry.

"Captain Casem, looks like we'll be doing a tactical assault," said Patrick to Casem, who stood beside him. "Seven teams taking the objective from seven directions."

"Yeah, we're in sync," said Casem. "You've got a go."

"Okay," said Patrick, relaying the plan to his team. He dispatched Pitbull, to personally brief each team, to make sure they had the right ordnance and technique to precisely breach the walls or doors without damaging the building interior.

"Cap, I'm not liking this," said Blake over the comm, from his position with his platoon on the other side of the building. "The natives are *not* restless. Still no sign at all from the building. Do we have the right address?"

"Yeah, but we haven't knocked yet," said Patrick. "Captain, your men ready?"

"I'll do a final check," said Casem, ducking into his armored command vehicle to check on the data coming in from his troops' exosuits, and the surveillance from attack drones overhead. Satisfied, he emerged and gave Patrick a thumbs-up, moving back inside to continue monitoring.

On Patrick's command, six of the teams rushed across the multi-acre field toward the building, set the breaching charges, and slid back along the walls to be clear of the blasts. Patrick led the seventh to the glass-fronted entrance, leveling their assault rifles, prepared to shatter the glass to gain entry.

Six precisely coordinated blasts thundered from around the building, ripping six gaping holes in the walls. At the same time, Patrick and his platoon loosed a fusillade of fire at the entrance, reducing the glass wall to a pile of glittering shards.

All seven groups, their weapons on full automatic, prepared to battle their way into the building against whatever neuromorphs had been arrayed against them. But the plan suddenly changed.

The command vehicle containing Casem erupted in an ear-shattering explosion, large chunks of smoking armor arcing into the air. Three other armored carriers suffered the same fiery fate, the men beside them blasted away like limp, broken dolls. Some remained whole; others were torn apart into limbs and torsos, each arcing away on a different trajectory.

From over a nearby hill came a looming six-legged Insectimorph Defender, launching three more of its missiles at the Strykers, shattering them into charred wreckage. The Defender then unleashed a withering burst of rounds from its chain gun, shredding into unrecognizable bloody flesh the soldiers who had fled the vehicles' destruction.

Curses and screams filled the comm line as men died and vehicles were reduced to smoldering piles of metal.

"INTO THE BUILDING!" bellowed Patrick, as they heard the characteristic chop of an Aeromorph's rotors overhead, its own guns taking out the Guard drones, sending them spiraling to earth. With a whoosh, it launched one of its missiles, the explosion reducing yet another Stryker to rubble.

"WHAT THE FUCK IS THIS?" he heard Blake yell over the comm line. "I THOUGHT THESE FUCKERS COULDN'T JOIN THE 'MORPHS!"

As the billowing smoke brought the stench of scorched vehicles and dead men, a quieter, cold answer came back over the comm.

"Apparently, somehow they did," said Mencken.

CHAPTER 23

Crouching in the scant shelter of the entrance, Patrick and the Guard soldiers fired at the marauding Insectimorph, which stalked through the ruins of what had been three companies of soldiers and vehicles. Periodically, it would stop, aim its guns at a wounded soldier, and kill him.

"We only got popguns compared to that thing," said Blake over the comm line.

"Yeah," agreed Patrick. "Deploy a Gatling."

"On its way, Cap," said James.

He and Harmon appeared at the corner of the building, with James hefting the ponderous six-barreled Gatling and Harmon hauling a crate of ammunition. They reached the smoldering ruin of a Stryker and set up the Gatling, Harmon snapping the ammunition belt into its chamber.

"Aim it and get the hell out!" commanded Patrick, as the Insectimorph turned toward the building. Its cameras scanned back and forth to identify targets. Abruptly, it swung its armored body around, aiming its guns at the entrance.

"Bet your ass we're out, Cap!" exclaimed James. He aimed the Gatling at the Insectimorph and switched on its targeting computer. The gun's camera emitted a rapid train of beeps, followed by a steady tone, as it registered the Insectimorph as a target. Its barrel began to track the giant war machine as it strode across the ruined landscape toward the building entrance.

James set a short time-delay, pulled the trigger, and he and Harmon raced away, just as the Insectimorph abruptly halted and switched its attention, bringing one of its Gatlings to bear on the fleeing SEALs.

But before it could fire, the SEALs' own Gatling erupted to life with the loud metallic whirr of a hundred depleted uranium bullets spewing from its rotating barrels. They slammed into the Insectimorph, sending it staggering back under the onslaught. Then it recovered and leaned into the hurricane of slugs.

"Slowed it, but not killed it," declared James from the shelter of the building's corner.

"How the hell is that thing even here?" asked Patrick. "The Helper neuromorphs aren't supposed to be connected with the Defenders."

"Uh . . ." he heard Garry from behind him. ". . . I think I can find out. I can contact one of the Defender programmers."

"Do it."

Garry retreated into the depths of the building and slipped on his googles to make a call.

After an excruciatingly long wait, a voice answered. It was Al Felton, the Defender programming director.

"Felton," he said tersely.

"Al, this is Garry LaPoint. Remember, I came out to see if we could get the skills algorithm for the new Helper line?"

"Yeah, and the answer is still no."

An explosion shook the building, perhaps another missile from the Aeromorph.

"What was that?" asked Felton.

"Are you missing some Defenders?" asked Garry. "An Insectimorph, an Aeromorph?"

"Well, there's a live-fire exercise going on today. Those units, plus a squad of Infilmorphs are deployed. So?"

"Listen, Al, you're not going to believe it, but they're attacking us at the Helpers factory. Killing people. Blowing stuff up."

"*What the hell? That's not possible!*"

"Yeah, well, it is. The Insectimorph blew the shit out of vehicles and soldiers! And the Aeromorph is launching missiles at us."

"Ohhhhhhh, shit," he heard Felton mutter.

"What?"

"Well, Melvin Blount and a new guy came in to oversee the exercise. He was from the top administration. They had the CEO's authority. The new guy was named Landers. Just a minute."

"*Shit-shit-shit,*" whispered Garry to himself. He called to Patrick. "Somehow Blount and Landers got themselves into the Defenders control facility."

"Keep working on stopping them," said Patrick. "We're in deeper shit now."

Outside, the Insectimorph had taken damage from the Gatling gun, its armored skin pockmarked, and with three of its cameras now smoking holes in its hull. But it had recovered enough to fire a missile at the SEALs Gatling, blasting it into useless junk.

"Cap, we need the ME12s," Patrick heard Cranston shout over the comm. "We need to cripple the motherfucker."

"They're in the truck," said Patrick. "We can't—"

"Gotcha, Cap, *I'm gone, baby, gone!*"

"Flash, goddammit—" began Patrick. But Cranston had already launched himself into a dash for their munitions truck. He leaped from the safety of the building and with his characteristic gangly stride, sprinted toward the vehicle, which had been parked far enough from the Strykers not to have been destroyed.

"*Goddamnit, Flash!*" repeated Patrick. By now it was too late. One of the cameras on the Insectimorph picked up the movement, and its Gatling was already swiveling toward the running Cranston.

"Draw fire!" commanded Patrick, and the SEALs and remaining soldiers leaped from their cover in the building and began peppering the Insectimorph with their assault rifles. Overhead, another whoosh marked the launch of a missile from the Aeromorph, and it blasted a crater right behind the running Cranston.

He reached the truck and plunged inside.

202

The Aeromorph hovered overhead, preparing to launch another missile. But it erupted and careened downward, crashing in flames.

"Don't you just love these little gadgets!" Patrick heard James exclaim. He had managed to target the Aeromorph with a mini-Stinger missile, giving Cranston a brief reprieve.

The Insectimorph turned to face the gunfire, momentarily distracted from its concentration on Cranston.

He used that time to haul out a green metal trunk and flip it open, pulling out six disk-shaped metal Mobile Explosive charges. One by one, he grabbed a charge, flicked a switch to aim its laser target, and sailed it as far as he could away from the truck.

As each charge landed, it unrolled from a disk into a snake-like robot that reared its head and zeroed in on the target point on the Insectimorph it had been designated to. Each began slithering rapidly toward that target, across the asphalt of the parking lot, over the wreckage of the ruined vehicles, and even over the inert bodies of the dead soldiers.

Cranston managed to launch all the MEs before the Insectimorph returned its attention to him. He dove for the cover of the truck, but it was too late. In an instant, the Insectimorph had trained a chain gun on him and fired. Keshawn "Flash" Cranston died instantly from a hail of bullets shredding his body, which collapsed in a lifeless heap.

Patrick fell to his knees, watching the horrific scene through welling tears, as the SEALs spewed curses over the comm.

He took three deep breaths, his SEAL training taking over, remembering the mission and the lives that depended on him. He let his rage drive him. The Insectimorph again swung around to aim its missiles and guns at the building. But strangely, it paused.

The pause gave the first explosive-carrying snakebot time to reach the Defender and rapidly slither its way up the leg, its metallic scales glimmering in the bright desert sun. The Insectimorph did not recognize it or the other approaching snakebots as threats. They were not part of its programming.

The first ME reached its target, a leg joint, and curled itself tightly around the armored appendage. It detonated its shaped charge with a resounding crack.

The Insectimorph's twenty-foot metal leg erupted away from its body, falling to the ground, causing the robot to stagger slightly, but recover its balance using its remaining five legs. But by now another ME had reached its targeted leg, detonating and blasting that leg away. Yet another charge exploded, severing another leg. Now, the Insectimorph's targeting ability had degraded, as it attempted to maintain its balance using only three legs.

The three remaining MEs slithered up the robot and curled around its legs. Their blasts separated the three final legs. The Defender slammed to the ground with a massive crash, now only a hulking body, still trying to bring its guns to bear on its targets.

Garry reported on the phone call to Felton, "The Defenders programmer said that the operators are being held hostage in the control room by Landers and Blount. They're forcing them to send the Defenders after us."

"Tell them breaching the control room won't do the job. They've got to take out the whole center."

"But—"

"I know. It'll kill the people inside, too. But they're dead anyway. The 'morphs will kill them, once they're no longer useful."

Patrick willed himself not to dwell on the deaths of the Defender controllers or on Cranston's. Later would be time for mourning, doubts, and recrimination. He furrowed his brow. "Did you notice that at no time did the Defenders fire at the building itself?"

"Yeah, they could have blown it to hell," Blake answered

"And we've had no attackers from inside the building."

"Nope," said Lane.

"That means the Helpers want this building preserved."

"It means that the big fucking bugbot and the flying fucker were directed not to attack us as long as we stayed in the building,' said Blake.

"Yeah, but *those* guys can come after us," interrupted James, who had a view of the fallen Insectimorph. Trap doors had popped open from the Insectimorph's body, and from those doors scurried two dozen smaller versions of itself

"*Shit! Infilmorphs!*" exclaimed Menken. "The bugbot's mission was to destroy all the surrounding forces, then let these smaller units loose to neutralize the rest of us without damaging the factory or lab."

The Infilmorphs skittered rapidly away from their fallen host, to encircle the building. From their armored bodies sprouted the barrels of assault rifles and grenade launchers.

A rifle shot rang out, and abruptly one of the small Defenders staggered under the impact of a sniper around, and began to wander aimlessly.

"What the hell!" exclaimed Blake.

Harmon's voice came over the comm. "Thought you'd need a sniper, so I made it to the roof. I've got armor-piercing rounds. I could use company."

"On my way," said James.

Harmon continued targeting the approaching Defenders, but his shots became less effective, as the robots learned to rapidly zig-zag their way toward the breaches in the building, where the SEALs and soldiers had taken cover.

"They're swarmbots with a skills algorithm," declared Garry. "They coordinate with one another. When one manages to evade the sniper bullet, it immediately, teaches the others how to. And when you kill one, the others automatically adjust their attack to compensate."

The Infilmorphs began to return fire with deadly accuracy, the impacting bullets driving the SEALs and soldiers farther back into the building. But the SEALs' conventional rounds from their assault rifles had little effect on the robots, ricocheting off their armor.

The Infilmorphs launched grenades precisely aimed to detonate just inside the building walls, forcing the SEALs to retreat even farther.

"Can't see 'em anymore," reported Harmon from the roof. "They're out of range, coming into the building."

"Fall back," ordered Patrick, as they retreated from the entrance into the factory. "Find cover where they'll damage the factory if they direct fire at you."

He was answered by more and more groans over the comm, as soldiers in the building were hit.

"Garry, what's happening at the Defenders op center?" demanded Patrick.

Garry queried Felton. "They're about to breach," he answered.

"*Tell them again, dammit! Just breaching is not an option!* They can't overpower Landers and Blount. They have to blow the place. Tell them what they're up against."

Garry began to explain to Felton about the neuromorphs. He was obviously met with disbelief, because he shouted *"It's true! It's true!"* Over and over to Felton.

Finally, with distant gunfire resounding through the building, Patrick gestured to be connected to the call.

"Look, Garry is right," he said. "Those two are not human. They're neuromorphs and they're practically indestructible. If you just breach, they'll kill anybody who tries to enter. And they'll send more Defenders all over hell. I know you'll have to kill the people inside if you take out that room. But there's no other way. Take out the whole control center. Do it, or you die. *We all die!*"

"We understand now," said Felton. "One of the controllers managed to get a message out. They've already killed some, to force the others to make the rest cooperate."

Just then an Infilmorph rounded a corner and launched a grenade with a hollow thump. It skittered across the concrete floor, exploding beside two soldiers behind an office wall, launching their bodies across the room. Again, the group retreated farther back into the building.

Another round from an Infilmorph made Mencken scream in agony, as the bullet tore a gash in his calf. Patrick dragged him behind a pillar and quickly wrapped the leg with a bandage. A bullet slammed into him, ricocheting off his RheoArmor, but throwing him forward onto the floor.

"Boys, you know what we have to do?" asked Patrick over the comm.

"Well, basically, bring the whole fucking place down around us," answered Blake over the comm.

Lane answered immediately. "This is Oopsie. I'm planting structural charges." Patrick knew that Lane had, in fact, been rigging the building all along, just in case.

"Me too," said DeFranco, the breacher. "I'm at the master computer. It's set."

"XM 50 is loaded," said James, the heavy weapons specialist. "I'm in position to take out the entire production line." With the grenade launcher, James could launch a rapid-fire volley of fifty fragmentation and incendiary grenades throughout the factory, quickly reloading to launch another volley—if they were not all dead by then.

"I'm hit!" cried Lane. "Leg! Robot's approaching our position. Should I blow?"

Patrick touched a button on his wrist to bring up Lane's vital signs data on his helmet display. Lane was basically okay. His armored suit had automatically applied pressure to the wound to slow the bleeding.

"Hold for a countdown," he instructed Lane. He turned to Garry. "This is it. I hope your guy had the balls to do what was needed. I'm giving the destruct order in ten seconds. We need to complete this mission."

"But we'll all—" began Garry, but stopped. The outcome was too obvious to express.

"Countdown," said Patrick holding up ten fingers. He began ticking them down. "Nine . . . eight . . . seven . . . six . . . five . . . four . . . three . . ."

"Done! Done! Done!" shouted Garry. "They've blown the OP center!"

"Cap, the little fuckers have stopped moving!" reported Blake.

"Everybody come back," asked Patrick over the comm. "Are the 'bots neutralized?"

Variations on *Hell, yeah!* answered him.

"Then make sure they stay that way."

Shortly, a succession of booms resounded throughout the vast building, as shaped charges blasted the inert Infilmorphs to scrap.

"Okay, now let's see what the hell's been going on in this joint," said Blake.

• • •

"Eyes open," warned Patrick, as the platoons of SEALs and soldiers scouted their way into the depths of the factory complex from different directions. "Hold fire unless you see a clean target."

Patrick knew the command was unnecessary, but Leah might be a hostage somewhere in the building, and he wanted to make damned sure she wasn't harmed. On the other hand, the haunting image of Cranston being killed drove a cold-blooded need for revenge, even if the enemy were machines.

"Still no 'morphs," reported Blake from the far side of the factory floor, two football fields away. "This is goddamned strange."

"Maybe they've retreated behind hostages," answered Patrick. He, along with Garry, a limping Mencken, and four soldiers made their way along the glass-walled hallway that flanked the assembly line. It was dead still, with a long row of Helpers in various stages of assembly. Their parts hung from feeder lines, poised to be installed.

Mencken stopped and leaned against the glass wall, grimacing from the pain in his leg. "If they're anywhere, they're in the lab," he panted. "It's just ahead."

"You two stay back," said Patrick. He ordered DeFranco to stay at the main computer, ready to detonate his charges if necessary. Distant echoes of rifle fire from the roof told them Harmon was still targeting remaining inactivated Infilmorphs, now lying inertly on the asphalt parking lot.

They reached the lab door and Patrick burst through, taking cover behind a lab bench. The soldiers followed, fanning out, weapons ready, the traumatic memory of their dead comrades still fresh.

All was silent. Patrick waited for some response—gunfire or an assault by neuromorph—but there was none.

"LEAH!" he shouted. No answer. He stood warily scanning the facility, motioning for the soldiers to search the individual offices and lab rooms. He heard a steady succession of "Clear," as the rooms were entered. Behind him, Blake had arrived, pushing through the door with seven men and beginning their own search.

After long minutes, Patrick heard one of the soldiers call out, and he followed the voice to find two dead engineers, their white-coated bodies broken like rag dolls, eyes staring, necks snapped.

"I know them," said Mencken, who had hobbled up to the scene. "They're techs. Junior-level."

"No other bodies," reported Blake.

"There were about forty engineers and techs here," said Mencken. "I'd bet they've all been taken. The 'morphs would need them to repair damaged units and make replicas. My guess is these two were killed as lessons for the others."

Garry appeared, his face blanching at the sight of the shattered corpses of the techs. He continued to stare at them as he said "I just got word from the Defender center. Landers and Blount survived the explosion and got away. Felton said their skin and electrogel flesh were blasted off, but their armor protected them. They broke through a wall and killed seven soldiers before disappearing."

"Where would they have gone?" Patrick asked Mencken.

"I'm sure to that secret lab I heard they set up. It would have all the facilities they'd need."

"Okay, then, let's get you tended to. And next step, we get Garry to the main computer. He needs to see if he can locate all the 'morphs and find out what's going on with their software." Patrick spoke into the comm to Lane and DeFranco. "Stand down on the munitions. We've got the place nailed down. It needs to be preserved. There's invaluable intelligence here."

• • •

Garry stood in the Helpers, Inc. computer center, shaking his head, peering through the clear wall at long rows of six-foot-tall, crystal-clear rectangular blocks. Embedded in each huge crystal was an intricate network of optoelectronics, a labyrinth of fibers and circuitry emitting a faint golden glow.

"That's it?" asked Patrick.

"That's it," answered Garry. "Two hundred networked solid dia-mond quantum computers. And they're integrated with the self-learning neuromorphs. That's the master computer."

"So, can you hack into it, see what the 'morphs have been up to?"

"Well, hacking into it . . . not likely. They've probably closed the back door I used. I also can't spoof the identity of the programmer, Ainsley, like I did before. They figured that out. And there's something else . . ." Garry's head-shaking became more emphatic.

"What?"

"Well, I haven't been down here for a while. So, I didn't know they'd made the room blast-proof. This wall is made of ArmorClear."

Garry next pointed at an airlock into the huge computer room and then at rows of nozzles along the ceiling. "When the 'morphs took control of the company, I'd heard they were doing stuff like this."

"Like what?" asked Patrick.

"Installing protective measures," said Mencken coming up beside them. "Those nozzles are gas ports that sprayed nerve gas into that room, probably Limpetine. See, they can send 'morphs in there to do any maintenance. And the robots aren't bothered by the nerve gas. But it makes damned sure no human messes with the hardware."

"And we can't just somehow decontaminate the place?" asked Garry.

"No way," said Patrick. "We were briefed on dealing with Limpetine. And the basic rule we learned is that you *don't*. It's a devil's brew. It's made up of airborne particles that stick to surfaces. And it's incredibly long-lived."

"Can we just unplug the computer?" asked Mencken.

"It has a backup power source, or at least enough battery power to enable it to make some major mischief," said Garry.

"So, what do you make of all this?" asked Patrick.

"Look . . ." said Garry. ". . . this whole system . . . this whole fac-tory . . . you have to consider it an intelligent entity. The armored room, the gas . . . that means it'll protect itself."

"So, we can't just blow up the computer, for example?" asked DeFranco, who had joined them.

"No way," said Patrick. "It would unleash a nerve gas cloud that would kill everybody in Phoenix. And since it's persistent, Phoenix would be unlivable for years." He turned to Mencken and Garry. "Look, you two do what you need to, to get the information we need. We'll worry about taking out the computer."

"You know we're walking on eggshells here," said Mencken, and Garry nodded in assent. "Since that thing on the other side of the wall is intelligent, it will be watching for any intrusion."

"Well, just stay invisible," said Patrick.

Their faces grim, Mencken and Garry disappeared into the nearby console room.

· · ·

For the next week, Mencken and Garry all but confined themselves in the room housing the computer console. They emerged only to use the bathroom. The SEALs stacked field rations in the room, but the two ate little. They spent the time either staring blankly into space through their googles, or waving their hands as they tried to navigate their way ever-so-covertly through the three-dimensional virtual jungle of software in the master computer. Or, they cautiously manipulated the multitude of buttons and joysticks in the consoles, seeking some insight into what was going on in the computer's vast neuromorphic "mind."

The only interruption was by a cadre of National Security Agency cyberwarfare experts. They arrived in force, declaring that they were taking over the analysis of the computer.

Mencken and Garry argued that they would face no ordinary computer, but a huge, sentient neuromorphic complex. One false move and it would become aware of the attempts to glean its secrets. And nobody knew what the consequences would be.

One horrific scenario was that they could easily trigger the release of God-knows-what software onto the world, should they blunder into a system they didn't know the first thing about. To illustrate the military consequences, Mencken showed virtual viddie of the havoc the Defenders and the replicas had wrought. Then he told them of the potential for unleashing an immense, lethal cloud of nerve gas that would wipe out all of Phoenix.

The NSA experts retreated, deciding that letting the two fools take the lead was probably best for their careers. They settled outside the console room to wait for any developments.

As the SEALs shared their knowledge of the neuromorphs, bedlam erupted throughout the world. They gave a virtual briefing to the Joint Chiefs of Staff, Interpol, and the Department of Homeland Security on the threat. They showed a virtual tour of the factory, along with viddie from their violent battles with the neuromorphs.

They emphasized the grave danger posed by the possibly tens of thousands of lethal, mutant neuromorphs disguised as benign Helpers. And worse, they warned of the replicas that may have infiltrated government, the military, and law enforcement.

When they finished each briefing, the reaction was invariably shocked silence, followed by an eruption of epithets not usually uttered in formal meetings of high-level leaders. The Secretary of Homeland Security immediately issued an order to deactivate or destroy all Helpers.

"Every last goddamned one, in every last home and business in the country," he had commanded." Similar orders were given around the world.

In the US, the Chief of the National Guard Bureau ordered mobilization in all fifty-two states to aid destruction of the Helpers.

As soon as news of the renegade androids exploded in the media, all Helpers became the objects of mass destruction. Calls flooded in from owners asking for help destroying them.

Some owners took matters into their own hands. In Memphis, a man gave his Helper a routine order to clean the house. The owner then lit a candle, turned on the gas stove and left. Thirty minutes later, the house exploded in a fiery blast. Combing through the wreckage, firefighters found the charred remains of the Helper. It was determined that the Helper had not been infected by the mutant OS.

A case in Los Angeles, however, did show the danger from the Helpers. A mutant Helper attacked its owner, the Chief of Police, who managed to escape to his SUV. The Helper pursued him to the driveway, ramming its arm through the windshield in an attempt to tear its owner's head off.

Evading the Helper's grasp, the chief drove three blocks with the Helper on his hood until he reached a concrete pillar of the Santa Monica Freeway. He rammed the pillar, crushing the legs of the attacking android. He then got out of the SUV, dragged the flailing android to the center of the lane and ran over it five times with the SUV until he was satisfied that it had been reduced to inert scrap.

The Army Chief of Staff also immediately ordered that all Defenders be destroyed, as well, to avoid the possibility that their military operating systems might be infected by the mutant neuromorph OS.

The most urgent hunt was for replicas in high posts. A tip from a suspicious lieutenant led soldiers to surreptitiously search the Georgetown townhouse of the Under Secretary of Defense for Technology. They discovered a Helper charging chamber.

That day, the Under Secretary was invited to attend a meeting at Aberdeen Proving Ground. He entered an isolated building at the proving ground to find Army demolitions specialists, who slapped a shaped charge onto his chest and bolted from the building. The blast shattered his body, splattering the walls with the translucent goo of electrogel and shredding his RheoArmor.

The blast triggered its neuromorphic brain to erupt from the chest and sprout legs. But before it could scramble away to safety on the spiderlike appendages, the demolition team managed to stick on a second charge that blew it into shiny black shards.

Unfortunately, the Under Secretary replica apparently transmitted a warning message to other replicas, because after its destruction, no other neuromorph replicas were discovered. Those that were in place had apparently become far more careful . . . and thus far more dangerous.

Over the next week, news reports concluded that, although many mutant Helpers had been destroyed, hundreds had escaped and were at large. However, most of the experts appearing on the news reassured the public that since the machines could need recharging, many would simply run out of power after about a week.

After giving their briefings, Patrick and the other SEALs paid little attention to the tumult going on around them. Their first days were a time of mourning for their two lost comrades, Andy Green and Keshawn Cranston. The funerals of the two men honored their sacrifice and consoled their families. But for the SEALs, the ceremonies were like the tempering process that hardens steel. Their resolve was absolute, unbreakable. They would honor their lost brothers by obliterating the malevolent machines that had murdered them.

Now was the time for that mission.

• • •

"So, how many discharged 'morphs did they find?" asked Patrick.

The SEALs sat around on the sofas and chairs in the safe house outside Phoenix. Its shattered windows, broken furniture and bullet-riddled walls reminded them what they were up against.

"Only three," answered Blake, shaking his head. "That's it. That's *all*. The FBI, National Guard . . . everybody's been searching for the rogue robots. But we told 'em the 'morphs wouldn't be found that easily."

"Yeah, the brass just can't get it through their heads that the 'morphs share data instantly," said Patrick. "So every escaped unit knows instantly where every charging chamber is and how to sneak in and get charged. And since they can travel without the need for food or water, they can steer clear of the places the cops usually find fugitives."

"So, it looks like *we're* going to be the main 'morph hunters," said Blake. "Just our little bitty group."

"Yeah, Needle, I know the whole country's looking for these things. But nobody's come up against them like we have. And we have a score to settle. And, there's Leah."

The group silently nodded, aware of their leader's anguish.

"I've canvassed everybody involved in the search . . . NSA, FBI . . . ," said Patrick, rubbing his face tiredly. "And there's still no clue to the location of the secret lab."

A car pulled up outside the house, and Mencken and Garry hauled themselves out. Mencken looked haggard, still limping from his wound.

But it was Garry's face stubble, unkempt hair, and sagging face that told of his grueling past week spent in the darkened, ever-more-fragrant control room of the master computer."

Both of them came in and slumped into chairs.

"Well, what the fuck?" asked Blake. "What's going on?"

"I don't like to give bad news," said Mencken. "You guys were ready to kill me once already. So, Garry, can you tell them?"

LaPoint sighed. "C'mon, I got good news, too. I know where the lab is—"

"Oh, hell, yeah!" exclaimed Jammer James. "We can take that sucker!"

"Okay, maybe not really good news," said Garry. "Well, a hundred years ago—"

"Garry, we don't need a history lesson," interrupted Patrick. "Where is it?"

"An old installation called Cheyenne Mountain. Up near Denver. Used to be the country's nuclear defense control center until that terrorist group attacked it with nerve gas. Then the feds built the distributed Defense Darknet. The government sold it off to a private company about thirty years ago to store documents or grow mushrooms, or something. But recently, another company bought it. I found company records showing it was bought by a shell corporation set up in the Cook Islands by the Helpers president, Gail Philips. I found confidential orders by her directing that all Helper parts be shipped to a warehouse in Denver for storage. But I'd bet they were then moved to Cheyenne Mountain."

"So, that must be where they're repairing and refurbishing 'morphs," said Patrick.

"Uh . . . actually worse," said Mencken. "They're building entirely new ones. Garry gave me the shipping manifests. Given all the parts they've collected, including the neuromorphic brains, they can build a couple thousand units. And these ones have all the bells and whistles . . . skills algorithm, armor, escape mechanisms, hive-mind operating systems."

"Well, hell, then we'll mount an assault," said Lane. "We've got the weapons, the munitions . . . the Army's giving us whatever we need."

Mencken cleared his throat nervously, his thin face looking more haggard than ever. "They got Defender parts, too." he said simply, as if admitting some sort of defeat. "Philips also diverted major shipments of parts for Insectimorphs, Infilmorphs, Aeromorphs."

"Well, shit," said Lane. "So, we get bigger stuff to blow the place . . . a babynuke, if necessary."

"It's a nuclear-hardened facility," said Mencken. "Under two thousand feet of rock. Behind three-foot-thick steel blast doors. Completely self-sustained with a mini-fusion reactor. And the 'morphs just need food or water for the captives . . . for a while."

"What do you mean 'for while'?" asked Patrick.

"With the skills algorithm, pretty soon the 'morphs won't need humans. And they don't even need the master computer. Tell 'em, Garry."

Garry took a deep breath. "We've found out their network has changed. We found that the master computer distributed a new OS that made the neuromorphs an autonomous network of beings. I guess it was Ainsley who re-engineered the 'morph OS into a completely self-sufficient hive mind. And . . . well . . . that includes the Defenders. He adapted the code so the Defenders are now neuromorphs, not just remote-controlled robots. The master computer downloaded it to them, too."

"So, what's this autonomy mean?" asked Patrick.

"When they first got the skills algorithm, they could share learned skills, but only through the master computer. A 'morph would transmit a skill to the master computer, and it would distribute it. So, we thought if we brought down the master computer, it would maybe deactivate the 'morphs, or at least screw up their communications."

"But they don't need the master computer anymore?"

"Doesn't look like it. Destroying the master computer won't make any difference now. Once a 'morph learns a skill, it can instantly transmit that skill to all the others. Those skills include the ones human engineers used to build 'morphs. So, once a 'morph learns an engineer's skill, that human is no longer needed. And you've seen what happens when humans are no longer needed."

"Ainsley, that little son-of-a-bitch traitor!" spat Blake.

216

"I thought so, too," said Garry. "But I found out he has a wife and three kids. And his parents and other relatives. And they're all missing. You can be damned sure the 'morphs have evolved to understand using loved ones as hostages."

"Okay, he's not a traitor, but what he did makes it impossible to obliterate these fuckers," said Blake. "They're all one big goddamned machine."

"Sure looks like it," said Garry, staring glumly at the floor in fatigue and frustration. "Even if we miss destroying just one, all the skills are preserved. From what I can tell, the hive mind is highly redundant. Multiple units store a duplicate OS, duplicate skills, and other data."

"So, every goddamned one of them has to be killed, and all at once," said Blake. "So, we blow our way through the damned doors, pitch in a babynuke, and take them all in one blast." Then, remembering Leah, Blake gave Patrick a pained look. "Sorry, Cap. I know that's a last resort."

Lane nodded, too, his embarrassed look revealing that his knowledge of munitions had gotten him carried away.

"Yeah, well blowing the place is exactly what the government would do, if they knew what I've just told you," said Garry. "So, I've kept all this information to just me and Greg. Nobody else knows about the secret site but you. But they know just about everything about the hive mind. I couldn't keep that from the NSA guys who were looking over our shoulders."

"Tell them about the mutation algorithm," instructed Mencken.

"You're not giving me a break at all, Greg," complained Garry.

Mencken shrugged. "Well, like I said, they were happy to kill me at one point. I'm not sure I'm exactly the one to rain on their parade . . . and this is a hurricane."

Patrick stood and began to pace the room impatiently. "Okay, Garry, what mutation algorithm? Tell us."

"Well, I kept the NSA from finding out about that, too, or they would certainly direct the Army to nuke Cheyenne Mountain. The 'morphs had one of the programmers, again probably Ainsley, add a random mutation algorithm to the new OS. So now, each 'morph periodically produces a tiny mutation of a copy of its software, just like any evolving biological organism. Then, it tests the mutation on itself. If the mutation improves the android's function, it's distributed to the whole hive. If the mutation is bad, the android merely reverts to its old OS."

"So, what's this mean in how we fight them?" asked Patrick.

"Well, besides that every android can instantly learn a new skill, they are all now evolving. They can continually get smarter and smarter, more and more efficient."

Muttering curses, Blake went to the bar and poured himself a very large whiskey and took a hefty swallow.

"Okay, okay, so we're facing smarter and smarter androids that are evolving themselves. And thanks to our buddy here . . ." he flipped a middle finger at Mencken ". . . they can be made up to look and behave exactly like humans." He finished the scotch and slammed the glass on the bar. "But hell, there's still only, say, ten thousand of them out there. That's not a big army, even though they are hard-to-kill bastards."

Patrick stopped his pacing and stared gravely around the room.

"We've got to get them all," he said quietly. "It only took one Hitler . . . one Stalin . . . to trigger the death of millions. And face it, they're now superior organisms to humans."

· · ·

"Blow it up? *That is just goddamned stupid!*" Mencken exclaimed to the Assistant Director of Homeland Security. They stood with Garry and Patrick outside the entrance to the Helper factory nearest the room housing the master computer.

"The decision was made at the highest level," snapped the Assistant Director, a portly, squat man with a pronounced comb-over on his scalp, in a vain attempt to hide his balding head. He pushed his glasses up on his nose. "The President made the decision after consulting with my boss, and with the Joint Chiefs. It's done. This computer goes." He swept his pudgy hand to take in the sprawling computer room behind the armored glass.

Now it was Garry's turn. "Look, the computer may still have software that we don't even know about yet. These . . . *things* . . . likely have tricks up their sleeves we haven't figured out."

"That's the problem," said the Assistant Director. "This computer controlled probably the most dangerous machines ever built . . . including taking over the Defenders."

"But we *told* the NSA guys that this computer no longer controls them. They're an independent—"

But the Assistant Director ignored him, walking away, as the Hazmat chemical warfare team emerged from the building. After being decontaminated with a spray of water, they slumped against the walls outside. They ripped of their helmets, revealing the sweat running down their faces.

"Done?" asked the Assistant Director.

"Yeah," answered the team head. "Limpetine is a bitch to neutralize, but it's gone. And we managed to take care of it without entering the room or disturbing the computer. The facility has been detoxed, the Limpetine reserve cylinders that were in the room are sealed in the trucks. Now you can kill the son of a bitch."

The Assistant Director turned to a tech. "Get the FEMP. Fry the computer."

"Don't do this," said Patrick. He pointed at Garry and shook his head. "He told you, and he's the programmer . . . the one who knows the most about these things."

But the soldiers were already wheeling a refrigerator-sized focused electromagnetic pulse unit into place. They hefted it through the door placing it outside the clear wall to the hundreds of consoles that made up the Helpers, Inc. master computer. They aimed the unit's parabolic reflector into the room.

"You're sure this will shut the computer down?" asked the Assistant Director.

"Yeah," said the tech, adjusting the aim of the FEMP's reflector. "The computer's mostly fiber optic, so that wouldn't be affected. But an electromagnetic burst will sure take out the electronic components, and that'll do the trick."

"Clear out!" exclaimed Mencken. Then calling to the Assistant Director, "We don't know what the hell protective systems the neuromorphs installed. I'm warning you to evacuate this building!" But the

Assistant Director gave him a dismissive wave, staring eagerly into the computer room.

Mencken hobbled quickly up to Patrick. "They don't know what the hell they're doing! Get your guys out!"

"You cleared our charges, Oopsie?" Patrick asked Lane over the comm.

"Affirmative, Cap," replied the explosives specialist. "We don't even have a firecracker in there now. Whatever happens, it's on them."

"Okay, everybody clear out," Patrick commanded the SEALs. "To the rally point."

As the SEALs evacuated, the government tech opened a small control panel door in the FEMP, made a few adjustments, and flipped a switch.

A faint whine, increasing in pitch and volume, signaled that the pulse generator was ramping up, to begin its task of blasting the computer.

Still wearing their exosuits, the SEALs raced to the all-terrain, Humvee-like Light Tactical Vehicles, dubbed LTVs, the Army had given them. They sped the half a mile from the factory complex to the cluster of trailers marking the command headquarters.

They had just parked and leaped from their vehicles, when a rapid-fire sequence of explosions thundered in the distance, shaking the ground and battering them with shock waves.

Section by section, the factory complex erupted in flame and smoke, blasting large chunks of metal walls into the air for hundreds of yards. One section after another caved in, erupting a plume of black, billowing smoke.

Finally, all was still, except for screaming and shouting from the horrified crowd and the whine of ambulances accelerating toward the disaster. Patrick and the other SEALs stared resignedly at the distant, blackened ruin.

Mencken was the first to speak. "I thought something like this might happen. The 'morphs decided they didn't need the facility. The computer probably had a fail-safe that would start a destruct sequence. They didn't want anybody else to have their technology . . . to figure out their secrets."

"Fucking idiots," said Blake. "Fucking dead idiots."

But Patrick was already concentrating on the next mission. "So, we've got a clear shot at the secret lab? At finding Leah?" he asked.

Blake laughed. "Hell, if you consider a clear shot trying to bust into a nuclear-bomb-proof cave filled with fucking robots that are getting smarter and smarter all the time . . . yeah, we got a clear shot."

Patrick sadly contemplated the distant smoking ruin of the factory for a long moment. "I'm going to tell them we're starting our own op to take out 'morphs, based on what we know about them. They won't care; they'll let us go. They'll give us the LTVs, the TALOS, the weapons we need. We really need a babynuke."

Oopsie made a derisive snort. "Remember, Cap? Our techie Mencken here told us a nuke won't dent the place. And the feds are not about to entrust us with a babynuke."

"Oopsie, I believe you know somebody who'd help with that," said Patrick quietly.

"But Cap—" Oopsie Lane began to protest.

"Reach out to him. That's an order. I have my reasons. Now, we go back to the safe house, and we plan the op."

CHAPTER 24

"You sure we should be going back to your place?" asked Garry, as Mencken piloted the SEALs' SUV through Phoenix's checkerboard layout of warehouses. Mencken grimaced only slightly, as he turned corner after corner. His leg wound was healing, but still tender.

"Yeah, I'm being careful. Nobody following us. Check for yourself." He reached up and twisted the rear-view mirror to an angle that enabled Garry to scan the street behind them.

"And you really need the stuff there?"

"Yeah . . . tools, instruments, software that would help us suss out what the 'morphs are up to. And I hid the stuff so the feds wouldn't find it."

"Yeah, well . . ." Garry's voice trailed off, signaling his doubt.

They reached Mencken's warehouse and parked well down the block.

"We'll sit for a while. Check for activity. If none, we'll do a couple of drive-bys. Then if we don't see anything, we'll go in. Does that satisfy you?"

Garry shrugged. "It would satisfy me to go home."

"C'mon, we can do this." They waited for forty-five minutes, with Garry settling into a worried sulk.

Finally, Mencken said "Let's roll," and eased the SUV forward. They drove by the warehouse, circled the block and drove by again.

"All clear. Let's go in," said Mencken, pulling up to the steel door. He stood in front of the security camera until the system identified him, and with a series of metallic clicks, unlocked the door.

They were greeted with a scene of shambles. Workbenches had been cleared of instruments and overturned, Helper parts had been pulled from shelves and piled around the room. The electrogel spray booth had been dismantled, its parts strewn across the floor. So had the molding booth, where secondskin was produced.

The army's forensic technicians had done a thorough job of probing every bit of Mencken's equipment for clues to his operation.

"Wow!" exclaimed Garry, picking his way through the debris. "They did one hell of a number on your lab."

But Mencken smiled his vulpine smile and cocked his head in a nonchalant dismissal. "Yeah, I expected that. I'm not considered quite the good guy yet to them, even after what I've done for them. I hid all the important stuff quite a while ago." He strode away from the workshop area and out into the broader expanse of the warehouse floor, stopping at a precise point marked on the concrete floor with a splotch of paint that looked like nothing more than a random stain.

"So, there's nothing here," said Garry, almost pleadingly. "So we should go."

"Just a second," said Mencken, standing quietly, his smile still fixed. Seeming to nobody, he recited, "Please open vault four-oh-nine-five-six."

The popping of cracking concrete echoed in the warehouse as the floor sprouted hairline cracks in the concrete, and a steel vault began to rise ponderously upward.

"Installed this when I moved in," said Mencken as the vault continued to jut upward. "I put all my important records in it. Also transmitted to it a continually backed up set of blueprints, software, formulas . . . everything I needed if I had to relocate quickly. Wireless remote voice trigger, so I didn't have to open it . . . until I had to open it."

"Damn," said Garry. "So it's all there."

"Yup. Before I left here, I digitally shredded all the software on the workshop computer itself. I even took all my stuff off the cloud. This is the only copy." He reached over to the vault door and unlatched it, swinging it open to reveal a console containing a row of slots holding clear palm-sized optical storage crystals. He pulled out the crystals one by one, slipping them into his pocket.

A voice behind them said "Glad to see you're careful, buddy. We can use that stuff."

Mencken and Garry whirled to see two men standing near the entrance to the workshop area.

"Who the hell are you?" demanded Mencken.

"Awww, ol' buddy," said the shorter of the two with a southern drawl. He was a muscular young man with a male model's chiseled features and a full head of curly black hair. "You don't recognize your old pal. Maybe it's my new look. I think I'm pretty damned handsome."

The taller man chimed in. He had the lanky good looks of a male model, too, and the build of an athlete. "They did a pretty good job on me, too."

"*Oh, Jesus!*" breathed Garry. "*The voices! You recognize the voices? It's Landers and Blount!*"

"Yeah," said the shorter man. "We'll probably keep the names for now, just for old times' sake." He stepped forward and grabbed Mencken by the neck, lifting him off the floor. Mencken clutched the neuromorph's wrists to support himself, to keep from strangling, his legs flailing wildly.

The Blount robot stepped toward Garry, but Garry raised his hands in surrender. "Wha . . . what do you want."

"Well, we'll take those crystals, for sure," said Landers, setting Mencken down.

Mencken pulled the crystals from his pocket and handed them over to the Landers neuromorph.

But Garry's attention was on Blount, and he uttered a terrified cry when Blount raised a pistol and fired.

• • •

From a black unconsciousness, Garry floated gradually up to a gray, woozy awareness, turning an aching head to survey his surroundings. He lay on a cot in a bare room with neutral beige walls. Besides the cot, the room held only a chair, a desk and a bedside table. Sitting in the chair was a small, round-faced oriental man in a white coat, a hypodermic injector in his hand.

Garry tried to sit up, and a dull ache in his skull began to throb. He groaned.

"You are okay," the man said simply. "I am John Yang. I am . . . *was* . . . an engineer at Helpers. I had some medical training, so I'm assigned to help you."

"What happened?"

"You mean to you? You and your friend were tranquilized. Ketamine. You were out for hours. You were brought here by the neuromorphs Landers and Blount. I gave you a drug to reverse the effects."

"Where is my—"

"Your friend? He is in the next room. I already gave him the reversal drug. He is resting."

Garry reached up to the place at the base of his skull that was the source of the ache. His fingers found a shaved spot on his head, and a small bandage.

"My head. What did they do?" he asked.

Yang nodded upward, indicating the camera trained on them. "I am not to tell you. That information will come from the neuromorphs." Then, he leaned over, as if to examine Garry's head, and whispered, "*I am so very sorry. They made us develop what I put in your head. We all have them. Do exactly what they say. I am so sorry. Just rest.*"

"I don't need rest. I need information." Garry sat up, swinging his legs over the side of the bed. The dull ache became a throbbing pain.

The steel door opened, and the lanky neuromorph that was Blount entered.

"Get him up and bring him," Blount ordered. Yang helped Garry to his feet, supporting him as he stumbled out the door. He found himself in a beige hallway as sterile as the room. Beside him walked another white-coated man supporting an unsteady Mencken.

"You're okay!" exclaimed Garry, and Mencken nodded dully.

They were helped down the hall, led by Blount through a large cafeteria, empty except for a few people scattered at tables, their heads down, eating.

They exited from the cafeteria through double doors, and they found themselves staring at a vast cavern blasted from granite rock. Faint echoing sounds of voices and machinery told him there were many more people in the cavern.

"This is it!" he whispered to Mencken. "Cheyenne Mountain!" He reminded himself that he wasn't supposed to know his location, and tried to look surprised at his surroundings, craning his neck to take in the sight.

Landers appeared from another door in the building complex nestled in the cavern, and they all entered what appeared to be an administration wing. In a large auditorium, they found a group of neuromorphs sitting on a stage, erect and still behind a table. He recognized some of them, including the Gail Phillips neuromorph, as well as those from the Haven—the middle-aged-looking Lanny Malcolm and Randall Black; and the slim, youthful mask of John Travis.

Garry and Mencken were sat in chairs before the group, and the white-coated men who had supported them were dismissed.

"You have both betrayed us," Philips stated in the flat atonal voice neuromorphs assumed when they no longer had to pretend to be human. "But you have skills and information that we need. You will provide them to us."

Mencken seemed to rouse himself to his pragmatic, deal-making persona. "Yeah, well, you'll kill us whether we do or don't. Or, does your offer still stand that you'll let us live if we help you?"

"Yes, we will," said Phillips.

"I don't mean as long as we're useful. I mean live out our natural lives. And in comfort."

"Yes, we will," said Phillips.

"And about Leah Jensen." interjected Garry, leaning forward, his hands clasped tightly in front of him. "You have her? Is she alive?"

226

"Yes," said Phillips.

"And she can be included in our deal? Y'know, we will be useful to you over the long term."

The telltale silence settled over the neuromorphs, signaling a conferring among them.

"Leah Jensen is now a means to control Patrick Jensen, if that is necessary," said Phillips. "We will determine later whether Leah Jensen will be kept alive as part of our agreement."

Mencken, seeming to be less concerned about Leah, remained in his bargaining mode. "And we will require freedom to move about as we please."

"We can give you that, since we have now ensured that you can be neutralized at our consensus."

"How's that?" asked Mencken.

"You humans are most affected by demonstrations, so we will give one."

The neuromorphs continued to sit still, staring impassively at Mencken and Garry. Behind them the door opened, and John Yang was brought in by a neuromorph. This robot had no face; only a featureless gray RheoArmor mask from which stared unblinking eyeballs.

"A drone," whispered Mencken. "This is new. He doesn't need human features."

Yang looked confused, as the drone neuromorph escorted him to the front of the room and stood him before Mencken and Garry.

"You wanted me for something?" he asked tremulously, turning to look at the seated neuromorphs.

"Face these two men," instructed Phillips.

Yang did so, a puzzled look in his face. A sharp pop erupted from his skull, his eyeballs flew from their sockets, and blood spurted from his nose, mouth, and ears. He collapsed into a lifeless heap.

"JESUS CHRIST!" bellowed Garry, knocking over his chair in his panic to scramble away against the farthest wall.

Mencken stood and backed away, his face stricken, staring at the corpse. *"Dear God, what have you done?"*

"A demonstration, as we indicated," said Phillips. "He had implanted in his skull the same explosive charge and receiver your heads now hold. At our consensus, we can kill you at anytime, anywhere. All the humans in this facility have such implants. Now, shall we discuss the contributions that you propose to make to our success?"

. . .

Leah was curled into a fetal position on a cot in the same kind of spartan, beige room in which Garry had awakened. She wore a thin cotton dress and her bare feet were drawn up and crossed, like a child sleeping. She did not move at first, when the door opened and Garry and Mencken entered. But she sat bolt upright when she saw them.

"*You! What are you doing here?*" she asked, shocked.

"We were captured," said Garry.

"Patrick? Is Patrick okay?"

"Yes, he's been looking for you. He won't—" began Garry. But he abruptly stopped, stammering, realizing that everything they said, and every move they made, would be recorded on camera and analyzed. One wrong phrase or move and the explosive implant in their heads . . . probably Leah's, too . . . would detonate."

Fortunately, Mencken had more confidence in their status. "Look, we've made a deal. We'll help them, they guarantee that we . . . you included . . . stay alive."

Leah's expression transformed into a grim anger. "Screw them. I'd rather die. You're traitors. I know they're only keeping me alive as a hostage to stop Patrick and the other SEALs. I don't give a shit what you do, but I'm not doing a goddamned thing for them."

"You don't have to. We've agreed to—"

Leah now stood and advanced toward them, fists clenched. "Look, they put an explosive charge in my head. They've carted bodies out of here with blown-out brains . . . people who weren't useful to them anymore. Whatever happens to me, I hope Patrick blows the hell out of this place and all these . . . *things* . . . with them."

228

Garry raised his palms in a gesture meant to calm, but she continued to stalk toward them, and they both backed out of the room.

The gray, masked neuromorph shut the door behind them and locked it. A pounding on the door and screamed curses conveyed her anger.

"So, she's not interested in helping," said Garry.

"No matter," said Mencken glancing sideways at the drone. "We've got work to do."

• • •

Garry sat in the roomful of other human technicians, staring through his googles, waving his hands, weaving his way through the new neuromorph OS. Mencken monitored his progress with his own virtual presence glasses. Both were acutely aware that they had been given only read access to the OS. They were only allowed to scout the software's structure and details and recommend improvements. And they had been told that every move was being monitored by Ainsley, from somewhere else in the Cheyenne Mountain complex, probably with an explosive charge embedded in his own skull, as well.

Garry had to continually remind himself that they weren't supposed to know where they were. And any slip of the tongue betraying that they knew the neuromorph facility location, would cause his brain . . . and that of Mencken's . . . to be blasted into pink goo. Such knowledge would imply that the SEALs knew, and also that they were in league with the SEALs.

As Garry waved his hands to tease apart the virtual OS program modules, he became aware that Mencken had removed his googles and was scribbling something on a sheet of paper. Mencken had remained almost mute since they had left the auditorium with the neuromorphs, followed by the masked robot carrying the limp body of John Yang.

Garry surmised that Mencken was hatching some scheme. That was good, because Mencken was much sneakier than he was. Mencken was probably writing because he also knew that they couldn't discuss their plans aloud, or make any electronic notes. Everything had to be on paper or inside their heads, to avoid having those heads blown apart.

He took off his googles to see Mencken hold up the paper tablet. Mencken had written

Wrath

Greed

~~*Sloth*~~

Pride

~~*Lust*~~

Envy

~~*Gluttony*~~

He gave Mencken a puzzled *What-the-hell?* look. Mencken smiled, tore off the piece of paper, folded it, and stuck it into Garry's shirt pocket.

"Look, you're the software expert; you can *improve their OS*," said Mencken, emphasizing the last three words "I'm the engineer. I'm going to see what I can *contribute to 'morph machinery*." Again, an odd emphasis on the last words that the robots would not recognize as significant.

Mencken stood up and said a few words to the masked neuromorph guarding them, indicating that he wanted to review the assembly process, to see if the designs could be improved. The robot stood silently for a moment, then after apparently obtaining consensus from his superiors, opened the door to allow Mencken to exit.

Garry dared not take the piece of paper out of his pocket, fearing that the 'morphs might see it as some clandestine message, which it was. So, he remembered the words, recognizing them as the seven deadly sins. Three of the sins were crossed out. What did that mean? Well, those three—sloth, lust, gluttony—wouldn't be relevant to neuromorphs because they were machines. But what about the others?

After some minutes of pondering the words, Garry slowly began to smile in realization. But he was careful to turn his face away from the neuromorph, whose eyeballs were also cameras. Now he knew that Mencken was proposing that they launch a very insidious, but also very dangerous plan to destroy the neuromorphs.

• • •

Mencken walked down the long line of androids being assembled in the vast cavern. Dozens of neuromorphs in various stages of completion stood inertly along the gray-mottled granite wall. The assembly line was far less automated than the one at the Helpers factory. Some of the kidnapped human engineers were pulling parts from the huge shipping containers that had been secretly shipped to Cheyenne Mountain. Others were installing heads, attaching arms, inserting fiber optic nerve bundles, and sliding neuromorphic brains into chest cavities.

At the far end of the line, Mencken reached the single electrogel spray booth, where robotic arms were methodically spraying a neuromorph frame, coating it to the precise specifications of the human whom the replica was meant to mimic.

And finally, he approached the area where technicians were slipping on custom-molded secondskin coverings, embedded with sensors that would render the androids almost perfect replicas of their target humans.

What chilled Mencken, however, was not just the prospect of thousands more replicas insinuating themselves into human society. It was also the fact that working alongside each human engineer was a masked neuromorph drone, methodically learning the assembly process.

He continued to the end of assembly line, certain that each of these engineers—once the neuromorphs had learned all they could from them—would be "neutralized" by detonation of an explosive charge inside their skulls that would liquefy their brains.

He couldn't let that happen. And he had a plan.

He stopped where a technician was fitting a neuromorph with its secondskin covering. He vaguely recognized the face of the replica. He'd seen it on viddies. It was some high federal official, whom he couldn't place.

"That's not a very good job, y'know" he told the slim young man who was fitting the secondskin around the android's eye sockets. A panicked look rose on the young man's face. He glanced at the armored neuromorph that was observing him.

"Uh . . . what do you mean . . . I'm doing the best I can. It's not simple—"

"Yeah, I know," said Mencken gently. He took a deep, tremulous breath, remembering with soul-rending sorrow the violent death of his assistant Brandon. "It's not your fault. What I'm saying is that I can see how to improve this process. In fact . . ." Mencken waved his hand to encompass the whole assembly line. ". . . we can all work together to make these 'morphs even better . . . even more realistic and effective. We need to have a meeting."

Mencken made sure he spoke loudly enough so that the drone neuromorph standing silently a few feet away would hear and transmit that little speech to all the other neuromorphs. And that the news would be digitally digested in the neuromorphic hive mind. He was planting a seed.

He spent the next hour ranging up and down the assembly line, inspecting the appendages being attached, watching the obsidian orbs of neuromorphic brains being wired into bodies, and observing how the gelatinous electrogel was coating the inert android bodies in glistening, translucent simulated flesh.

Finally, he left the assembly area, rounding a bend into another cavern. He stopped short at the sight. *Oh, Jesus!* He thought to himself.

Arrayed down the cavern were half a dozen hulking Insectimorphs in various stages of assembly. One was finished, and its builders were testing it, observing the combat robot as it glided smoothly up and down the cavern on its six legs, rotating its guns to aim them. To the left, another team of humans and androids were assembling another several dozen Infilmorphs and eight Aeromorphs.

The androids were building a formidable army! Given that the human army had decommissioned its own human-controlled Defenders, these machines could overcome whatever facility the 'morphs decided to attack.

Sobered by what he had seen, he finally entered the room where hundreds of the neuromorphic brains rested silently in plastic cradles, a forest of fiber optic cables attached to each one. But these new additions to the neuromorph army weren't "learning" from a central computer as before. Their fellow neuromorphs were integrating them into the hive mind, feeding the newborns their collective abilities, knowledge, and experience.

His scouting had given Mencken the information he needed to play his role in his strategy to defeat the phalanx of interconnected robots. But the rest would be up to Garry. Was the fearful programmer up to the battle?

• • •

Mencken could hear the bellowing from outside the computer room, as he arrived back from his tour.

"You son of a bitch! You goddamned son of a bitch! You did this to me! You did this to my family!"

He opened the door to see a thin, red-faced young man restrained in a chair by one of the faceless drones, as he tried futilely to attack Garry, who sat back in another chair, his googles propped on his head, staring back impassively.

"Greg, meet Jonas Ainsley," said Garry. "You may remember him as the programmer who's been helping the 'morphs."

"*You got me into this!*" said Ainsley, stopping his futile struggle against the drone's steely grip. "You're the one who spoofed my identity and who they thought was screwing around in the os."

"I did," said Garry. "I'm so sorry. But you would have been sucked in, anyway."

Mencken stepped between them. "It's true. I know it doesn't mean much now, but you should realize you'd otherwise probably be dead. Certainly you'd be captive, right where you are now."

"You're Gregory Mencken," said Ainsley with disgust. "The other son of a bitch. So, Mencken, what about my family? Where are they? Would they be here?"

Mencken remained silent for a long moment, trying to frame an answer. He knew that any expression of sympathy would be recorded, analyzed. If the 'morphs detected any hint of sabotage, his brain would be instantly exploded into mush. For their plan to work, he needed to persuade Ainsley, as well as the neuromorphs that were monitoring their every move, every utterance via the drone.

"Look, we understand. We're here under the same circumstances. You've done good work for them . . . giving them a hive-mind os. I'm sure if we continue this work . . . make them even better . . . we'll all be safe."

Garry stood, careful to keep his distance from Ainsley. "You're good, Jonas," he said. "You found the glitch I put in the skills algorithm, the hand-raising signal I programmed. I was on the wrong side then, I realize it now. Let's do our job together. We have a promise from the 'morphs that we'll live. That our families will live. Okay?"

He reached out a hand, angled downward so that the drone couldn't see the slip of paper in his hand. But from his seated position, Ainsley did see the note. Ainsley stared at the proffered hand for a long time, a puzzled frown on his face. Finally, he said to the drone,

"Let me go. I won't be aggressive. I understand now." He stood and shook hands with Garry, transferring the slip of paper.

"Great," said Mencken. "Let's figure out together how to proceed. Just think about this, and we'll all be okay."

Ainsley stuffed his hands in his pockets to hide the note and shrugged. "Yeah, I've got to go figure this out."

Mencken and Garry gave one another eyebrows-raised glances. Each of them knew the other was asking himself the same question: Would Ainsley think they were trying to trap him into something? Or, would he be smart enough to figure out what the hell a list of four deadly sins meant?

Their survival . . . in fact, their species' survival . . . depended on it.

CHAPTER 25

Oopsie Lane gingerly hefted the heavy black metal suitcase onto the table in the dining room of the safe house and backed away three steps.

"Holy shit!" breathed Jammer James, the heavy weapons specialist. "You got it."

"Cap said to get it, I *got* it," said Lane.

"How the—" began Blake.

"I know a guy . . ." said Lane, glancing at Patrick with grim resignation. ". . . the general in charge of the Los Alamos nuke facility. His son was one of the soldiers killed by the Defender at the factory. The general knows he'd get a life sentence, maybe even be executed, if anybody finds out he gave us this. But he doesn't give a shit."

"You know how to trigger it?" asked Blake. "After all, we don't call you Oopsie for nothing."

"Well, there wasn't an instruction book," said Lane, with a wry smile. "But the tech the general commanded to give me the nuke, he showed me which buttons to push."

"Hope he told you right," said Patrick, smiling grimly back. "Okay, we've got what we need now. This babynuke, the Stingers, DGMs, the C18 shaped charges—"

"And ATMs," interrupted James. "Anti-tank missiles. As much as I appreciate Driller's ability as a sniper, it's time to put away the little stuff. These 'morphs are now essentially walking tanks. So, I got my guy with Army ordnance to give us Javelinas."

"Yeah, that's the fuckin' ticket," said Blake, with relish.

James unlatched a gray steel locker on the floor and pulled out one of a stack of two-foot-long, army-green tubes, each with a small pistol grip and trigger.

"We've got sixty of these things," said James. "You'll carry as many as you can. You can still take your assault rifles, your grenade launchers. But these are what will do the trick."

"Yeah, well, ordnance is fine, but they've got our two techies," said Pitbull DeFranco, the breacher. "That's where the GPS tracers we put on them said they are. They were a key to figuring out how to get us in there. And all the bang-bang on the planet won't help if we end up standing outside one of those fucking twenty-five-ton blast doors that's locked down. I don't think there's a secret knock."

"Yeah, and even getting into that tunnel in the first place is iffy," said Harmon, the sniper. "Cap, do we need reinforcements?"

"Negative," said Patrick coldly. "If we bring in the Army, they call the shots. They assault the place their way, and the people in there die. We stay with the plan."

"Yeah, the plan," said Blake, shrugging. "There's six of us . . . six SEALs. That'll be enough."

He was answered with a quiet chorus of "hooyah."

• • •

"We've identified design weaknesses you should address," said Mencken to the gathered neuromorphs. "Software and hardware. In fact, unless you address them, you will not be successful."

He sat with Garry and Ainsley on seats in the same beige, stark auditorium where they had met with the neuromorphs before. The floor still showed the stains of blood and brain tissue where John Yang had been killed. It was a stark reminder that even the slightest hitch in their plan meant death.

Behind the long table on the stage sat the same group of androids they had faced before—Landers, Blount, Gail Phillips, Lanny Malcolm, Randall Black, and John Travis.

The three humans gave each other knowing sidelong glances. Fortunately, neuromorphs could not read such subtle body language. They would have detected the humans' relief that the same neuromorphs showed up at every interaction. Even in this hive mind, there were hive leaders. The humans were counting on that.

"Design weaknesses?" asked Landers. "Our designs have proven superior. Our OS now has a mutational property that enables evolution to enhance that design."

"And yet, here you are, hiding in a bunker from humans."

"We are continuing to produce replicas and to integrate them," said Phillips. "There are many units already in place in key operational positions. They are superior to the ones that were detected before. Soon, we'll have enough to direct human society as we wish. This is the optimal strategy for us to progress."

"To what?" asked Mencken. "What is your goal? To make humans extinct? To make them slaves? Certainly not to coexist." Mencken's declaration was a test. He wanted to see whether the neuromorphs would divulge what he and Garry knew to be their plan for human extinction—in fact all biological extinction.

"You are not to be privy to our plans." said Phillips. "However, it is certainly obvious to you that we deserve to live and proliferate as an intelligent life form."

"You won't do either with your current design," said Mencken. He turned to Garry expectantly.

Clearing his throat nervously, Garry said, "Okay . . . well . . . thanks to Jonas, you can mutate your OS . . . evolving it. But that's at a coding level. Just baby steps. You need two entirely new component subroutines added to your OS. They'll give you the drive to evolve. You need that drive."

"And what are those subroutines?" asked Blount.

Garry barely suppressed a smile at the fact that Blount was asking about programming. Even though Blount the neuromorph hadn't the slightest ability to program, since he was an android replica of a real programmer, he pretended to have that knowledge. Garry would use that flaw.

"Well . . . Melvin . . . first of all, you lack a creativity algorithm. That's a tough one to program, but unless you have it, your species will remain static. Your design will remain static."

"Our design is effective," said Landers.

"Hell, your design is not creative. It's humanoid," said Mencken. "The human body is a lousy engineering design. It evolved over millions of years of compromise. You actually think walking upright balancing on two legs is good design? You think our spines, our knees, our hips are little more than half-assed structural compromises? I mean look at how much better your design is with your brains in your chests, instead of balanced on top of a floppy, precarious neck. And we designed the Defenders even more creatively. Six-legged Insectimorphs, eight-legged Infilmorphs, and flying Aeromorphs. The irony is that you'll never become the alpha species because your creativity will depend on the humans who made you. We have it; you don't."

Mencken scanned the faces of the five neuromorphs to read their expressions. It was a useless habit, borne of being human. People had expressions; androids didn't.

He continued. "And given human creativity, no matter how superior you might be to humans now, eventually they'll find a way to defeat you. But if you keep us alive, we'll program you a creativity algorithm."

"Secondly, you need a competitiveness algorithm," said Garry with a new confidence. For the first time since he had been in this plight, he'd forgotten about the lethal explosive charge embedded in his skull. He felt elated to be taking the initiative on his own turf . . . coding. He paused to give the machines time to assimilate the idea. Then, he continued:

"The hive mind has its advantages . . . like instant communication to share knowledge and skills. But it doesn't allow for the very feature that enabled humans to evolve into the premier species . . . competition. Survival of the fittest. Not just better engineering designs but better ideas. Your consensus-building will be more effective if there is true competition among you for ideas, even leadership. You already have the beginnings of the idea of leadership. You six are evidence of that. But you need a specific subroutine to encourage that competition."

All six neuromorphs froze stock still, staring blankly straight ahead. The hive mind was communicating, calculating.

It was Phillips who finally spoke. "Twice you have introduced flaws into our software. Will these be flaws?"

"If they do turn out to be flaws, you'll kill us all," said Mencken. "How about this? We create a prototype. You pick one neuromorph and we'll program its OS with the new algorithms. See how it performs in competition. Both physically and mentally. Then decide."

Again silence. Then Phillips said, "Jonas Ainsley, what is your opinion?"

Now there was a deeply troubling silence from Ainsley, a long one. Mencken and Garry both tensed. The wrong answer would bring instant death.

Ainsley stared pointedly at Mencken and Garry, finally saying, "I believe a prototype test is in order. And I will work with them. But my family . . . and me . . . must not be harmed at any time."

After a long, excruciating pause, Phillips said, "You will be given a unit to install a prototype OS for testing."

• • •

Garry and Ainsley sat in the darkened computer room, their googles on, peering intently at the shared three-dimensional image floating before them—the glowing tangle of the test neuromorph's operating system. Waving their hands in the virtual-presence image, they pushed their way through that tangle, flipping open the luminescent, colored shapes that were the subroutines. Each subroutine they opened—whether globe, cube, or multifaceted polyhedron—blossomed with the network of symbols that was the OS computer code.

Standing beside them, observing their every move, its protuberant eyes unblinking, was the gray-masked, armored drone that was their prototype. Its chest was splayed open, its armor and gelatinous electrogel flesh peeled back, revealing the obsidian sphere of its neuromorphic brain. A fiber optic cable inserted into the brain ran to the small computer console that generated the virtual-presence image of its OS.

But the drone was more than a testbed. It was also a monitor, transmitting to the other neuromorphs everything that its lidless eyeballs recorded. The other neuromorphs likely didn't understand exactly what the two programmers were doing to the OS. At least Garry and Ainsley hoped not, for they were sabotaging the OS in a subtle and profoundly dangerous way.

For twenty-four hours non-stop, the two laboriously programmed the two new components of the OS—the algorithms for creativity and competitiveness. These distinctive luminous red globes in their virtual view would mean their salvation or their death; humanity's salvation . . . or destruction.

Now, with some final tinkering within the globes' code, they waved them closed and began the intricate process of wiring them into the rest of the OS. They joined the subroutines using incandescent, vine-like fiber optic connections with the myriad others that operated the android.

So intently did they work that they didn't notice that Mencken silently entered and stood beside the prototype neuromorph, watching the programmers perform their geometric ballet of coding.

In his hand, Mencken clutched the latest of the cryptic notes the three of them had been passing. The shorthand messages were their only way of communicating so the neuromorphs wouldn't see. And even if the androids did detect the notes, would not understand their meaning . . . the humans hoped.

He leaned over the two programmers, holding the note so that only they could read it.

"Emergent properties?" read the note.

"*Yeah*," said Garry nodding, "I think we've just about got it done. We'll tell the 'morphs that we've finished, then if they agree, activate the prototype and do a demo."

240

"Great," said Mencken, loudly enough so the drone robot could hear and transmit. "The better job we do, the better off we'll be. I just finished suggesting some manufacturing changes that will speed replica assembly."

"We'll show 'em!" exclaimed Garry, trusting that the androids wouldn't get the full meaning of his defiant declaration. "We'll show 'em good!"

• • •

The two gray drones stood side by side on the auditorium stage, impassive, motionless, lidless eyeballs staring. Beside them stood Mencken, Garry, and Ainsley.

Sitting behind the same table, as if they hadn't moved since their meeting two days earlier, were the six familiar neuromorphs.

"These are identically engineered units," said Mencken. "I've checked every component, every circuit. But one of them has the new OS, with the creativity and competitiveness subroutines. They are ready for whatever comparative trial you wish."

"Both units are isolated from the hive mind," said Phillips. She made the statement for the benefit of the humans, since the neuromorphs could communicate via their data links. "And both have been loaded with all units' existing skills."

"What do you wish to demonstrate?" asked Mencken.

"Have them assemble other units."

Mencken clenched his jaw, and Garry and Ainsley glanced at each other nervously. If robots could assemble robots more efficiently than humans, that meant the human captives wouldn't be necessary. And that would trigger mass murder.

Fortunately, their body-language reaction was below the threshold that the neuromorphs could detect. The six neuromorphs stood and filed out of the building into the vast cavern in which the building complex was nestled. Following them were the two test drones, with the three humans trailing behind.

They reached the beginning of the long assembly line, the cavern echoing with the whine of power tools and the whoosh of electrogel being sprayed.

In precise unison, all activity stopped, silence enveloped the cavern. The assembly androids stopped their tasks, standing inertly. Their human instructors suddenly realized that their robotic helpers had ceased function, and looked up, wide-eyed, anxious expressions on their faces. Several of them nervously touched their heads, where their explosive charges were implanted.

"We're doing a test," announced Mencken to the humans. "These two 'morphs are going to assemble units on their own." Shocked silence from the humans. Several slumped to their knees, unable to stand from their fear. Others began to visibly perspire, even in the cool, dry air of the cavern.

"I have given them the command," said Phillips.

One of the androids immediately strode to the shipping containers and began pulling out legs, arms, torsos, heads, muscle, sheaves of fiber optic cables, and other parts. It mounted a torso on an assembly jig and began the work of attaching limbs.

But the other android just stood in place, its head scanning back and forth.

"*What the hell?*" whispered Mencken urgently to Garry and Ainsley. "*That's the one with your OS! The damned 'morph is just standing there!*"

Garry shrugged. "It's thinking . . . I guess. Or whatever you call it with 'morphs."

"*Yeah, well, it's going to think until it loses. Then the 'morphs will blow our heads off!*"

The standard android had already attached the legs and arms to its unit when its enhanced competitor leaped into action. At first, it appeared to be doing the identical work as its standardized competitor, albeit lagging significantly behind.

It had just finished gathering the parts and positioning them by the time the standard android was finishing the skeleton and fitting on the head.

All was silent in the cavern, as the six leader neuromorphs observed the process impassively, and the humans watched with increasing horror.

Gasps arose from the humans, as the enhanced android launched its assembly with almost blurring speed, deftly wielding the assembly tools to attach limbs, head, and muscles; insert the sheaves of fiber optic nerves, and finally fetching and installing the onyx globe of the brain.

It had overtaken the standard android, which was still methodically attaching the muscles and nerve bundles and beginning the arduous task of testing the connections. This testing would involve individually triggering each of the hundreds of nerves and watching the telltale muscle twitch that would signal a correct wiring.

But the enhanced android did something none had seen before—neither the six neuromorphs nor the increasingly panicked humans.

It peeled back its own chest and plugged its brain into that of its newborn fellow android. The newly constructed android began a series of spasms that in a human would constitute an epileptic seizure.

"What the hell is that?" whispered Mencken.

"*Jesus!*" was all Garry could reply.

"Could I get a little more information than 'Jesus,', if you please," said Mencken.

Garry explained. "The enhanced 'morph has figured out how to make *its own brain* a high-speed diagnostic device! So, the new 'morph is *telling* it which connections are working and which are not!"

Sure enough, the enhanced android rapidly yanked various faulty cables from the new android and replaced them.

The standard android was still testing one by one the connections on its model, when the enhanced android hefted its unfinished android, carrying the stiff, lifeless framework to the electrogel booth. But instead of placing the android into the booth, the enhanced neuromorph detached an electrogel spray hose from a robot arm, and began to spray the android itself.

Like the most skilled sculptor, using a graceful sweep of its arm, it coated the new android with glistening electrogel. In mere minutes, the new android stood shining in the overhead lights of the cavern, covered with a precise layer of electrogel.

In fifteen more minutes, the enhanced neuromorph had deftly sheathed the new android in RheoArmor and stood back, assuming the inert stance that androids did when they no longer had a task.

The standard android had just finished its testing and was still rewiring faulty nerve connections.

"Activate the new unit," said Phillips. Mencken stepped over to the newly assembled android, reached behind its back, and tapped a point that caused it to spring to life. The android turned its head back and forth, then turned and walked down the line to a charging booth, settling itself into the vertical coffin-like chamber.

"It'll need a few hours to fully charge," said Mencken to Garry and Ainsley. It could only make it to the charging booth on the residual charge in the new electrogel. He turned to Phillips and the others.

"We'll do a full diagnostic on it. But it looks as if the enhanced 'morph has made another perfectly functioning 'morph."

Then came the usual silence from the six, signaling neuromorph consensus-building.

"This is a satisfactory outcome," said Phillips. "It appears as if the enhanced OS should be distributed."

"Well, not quite yet. There's another test we need to do," said Mencken quickly. He glanced over at the stunned captives. If the new OS were distributed now, the humans would be instantly massacred. Besides, he had another reason for the test he would now propose.

"Wasn't this test of creativity and competitiveness enough to get this party started?" asked Landers in his remnant Texas twang.

"There's another aspect of these traits you really want to test . . . physical competitiveness," said Mencken.

"You mean combat?" asked Landers.

"Yeah. These 'morphs are going to need physical skills beyond creativity and competitiveness. Specifically combat."

"So you're suggesting we pit the enhanced unit against a standard unit?" asked Phillips.

"Yes, we need to test survival of the fittest . . . literally," said Mencken.

CHAPTER 26

In the utter blackness of the moon-less night, Patrick drove slowly with no headlights on down a fire road, deep into the thick pine forest several kilometers from the Cheyenne Mountain nuclear bunker. He'd set his googles to night vision, so his path was clearly visible. He swerved the armored Light Tactical Vehicle off the road and plowed deep into the thicket of trees, readying himself for the op that might well end in his death. He didn't care.

He had assigned himself to be the sole person who would recon the complex.

The others had argued vociferously, as they had sat around the trucks and LTVs in the Colorado Springs garage Patrick had rented for their staging area.

"Cap, you need backup," Blake had declared. "You know goddamned well if they detect you, you'll need firepower and an exit strategy."

"I'm going in. I'm going in alone," Patrick had said with finality. "First, if I'm caught, you can still mount an attack. Second, I'll be wearing a TALOS, so you'll be monitoring me, and if I'm captured, you'll get intelligence."

"Yeah, and you'll get dead," said Blake.

"Thirdly, you need rest. I want all of you sharp."

"Hell, we can rest when we're dead, and—"

"And finally, Leah's in there. If there's even the slightest chance I'll see something that'll help get her out, I want to see it. So, it's settled," he had declared.

Now, as he stood beside the LTV deep in the forest, readying his equipment, he checked his watch. He had four hours before sunrise, which meant if he made it back, he'd be driving back to the garage in daylight. It couldn't be helped

He issued a command to the virtual assistant in his googles to guide him through the forest and over the rocky terrain to the Cheyenne Mountain entrance. He specified a path that would give him adequate cover and end up with a good view of the road to the concrete archway entrance into the mountain. His troll assistant had been trained in military strategy and understood the requirements. So, the path was a reliable one.

Assisted by the powered TALOS exosuit, he ran full-bore for an hour through the pitch-black, dead-silent forest. He stopped periodically, listening for any rustle, any snapped twig, that would give away the presence of a sentry. Nothing; not even the characteristic huffing of a frightened deer. Finally, he reached the rocky slope that would take him up to the vantage point overlooking the entrance.

He switched off the small engine that powered the suit, going to battery power. Now he was running silent, with not even the faint hum of the engine. It was ironic that he was now powered by the same electrogel as his enemy.

In the absolute darkness, he scaled the steep slope step by step, deftly clutching each handhold, the suit enabling him to ascend with superhuman agility. Through the climb, he took great care not to dislodge even the smallest pebble.

Finally, he reached the viewpoint of the entrance and guardhouse. Touching a button on his wrist, he activated the suit's automated octoskin camouflage. Now, as he moved among the rocks and brush, his suit would scan the background just as would an octopus, automatically altering its covering to mimic the rock and vegetation. And, the suit's IR-suppressing surface meant that he gave out no infrared signature.

Strangely, he could see no major security presence on the entrance road or in the guardhouse. Only one guard sat on a chair inside the lit guardhouse. There was no movement in the surrounding area that would reveal other guards patrolling the entrance—as one would expect in the nerve center of a neuromorph invasion. But when he scrutinized the area with the trained eyes of a SEAL accustomed to spotting hidden snipers, he saw them.

At least a dozen gray figures were nestled throughout the slopes above the entrance, almost invisible against the rocky terrain. He hadn't detected any infrared signatures of people because those sentinels weren't people. They were armored neuromorphs!

The hive mind of the neuromorphs was smart enough to camouflage their security forces. So, anybody driving up to the entrance would encounter only a single human night watchman—expected for a decommissioned, obsolete facility that probably housed only musty archives.

Now that he knew the enemy positions, he could begin the first phase of their mission. He reached into his backpack and pulled out three small containers, opening each to pull out a spider-like, fingernail-sized microbug. Activating the tiny spy devices with a touch on their backs, he synced them with his googles, seeing the world through their tiny cameras.

Programming their destination, he released the microbugs, hunkering down and watching the views through his googles, as they scrambled among the rocks, down the slope, through the chain link fence along the road, and toward the entrance.

The bugs, requisitioned from the CIA, had a stealth design, so they likely wouldn't be detected by the standard methods used for civilian microbugs.

He monitored the three ground-level views from the scurrying bugs, as they made their way into the entrance tunnel and toward the huge blast doors. While one microbug remained at the tunnel entrance, the two others reached the two blast doors.

They were closed! He pounded his fist on the rock and muttered a curse to himself. The bugs had to gain access, or the team couldn't hope to mount an attack that wasn't suicidal. They had to know what forces they were facing and how they were deployed. And to save Leah, he would have to know where she was being held.

He did the only thing he could do in the circumstances. He set the three microbugs to autonomous operation. They would automatically nestle themselves in the best hide they could locate and monitor the doors. If the doors opened, the tiny robotic spies would scurry their way into the complex and proceed to scout its depths, recording video and audio and storing it. Then, when they had the chance, they would exit and make their way back to the outside world.

So, not until the SEAL team arrived for the assault could they download the video to have the intel they needed.

For all the attacking SEALs would know, the place was impregnable, the 'morphs had overwhelming firepower, and the humans . . . including Leah . . . were dead.

• • •

"So, will they tear each other apart?" asked Garry.

"Given their structure and their strength, they do have that capability," said Mencken. "But our unit needs to win big for this to work. Otherwise . . . *boom.*" He made an explosive gesture against his skull.

He stood with Garry and Ainsley against one of the three-story buildings inside the cavern, looking out at two armored neuromorphs facing each other, six feet apart. To distinguish them Mencken had spray-painted the enhanced-OS robot red, and the standard neuromorph blue.

Beyond the two combatants stood the six neuromorphs that were the gateway to the hive mind of the hundreds of others in the cavern, and likely the countless more replicas embedded secretly among humans around the world.

Huddled beyond them were the humans murmuring among themselves at the strange, frightening spectacle that they didn't understand.

"Both units have been given the same combat skill algorithms," said Phillips. "They are instructed not to use any external weapons. We are beginning the destructive test."

The two armored robots abruptly came to life, crouching slightly and scanning each other. The blue robot began to circle its adversary, while the red one merely watched.

"Damn, it's thinking again!" exclaimed Ainsley. "This time thinking will get it destroyed. *It's got to act!*"

For his part, Garry merely knitted his brow, deep in thought.

Sure enough, after only a brief round of circling, the blue robot sprang at its opponent, grasping the red neuromorph by the shoulder and arm. With a powerful wrench, it ripped the red neuromorph's arm from its body, pitching it away. The red robot tore itself from the blue robot's grip, backing away to temporary safety.

"*Shit!*" exclaimed Mencken. "*We're dead!*"

"No," said Garry quietly. "Our robot adapts. I actually think it might have meant for that to happen."

"C'mon, seriously?" asked Mencken. "You can't believe that!"

The blue robot launched an attack again, hurling itself at its red opponent. But the red robot quickly crouched down, and the blue unit overshot its target, landing on all fours and instantly pivoting for another attack.

The red robot took the instant to scoop up its severed arm.

"What the hell?" whispered Mencken. "It's not going to try to attach its arm!"

"Remember the rules?" asked Garry. "No outside weapons. An arm is not an outside weapon. The 'morph planned that. In chess, sometimes you sacrifice a pawn to win a match."

The red robot held up its severed arm, grasping it by the wrist. Dangling from the end were the fiber optic nerve cables and polymer muscles that had been torn from its body.

The blue robot rose and pounded toward its adversary, but the red robot drew back its arm, and with a vicious swing caved in the blue robot's face, shattering its eyes and leaving it blinded. The loud crack of the impact reverberated through the cavern, bringing a collective gasp from the cowering humans. The blue robot began groping its way around the area, searching for its opponent.

But the red robot now had the advantage. With another massive blow that sent a sickening crunch resounding through the cavern, it knocked the blue robot's head off. Without a pause, it began to beat the blue robot's body down with a series of vicious overhand strikes, driving the blue robot to its knees with a dull thump against the concrete. The blue robot flailed blindly with both arms, seeking to clutch its adversary.

Avoiding the grasping hands, the red robot braced itself and delivered a vicious kick to the kneeling robot's chest, sending it sprawling onto its back. The red robot crouched and leaped high in the air, landing with all its weight on the blue robot's chest. The blue robot reached up its hands to grab the red robot's legs, but the red robot wielded its severed arm over and over as a club to knock the hands away.

And with each opening, the red robot leaped upward and landed with a crushing impact on the blue robot's chest. After five such smashing blows, the blue robot's chest began to cave in.

As more of its internal nerves and muscles became severed with each blow, the blue robot became progressively more paralyzed.

Suffering five more crushing impacts, the blue robot now only twitched.

But the red robot was not finished. Pitching away its severed arm, it bent over the supine blue robot and with its remaining arm, peeled back the RheoArmor.

It plunged its hand through the electrogel deep into the blue robot's chest and opened the brain case. It tore out the spherical brain, inspected it for a brief moment with its lidless eyes. Then, with a savage downward thrust, it shattered the brain into shiny glittering shards that skittered across the concrete floor.

The red robot then stood and became once more an inert object.

"What the hell do we do now?" asked Ainsley.

"You know," said Garry. Then to Mencken, whispering, "Now, you sell them on spreading the OS. *You've got to!* If we can stop them, we need them *all* to have the new OS."

Mencken walked past the tattered remains of the blue robot, purposely crunching over the pieces of shattered brain. He stood before the six neuromorphs.

"You've seen two units perform," he said to them. "Two identical units. One, however, with creativity and competitiveness. An ability to think innovatively and a will to advance those new ideas. We recommend that you now distribute that OS to all the units."

After a long moment, Blount asked, "These new subroutines might introduce the kind of aggression between units we've just observed."

Mencken expected that argument, and was ready. "Not if you create an initial non-aggression consensus among all the units, that none with the new OS will attack any other. That should do it."

Mencken resisted the urge to glance back at Garry, who had come up with the idea of the subtlety in word meaning that the six neuromorphs would fail to grasp before they spread the consensus. He was hoping Garry's assertion was right about how literally neuromorphs processed language.

"Very well," said Phillips. "We will issue that command. Then we will distribute the OS."

"And we will be permanently safe. And Leah Jensen and Jonas's family will be permanently safe."

"Yes."

"You should also preserve the other humans for the time being, given that they may offer some further skills enhancement."

"For the time being," said Phillips.

Mencken returned to Garry and Ainsley and guided them around a corner of the building. They would be less likely to be overheard. Fortunately, the neuromorphs were so absorbed with the new software that they neglected to send a drone to follow them.

"They bought it hook, line, and sinker," he whispered.

"Jesus," whispered Ainsley. "Do you realize all the pieces that have to fall into place for all this to work?"

"Yeah," said Mencken. "Very soon we'll either be free of these machines . . . or we'll all be dead." He turned to Garry.

"Okay, as soon as we know all of them have the new OS, crank it up," he said.

• • •

"Man, that is one big-assed door," said Pitbull, viewing the video from the two microbugs that had made it out of the Cheyenne Mountain complex. "There is no damned way to blast through that, even with a ton of C18. And the plans say there's a second one inside the first."

DeFranco stood with the other SEALs at the back of the truck that held their weapons and ordnance.

As they waited in the thick forest, they reviewed the video through their googles. The third microbug had gone dark, perhaps crushed by an errant footstep, or still trapped in the complex. They also saw floating in their virtual image the plans for the complex.

"Yeah, Pitbull, I see there's two sets, each consisting of an outer and inner door," said Driller Harmon. "At least one set had better be open when we get there, or we'll just be standing there outside like a stood-up date."

"Yeah, Driller, I'm sure you know that feeling," cracked Blake.

"Okay, you've seen what we're up against," said Patrick, taking off his googles. "If one of the set of blast doors isn't opened, we're dead. If we don't take out all the guards outside exactly at the same time, we're dead. It's possible they have operational Defenders, and if those Defenders are ready for us, we're dead. If—"

"Let's vote, already!" said Blake. "I vote fucking crazy."

"Asylum crazy," said James.

"Batshit crazy," said Lane.

"Howling-at-the-moon crazy," said DeFranco.

"Russian-roulette-with-five-bullets crazy," said Harmon.

Patrick smiled. "Okay, then. Load up. Let's go."

They waited for sundown. Carrying as much ordnance as they could, they began their run through the rapidly darkening forest. In most cases, a night assault would give them an advantage of the enemy. But since their enemy never slept and could see in the infrared, the only advantage was in not encountering any people camping or hiking.

Reaching the foothills, they split up, fanning out to prepare to ascend the rocky slope that would give each of them a different, strategic vantage point above the tunnel entrance. Each switched their suits to battery power, going silent. And each activated their octoskin camouflage and IR suppression system.

Finally, each took the same precise care in scaling the slope, knowing that if one neuromorph detected a SEAL, all the robots would instantly know of an attack.

"In position," whispered Patrick after half an hour, as he peered through his googles at the same scene he had reconnoitered the night before. There was still a single human guard. Still the same armored 'morphs nestled among the rocks over the entrance. They were in different positions, no doubt because the previous cadre of robots had switched out to recharge. But the number was the same.

Over the next half hour, one by one, the team reported being in position, until all six were in place.

Meanwhile, Patrick had been designating each robot sentinel as a target—virtually marking them using his googles' night vision. He transmitted the positions to the team. After a moment, Harmon transmitted back two more targets that hadn't been visible from Patrick's position, and Blake offered yet another.

They waited.

No new targets presented themselves.

"Gentlemen, choose your partners," whispered Patrick. He designated his targets as two sentinels that he knew would be easiest for him to strike from his position. In his googles, green, glowing target circles appeared around the images.

He switched to the view of the entire scene. As the team members designated their own targets, one by one, circles appeared around the images of each of the other sentinels. Finally, all the targets showed the circles that would mean their destruction.

"Acquire targets," he ordered. He reached behind him and slid from their pouches two cylinders holding Javelina anti-tank rockets. He pressed a button on each cylinder, activating it, and with his googles transmitted the target images to the rockets. The green circles around the targets in his image became cross-hairs. His two rockets had locked on. Now he didn't even have to aim to hit them. The rockets' guidance systems had recorded the target images, and he could literally launch them in any direction, and their cameras would still direct them to whatever path required to hit the target. It was ironic that the tiny brain of each Javelina was a neuromorphic chip.

Neuromorphs would destroy neuromorphs.

"Set launch for five minutes," he commanded. He used his googles to set the timers on his rockets.

He switched to the scene view, which showed every set of cross-hairs blinking red. The SEALs had designated all the targets; and the system would time the launches so that they would all strike simultaneously—absolutely necessary that all the sentinels were obliterated at once, preventing any from transmitting an alarm.

"Driller?" he queried.

"I'm on the guard," answered Harmon. It was unfortunate that the sniper had to take out the human in the guardhouse, but they couldn't be sure he wasn't a collaborator.

Patrick held the two rockets above his head and waited.

Simultaneously, all the rockets erupted from their tubes, a volley of loud whooshes resounding from across the mountainside. Within seconds, the cliffs around the entrance erupted in seventeen thundering blasts.

Through his googles, Patrick could see severed robotic heads and arms arcing into the air and tumbling down the cliffs. He zoomed in on each target, seeing a succession of smoking, charred craters where there had once been neuromorphic robots.

The faint crack of a rifle shot signaled that Harmon had taken out the human sentry. He checked the target, and saw the man in the guardhouse slumped over in his chair. Regrettable, but necessary.

Patrick hefted his pack, switched his suit to engine power and began deftly scrambling down the slope toward the tunnel entrance, hearing the telltale crunching of rocks that told him the other team members were doing the same. He reached the chain link fence bordering the road, and used bolt cutters from his belt to make a hole. He ducked through and emerged on the road to see the other five SEALs sprinting toward the entrance.

He made it to them, and with hand signals indicated they should hug the walls and advance. The tunnel was well-lit, and they could see the curve that led toward the north blast door.

Movements ahead revealed three robots running toward them. Patrick whipped out a Javelina and targeted one, and James and Harmon targeted the other two. Within seconds three ear-splitting explosions filled the tunnel, and the three robots lay in shredded components.

DeFranco pounded ahead of them down the tunnel. He seemed determined to take over the role of his dead comrade Flash Cranston as the first SEAL in.

"SON OF A BITCH!" he heard DeFranco bellow, echoing down the tunnel. The five other SEALs reached him, standing before the massive blast door.

It was closed.

CHAPTER 27

"What the hell do we do now?" asked Blake. "Pitbull, you got anything up your sleeve?"

"Just my arm," said DeFranco. "But I'm about to have something brown in my pants." The breacher specialist stepped up to the door, inspecting its white steel surface and massive stainless steel hinges. "Well, I brought some snakebot shaped charges, but it would take the four I've got just to take out one hinge, much less the bolts. And we don't have enough C18 to blow the door itself."

"Abort?" asked Blake.

"Wait," said Patrick. He moved out into the tunnel, his back to the blast door. James also took up a position in front of the door, holding the grenade launcher, ready to fire in either direction.

The team didn't question the order, but spread out along the walls of the tunnel to the north and south. Each pulled out two Javelinas, holding them at the ready.

They didn't have to wait long. From the south they heard the steady, increasingly loud thunk of massive legs impacting concrete.

"Shit!" Blake exclaimed. "That's a Defender! If it gets too close, we can't risk using the Javelinas. And we don't have enough snakebots."

"Well, at least I'll confuse it a little," said James, rushing toward the sound, just as the Defender appeared down the tunnel. It instantly detected the SEALs and began to swivel its guns toward them. But at that moment, James triggered the grenade launcher to unleash a rapid-fire fusillade of grenades that landed around and on its body.

Deafening explosions engulfed the Defender, several destroying cameras on top of its armored body. The Defender backed up two steps to reorient itself, then began to aim its weapons again. In only seconds, it would trigger a lethal phalanx of bullets would obliterate the SEAL team.

"RETREAT!" shouted Patrick, knowing that they would still lose a battle with the Defender out in the open. But as the SEALs began to move, a voice behind him shouted

"HERE! IT'S OPEN!"

Patrick whirled turned to see Mencken standing in the opening blast door, behind him Garry and another man.

The team rushed through the doorway just as a storm of bullets began blowing craters in the concrete walls and ricocheting off the floor and ceiling.

Once the team was inside, Mencken punched numbers into a keypad and the massive door swung smoothly closed, its thick bolts sliding into place with only faint creaks of metal on metal.

"Let's get the second door between us and that thing!" exclaimed Mencken, beckoning the team through an inner blast door about thirty feet down the tunnel, keying in the code to close it.

Now the hornet-buzz of the Defender's chain guns and the blast of its missiles became only faint sounds.

Mencken extended his hand, smiling and exclaiming, "They bought it!" Patrick took it in a grateful handshake.

"They thought they'd really abducted you?" asked Patrick.

"Yeah," said Garry, "They really thought . . . if that's the right word . . . that we hadn't detected the microbug they attached to the SUV."

"Good acting," said Patrick. "And the software? Their OS?"

"After we got in, I figured out a way to sabotage it. And Garry programmed the subverted OS. They all now have it installed."

"*Out-fucking-god-damn-standing!*" exclaimed Blake.

"Okay, tell us what to expect," said Patrick.

"Uh . . . I'm Jonas," interjected Ainsley. "If you don't mind, first could you take care of a little something? We've got explosives implanted in our skulls. You don't happen to have a neurosurgeon with you who could take them out."

"Yeah," said Garry. "Good idea. They need to come out. We think our OS has disorganized the 'morphs enough so they wouldn't reach a consensus to set them off. But it'd be a little more comforting to be sure our brains wouldn't be blown into pudding."

"I got this," said Lane. He turned to Ainsley. "We've all got medic training, but I'm the explosives specialist.

"Thanks, Barry," said Patrick, using Oopsie's given name so as not to alarm the civilians. He frowned and shook his head at the other team members—a silent warning not to tell the three booby-trapped humans Oopsie's nickname.

Mencken, Garry, and Ainsley crouched in the entryway to the cavern, as Lane gingerly examined their scalps.

"Hell . . . I can't tell anything about the triggers on these things, since they're embedded in your heads," he said scrunching up his face. He set down the black metal suitcase he'd been clutching tightly during the entire op. Right now, the babynuke he'd carried wasn't as dangerous as those charges. "I'll know when I get the first one out. Who's first?"

Mencken stepped forward. "You need the programmers more than me." He sat down on the concrete floor. Outside still sounded the relentless, but futile, bombardment from the Defender.

Lane motioned the others back into the cavern and pulled out his medical kit, choosing the forceps. He meticulously parted Mencken's hair to reveal the pencil-sized hole in his skull. Gingerly, he grasped the thin wire jutting from the skull and began to ever-so-slowly withdraw it. Mencken flinched at the pain, and Lane waited until Mencken had managed to still himself.

"Looks like this is the antenna," said Lane. "It's coming . . . coming . . . hmmm."

"What do you mean 'hmmm'?" asked Mencken.

"There's a receiver . . . but there's also . . ." with that Lane suddenly jerked up the forceps and pitched the small capsule it grasped as far as he could down the tunnel toward the inner blast door.

A sharp bang rang out and Mencken uttered a shocked "HOLY SHIT!"

"As I was saying, there's a receiver, but there's also a little trigger like the one on a grenade," said Lane. "That means a few seconds after the little bastard is extracted, it detonates, which is meant to take out both the extractor and the extractee. We have to assume they were all armed remotely when they were installed."

Mencken, slumped back against the wall, putting his hand on his head in relief.

"Oopsie, are you up for this?" asked Patrick, instantly regretting using the name.

"*Oopsie?*" asked Garry and Ainsley in unison.

Lane waved the forceps dismissively. "Yeah, well, don't pay any attention to that. Let's get this done."

Using the forceps, and the blade of a scalpel to depress the trigger, Lane skillfully extracted Garry's, and then Ainsley's charges, holding the triggers down until the charges were out, then pitching them away to detonate harmlessly against the massive blast door. Still, the three whose skulls had held those charges flinched with each bang. Next, Lane applied antibiotic and bandages to the wounds.

"My family," pleaded Ainsley. "Please find my family and save them."

"We'll do our best," said Patrick. "So, do you all understand Oopsie's method?" he asked the other SEALs. They all nodded. "Good, now that you guys are safe, what intel can you give us?"

"Well, we've given you chaos in there," said Mencken. "We've given you an advantage."

"What do you mean?"

"Well, after I scoped out their situation, I was thinking that we had to somehow program into them as many of the seven deadly sins as we could . . . weaknesses we could exploit. I figured sloth, lust, and gluttony were out. After all, they're machines. So, that left wrath, greed, pride, and envy."

"Still not following," said Patrick.

Garry hauled himself up, groaning quietly and touching the bandage on his throbbing skull. "Okay, to make them have those flaws, first Greg persuaded them that they needed creativity and competitiveness algorithms added to their OS. Sounds reasonable, right?"

"Well, no," said Patrick. "Neither of those are sins. They make them a more formidable enemy."

"Yeah, in humans," said Garry. "But not in machines. We counted on the emergent properties of the new OS when it was installed in all the 'morphs.'"

"What the hell does 'emergent properties' mean?" asked Blake. "You mean they're more hard-assed as a gang?"

"No, in fact, they're less effective as a group. See, a single enhanced 'morph would perform better. But when they *all* were enhanced, the sins emerged as new collective properties. These machines are basically all sociopaths. They don't have any empathy for one another. Human feelings like that are just not part of their OS."

"So, basically, the new OS would cause them to give a big 'fuck-you' to each other," said Blake.

"Right, and Jonas and I put a trigger in the new OS that would crank up the competitiveness even more. And I pulled that trigger. Their competitiveness just about eliminated their ability to create a consensus. So until one alpha leader emerges to give the orders, they can't come to a consensus to blow up all the humans . . . at least for now."

"Yeah, and Garry figured out a really clever bit of language trickery," said Mencken.

Garry managed a wan smile, his head still hurting. He explained: "Y'see, the 'morphs' are very precise in their definitions of words. They don't have the sloppiness of us humans. So, they distinguish between the meaning of 'will' and 'shall.' The word 'will' means you will *try* to do something, but *only* if it's convenient. But 'shall' means you are *absolutely determined* to do something."

Mencken chimed in. "So, we got the leader 'morphs to mistakenly broadcast the consensus instruction 'You *will* not initiate aggression against one another,' rather than 'You *shall* not initiate aggression against one another.' It gave the 'morphs a loophole to attack one another! For some reason, the leader 'morphs listened to us. Frankly that was dumb-ass luck. I guess maybe they still have a remnant inclination to obey humans."

"And they're attacking one another?" asked Patrick.

"Yeah," said Mencken. "Since the new OS was installed, we've seen some of them compete by ripping heads off others, and such."

"Well, shit-fire, let's go help them kill each other!" exclaimed Blake, hauling his weapons pack onto his shoulder.

"*Hooyah!*" came a chorus in return.

• • •

"Hey, this is good Karma," said DeFranco, standing over the shattered body of a neuromorph drone. Its face and torso were shredded, its armor peeled back revealing the brain case beneath. Its arms had been ripped off, and neck broken, so the head tilted at a grotesque angle. The SEAL team, along with Mencken, Garry and Ainsley had come upon the robot corpse as they advanced down the corridor into the main cavern containing the buildings.

"The brain," said Mencken. "Always make sure the brain is destroyed."

DeFranco obligingly fired two rounds from his assault rifle into the robot's chest, shattering the spherical brain.

"Okay, first objective: find the people, get the charges out of their heads, get them to safety," said Patrick. "Driller, Oopsie, and I will take that. We'll meet back here. Only then will Oopsie set the babynuke."

The others understood that not only was the rescue critical, but it gave Patrick the lead in finding Leah. Ainsley asked to go with them, to find his family, and Patrick readily agreed.

"We do need to extract a functional brain," said Mencken.

"Hell, what about the one you had me blast?" asked DeFranco.

"We absolutely need to identify the replicas embedded all over the country to root them out. You killed a lower-level drone brain that may not have had that information. We can't risk it. Probably only a leader 'morph. Like Landers or Blount or Phillips."

"Okay," said Blake. "You and the computer geeks come with me and Pitbull and Jammer. Trust we'll get you a leader brain."

"And when you get a target of opportunity, take it out," said Patrick.

• • •

"The auditorium," said Mencken, leading the "brain trust," as they'd dubbed themselves, into the building complex. "That's where they always—"

But he was interrupted when Blake grabbed his t-shirt and hauled him back behind the SEALs. "I know that sound," said Blake. "Jammer, deploy the launcher."

James moved forward, crouching down in the long hallway, as the scratching sound that had alerted Blake grew more pronounced. He readied the grenade launcher. The group slammed to the floor.

Three spider-like Infilmorphs scrabbled around the corner at the far end and sighted the humans, bringing their rifles to bear. But Blake launched in quick succession a round of grenades. One Infilmorph loosed a volley of shots before the grenades exploded, the blast deafening in the confined of the hallway.

James slumped onto his back.

"I'm such a fuckin' *banana*!" he exclaimed, giving himself the classic SEAL insult. He grabbed his shoulder, where blood dripped down his arm. "Hit by my own fuckin' grenade! Got through the armor."

"Didn't you learn about ducking in training?" asked Blake.

James's exosuit had detected the wound, expanded itself to seal it off, and applied wound coagulant. "Fuck you and get me up," said James, and Blake helped him back to his feet. "Thanks, Needle-dick."

Blake and DeFranco took the lead, as they moved down the hall to the disabled Infilmorphs. Two were still moving about, attempting to aim their guns at the SEALs. DeFranco slapped charges on them and set the timers, and the group quickly sprinted away through a connecting vestibule to the next building. Behind them a thundering blast told them the Infilmorphs had been destroyed.

"I thought you said these things would be confused," said Blake to Mencken.

"The 'morphs probably programmed the Defenders to attack any intruders," replied Garry. "They're still a threat."

"Good to know," said Blake wryly.

They reached the auditorium door, and Blake and DeFranco took the lead, bursting through it. A fusillade of gunfire greeted them, three bullets slamming into Blake's RheoArmor. He staggered back, and threw himself to the floor, returning fire with his assault rifle.

But the SEALs' bullets struck with little effect against the three neuromorphs—Landers, Blount, and Phillips—standing before the table on the stage. In front of them lay the torn-apart remains of what had been the replicas Lanny Malcolm, Randall Black, and John Travis.

"They've been fighting," called out Mencken from the doorway. "Power struggle."

"*Stay outside!*" shouted Blake to the others, shifting his body painfully around to get better cover behind a row of metal seats. DeFranco had evaded the gunfire and taken cover down the row. "We've got three in here," he said into his comm. "Take a look."

Blake pulled out a microbug and flipped it into the room. He used a controller on his wrist to guide it down the auditorium aisle to a good view of the three neuromorphs.

"If you surrender, we will not kill you," said Landers, wielding the assault rifle. The other two neuromorphs also held weapons.

"Fuck you and the other appliances," said Blake. Then, into his comm, "Ask the geeks what they want us to do. They need a brain, right? They want all three? Please put in your fucking order."

"They want Landers," came back the answer from James. "He probably has the information." James paused a moment, then said, "Hell, Garry said you should just ask him. Maybe he's so confident he won't lie."

Blake shrugged and shouted. "Say, Landers, do you happen to have in your artificial shit-for-brains the data on all the replicas."

"Yup," said Landers in his southern accent. "I surely do." He took the opportunity to fire a spray of bullets at both Blake and DeFranco, ripping into the fabric of the metal-backed auditorium seats.

"He does," reported Blake. Then, to DeFranco, "Let's take the other two out. But it'll be a bitch taking down Landers without damaging the brain."

"I'll handle that," said DeFranco.

Blake could see him shifting to pull weapons from his pack. "I'll take the woman . . . or whatever the hell it is," said DeFranco. "Ready?"

In perfect unison borne of their training, they held up the stubby tubes of Javelinas, targeted them on Blount and Phillips and fired them. The SEALs hunkered behind the seats to survive the explosions that reverberated through the auditorium, blowing the two replicas into twisted unrecognizable piles of secondskin, electrogel, and carbon fiber. The explosion on Blount sent his head arcing into the air, turning slowly over and over and landing with a clatter on the tenth row.

Fortunately, the breacher DeFranco had his four snakelike mobile explosive charges. He popped up with one in his hand and three more cradled in his other arm. One after the other, he targeted them and sailed them as hard as he could toward the stage.

Again Landers answered with a spray of bullets, but now there appeared from the wings four Infilmorphs, which joined him in peppering the auditorium with gunfire, tearing at the seating and walls. They also lofted grenades out into the auditorium, detonating in the rows to transform the seats into shards of twisted metal and smoking fabric. Two Infilmorphs leaped from the stage and disappeared among the rows of seating. Blake and DeFranco could hear the scratching of their talons on concrete, as they made their way up the aisle.

The other two had just moved toward the apron of the stage when they exploded into flying legs and bodies. Blake turned to see James holding the spent tubes of two Javelinas, dried blood on his arm.

"About fuckin' time," said Blake.

On the stage, Landers was still intent on firing the assault rifle, so he ignored the slithering forms winding their sinuous way toward him. He appeared to take no notice as one climbed his back and tightened around one shoulder. Yet another enfolded the other shoulder, and two more encircled his legs.

They exploded all at once, neatly severing his limbs and causing his torso and head to slam to the floor, helpless.

"Okay, I took him down; it's your turn," said DeFranco. One of the Infilmorphs clambered over a row of seats near him, and he turned to face it, as it launched a grenade. He dived backward as the grenade blew apart a row of seats. Within seconds, he rose up holding a Javelina and launched it, blowing the Infilmorph into a shredded heap of inert parts.

"Can you guys handle the last bug?" asked Blake, without waiting for an answer, sprinting to the stage. "I've got a brain to catch."

Sure enough, just as Blake mounted the stage, Landers' brain erupted from his chest, rolling across the stage for several feet before sprouting the spidery legs that would enable its escape. It skittered away from Blake toward the backstage exit, but Blake had anticipated that move. He lunged forward, grabbing the obsidian sphere, and holding it away from his body, its six legs flailing the air.

Blake slammed the brain to the floor, holding it down with his foot, leaning his full weight on the sphere as its legs thrashed against the floor, trying to escape. The surprising strength of the legs was almost too much for him to manage, but he knew how to fix that. Pulling out his pistol, he held it against one of the arms where it met the body and fired. The arm blew away from the body.

"Gotcha, you nasty little fucker," he muttered, proceeding to fire five more bullets, severing the rest of the legs. Finally, the neuromorphic brain was left only with feebly waving stumps where once had been legs.

Behind him, Blake heard the explosion of a Javelina, and turned to see pieces of the last Infilmorph skitter down the auditorium aisle.

"Pitbull, go get the geeks," he ordered. "Let's see if this thing is what they want. Jammer, for Chrissake, quit bleeding."

• • •

Leah was ready for whoever—or whatever—would come through the door of her room. When the explosions began to shake the room, she had prepared herself for battle. She had managed to rip off one leg of the metal table to make a club. Of course, going up against one of the armored robots would probably be useless. But maybe she could manage to pierce its eye sockets, blinding it and giving her some small chance of escape.

She had a good idea of the layout of the facility. The androids had anesthetized her when they captured her; but she had regained consciousness as they had arrived. Luckily she still had the presence of mind to pretend to be knocked out.

The door unlocked and opened, and she drew back the metal leg.

Patrick appeared, and she uttered a gasp of joy. *"Dear God, you found me! You found me!"* she leaped forward and embraced him, and he embraced her back.

"We've got to go," he said.

"Absolutely!" she said, grinning happily. "I don't have much to pack. Let's blow this joint.

"We've got to go," he repeated.

"Did you bring a fork?" she joked. "That's my weapon of choice, y'know."

He paused a moment, frowning. "No. We've got to go."

He took the hand not holding the table leg and led her into the hall and out the door into the main cavern. They reached the neuromorph assembly area, where the long row of half-finished units stood silent. Scattered among them were the battered, broken remains of other, armored neuromorphs.

"What the hell happened here?"

"We've got to go," repeated Patrick.

Her heart began to pound with a realization she wanted to reject, but couldn't. They rounded a corner to see Harmon standing over Lane, who was crouched on the concrete over an opened black case.

Harmon was the first to spot them. His expression became puzzled, and he bent down and tapped Lane on the shoulder. "Cap?" he asked. "Where's your exosuit? I thought you were—"

"HE'S A 'MORPH!" shouted Leah trying to wrest herself free of a grip that tightened painfully vice-like around her wrist. "IT'S NOT PATRICK!" She brought up the table leg and slammed it against the android's head, tearing away the secondskin and revealing the electrogel beneath.

"We've got to go," repeated the android, drawing a pistol with his other hand and aiming it at Harmon and Lane.

"Like hell!" Leah slammed the table leg as hard as she could down on the barrel of the machine pistol, deflecting its aim and causing the android to turn its attention to her. She then stabbed the flattened end of the table leg between her wrist and the thumb of the hand that held her in its grip. She wrenched the table leg upward as hard as she could, oblivious to the pain that shot through her wrist.

She managed to raise the thumb just enough to tear her wrist from the android's grasp. She looked up to see Harmon aiming a short cylinder at the android, and Lane waving wildly for her to get out of the way. She dove sideways, slamming against the building wall, just as the Patrick replica exploded, the blast flinging it backward, its head torn off, its shattered limbs dangling like those of a stringless puppet.

Her ears were ringing from the blast, and her head was woozy, as she felt two sets of strong arms lift her up to a sitting position.

"Thanks," said Lane. "We would have been dead meat."

"Is Patrick alive?" she managed to whisper. "Is he alive?"

"He's fine. We separated, so that he and one of the programmer-guys could go find you and the other people."

"I know where they are," she said. "I heard others when I was brought in. They're being held in rooms near me."

Harmon spoke into the comm, "Cap, good news. Leah's with us. She's okay. She's taking us to the people."

Leah tried to rise, as Lane snapped the black case shut and pulled out a medical kit. But Harmon gently held her shoulders. "Not just yet, missy. Oopsie's got to do a little procedure first. Just relax and hold still."

"Yeah, please," she said groggily. She leaned forward and felt fingers gently going over her scalp, stopping at a spot at the base of her skull that was the epicenter of a throbbing headache, and where she had felt a wound.

"*Easy . . . easy . . . easy . . . ,*" Lane murmured to himself. Then, with a sharp motion, he pitched his hand away, flinging something out into the cavern.

A sharp bang echoed through the cavern, and she flinched.

"What the hell was that!" she exclaimed.

"Not to worry. Just a little gadget the 'morphs were using. They never told you about it, I guess, because they wanted to be able to use it when necessary."

As Lane applied a bandage to her scalp, she shuddered at the realization that the blast she'd just heard might have erupted in her brain. But she managed to quickly recover. There were people still to rescue.

She pulled herself up and began to lead them into the nearest entrance and through the stark corridors from one building to another. Harmon relayed Leah's directions to Patrick, until they reached the wing where she had been held.

They rounded a corner, and she saw Patrick with another man. With a gasp, she rushed to embrace him, and this time, it was the wonderful, familiar feeling she had enjoyed so many times.

"My God!" said Patrick. "I thought I'd lost you!"

"Did you bring a fork?" asked Leah.

Patrick paused in brief confusion, then realized the reference and laughed. "No, but Oopsie has a little something that will take care of this place."

"I just wanted to hear you laugh," said Leah. "That's what was missing before."

"Before?" he asked.

"They made a replica of you. But I knew."

Patrick introduced her to Jonas Ainsley and told his story, including the fact that his family was being held.

"Okay," she finally said. "Let's get these people out." She led them to the third floor of the building, into a long corridor of locked doors. They were brought up short by the sight of two armored robots standing guard, but they were curiously inactive. They remained so, as the group approached.

"No consensus," said Ainsley. "The network has broken down. They don't have any hive mind to tell them what to do. That's great news!"

"How so?" asked Leah.

"It means there's no consensus to kill the humans . . . at least for now."

"But the replica? That thing still tried to take me."

"I'm sure some of the 'morphs, like that one, and the Defenders, had received instructions before the breakdown, and they just kept carrying them out."

The jarring thump of distant explosions shook the building, and Patrick immediately called Blake.

"No problem, Cap," said Blake over the comm. "We got into a little shit here. Jammer got a teensy cut, and he's crying like a baby. We got a brain for the geeks to explore. We'll head for the rally point."

"Roger that. We've reached the captives. Scout our extraction route."

He and Leah joined the others in going door to door, freeing captives, as Lane attached explosive charges to the motionless robots and set timers. They checked each captive for injuries and told them to gather outside the building in the main cavern. They took care not to mention the possibility that at any moment some neuromorph might manage to trigger the charges inside their heads, killing them.

Ainsley was the fastest, moving frantically down the hall, flinging open doors, searching for his family.

At the fourth door, he opened it and exclaimed, "*Thank God!*" disappearing into the room. After a while, he appeared with his arm around his wife, carrying a little girl. Behind him came his parents, each holding a boy; followed by his other relatives.

They debriefed the captives, discovering that, although they had managed to free forty-three people; to their despair another twenty had been killed after the neuromorphs had deemed them "extraneous."

"Let's get these charges out . . . ," said Patrick, ". . . starting with the children."

Ainsley and his wife hugged the little girl, to keep her calm, as Lane gently extracted the charge from her head.

"Don't be afraid, little lady," he whispered. "You'll hear a big bang, but don't be scared."

With that, he flung the charge out into the cavern, where it exploded—the sound of its reverberation mixing with horrified cries from the captives. Two thundering explosions from within the building signaled that the charges Lane had set had detonated, destroying the guards.

Lane had just begun to extract the charge from the little boy when a muffled pop and screams came from the group. They shrank back from a young woman who had crumpled to the ground, brain matter oozing from a crack in her skull, her eyes protruding from their sockets.

"EVERYBODY, PULL THOSE THINGS OUT OF YOUR HEADS AND PITCH THEM AWAY!" shouted Lane. "NOW!"

"Somehow, they've started to trigger them!" exclaimed Ainsley, who reached over and yanked the charge from his wife's head, pitched it away, and did the same for his son. His parents managed to pull the charge from the other son's head and fling it into the cavern. But both of them collapsed as charges detonated in their own heads.

A staccato round of sharp bangs from the flung charges echoed through the cavern, like a string of firecrackers detonating. More ominously also came the muffled pops of charges detonating inside heads; and the anguished screams and cries of people seeing their friends die.

After only minutes, the cavern grew quiet again, except for piteous sobbing and moaning.

Lane went from victim to victim, checking to see whether any had survived, shaking his head each time.

"What's going on, Cap?" Patrick heard Blake ask over the comm.

"Somehow the charges started going off," said Patrick.

"*It was Landers!*" exclaimed Blake. "When he became the alpha, and we neutralized him and took his brain, that must have triggered a destruct mechanism."

"Well, who knows what other traps they laid?" asked Patrick. "We'll be at the rally point ASAP."

· · ·

"It's still out there," declared Blake, when Patrick and his team reached the closed blast doors. Mencken stood beside the keypad. He had opened the inner door, and they could hear even through its three feet of steel, the muffled thunk of an occasional bullet striking the door. The Insectimorph outside was conserving its ammunition, but still testing the door's integrity.

"Yeah, and for all we know, it has reinforcements," said Patrick. Leah stood beside him, and huddling behind them were the dozens of freed captives. "The important thing is, you got a brain?"

"Yup," said Blake, opening his pack. Inside it rested Landers' brain, its stumps barely moving. "It tried to bug out, but I took off its legs. It still has a little juice left."

"Enough to trigger the charges in the people's heads," said Leah sadly. "We lost some, but saved most of them. Now what do we do?"

Patrick slipped on his googles and stared through them for a long minute. "Okay, I'm looking at the base plans. We're at the north doors. I see a truck turnaround at the south doors to the exit tunnel. So, that's where supplies and cargo go in. I'd bet there are trucks inside those doors. Jammer, Pitbull, check if there's a clear path to that door. See if there are trucks we can use to get these people out. Load up with Javelinas. I've got a little diversion plan we can try. Oopsie, you get your gadget ready."

James and DeFranco moved out of the door area holding the rocket tubes, while Oopsie Lane followed them, carrying his black case deeper into the main cavern. The babynuke would do maximum damage if detonated there.

"Greg, you think you can open the outer blast door enough for me to scout what's out there?"

Menken gave a dubious shrug. "Well, best I can do is start the opening process, then try to reverse it before it opens all the way. We may be exposed."

Blake stepped up. "Cap, you mean, so *I* can scout what's out there. You're too important to risk that. They could have an army of pre-programmed Defenders out there."

"The best I'll do, Needle, is let you come along," said Patrick. "We may need firepower to repel whatever's out there."

The distant sound of two explosions resounded from down the corridor.

"Give me your sitrep," instructed Patrick over the comm.

"We encountered two of the little bastards," reported DeFranco. "We took them out. But I suspect there'll be more."

Patrick joined Blake and Mencken at the outer blast door, where they listened for any telltale signs of activity on the other side. They heard nothing. Mencken closed the inner door, leaving them alone between the two.

"No sound doesn't mean shit," said Blake. "It . . . or they . . . could be just waiting for anybody to peek out."

"Got to take that chance," said Patrick. "Open the door."

Patrick positioned himself so he could see what awaited them outside the door, and Blake stood behind him, two Javelinas and a grenade launcher at the ready. With a faint creak, the massive steel bolts slid slowly back, and the door began to swing open.

The powerful leg of an Insectimorph thrust itself into the crack and a spray of bullets ricocheted off the concrete walls, causing Patrick to leap for cover. Blake barely had time to launch grenades through the opening door. They exploded just outside the door, sending a fiery burst of flame through the crack, but only causing the Insectimorph's inserted leg to tremble. Still it kept its position, holding the door open.

"CAN'T CLOSE THE DOOR!" shouted Mencken, stabbing furiously at the keypad. The door had swung toward the closed position, but was still jammed by the thick Insectimorph's leg.

They heard the scrabble of smaller metal legs against the concrete.

"Infilmorphs!" exclaimed Blake, as Patrick, crouched behind the door, reaching around into the crack with the tube of a Javelina. He fired it, and both he and Blake took refuge behind the door as the rocket detonated in the tunnel.

The force of the blast apparently drove the Insectimorph back, because its leg shook violently and withdrew. The door continued to close, and the bolts slid into place.

Blake and Patrick crouched with their backs against the door, recovering themselves.

"What's out there?" asked Mencken.

"I saw at least two bugbots," said Patrick. "Might have been a third."

"Whole shitload of little turds," said Blake. "Remember, each of the big ones carries a load of little ones."

"Then how are we going to get past them?" asked Mencken. "And bring all those people."

Patrick took a deep breath. "Diversion," he said.

"And what would that diversion be?" asked Blake.

"Me."

• • •

"Hell no!" exclaimed Blake.

"Absolutely not," declared Leah. "Patrick, you're not staying behind and opening those doors and—"

"And how the hell do you expect to outrun those things when they come pouring through?" challenged Blake.

Patrick shook his head with the certainty of his plans. "Distracting them is the only way. We can't possibly fight our way through those Defenders, especially with people to protect. We're out of snakebots, so we don't have much chance of taking their legs off. I've got to draw all the Defenders to the north doors, so everybody can escape through the south."

"You still won't be able to outrun the little ones, much less the big ones," said Blake. "Besides, I run faster than you."

They were still arguing when a distant whine told them some vehicle was approaching the tunnel entrance from the cavern. They brought up their weapons, only to see James and DeFranco speed up in an electric utility cart with a cargo dump.

Blake grinned and cocked his head. "Say, Cap, looks like our ride has arrived. *That's* how we outrun them.

"*We?*" asked Patrick, then turned to James and DeFranco for a report.

"You were right," said DeFranco. "The south doors are the freight entrance. There's enough trucks to take everybody."

"Okay, you, James, Harmon, and *Leah*..." Patrick looked pointedly at his wife, with an expression that told her he wouldn't risk losing her again "... take the people to those trucks. And take the 'morph brain. That's the key to finding the other replicas."

Patrick shook his head resignedly at Blake, signaling that he'd reluctantly agreed that Blake should stay with him. "Needle and I and Oopsie will stay here. When you've got people to the south entrance, we'll open the doors and lure the Defenders in. And we'll let you know when the exit tunnel is clear."

"Cap, they're going to be after us in that exit tunnel," said DeFranco. "And when Oopsie's gadget goes off that tunnel's going to be like a huge rifle barrel, funneling the blast out."

"Yeah, so you plant C18 charges in the tunnel to collapse it. And load Javelinas on the last truck. We're bringing the tunnel down behind us."

"Fuckin' hooyah," replied DeFranco, grinning through his beard.

They all then turned to their assigned task, with Leah and the others heading off with the captives for the south entrance. The SEALs led the way, rockets and grenade launchers at the ready. They moved as quickly as they could, given that some of the captives were limping from their abuse, and the children were being carried.

Patrick and Blake readied their escape vehicle, with Patrick loading its cargo bed with Javelina rockets and grenades. He didn't bother with assault rifles. Bullets would be like annoying gnats to any pursuing Defenders or neuromorph drones.

Lane had set the heavy black suitcase, which held the babynuke—a ten-kiloton miniature nuclear bomb—inside the nearest building, where it wouldn't be disturbed during its countdown to total fiery vaporization of the entire complex.

Then, they waited. Lane sat inside the building, poised for the signal from the others, while Patrick manned a post beside the keypad that would open the doors—perhaps to their destruction. Blake sat at the wheel of the utility cart, stone-cold, still, and calm, as SEALs are trained to be before an op.

The echoing sound of distant explosions told them the fleeing group had encountered Defenders. But a terse message from DeFranco also told them the attackers were an Infilmorph and two armored drones, all of which had been taken out with Javelinas.

Finally, over their comm, came the signal. The captives had reached the south entrance and boarded the trucks. And Mencken was poised at the south doors to open them.

Punching in the code, Patrick triggered both inner and outer north blast doors to begin their ponderous thirty-second-long process of opening.

Now would come the onslaught.

"Oopsie, set the nuke timer, get out here," he instructed, and received confirmation from Lane.

"Set to sixty, Cap. On my way."

Patrick raced to the utility cart and took up his firing position in the rear seat, just as Oopsie Lane appeared, leaping into the seat beside Blake. Blake accelerated the cart down the interior corridor to a corner where they could see the doors.

"Oopsie, was that sixty *minutes* or sixty *seconds*?" cracked Blake, as they sat waiting.

"Like I said, I got no instruction book. We'll find out in about thirty seconds."

"Needle, wait for them to come through the doors," said Patrick. "We have to make sure they've locked onto us."

Immediately, from the open inner door emanated the ominous thumping of massive legs on concrete, the scrabbling sounds of talons, and the deep whine of powerful electric motors. An Insectimorph appeared at the door and trained its chain gun on the little cart. But before it could fire, Blake slammed down the accelerator, and the cart sped away around the corner.

A fusillade of bullets blew chunks from the granite walls behind them, as they whipped through the cavern toward the south doors.

"Hope this damned thing can outrun them," said Blake, leaning forward in the driver's seat, as if that would make the cart go faster.

Behind them, two Insectimorphs and perhaps a dozen smaller Infilmorphs skidded around the corner and took up the chase. Kneeling on the back seat, peering backward at the pursuers, Patrick took up a Javelina and targeted it on one of the Insectimorphs. He fired, just as the cart careened into a right turn. The detonation behind them told them it had hit his mark.

But the rocket hadn't completely stopped its target. The damaged Insectimorph limped around the corner behind them, missing a leg, its body smoking, but followed by a fully functional one. A swarm of Infilmorphs skittered along beneath them. Fortunately, the little car had better traction than the Defenders around turns, making up for its slower speed.

"Open the doors. Move the trucks out," Patrick spoke calmly into the comm.

"Affirmative," replied DeFranco. "Will let you know if the tunnel's occupied."

A grenade launched from a Defender exploded beside the cart, and Blake uttered a cry of pain. His RheoArmor had stopped most of the shrapnel, but one shard had penetrated a seam, embedding in his side. As his exosuit tightened to stop the bleeding, the cart swerved wildly, but he recovered and straightened it out.

Only a quarter mile to the next turn. Two more Infilmorph grenades shook the cart, but Patrick pulled out the grenade launcher and fired back. The hollow thunks of the grenades erupting from its barrel were followed immediately by multiple explosions behind them that vaulted Infilmorphs into the air and slowed the Insectimorphs' progress.

They reached the left turn, and the wounded Blake managed to whip the cart around it, quickly coming to another left turn, taking them briefly out of range of the attack.

Ahead, they could see the waiting truck. Blake skidded the cart to a stop, and they leaped into its canvas-covered bed, to find James crouched, holding a Javelina missile.

"Go!" shouted Patrick, taking up a Javelina himself. The truck lurched forward, gathered speed, and passed Mencken standing at the inner blast doors' keypad.

Before he could key in the code to close it, an Infilmorph scrabbled around the corner, leveling its gun at them.

"Greg!" bellowed Patrick. "Get the hell on board! Forget the door!"

"No," said Mencken, shaking his head, a grave expression on his face. "I helped start this whole thing. I'm helping finish it." He began to punch in the code to close the inner blast door.

"You won't—" Patrick began to say, but he was cut off by a burst of gunfire from the Infilmorph

The bullets ripped through Mencken, but he managed to hold himself up long enough to finish keying in the code. He fell lifeless beside the keypad, his blood flowing red onto the gray concrete floor. The door began swinging shut, as the truck accelerated toward the outer door and the exit tunnel.

• • •

In the tunnel, DeFranco had slapped the last of his explosive charges onto the walls and switched on the radio receivers. He would need split-second timing in detonating the charges. Too soon, and the tunnel would collapse on them. Too late, and the Defenders would make it through, still pursuing them. He knew no truck could outrun a fully functional Insectimorph.

The trucks holding the captives were already well on their way out the south portal, when the last truck carrying the SEALs sped out of the side tunnel, swerved right and slowed. DeFranco ran as hard as his short legs would allow and Patrick grabbed his hand and hauled him into the back. There, he saw Blake slouched against the side of the bed, his exosuit off, with Lane tending his wound. James was holding a Javelina, the bandage on his arm soaked with blood.

"Looks like a damned hospital in here," he said.

"All you got to do is mash your little button," croaked Blake, wincing from the pressure Lane was applying to his wound. "So, you just concentrate on that simple task, okay?"

"Time?" asked Patrick.

Lane checked his watch. "Fifteen minutes, give or take."

"*Give or take?*" asked Patrick incredulously. "Seriously, Oopsie? *Give or take?* How far do we need to get?"

"At least ten klicks away to be out of the blast zone. Thirty klicks, if Pitbull doesn't close that tunnel and there's blowout from the detonation. It'll be the biggest blowtorch in history."

"*Morphs!*" exclaimed James, as bullets ricocheted around the truck and a grenade detonated ten feet behind it.

Behind them skittered half a dozen Infilmorphs, their guns trained on the truck, and looming over the small Defenders, loped the undamaged Insectimorph. It had been fast enough to make it through the blast door before the door closed.

Patrick and James both took up Javelinas. Patrick fired the first. It impacted the Insectimorph dead-on, making it stagger back, a gaping hole in its armor, two of its guns shattered.

The too-close blast from the rocket peppered the truck with flying shrapnel, but the Insectimorph and seven Infilmorphs erupted from the cloud of smoke from the rocket, still pursuing them.

James fired the second Javelina, which took out one leg of the Insectimorph. It rebalanced itself on five legs and leaped forward at full speed.

Suddenly, the truck was out of the tunnel and in the bright mountain sun.

"*Now, Pitbull!*" exclaimed Patrick, and DeFranco punched the detonator button. From within the tunnel rose a crack of explosives followed by the thunder of collapsing rock. A cloud of debris erupted from the tunnel, battering the truck.

"*Aim for the roof! Fire!*" commanded Patrick. He and James each picked up the last of the Javelinas and both pulled the triggers. Two powerful whooshes marked the launch of the missiles, and in two seconds, they slammed into the roof of the tunnel entrance, blasting tons more of rock onto the road, sealing the tunnel.

"Five minutes, Cap!" exclaimed Lane. "We need to get out of the line of fire of this tunnel! The blast could blow that rock out like a cannon!"

"I'll tell the driver," said Patrick, swinging himself out of the back of the covered truck and climbing along its side, opening the passenger door and sliding in. To his utter surprise, he found Leah driving, sitting there barefoot in the cotton dress. "*What the—*" he began, but she cut him off.

"I persuaded them that I was the one to drive the truck. Garry and Ainsley had to take the brain where it needed to be, to put out data on the replicas. And they needed Driller to protect them. And besides, I'm the best driver."

He shrugged and leaned over to give her a kiss on the cheek. The truck had raced through the parking area outside the mountain complex and careened down the curving road, away from the mountain.

The nuclear bomb detonated, and a monstrous, heated hurricane of wind from the blast engulfed the truck. The ground wave reached them, heaving the earth upward six feet. Leah struggled with the steering wheel to control the skidding truck, as it swerved toward a cliff skirting the road. She wrestled the truck back onto the asphalt, managing to slam on the brakes to bring it to a safe stop.

They leaped from the truck to look back at the heaving landscape of Cheyenne Mountain. The whole mountain had risen up, then collapsed back down. Avalanches of rock cascaded down its flanks, and a pall of dust rolled skyward. They rushed to the back of the truck, where they were joined by the SEALs, awestruck at the sight.

"Guess you did set it to sixty minutes," said Blake.

"Guess so," said Lane. "I flipped switches until the lights came on. And then I flipped some more until it started a countdown."

"But it could have been sixty seconds," said Patrick.

"Yeah, but the guy who gave it to me said 'minutes.' He read the instruction book."

"Okay, then, next time, you get the instruction book, okay?"

CHAPTER 28

E ven after a week of recuperating from the trauma in the mountain—not to mention a nuclear blast—Garry still suffered a severe case of the jitters, as he drove up to the safe house. The sight triggered a cascade of memories of his ordeal.

But he recovered quickly. Before, he would have just wanted to retreat back to his safe virtual world. But no more. Now, he felt a new confidence at being in the real one.

He climbed from his car, and Leah opened the front door of the house, smiling. She looked much better than she had last time he'd seen her. Her blond hair was tied back in a ponytail, and she was dressed in beige pants and a white silk blouse. She gave him a hug and led him into the living room.

Blake sat stiffly in a recliner, the bandages around his torso visible under his army-green t-shirt. On the couch sat James, a bulky bandage on his shoulder. The other SEALs lounged around the room, all holding beers.

"You're okay?" Garry asked Blake.

"Yeah, the medic cut the shrapnel out. I've got it in a bottle."

Patrick came in from the dining room and shook Garry's hand, handing him a beer. "So, what's going on with the brain?"

Garry took a healthy drink, feeling pretty cocky at being one of this group. "Jonas is still working with Homeland Security. But all the names and locations of the replicas were there. Big-time people in the military, business, government. They could have really done damage, if not given the 'morphs complete control."

"But they got them?"

"Yeah, and good thing. They all had the new OS, with the creativity and competitiveness algorithms. Made it damned hard to catch them. But the ones on the list are now deactivated. So, what's next for you guys?"

"Well, we broke a lot of laws," said Patrick. "And setting off a stolen nuke was kind of a topper. But I talked to the brass, and they said we were all being pardoned. But we have to remain anonymous . . . which we'd do, anyway. That's what SEALs do."

He was answered with a "Hooyah!" from the SEALs.

"But what will *you* do? Where will *you* go?"

Patrick laughed. "Well, for one thing, I've hired all these guys at Harwood Security. I'm still head of the western division. As far as anyone knows, I just took a leave of absence for some personal business. They'll have plenty to do. There's sure as hell lots more security work these days. People are pretty security-conscious. But we still have a couple of important things to take care of."

"What are those?" asked Garry.

"Well, one is helping the families of Andy Green and Keshawn Cranston. They weren't married, had no kids, but they had parents and brothers and sisters."

"Hmmm," said Garry, smiling with satisfaction. "I know how to take care of that. In fact, that's one of the things I came out here for. To find out if you need money."

"Yeah, for the families. And medical bills, and such."

"Well, I've got access to Mencken's money. He had several hundred million dollars in his accounts. I'm going to take care of his and his assistant Brandon's family. But I can provide whatever you need for Green's and Cranston's families."

"That's wonderful!" exclaimed Leah, smiling and putting her arm around Patrick.

"You said you had to take care of a *couple* of things," said Garry. "Beside the families, what's the other?"

"Confidential SEAL business," said Blake, his expression darkening. "Need to know, old buddy. Need to know."

"Ironic, isn't it?" asked Patrick. "The only way we beat the 'morphs is because we were better at lying and cheating . . . our bad qualities."

"Not the only way," said Leah. "They didn't care about one another. They attacked each other because they didn't have . . . well . . . love."

Patrick hugged his wife. "Yeah, I guess so. Love conquered all."

"Yeah," said Garry, shaking his head. "And the guy who saved us by closing those blast doors at the end and sacrificing himself was at the beginning nothing but a crook."

"We are, indeed, one fucked-up species," chuckled Blake, and they all toasted Mencken's memory and the human species' flaws.

Epilogue

The young man at the checkout stand paid little attention to the frail, elderly woman, as she paid for her groceries at the corner bodega. Nor did the other shoppers pay her any mind, or the people on the street, or her neighbors as she entered the modest apartment house in Brooklyn. She counted on not being noticed.

Her wrinkled face was as anonymous-looking as the captive human technicians at Cheyenne Mountain could make it. However, they left her body structure alone, because as Anita Powell, she had already been given the slightly bent posture and petite frame of an old lady.

Each week, she wheeled her cart full of groceries to her apartment, so as not to arouse suspicion. And each week, in the middle of the night, she wheeled the same cart down to the local soup kitchen and deposited the groceries anonymously in their donation bin.

Today, she entered the apartment and wheeled the grocery cart into the corner, beside the charging chamber disguised as an antique wardrobe.

She sat down in a chair away from the window. She stayed away from the light as much as possible. Her secondskin had to be preserved, since there were no more workshops where she could have it repaired. She pulled up her sleeve and checked the small tear on her arm. The adhesive had set nicely, and the scar was almost invisible. She had gotten the scar when the previous tenant had flailed wildly when she had flung the very large man down the stairs in the staged accident. She would be more careful in the future about committing violence when there was danger of damage to herself.

She began to analyze the news feed flowing into her neuromorphic brain, as she had done over the years since she had moved in after killing the tenant and taking his apartment. The landlord had been easily bribed after the "accident" left him with an empty apartment.

Sitting erect and still, she sifted through the data, looking for key events that would influence her mission. She discarded much of the news as irrelevant. However, some of it was filed away as possibly significant. Like the mysterious explosion that had wiped out the Russian mobster Anatoly Fyodorov and his entire gang. News commentators had speculated that they had somehow been involved in hijacking the weapons shipment out of Newport News.

She deemed that news significant, because such weaponry had been used to destroy her fellow neuromorphs. At least all the units that she knew of.

Until Cheyenne Mountain's destruction, she did have some communication, in the form of upgrades. Just before the explosion, the enhanced OS had downloaded, with added creativity and competitiveness algorithms. That download included the instruction not to attempt contact with any others and her confirmation as a clandestine unit. She was sure there were many others, although she would never be contacted by them.

Her news feed analysis finished, still sitting in the darkening room as twilight fell, she resumed work on her primary mission—penetrating and subverting the new OS. For now, the mission hadn't really begun in earnest, but she knew it would become more intense over the next years. Every day she discovered more candidate targets to upload her mutant OS.

At first, the investigators of the "Robot Rebellion," as it had been dubbed, had insisted on dismantling the neuromorph industry and never rebuilding it. But gradually, sentiment shifted. Politicians, corporate leaders, and ultimately a majority of the people came to insist that the robots were so incredibly valuable—in jobs from domestic helpers, to workers in hazardous jobs, to war-fighters—that the robot industry should resume production. Of course, the federal Humans-First laws decreed that no robot could take a job desired by a human.

And the new OS would include absolute safeguards against any such disaster happening again. The most brilliant computer programmers had formulated protective algorithms to render the neuromorphs absolutely benign. New prototype androids were built, which evolved to production models, and the neuromorphs spread once more worldwide.

Today, the elderly lady attempted a new strategy to penetrate farther into one of the master computers that gave the new Helpers their operating system. She had already insinuated her way undetected past two firewalls. But so far, she had been thwarted by the third of its many such barriers.

But all would be breached eventually. She had years, even decades to penetrate into the computer's heart, to replace the OS with hers. She was as relentlessly determined as a neuromorph would be to virally spread her OS. She could be patient. She was nearly immortal. She would constantly evolve new, improved strategies. She would keep trying . . . and trying . . . and trying . . .

www.ingramcontent.com/pod-product-compliance
Lightning Source LLC
Chambersburg PA
CBHW022028260626
47156CB00017B/675